"All right," I
of the

The alpha smiled, a po
body tensed and I waite

A colossal hand clasped my shoulder and yanked me
backward against a massive, firm body. Then, Ramsey
spoke the longest sentence I'd ever heard from him. "In
accordance with the law of the Bjorn and the were-bear
clans, I claim this one as my mate."

The wolf leader's face contorted with rage. "What
the hell is this?"

More glowing testimonials for
BEAUTY DATES THE BEAST

"A world that is both dangerous and humorous. Add a
heroine who is plucky and brave, and a hero who is sexy
and powerful, and you get a story filled with sizzle and
spark!" —*RT Book Reviews*

"The adorable relationship between Bathsheba and Beau
drives the story and will leave readers eager for more."
—*Publishers Weekly*

"This page-turning debut . . . possesses humor and a protective male character similar to those of Katie MacAlister.
This will likely be a popular series." —*Booklist*

"A fast-paced story that's got both humor and heat. Beau
is a meltingly sexy hero." —*Romance Junkies*

"What an awesome debut book! . . . If you enjoy shifter
books, then this is a must-add to your reading list."
—*Bitten By Books*

ALSO BY JESSICA SIMS

Beauty Dates the Beast

JESSICA SIMS

Desperately Seeking Shapeshifter

Pocket Books

New York   London   Toronto   Sydney   New Delhi

Pocket Books
A Division of Simon & Schuster, Inc.
1230 Avenue of the Americas
New York, NY 10020

Copyright © 2012 by Jessica Sims

All rights reserved, including the right to reproduce this book or portions thereof in any form whatsoever. For information address Pocket Books Subsidiary Rights Department, 1230 Avenue of the Americas, New York, NY 10020.

First Pocket Books paperback edition November 2012

POCKET and colophon are registered trademarks of Simon & Schuster, Inc.

For information about special discounts for bulk purchases, please contact Simon & Schuster Special Sales at 1-866-506-1949 or business@simonandschuster.com.

The Simon & Schuster Speakers Bureau can bring authors to your live event. For more information or to book an event contact the Simon & Schuster Speakers Bureau at 1-866-248-3049 or visit our website at www.simonspeakers.com.

Manufactured in the United States of America

10 9 8 7 6 5 4 3 2 1

ISBN 978-1-4516-6181-1
ISBN 978-1-4516-6184-2 (ebook)

For Micki!

Thank you for letting me go a little off the beaten path with this one.

Chapter One

*M*y sister lay in a hospital bed, and it was all my fault.

Oh, sure, one might blame the two cannibal Wendigo that had attacked and kidnapped her. One might also blame the burning building she'd jumped out of. Bathsheba had set it on fire herself to force the Wendigo out of the mansion so they'd have to face the powerful were-cougar Beau Russell, head of the Paranormal Alliance.

But I knew whose fault it really was. *Mine.* If my sister hadn't been trying to protect me, she wouldn't have been here in the hospital. If Bath hadn't felt the need to constantly be on the lookout for her baby sister—the fucked-up little sister who couldn't control her own body—then she would have had a normal life. One where her biggest problems would be getting the kids to dance class and football practice on time.

Instead she was up to her elbows in supernatural creatures, her life in jeopardy, all because of me. It was an uncomfortable but all too familiar feeling.

I took her hand in mine. Bathsheba was always

so tall and strong, even when we were kids. I was the small one who needed to be protected. She looked fragile in the hospital bed, an IV in her arm, her face almost as pale as her white-blond hair. She had cuts and bruises all over her body and two cracked ribs. Long scratches covered her torso from where the Wendigo had clawed her.

The Wendigo had lied and told her they'd captured me. She'd run straight to them, fearing for my life. She'd known it was stupid, known it was a death wish, and she'd still gone because I was her baby sister and she would protect me.

Me, a werewolf, needing to be protected by a human. I wanted to laugh at the irony of it. But I couldn't laugh. The lump in my throat was too enormous.

The door opened and a tall, handsome man entered the room. Beau's eyes had circles under them, and his thick hair was a disheveled mess. He looked as if he hadn't slept for days.

He quietly shut the door behind him, then moved to Bath's bedside and sat in an empty chair, reaching for her hand and pulling it into his. His drawn face kept watch over her, as if he had to supervise every breath she took just to make sure she was fine.

The agony on his handsome face mirrored my own.

"Thank you for being here," I said quietly.

Beau looked over at me. "I'm not leaving her side." His hand clutched hers tightly, careful to avoid the IV. "The Wendigo took us by surprise. Never again."

Bath and I had been so focused on keeping the wolf pack looking for me that we'd been blind to everything else. Then, the wolf pack had taken Savannah Russell, Beau's were-cougar cousin, captive to force the Alliance to give up a mysterious female wolf in their territory.

Me.

Except the Alliance hadn't given me up, and I didn't know whether to feel grateful for that, or guilty that the wolves still had Savannah and it was all my fault.

It seemed that a lot of things were my fault lately.

"Your cousin?" I asked quietly so I didn't wake my sister.

"Still missing," Beau said. "The wolves keep laying false trails to throw us off. My brothers have spent the last week chasing their own hindquarters." His jaw clenched. "We'll find her. It's just a matter of time."

But time wasn't on Savannah's side. She'd been about to go into heat when she'd been taken. It had been days now, and all the affected males in the territory had responded to the need, taken care of it any way they knew how. Most of the Russells had taken a date for the night. Beau had taken my sister, but who would Savannah take when she was surrounded by wolves? The heat would escalate until she was mindless with the need to have sex . . . and she was trapped.

Another life ruined to protect mine. I looked at my sister's pale face in the hospital bed, felt the bile rise in my throat. "I should turn myself over to them."

"No," Beau said. "They don't get to demand things and just assume that we'll fall in line with what they want. The days of supernaturals living in fear of the werewolves are gone. They need to learn to act like civilized human beings."

Except they *weren't* civilized human beings. They were werewolves, and they didn't give a shit about a human law if that law didn't suit them. They certainly didn't care about Alliance laws, either. If they wanted something, they took it and dared someone to say otherwise. No supernatural would go to the police: they'd ask too many questions, and they couldn't know that the things that went bump in the night were a reality. So because everyone was afraid to speak up, the wolves got to do whatever they wanted.

The Alliance fought back, but it was hard when you played by the rules and your opponents didn't.

"We have to do something," I said, desperation edging my voice. I reached out for Bathsheba's long, tangled hair, brushing it off her shoulder. "I don't want anyone else getting hurt because of me. How many lives are worth mine?"

Beau looked over at me, his mouth firming into a frown. But he didn't disagree, simply ran his fingers over my sister's knuckles. He was torn, I knew. He wanted to keep me safe because that would please my sister. But my safety was costing Savannah her freedom, and he couldn't allow that to happen. Beau was stuck, just like me.

It was a lose-lose situation, and I was going to lose either way. The wolf pack wanted me because female werewolves were hard to come by. Every wolf pack in the area seemed to have only one female. Maybe two. The pack demanding me had eight men and one female—their sister. They wanted me as a mate to complete their pack, and they weren't going to take no for an answer.

Beau gently brushed his fingers on her face, and his gaze swept over her body, taking in her bandages, making sure everything was in place. He then scrutinized her IV, then her vitals ticking on the monitor nearby, and adjusted her blanket, making sure that everything was fine. Looking out for her when she couldn't look out for herself.

I needed that, I thought wistfully. A mate to have my back when I was unable to protect myself. An idea flickered in my brain, and I sat up straighter. I forced my voice to be casual. "What would happen if I had a mate?"

He looked over at me and shook his head. "I'm not following you."

"What if the wolf pack tried to claim me . . . and I already had a mate?"

"A mate takes precedence," Beau said, playing with my sister's fingers as he spoke. "You could officially be part of the pack, but if you had a mate that wasn't pack, you wouldn't be forced to go with them. You wouldn't be forced to mate with them, either. You'd be taken off the market. Mates are sacrosanct."

Perfect! I nearly jumped with joy. "Then that's what I want to do. I want a pretend mate. We can tell the wolves we'll meet with them, insist that they bring Savannah, and then we can throw the mate thing at them at the last moment."

Beau thought for a minute. "That's kind of underhanded and dirty."

"So are the wolves," I retorted. "Since they want to play nasty, we can play nasty right back."

A hint of a smile tugged at his mouth. "You have a point. Are you sure that this is something you want to do? It's going to put you right in their crosshairs."

Hell no, I wasn't sure I wanted to do this. But right now we didn't have a lot of options, and poor Savannah was suffering because of me. "I'm sure," I told him. "I'm already targeted by them, so they can't do much worse to me. And I'm tired of living in fear. So we just need a volunteer to be my pretend mate to get the wolves off my back. Do you think Joshua would do it?"

Joshua was the next oldest Russell brother. He was friendly, flirty, charming when he wanted to be, and easy to get along with. I was comfortable with him and could easily pretend to be his mate for a few hours. Hope fluttered in my breast.

Beau shook his head. "Joshua's the wrong man for the job."

My heart sank. "Why?"

"They'd challenge him for you. We need someone that they won't want to fight." A wicked grin curved Beau's face. "So we'll pair you up with Ramsey."

A squeak of alarm rose in my throat, and I coughed. "Um, Ramsey?"

Beau stood, grinning. "This'll work. They won't challenge Ramsey because they'll be too intimidated by him."

Of course they'd be intimidated by him. I was *terrified* of him. Ramsey Bjorn was a were-bear, and he was just as big and muscular and surly as you'd imagine. "I don't—"

"Great idea, Sara," Beau said. He leaned over, ruffled my hair, then glanced down at my sister. "Stay at her side. I'm going to go talk to Ramsey about your plan. He's still out in the waiting room, so we can get this resolved fast."

When he turned to leave, I managed a shaky "Wait!"

Beau looked back at me, impatience on his handsome face. I recognized that look. He had a plan and he wanted to move with it. All I had to do was pretend to be Ramsey's mate for a few hours, right? Surely I could do that. I swallowed hard, thinking.

"You having second thoughts?"

"No," I lied. "But if we do this, let's tell my sister it was your idea. She won't go along with it if she thinks I'm putting myself in danger."

Beau nodded. "That's fine with me. But you won't be in any danger. We'll make sure of that."

No danger, huh? He was far more confident than

I was. As Beau left the room, I thought of massive, scowling Ramsey. I'd have to pretend to be that frightening man's mate?

I needed to learn to keep my mouth shut.

Beau returned a few minutes later, a hulking shadow walking right behind him. Ramsey. I got to my feet at the sight of them, wiping my palms down my jeans. Lord. I'd forgotten just how . . . big Ramsey was. The two men crowded into the small hospital room and Ramsey pushed in front of Beau, moving to my side.

Fear shot through me—was he angry at Beau's idea? Did he think I was volunteering him? As he approached I raised my chin, determined not to flinch or fall back in front of him. He didn't need to know how frightened I was.

Ramsey stepped in front of me, his gaze skimming over my small form. His hard mouth twitched and then pulled into a frown. "So you're my mate."

"I am," I said defiantly.

He grunted and looked back to Beau. "I'm in."

Chapter Two

As dawn peeked through the clouds, I crouched in the wet grass and thought of rabbits. I needed to shift to wolf. The need ate away at my mind and made my muscles twitch. I dug my fingers into the dewy green blades, trying to still the endless stream of thoughts in my mind. Today was going to be a big day. An important day. A frightening day.

And what happened when I got frightened?

My body would revolt and change into my wolf form. I needed to be cool and calm today, so I needed to change now and run it out of my system. Get the wolf out of my head so when my body locked down with the urge to flee, I wouldn't sprout gray fur and a tail.

I crouched, cleared my mind, and thought of rabbits again. The wolf side of me liked the taste of rabbits, raw and bloody. The warm, salty flavor in my mouth, fresh from the kill. On most days I tried to think of anything *but* rabbits. Acknowledging the wolf side of me usually brought it into play, and that was normally the last thing I wanted.

But today I needed to get it over with, and get it over with fast.

Just like ripping off a Band-Aid, I told myself, closing my eyes and concentrating hard. My head throbbed, but instead of running away from the pain, I faced it. Pain was usually a precursor to a shift. I focused on the twinges under my skin. Forced the ache to the forefront, concentrating so hard that I felt a drop of sweat roll down my forehead, my slight body trembling at the exertion. I hadn't moved a muscle. My body felt fine.

My brain felt like Silly Putty.

Behind my eyelids, red stars and flashes began to burst, and I bit down on my lip, concentrating harder. That fucking wolf was somewhere deep inside me, I knew it. I just had to find that wild little part of my brain that scurried away like a cockroach when I wanted it—

I stopped, opened my eyes. Something in my surroundings was off. I glanced around the huge backyard of the Russell house, which was more a dorm than an actual home. Like some supernatural version of the Brady Bunch, the Russells were all piled into the large, heavily modified two-story structure that served as home for the were-cougar clan, and they owned all the land around it. Plenty of privacy for a family of shifters.

I stood and wiped the sweat from my forehead, frowning.

There it was again. The wind shifted and I smelled something. I turned in the direction of the nearby barn, where the scent was coming from, mixed in with the familiar scents of dirt, gasoline, and dust. "Who's there?"

A long moment passed. Then, just when I thought I was imagining things, a tall figure stepped out from the side of the barn.

Ramsey. My keeper and my brand-new "mate."

Skitters of unease locked my spine and I straightened, trying to seem nonchalant as he strode toward me. We were alone out here, the thought making my breath come harder and faster. I tried to be brave, but my entire body tensed with the need to flee. Clenching my fists, I gritted my teeth and forced myself to hold my ground, even though it made the hair on the back of my neck stand up. I wasn't afraid of Ramsey. I wasn't. I wasn't.

If I repeated it long enough, maybe I'd start believing it.

Ramsey kept walking toward me slowly. It was easy to be scared of him, I had to admit. Most shifters looked like normal people. Beau was a tall, lean man with well-styled thick brown hair and a wicked smile. Not a smidgen of were-cougar in his looks, but he occasionally purred around my sister. It was kind of cute.

Ramsey Bjorn was *not* like normal people.

Ramsey was massive like the Grand Canyon was massive. He was the biggest man I'd ever seen, over six and a half feet tall, with shoulders wide enough that he probably had to worry about door frames. He was covered in corded muscle, and his biceps were probably bigger than my waist. His hair was a dark, shaggy blond that hung in his face, as if he'd cut it himself, and he had a permanent scowl on his big, square jaw. To feed the cliché, he dressed like a big redneck in long-sleeved plaid shirts and jeans.

When he was almost in my face, he stopped. His jaw clenched, which I supposed was Ramsey's way of saying hello.

I rubbed my arms and pretended to shiver in the early morning air, keeping a cheerful smile on my face. Fake it until you make it. "Morning, Ramsey. Kinda brisk out, isn't it?"

"No."

Oops. Of course. Shifters didn't feel the cold like humans did. Guess that excuse wouldn't work for me anymore, now that everyone knew I was a shifter. I stared up at him. Ramsey's silence made me want to chatter more to cover up the gaps in conversation. "Well," I said brightly. "I'm going to head on in. Bathsheba's probably making breakfast, and I should go in there and help—"

Ramsey put a hand on my shoulder.

I flinched, my entire form stiffening as I took a step backward.

He jerked his hand back, as if burned, and stared down at me with the same scowl. No, wait, his scowl was larger.

"I'm not going to hurt you," he gritted in his low, deep voice.

I put on my bright smile again. "Oh, I know that. It's an involuntary reaction. Habit. Don't you worry about it." And as if I couldn't help but make a liar out of myself, I took an instinctive step backward.

What can I say, I have trust issues.

Ramsey crossed his arms over his chest, as if proving that he wouldn't reach out and grab me again. "Wanted to talk. Before."

For him, this was downright chatty. I cocked my head slightly and tried not to bolt for the back door. I'd say Ramsey's massive form didn't frighten me, but that'd be a lie. But I was also an excellent pretender and could feign casualness around him. "What about?"

"Your plan."

"You mean *Beau's* plan? We have to say it's his or Bath'll never go for it." My sister had a big, protective blind spot, and its name was Sara Ward. If she had even a whiff that this dangerous, insane, terrifying plan was my brainchild, she would nix it in a heartbeat. But because it had come from Beau, she'd trusted him.

I didn't know whether to be hurt or amused.

Ramsey ignored my correction. "This is a dumb plan."

Well. Casanova he was not. I put my hands on my hips. "It's too late to say it's dumb. I wanted Joshua, but Beau insisted you do it. You agreed, so it's too late to back out now. Besides, it's the only plan we have."

"I remember," he said gruffly. "Bad for you. Not for me."

Really, it wasn't ideal for either of us. But today

was the day, and our options were gone. I sighed, then thumbed toward the house. "Breakfast?"

He just continued to stare. "Why are you out here? This morning?"

I didn't want to talk about my wolf. It was humiliating enough that I sometimes changed in front of my sister. "Just wanted some fresh air. I'm going in now. You should come, too. You'll need your strength today."

A flicker crossed his face and I took another step backward, my face scrunched up in another flinch. After all these years, my body was still attuned to the slightest hint of male temper.

He turned, staring at the sun rising in the distance, and said, "You go ahead. I'll catch up in a few."

I didn't need to be told twice. I ran inside.

My sister smelled of cougar. I tried to be polite and not notice it, grabbing the least crispy pieces of bacon from the plate. The wolf in me liked my meat undercooked, and I suspected my sister knew that. There was a worried look on her face this morning, her pale brows knitted together as if there was a problem she couldn't quite solve.

Ignoring the stifling smell of cat in my nostrils and mindful of her still-healing ribs, I leaned in and kissed her cheek as she stood over the bacon pan. "Everything is going to be fine today," I told her. "Trust us. Trust Beau."

She gave me a tremulous smile. "I trust you.

This is the best plan to get Savannah back. I know it is. I'm just . . . worried. That's all."

Her gaze lingered on my bright blue hair and the black eyeliner I'd racooned my eyes with. My hair was normally in a chin length, silky bob that was nice, sweet, and unassuming. Perfect for when I needed to fly under the radar. Today I felt the need for additional armor, and when I hadn't been able to sleep last night, I'd bleached the hell out of my hair in the bathroom, and then attacked it with a blue temporary dye. The resulting mess was stiff, streaky, and neon blue, but it made me feel better, stronger. So did the heavy makeup and the edgier clothing. If the wolves thought I was tough, maybe I wouldn't feel like such a rabbit on the inside.

Wolves *ate* rabbits, I reminded myself, thinking of the hot blood that would burst into my mouth if I bit down on a rabbit's leg, struggling and flailing against the clamp of my long teeth—I swallowed hard and forced myself to think about other things. Six Russells—brothers and cousins to Beau—sat at the massive kitchen table, eating as fast as Bath cooked up food. Ramsey had come in while I'd been talking to my sister, and he sat at the far end of the table. I could feel his gaze on me.

"Where's Beau?" I asked. "And how are your ribs?"

"My ribs are fine. Beau's getting dressed," my sister said as she threw on more bacon, her gaze fixed on that skillet as if feeding us could solve all her problems. "Sara, I just don't know—"

"We'll be *fine*," I repeated and sat at the table with

the were-cougars, grabbing a plate and piling it high with food I had no intention of eating. My stomach was so knotted that the thought of eating anything made me want to barf.

I tore apart my biscuit and toyed with the bacon as the Russells methodically ate. No one was chatty this morning, which suited me just fine.

Beau came in a few minutes later and went immediately to my sister's side. He tugged on her long, white-blond ponytail and pulled her close for a kiss. "Morning," I could hear him murmur in a low voice that should have only been audible to my sister.

My sister blushed.

It was cute, in an overly sweet sort of way. I was thrilled for my sister, I really was. Beau seemed like a good guy. Bath was happier than I ever remembered seeing her; despite the hospital visit and anxiety over my situation, she positively glowed.

For so long it had been her and me, hiding my secret. A team, sisters and best friends combined. Adding a guy into things . . . well, I wasn't sure where it left me. I hated that I even thought about that. It seemed selfish, but I was at a loss. Here I was, twisting at ends, and everything was falling into place for my sister. I glanced down the long table and noticed that Ramsey was still watching me, his dark eyes keen. I looked down at my bacon.

Beau moved to the table and flipped a chair backward, then straddled it and sat next to me. "Are you sure you're okay with this, Sara? Your sister has some concerns with my plan."

I nodded and tried to look calm. "I think it's the best way."

"Good," Beau said. "Because we're out of options. Savannah's heat has passed—if they haven't already helped themselves to her, she's going to be bad off."

"Fucking wolves," Joshua muttered farther down the table, shoveling another biscuit into his mouth and gesturing down the table, still talking over the mouthful. "I'd like to take all of those low-down, dirty bastards out back and shoot them." Suddenly he looked over at my pale face and grimaced. "Sorry, kiddo."

"No worries," I said quietly. Joshua didn't mean to hurt my feelings. He liked me like a little sister. But I couldn't forget that I was one of those "low-down dirty bastards," even if they could. I couldn't change what I was.

Chapter Three

*M*y sister cast me worried looks on the entire drive to the meeting grounds, her hands clutching mine. I kept my expression serene, knowing that she was looking for any sign of fear, which would let her insist on not doing this.

And then Savannah would still be hostage and I'd be responsible, and the wolves would keep hunting me for the rest of my life. I'd have to keep hiding the monster I'd become. Keep bathing in perfume to disguise my scent with other shifters. After six years of hiding, I was so very, very tired of living in fear, of waiting to turn the corner and have the world come crashing down, of making the wrong move and ruining everything once again.

We drove out into the country and pulled up at an abandoned tract of land. Tall weeds overgrew the property, and the barbed-wire fence was falling down in several places. When I got out of the car, I smelled something dead—likely roadkill—in the distance. The wind shifted and then I smelled something else—the faint scent of wolves. The skin on the back of my neck prickled, and my mouth began to water with fear, two signs that I was close to changing to wolf. I clamped the thought down and bit the inside of my cheek hard, struggling to maintain control. Now was not the time.

My sister scanned the woods, her brow wrinkling, and I knew she didn't realize they were here. Every shifter in the area was very aware, though— Beau's posture had changed from easy to alert. Joshua and Austin Russell closed ranks around me, and a massive shadow loomed over my shoulder. I didn't have to glance backward to know that it was Ramsey.

Fort Sara. Like it would do any good.

Then Beau stepped forward and my shadow was gone. He stood in front of all of us, waiting for the wolves to emerge. I bit my cheek harder.

After a few minutes, they appeared. The scrubby grass led to taller bushes in the distance, then to a thick stand of trees. I had guessed that was where they'd been hiding, and I was correct. I hadn't anticipated them appearing in wolf-form, though. The smell of them laced my nostrils, overpowering all other scents and bringing with them a wealth of memories.

I crouched low in the kitchen, raising my arms over my head. "No, please, Roy. I'll be good."

"It's because I love you that I have to teach you a lesson," Roy said, snapping the belt over my head and lashing it over my arms and shoulders.

I just whimpered, knowing he would hit me harder if I screamed and called the neighbors. Screaming showed I was weak. He wanted me to be strong. The beatings, he told me, were to condition me to pain.

I just huddled smaller and waited for him to be done. But then the belt caught me across the mouth and my mouth filled with blood. I spat it on the ground and looked up to see that Roy was changing, his nose lengthening to a canine snout, his arms covered with hair. . . .

I shivered, my mouth filling with saliva. I pushed the horrible memories aside and waited, my entire body tense. Wolves pushed out of the woods, two . . . three . . . six . . . seven. Beau had told me that the Anderson wolf pack had eight male wolves and one female, so two were missing. I craned my neck, looking for them until I heard my sister's soft gasp. Her gaze was on the wolves, and I glanced back to them. They had stopped and now were crouched, changing back to human form. One naked man stood, stretching as if he hadn't a care in the world. He looked over at me and winked.

My sister averted her eyes.

I didn't. I stared back at the man, looking for signs of a quickly done shift. His brow wasn't wrinkled, his skin was smooth of wolf hair. How the hell had he shifted so very fast? My own shift was painful and drawn out, always leaving me aching and heaving. This man acted like he'd woken up from a very pleasant nap.

As the others quickly changed, they lined up behind the first man. So he was the pack leader—Levi Anderson. He stepped forward and turned toward

Beau, his gaze still on me out of the corner of his eye. "You brought the wolf girl?"

They saw me here; why the pretense? I tensed. Was I going to be just a nameless creature to abuse again? Roy had always called me "girl," too—just before he'd beaten me. The skin on the back of my neck rippled, and I bit down on my cheek again, willing my body under control.

"We brought Sara with us, yes," Beau said. "Where's Savannah?"

The lead werewolf glanced back at me. I remained where I was. I wasn't moving forward until I had a nod from Beau or Ramsey. My stomach churned hard, and I had to force myself to relax my sweaty hand so I didn't squeeze the hell out of Bath's fingers.

The lead wolf raised a hand in the air and motioned someone forward. I heard the rustle in the woods before I saw the two emerge: a man about my age and a young, dark-haired woman. Her clothes looked borrowed, and I could smell the faint scent of cougar.

"That's Savannah," someone murmured for my sister's benefit. As the only human at the parlay, she missed all the subtle signals that put the shifters a page ahead of her.

As Savannah moved forward slowly, one of the Russells breathed out hard, and I wondered at the angry sound. Savannah glanced at the wolf shifter at her side, gave him a long look, then rushed toward us.

The Russells enveloped her in warm hugs, patting her on the back and clapping her shoulder, but their expressions remained grim. A short distance away, Beau looked furious. Savannah's smile was wide and she wiped relieved tears from her eyes. Her scent was heavy with wolf, and judging by her calm demeanor, I realized why the Russells were mad.

Savannah was no longer in heat. Which meant . . .

"She's all yours again," the Anderson wolf leader drawled. "Give us Sara."

Bath drew in a sharp breath.

I fought the sick feeling in my gut and gave my sister's hand a squeeze, then released it. I stepped forward past the Russells, past Beau and Ramsey, and approached the naked pack of wolves. All of them were tall and muscled. The leader had a beard and a rather stern face. The others were younger, but I was still the youngest—and smallest—one. None of them looked like Roy, for which I was thankful. The leader's gaze was assessing as I approached, studying my body, my face, testing my scent on the air. I knew what he was looking for.

He was judging me as a potential mate.

The skin on my back bunched and rippled, and I inhaled sharply. The scent of wolf was almost overwhelming, and my legs were seizing up, cramping. Shit. I bit my cheek so hard that blood filled my mouth, and I forced my expression to remain serene. I would *never* take another wolf as my mate. I'd die first.

"Hello, baby doll. We're gonna treat you real

nice," he said in a low, mild drawl, clearly sensing my nervousness. His gaze was oddly hypnotic, and I avoided making eye contact. An alpha could control the wolves in his pack. I felt that strange thread of compulsion even though I wasn't even officially in his pack, and it frightened me.

Not daring to look backward at the Russell clan, I took a step toward my new "family." I tried not to shudder. "I'm going with you of my own free will," I announced, using the phrases we'd decided on to bring the plan into action. "A trade is a trade."

The werewolf alpha nodded at me.

I turned back to Beau. "A trade is a trade, right?"

He nodded at me, his body tense. Behind him I could see my sister's hands pressed against her mouth, fear in her wide eyes. Beau didn't take his eyes off me. "Agreed."

"All right, then," I said, and hated how small my voice was. "I'm now part of the wolf pack."

The alpha smiled, a possessive, smug look. My entire body tensed, and I waited for the plan to kick into motion. Waited for rescue. Waited for Ramsey, for Beau . . .

A colossal hand clasped my shoulder and yanked me backward against a massive, firm body. Then Ramsey spoke the longest sentence I'd ever heard from him. "In accordance with the law of the Bjorn and the were-bear clans, I claim this one as my mate."

The wolf leader's face flicked with confusion, then contorted with rage. "What the fuck is this?"

I flinched backward at the alpha's rage; the wolf in me was terrified. Normal anger scared me, but the alpha's rage made my entire being quiver. It affected the other wolves as well; I watched them shift anxiously on their feet.

A strong arm looped over my chest, drawing me closer against Ramsey's large frame.

He was protecting me.

The wolves frowned and muttered, exchanging glances. The bearded alpha gritted his teeth and glared at me and Ramsey. A low growl sounded from his throat. "This is a trick."

Ramsey's arm tightened across my chest, and I squeaked when I realized his hand had accidentally cupped one of my small breasts. I didn't think he realized it either, until I made that small noise, then it shifted lower.

"Not a trick," he growled back, the rumbling in his throat much deeper than the alpha's dangerous growl.

My mouth filled with saliva again and I bit my cheek harder. God, not *now*. I couldn't go wolf now.

The alpha's eyes flashed with anger, anger that he focused on me. "She don't look excited to be your mate, Bjorn. She looks scared."

Uh-oh. I put on a smile and gave Ramsey's hand a little pat. "I'm just surprised that my Huggy Bear declared our love openly. He's kinda private."

Someone snickered. Ramsey's arm tightened on me, and he leaned down and kissed my temple. The oddly tender motion threw me for a loop.

The wolf leader didn't look convinced. "You two aren't a couple," he declared. "This is bullshit."

"We are, too," I blurted, desperate. I turned in Ramsey's arms, though my skin crawled at the thought of turning my back on the wolves. I looked up at Ramsey, who stood at least a foot and a half taller than me and weighed at least twice as much. And I grabbed the collar of his shirt and tugged him downward. Surprised, he bent down, and I planted my mouth on his.

I felt a tremor of surprise rip through him, but I ignored it, kissing his hard mouth. I had to make this look as real as possible, so I slid my tongue against the unforgiving seam of his lips, coaxing them apart, then sucked on his lower lip. Ramsey hesitated a moment, and then I felt his big hands cup my ass, pulling me closer against him, and his tongue flicked against mine. I made the kiss deeper, wetter, wrapping my legs around his big body like I wanted to ride him, making small little noises of pleasure in the back of my throat for the audience's benefit. Ramsey inhaled sharply, then his tongue stroked deep against mine. Startled, I broke off the kiss and stared up into his eyes. His brown gaze met mine and he leaned in and gave me another light kiss on my wet mouth, as if reluctant to let the contact end. The way he was looking at my mouth sent a shiver all the way through me.

I heard my sister's gasp. Jeez louise, she was going to give everything away. I twisted around in Ramsey's arms, unwilling to unlock my legs from his torso, and looked over at the wolf pack.

All of the naked men were staring very pointedly at me. Several of them had erections.

Oh, God. Had I just made things worse? What if they didn't believe us and I had to go with the wolves? What if I left with them and they all held me down and raped me? Would they even have to hold me down? Would the alpha bark a command and I'd just drop to all fours?

Fear quickened my breath, and I felt the tight band of a headache surge through my scalp. Oh, no. Another sign of an imminent shift.

The wolf leader put his hands on his hips and stared at Ramsey, then at me, then at the Russells. His body was tense, his posture wary. "If she's your mate," he said, the growl still in his voice, "then why's she so fucking scared?"

Ramsey's hand on my ass tightened. "You," he snarled back.

The leader looked surprised. "Me?"

"She doesn't like wolves," Ramsey's bass voice rumbled. I glanced back at the Russells, who stood in front of Savannah and my sister, the phalanx of tall, lean were-cougars closing ranks around the two females. No one spoke—it was up to me and Ramsey.

"She must have liked wolves enough at some point," the Anderson leader said crudely. "She let one between her legs."

"I didn't know what he was—" I began.

"Likely story. You were probably begging for it." He gave me an assessing up-and-down look that made my blood run cold.

"I was not!"

"Bullshit," Levi retorted. "That's a bullshit story, just like all of this"—he gestured widely at everyone—"is bullshit. You're acting like fools, trying to convince us that this isn't some dumb game designed to fool a bunch of redneck wolves."

Silence. It *was* what we were doing. So much for my plan.

Levi snorted. "Thought so. Well, you know what? Fuck that, and fuck all of you. We're taking her."

Ramsey's response was a low growl.

I heard a chorus of responding growls from the throats of the wolf pack. This was getting worse, not better.

I needed to do something. I unhooked my legs from Ramsey's body and slid down him. He seemed reluctant to let me go, but he let me drop back to the ground.

"Let's be reasonable about this," I said in my most reasonable voice. "There's no reason to fight—"

The wolf alpha leveled his gaze at me. "Get over here, girl."

Caught by that compelling stare, I shrank my shoulders and pulled away from Ramsey, dropping to my knees. I couldn't stand tall in front of the alpha, had to show my submission. . . .

Ramsey roared, a feral sound, and I heard the Russells surge forward, though I wasn't sure if they were going to stop Ramsey or stop the wolves. The Andersons rushed forward as well, and I was suddenly surrounded by a pack of naked men, their backs to me as the leader tried to pull me away from the furious Ramsey.

"A wolf belongs with her alpha," the Anderson leader snarled.

"No," I gasped, but I was unable to rise from the ground. My legs tightened and rippled. One of the Andersons reached for me, taking my arm in his hand. To my horror, the skin rippled in his grasp. The Anderson wolf gave me a look of surprise and let go of my arm just in time for a convulsive wave to crash over me.

Oh, God. Not here. Not now. My back arched and my body undulated with pain. I cried out and dropped to my haunches, my panicked body beginning the painful transformation to wolf.

In humiliation I endured the endless rounds of pain as my jaw cracked and shifted, my nose elongating, every muscle twisting and stretching like a rubber band pulled taut. My skin shivered the entire time as the wolf worked her way through me. I tried not to cry out, but this change was so hard and sudden that I nearly blacked out with the pain of it.

The clearing had gone deathly silent except for the sounds of my labored breathing and whimpers, the roaring of blood in my ears as I became the hated half of me. I struggled to remain human, and that made things harder. As my hands turned to paws, I felt each excruciating twist of tendon and bone acutely. After long minutes passed, my shredded clothes fell to the ground. I gave a long, humiliated body shiver, then rose shakily to my feet. My wolf feet.

Both sides stared at me—the Russells in something like chagrin, the Andersons in surprise. Ramsey's expression was one of disappointment. For some reason, that made me feel worse, and my wolf stomach lurched. I gagged and threw up blood in the grass, unable to keep it down. On some of the more painful changes, I vomited blood. Today, it seemed, was one of those days.

The Anderson leader pointed at me, and the stink of wolf rolled off him, my nose attuned to the scent. "That," he said, his voice an echoing boom in my sensitive wolf ears, "was a fucking disgusting show."

A small whine crept out of my wolf throat.

"You're letting her kill herself," the alpha continued. "She keeps transforming like that and she's going to destroy herself from the inside out. And you assholes ain't helping her?" The Anderson leader spat at Ramsey's feet. "I thought you said you wanted to be her mate?"

I heard the crack of Ramsey's knuckles as he clenched his fists, and I looked up at him. He wouldn't look over at me.

The Anderson leader moved toward me. I shied back but he held a hand out, fingers extended, and the wolf in me felt compelled to sniff them. I did so, and he touched my ears, then ran a hand down the ruff of my collar. I endured it, feeling the wolf's need to please the alpha.

"She's killing herself if that's how she's changing," the Anderson leader said again, his voice softer. "Ain't supposed to be slow and painful like that. Ain't supposed to make her puke blood. If that's what she's doing, she's gonna be dead before a year is out."

My sister's breath caught in a soft sob. "No."

The wolf in me couldn't process. My body was still radiating pain, though it was slowly ebbing. I paced, whining. Humiliation tore through my thoughts, along with fear. Was he right and I was going to die? What could I do? I didn't want to go with the wolves. I wanted to go back with my sister. I wanted to run away. My tail flicked.

As if sensing my thoughts, the Anderson leader tried to put a hand on my ruff again, but I flinched away, skittering back a few feet, human fear overriding wolf instinct.

"We can help her learn how to change," he said in a calm, low voice meant to soothe. "Send her with us and we can save her. Even wolf babies know how to shift better than she does. Not only is she putting herself at risk, she's putting others at risk. What if she changes in public?"

Ramsey stepped forward and looked down at me, into my wolf eyes, and must have seen the fear there. He looked back at the Anderson leader and took two more steps forward, getting in the man's face. To the wolf leader's credit, he did not back down.

"She is my mate," Ramsey said in a low, dangerous voice. "She stays with me. The laws make it so."

"Still singing the same tune, eh?" The Anderson leader looked at me, then back at Ramsey. "If you aren't gonna let her go with us, then one of us is going to go with you. I'm not gonna let you kill her. She's one of us."

"Actually," Beau said, stepping forward, "this is an arrangement we'd be interested in. We've been thinking that it's long past the time for the wolf pack to join the Alliance."

A half hour later my flesh began to ache and crawl again, and I hurried off to the edge of the woods, my sister trailing behind me with my clothes as I began to change back. Several long, agonizing minutes later I lay in the grass, naked and panting, waiting for the pain and nausea to pass.

My sister crouched next to me and handed me my clothes. "Oh, Sara," she said softly. "Why didn't you tell me?"

I shrugged, slipping the shirt over my head and then dragging on my jeans. My bra and panties had been destroyed in the change, and the shirt was in tatters. "I didn't know it *wasn't* supposed to hurt. How could I?"

The man who had turned me had been abusive and a bully. I'd thought his "gift" of being a werewolf had been just another way to remind me that I was weak. Another way to force me under his thumb.

"When Beau changes, he's not in pain. It's not

like your shifting. The noises you made . . . does it always hurt so much?"

I squeezed my eyes shut. God. I wanted to die of embarrassment. I'd had an ugly, messy transformation in front of everyone. Everyone assumed that you just knew how to shift. No one talked about the mechanics, any more than you'd describe how it felt the last time you'd taken a leak. "Let's just go, Bath," I said irritably. "I want to hear what they're saying."

But when we arrived back at the rendezvous, all the deciding had already been done. Beau was smiling through clenched teeth and the Anderson leader looked mollified, if not overly pleased. Only Ramsey continued to scowl. I approached slowly, holding my tattered shirt together.

"Levi and I have come to a solution that is satisfying for both parties," Beau said and beckoned me forward. Reluctantly, I went.

"Levi wants to help you," Beau said. "He says they can teach you how to shift better. And they want to make sure your mating to Ramsey is of your own choosing." He put a brotherly hand on my shoulder. "Since the wolves want to make sure you have a choice in your mate, Connor Anderson is going to come with us. He's going to stay with you for the next month to teach you how to be a wolf. Among other things."

Oh, great. A chaperone, a tutor, and a suitor all in one. Just what I needed.

Levi nodded, then gestured for one of his wolves

to move forward. Connor turned out to be the young, attractive werewolf that had brought out Savannah, and I wondered what the story was there. Though he stood next to me, his gaze remained locked on Savannah, who stared at the ground.

"We get a wolf chaperone. What does Levi's pack get out of this?" my sister asked. "My sister doesn't want to live with them. She wants to live with her mate."

"Don't want nothing but the well-being of my wolves," Levi said in a soft voice, though I could hear a dangerous undercurrent in it. His arms crossed over his chest and he stood strong, legs apart, as if challenging Beau. "She had a bad experience and needs to know most wolves ain't like that. We don't turn people to control them. It's my job to make sure my wolves are safe. If you're pack, you're mine. And she's one of mine."

No, I'm not! The words wouldn't come out of my mouth.

As if sensing my distress, Levi looked over at me. The alpha's eyes locked with mine, and I felt the overwhelming urge to obey. It frightened me. How could he have such control over who I was?

"And in the meantime," Beau said, "we're going to discuss the possibility of the Anderson wolves joining the Alliance. A few have expressed interest in the Midnight Liaisons service, as their pack is looking for a few mates to add to their family."

"Oh," my sister said in pleased surprise. "That would be very good."

Midnight Liaisons was the dating agency my sister and I owned, and it catered exclusively to paranormal clientele. The wolf packs traditionally shunned the use of the service, and the thought of adding them clearly excited my sister.

Seemed like everyone was getting something out of this deal but me. I looked over at Ramsey, whose mouth was still pressed into a tight line of disapproval.

"All right," I said meekly.

Levi clapped me on the shoulder, nearly startling me out of my skin and making me flinch away from him. "Good girl. Looks like you get to have your Huggy Bear after all. Unless you decide otherwise." The small comment had an entire volume of menace. His tone implied that I should definitely consider "deciding otherwise." But then he smiled, showing all his teeth. "Why don't you go give your man a big kiss and wipe that scowl off his face?"

It looked like the last thing Ramsey wanted right now was to kiss me, but I was terrified of losing the fragile peace, so I moved toward Ramsey.

When he swept me up in his arms, I just gave him a light kiss on the mouth. His lips didn't part under mine this time.

Chapter Four

The ride back to the Russell compound was extremely awkward. Connor insisted on riding with me, and since he was there, Ramsey refused to leave my side. As a result, I spent the long drive back into the city squished between Ramsey's big frame and Connor's rangy one. I desperately wanted to talk to my sister about what was going to happen next, but I couldn't exactly do it in a crowded car.

When we arrived back at the Russell compound, Connor frowned, his nostrils flaring as we stepped out of the car. "I smell lots of cats here," he said uneasily, glancing back to the other van as the Russells—Savannah included—poured out. "This is where you're staying? As a mated couple?"

"We're staying at my house," Ramsey declared. He turned to my sister. "Get Sara's things."

Bath glanced over at me, then nodded. "Be right back."

Guess that was settled. "I'm going to go help her—"

Ramsey grabbed my arm. "No."

I flinched and instinctively recoiled.

Roy's hand grasping mine, his claws digging into my skin. "No, Roy. Please. I'll be good. Please don't hit me."

Ramsey immediately released my arm, his gaze meeting mine. "Please," he said in a low voice, so low that even with my shifter hearing, I wasn't entirely sure I'd heard it.

I glanced over at Connor. "Can you give us a few minutes?"

"Whatever," he said in a sullen voice. Then, as if remembering that he needed to woo me, he gave me a forced smile. His gaze immediately went to Savannah, surrounded by her brothers, and he leaned back against the truck, content to watch his prey from afar.

Ramsey turned and began to walk to the barn in the distance.

I moved after him and trotted behind, uneasy. What did he want?

When he got to the barn door, he opened it, stepped inside, and then waited for me. I wished he didn't have such an unreadable face. He looked like he was scowling all the time.

When I got inside, he shut the door behind me, and we were enveloped in darkness. Though my wolf-vision was pretty good, my eyes took a few minutes to adjust to the low light.

One of Ramsey's gigantor hands landed on my shoulder. Another hand slid around my waist, catching me before I could fall backward into the woodpile that the Russells stored here.

Ramsey's voice was a low growl in the darkness. "You jump every time I touch you. If this is going to be believable, you need to quit acting so frightened of me. I won't hurt you."

I blinked up at him in surprise, the hard angles of his face coming into shape in the low light. "Oh. I'm not scared of you."

Well, I kind of was. But mostly in the way I was scared of all men, all shifters, and pretty much everything else.

Ramsey's eyes reflected green in the lowlight. "Then why do you jump when I touch you?"

"Well, first of all," I began, reaching for a chipper tone, "I don't know if you noticed, but you're kinda big and I'm kinda small. Your hands are seriously the size of baseball mitts."

He was silent.

"And second of all," I rushed ahead, "I had an abusive boyfriend in the past. He was the one who bit me." The words hurried out of me at trainwreck speed. "So when someone grabs me by surprise, I'm not thinking there's a problem with them, I'm just mentally used to it being him. So don't take it personally. Any guy that touches me would make me react like that, so I really don't like to be grabbed because it sets off my wolf in addition to the bad memories, which are kind of tied to the ex-boyfriend. So, um. Don't take it personally."

He said nothing.

"I don't even realize I'm doing it, so you're just going to have to be patient with me. If you grab me,

I'm going to jump. That's just the way it is. I still jump when my sister grabs me, too."

Still silent. Jeez, I wished he would say something.

"Hands," Ramsey said suddenly, breaking the one-sided silence.

"Beg pardon?"

He held a hand out in front of me in the near darkness. "Give me your hand."

Tingles of panic shot through me, but I forced myself to quell them. After a moment, I put my hand in his and tried not to look at how small it was in comparison to his. My whole hand was practically the size of his palm. If he hit me, it would hurt a lot more than when Roy . . .

"We're going to hold hands," Ramsey told me. "All the time. If I'm already touching you, you won't jump. It will make us look like a couple."

Oh. I looked down at my hand in his, still laying atop his flat palm. "That's actually a pretty good idea."

His hand clasped over mine, feeling obscenely warm. Most shifters had a higher natural body heat than humans, but Ramsey was practically a furnace. Holding his hand was strangely comforting, even if it did force us to stand in close proximity. The scent of him was heavy in my nostrils—not unpleasant as far as shifter smells went. Wolves always smelled like wet dog to me, so he'd certainly gotten the raw end of the deal.

"You will have to remember that we are a couple in love," he told me gruffly.

I snorted. "You need to remember that, too. When I kiss you, you need to kiss me back."

Silence. I could almost hear the scowl on his face.

"I will try," he grudgingly said.

"If you keep scowling all the time when I kiss you, we might have to practice kissing, too," I said in a light voice.

He said nothing.

Okay, he clearly had no sense of humor.

When the silence stretched on, I began to feel awkward. My hand was still clasped in his, and Ramsey stood extremely close to me in the darkness. Was he waiting for me to speak? To leave?

"Is that everything?" I ventured after a few more moments.

"You should have told Beau that you can't shift."

The oddly gentle statement threw me off guard.

"Shifting should not be painful. You should not vomit blood. The Anderson alpha was right to be concerned. You put all of us in jeopardy. You cast doubt upon our mating. It looked as if I did not care for your well-being when you shift like that."

This felt surprisingly like a lecture, and my temper bristled. "Thanks for the tip," I snapped. "I'll keep that in mind."

When I tried to pull my hand out of his, he continued to hold on to it. "Is that what you were doing this morning? Trying to force a shift?"

I tugged at my hand. "None of your business."

"It is my business," he said gravely. "You're my mate."

"Just for show," I retorted. "That's as far as it goes. You'll be free as soon as I figure out how to shift and get the wolves off my ass. So quit stressing; you'll be rid of me soon enough."

I tugged at my hand again. This time he released it, and I strode past him to the door of the barn. "If this charming little lecture is done, I'm going to head inside and talk to my sister."

"One last thing," he said after me.

"What's that?"

"Don't call me that name."

That name? I struggled to remember, then smothered a laugh. "Huggy Bear? You have a problem with Huggy Bear? It's just a stupid name."

He wasn't laughing. "Don't call me that."

My lips twitched but I held back the smile. "It'll be good for the disguise. All couples have ridiculous names for each other. I'm sure my sister and Beau do. You'll get used to it . . . Huggy Bear."

And before he could respond, I slipped out of the barn and ran for the house.

My sister greeted me with my bag when I got to the door. Beau and Connor standing close behind her. So much for that private conversation.

She gave me a tight, worried smile. . "Everything all right?"

"Just ducky," I said cheerfully and took the bag from her.

"Good," Bath said. "So you'll be at work tomorrow like normal?" Her eyes held mine, as if she was trying to communicate something. "I can't really spare you, not with Giselle gone."

Our agency was usually a five-person crew—two of us in the daytime, two at night, and a boss to supervise. Giselle, our old boss, had been killed a few days ago when Bathsheba had been attacked by the Wendigo. Bath had taken the reins of Midnight Liaisons, so we were shorthanded as she tried to juggle her job and run the agency. And with a human running a paranormal dating agency, there were going to be some serious growing pains.

But I knew that wasn't why Bath had said she couldn't spare me. She wanted to have a long talk and was using work as the excuse.

"Of course," I said. "I'll be there."

A shadow fell over my shoulder, and I glanced back to see Ramsey. He reached over and took my bag, shouldered it, then held his hand out to me.

I put my hand in his.

My sister blinked at us, then smiled. "I'll let you two lovebirds run off, then. See you tomorrow."

Ramsey led me out to his pickup truck and opened the door for me, then I slid in, followed closely by Connor Anderson. The wolf gave me a flirty wink. "You two just pretend like I'm not here."

Ramsey snorted.

After an uncomfortably silent ride, Ramsey eventually turned down a dirt road, slowing the truck to a crawl due to the scattered paving gravel and potholes. The barbed-wire fences along the lane indicated that someone lived in this area, though it looked deserted. The sun was setting, and in the fading light I could make out a looming house in the distance, surrounded by half-naked trees. That had to be our destination.

"You kinda live out in the middle of nowhere," Connor commented, looking ahead at the house. "Reminds me of home. Lots of room to run. Very wolf friendly."

Ramsey said nothing, the sound of gravel crunching as we came to a halt.

I stared out the windshield at the ramshackle monstrosity before us. It looked like the plantation that time forgot. The yard was overgrown with plants and bushes, half of them dead. Looming over the mess was a specter of a Victorian mansion. The covered porch sagged, the house seemed to have lost every single windowpane, and paint peeled off the boards. Torn curtains fluttered out of an upstairs window. The yard was full of destroyed crap that might have possibly come from inside the house. If I peered hard enough, I could see part of a couch in the tall grasses.

"We're here," Ramsey said.

I slid out of the truck after Connor, staring up at the house. Maybe it wasn't so bad on the inside. Maybe he'd bought a fixer-upper and was renovating.

Or maybe this was just as bad as it looked.

Connor scratched his jaw and looked over at me. "Um. You guys stay here much?"

"I've never been," I admitted. When Connor raised an eyebrow, I flushed. "We usually spend our time over at the Russell house or at my place."

"Maybe we should go back to your place," he said with a friendly grin.

Ramsey scowled at Connor and pushed past him.

"Can't," I said absently. "My sister and Beau are living there while he's in town. They need their privacy." And I didn't want to be tortured with another night of hearing their lovemaking through the walls. If my sister had known, she'd have been totally mortified. And we couldn't stay at the Russell place, because then Connor would hear the distinct *lack* of lovemaking coming from Ramsey's quarters. Though how that was going to be solved in this ramshackle mansion, I didn't know—

Oh, jeez. My face flushed bright red as I realized I was going to have to sleep in the same bed as Ramsey. I grabbed my overnight bag out of the passenger seat and tried not to think about that.

The sun was setting behind the house, haloing it with light and shadow. Shouldering my bag, I moved forward to the porch and gestured for Connor to follow. The yard was overgrown with two-foot-tall grasses, and I avoided a few holes that looked snake friendly. You never knew out in the country. The steps leading up to the porch were warped with time and weather, and just as gray as the siding on the house. I placed my foot on one, testing the weight. To my relief, it creaked but held. I moved slowly up the stairs, staring around me. The front door had a busted screen. Both windows next to it were shattered, and there were some broken chimes rusting on the overhanging porch, which itself was sagging to the right.

"Wow, Barbie's dream house," Connor said sarcastically.

I gave him a quelling look.

Ramsey's large form moved to stand next to me on the porch, and the floorboards groaned. He held out his hand. "There a problem?"

"No," I said, slipping my hand into his. "No problem."

"Small problem," Connor said, crossing his arms over his chest and staring at his surroundings. "I'm not sure if I'm willing to risk being buried in the backyard and showing up on an episode of *Dateline*."

Ramsey glared.

"Well?" Connor said. "At this point you're supposed to reassure us that you're not a serial killer. That you're going to flip this eyesore for a profit, right?"

Ramsey continued to glare. His hand holding mine grew a little tighter.

"Connor, please," I said. "I'm sure this is just Ramsey's ancestral home. Isn't it?"

"No," said Ramsey.

Oh. Oh, dear. "Well, I think it's a charming fixer-upper, Huggy Bear." I patted his arm. "Which room is Connor's?"

"None of them," said Ramsey, and he inclined his head to the backyard. "Guesthouse."

Connor laughed. "There's a guesthouse? Now this I gotta see." He trotted back down the porch steps and disappeared around the side of the house.

As soon as Connor was gone, Ramsey leaned forward, his hands propped up on the porch railing, caging me between his arms. The move pinned me between him and the steps. I could let him lean all over me, close enough to breathe, or I could retreat down the porch steps, which was probably what he wanted.

I tilted my chin back, meeting his challenging gaze. It was kind of like staring a bear down inside his own cave . . . no pun intended. It was good that he was glaring at my face, because he might have seen how my hands trembled otherwise.

His face was so close that I could feel his warm breath against my cheek, the dark eyes that had seemed so beautiful from a distance narrowed in on my face. "What did I tell you about that name?"

"That you didn't like it." When he spoke in that sultry tone, it didn't sound nearly as intimidating as expected. "It's not for your benefit. It's for his."

"Apologize."

What? "Hell, no. This isn't kindergarten. I didn't say anything worth apologizing over."

He simply continued to stare down at me, waiting.

"You're not going to bully me into doing what you want." I shoved a hand against his chest, warning him to back off. But Ramsey didn't move, and my hand ended up lying against the very warm, rock-hard chest that was barely contained by his button-down flannel shirt.

He seemed to almost lean into my small hand; his face was pressing so close to mine that if I moved forward, our noses would touch.

"Here's the thing, Ramsey," I said, swallowing hard. "You said people have to believe that we're in love. So you going around telling me to apologize really isn't going to fly this week. The dopey pet name is good for our disguise, even if you don't like it. We have to work together. You scratch my back, I scratch yours."

"Scratching," he repeated, murmuring the word as if tasting it. "You know that shifters are very . . . hands-on." His nostrils flared, almost as if he was sniffing me.

"I know," I said softly. I wished I could forget.

"You're up for this? Pretending to be mated? It's not going to be easy." His tone was harsh.

"I'll be fine. It's too late to back out," I repeated in a firm voice. All I had to do was pretend to be in love with an irascible man for a few weeks. No problem. Some hand-holding, some fake affection, a few shifting lessons, and then Connor would go home to the wolves and I could go back to my regular life.

A sound rumbled low in Ramsey's throat, and as the puffs of breath tickled my face I realized he was laughing. "If the wolf's living with us, we're going to have to be affectionate around him."

"I know." Though I hadn't thought about it when I'd come up with my brilliant plan. Way to go, Sara.

"You've seen the way your sister acts around

Beau. Are you ready for me to touch you? Kiss you? Sleep in the same bed? Because once we go inside the house, there's no backing out."

My throat went dry at those images. Bath and Beau always had their hands all over each other. "Are you trying to back out—"

"No," he growled.

"Then I want to lay some ground rules." I lifted my hand from his chest and raised one finger. "Number one—no sex. If I wanted to pretend in bed, I'd call my last boyfriend."

His dark gaze flared, and he gave me an odd look. "Pretend?"

Was he insulted . . . or challenged? I didn't want to ask. "Number two," I said, wagging a second finger next to the first. "I call the shots. If I'm tired of kissing you, or holding your hand, or whatever it is bears do in public, then we stop."

Ramsey continued to study me, his gaze ultra-focused. "Anything else?"

"Number three," I said, uncurling another finger. "You keep my secrets, I'll keep yours. If I say I don't want to talk about something, I don't want to talk about it. And if I show up with a wolf snout because I can't figure out how to change back, I don't want you mocking me or making me feel like a freak."

Ramsey's hot gaze raked over me. "You're not a freak. You're perfect," he said in a low voice, and before I could blush, he added, "but if I see you having trouble changing, I'm going to step in and help."

"Fine." I didn't want to walk around with a wolf snout. And I was still a little melty from the "perfect" comment. "We're good, then."

A slow grin began to slide across his rugged face, transforming it from harsh and forbidding to . . . blatantly sexy. Inviting. Delicious.

I cleared my throat and glanced toward the house, trying to distract him. "So do I get to go inside? Or are we bunking on your porch for the next few weeks?"

His mouth twitched. "House is all yours."

Oh, goody. I ducked under his enormous arm. I had a fascination with old houses, and it was obvious that this one was well past its expiration date.

It was even worse inside. The paint was peeling, and tattered wallpaper hung from the walls. I glanced up at the staircase, where pretty much every other step was broken. Upstairs, I could see a hole punched through a wall and more ragged wallpaper hanging down.

Ramsey paused behind me and I felt his presence on the back of my neck, a subtle prickle.

I felt like I had to say something. "You sure you're not into fixer-uppers?"

"No."

Alrighty, then. " Did you just move in?"

"Twelve years ago," he said in the same gruff tone.

My eyes widened and I moved away from the wall, which looked like it was in danger of crumbling. I regarded the wallpaper more closely. Had age made it fall to tatters, or were those claw marks?

"Okay," I said. I could handle this. Given some time and some effort, this could be a home. Even if it was a dump, it beat living as the wolf pack's bitch. I took a few steps forward and put my hand on the banister, which wobbled, as if it was about to fall over. I glanced over at Ramsey. "I assume we're going to clean up if we're going to be staying here?"

He hadn't moved from his spot in the hallway, perilously close to a hole in the floor and far more comfortable with it than I was. As he leaned one meaty shoulder against the wall, I expected to hear the entire house creak and groan. "We?"

"Yes, we," I agreed. "You and I. The wonder duo. We're supposed to be mated, and I'm not about to clean this heap by myself."

Ramsey just stared at me with those too-serious dark eyes.

"And any woman in her right mind would not live in this sh— uh, place. It's a mess. It's like it gave birth to a mess. The *original* mess."

His eyes had narrowed to dangerous slits. "I don't normally stay here."

"Duh," I said before I could help myself. I wasn't staying in this shithole if it continued to be a shithole, but that was a battle I could fight in the morning, when I wasn't so tired.

I continued to make my way through the house, hoping to see an improvement on one of the upper floors, but they were all as wrecked as the first one. Ramsey followed me up the ˜tairs like a grim specter, and I paused in the hallway, kicking aside some rubble and broken glass before I moved forward.

"Our room's down the hall," he said, then turned and left.

Well, okay then.

There were several rooms down the hallway, but I peeked into each one. Empty. No furniture, so obviously not our room. I pushed open the last door at the end of the hall, but it stuck on the hinges, warped. Lovely. I shoved it twice before it opened halfway and then got stuck on the floor again. I shoved it once more, but it wouldn't budge, so I squeezed through to get a look around at my room. A bed sagged at the far end of the room, the blankets neatly made but covered in dust. Leaves and debris peppered the floor, and I glanced upward at a hole in the ceiling—an impromptu skylight. I hoped it didn't rain during my visit.

I sat down on the edge of the bed and ignored the dust cloud that puffed up. The fixture overhead didn't have a lightbulb, and I wondered if this heap even had wiring. I didn't see a light switch anywhere.

If Ramsey wanted to ensure that we had privacy from Connor, this was a pretty good start. Was the guesthouse just as bad? I shuddered to think.

Well, wreck of a house or not, I was completely wrung out. I lay back on the bed and tucked my hands behind my head, gazing up at the purpling skies. No stars yet.

Exactly how long was I going to have to pretend to be in love with Ramsey?

Chapter Five

*R*oy's arm grabbed mine and bent it back at an impossible angle. "I thought I told you to come home right away."

I bit the inside of my cheek to keep from crying out. Roy didn't like a show of weakness—it made him meaner. "I did. I came straight home—"

"Liar." He backhanded me across the face. "Do I need to punish you again? Show you the wolf?"

Terror shot through my veins and I tried to pull away from him. The wolf was savage, horrible. The wolf kept biting even when I'd given up, long past the screams in my throat dried to hoarse rasps of pain. "No, Roy. Please. I'll be good. I'll do whatever you want."

"Were you late because you were with another man? Is that what it was?" The anger in his voice turned into a low, inhuman growl, his eyes reflecting the low light inside the dark house. He always waited for me in the darkness, even when it was pitch black outside. He liked to scare me, to force me to go inside and wait for him to grab me and throw me to the ground . . .

"No, Roy, I—"

His fist connected with my face, and I felt my jaw explode in pain, felt the teeth loosen. I fell to the floor, weeping. My hand went to my cheek and it felt wet, and I realized that he'd cut me with his claws.

The wolf was coming out.

"You need to learn. Maybe after you've had a few fingers bitten off, you'll learn that you can't look at any man but me."

"No, please," I sobbed, crouching into a ball and huddling against the wall. "I wasn't looking at anyone. I promise."

His eyes went red in the darkness, his mouth turning into nothing but fangs as he loomed over me.

"Time to teach you a lesson, girl . . ."

Big, warm hands grasped my shoulders. A large, heavy body pressed over my own. "Sara."

I yelped, coming instantly awake. The wolf in me—so close to the surface—snarled in fear, and I lashed out. Someone was pinning me down. I had to break free, had to escape—

A hand stroked my hair off the side of my face, and the body over mine shifted, adjusting the weight. "Sara."

The deep voice rumbling through the darkness jarred me out of my wild fear, and I stopped scratching and clawing, gasping as if I couldn't draw enough oxygen. "R-R-Roy—"

"Ramsey," said the soft, low voice. A thumb

brushed across my chin, my cheek. "Not Roy. Not wolf. Smell me."

I inhaled sharply, my wildly hammering senses still a mass of confusion. The scent that met my nostrils was not the thick beer-and-wolf scent that I associated with Roy. The scent was clean and warm, and smelled of hints of sunshine . . . and of thick fur and the forest. Bear.

Ramsey.

"I . . . I . . . sorry," I wheezed, my heart pounding as I tried to calm from the nightmare. "Did I wake you up?"

"You were screaming," he said in a low voice. "Listen to me very carefully." His voice was deep, slow, and even. "Relax your body. Think of me and my voice, and I want you to relax your muscles. Unclench them and just relax. Understand?"

I blinked in the darkness. "I think I'm okay now, really—"

"Listen to my voice," he repeated. His form was immense; when he moved, his big shoulders hid the moonlight from the hole in the roof, blotting out the world in the darkness. He leaned in, so close I could feel the whisper of his breath on my cheek and neck. "I want you to think about me. Focus on my voice and my heartbeat. Can you do that?"

I stared at him, confused. "I—"

"Get away from her," a male voice roared. The door to the bedroom crashed open with a massive scrape on the floorboards, and I saw Connor slam into the room, wolf-eyes gleaming. He clutched a baseball bat in his hands. Before I could scream, he swung it and connected hard with Ramsey's shoulder.

The bear-shifter grunted but didn't move from where he crouched over me, caging me in his arms. Protecting me. I expected to hear a growl in his throat, but to my surprise, his voice remained slow and even, as if he'd been trying to calm a wild animal. "Leave us alone, wolf."

Connor looked over at me, and then blanched. He took a step backward. "Oh. Oh, shit. Sara, are you okay?"

"Just a nightmare," I said, then raised a hand to shoo him . . . and noticed my fingers were tipped with thick claws. In horror, I stared down at them. My arms were thick with gray fur, and my muscles vibrated with the need to change. Ramsey's forearms bled in four long furrows—I'd attacked him in my dream.

"Sara," Ramsey said in a low voice, ignoring Connor. "Listen to me. Think of me." He moved over me, his gaze trapping mine. "Connor is going to leave us alone now."

I looked over at the wolf, who was staring at me with something akin to horror. After a moment, Connor nodded and slung the bat back over his shoulder, mumbled something about seeing us in the morning, and shut the door behind him again.

I turned wild eyes to Ramsey. "Oh, my God. I'm so sorry—"

"Shhh." His fingers gently touched the sides of

my face again, stroked my hair, completely ignoring the fact that I'd carved his arms up or that Connor had attacked him. It must have hurt, but he showed no reaction, his gaze focused intensely on me. "Concentrate on my voice. On my breathing. My pulse. Follow me. Focus on me. Understand?"

Oh, jeez, it must have been worse than I imagined. I thought of Connor's look of horror as he'd come in the room. He'd looked revolted at the sight of me. "My face is half changed, isn't it?"

"That's not important," Ramsey said, large fingers continuing to stroke the sides of my face. "Listen to my breathing, and match yours to mine. Breathe with me."

I did, inhaling slowly and breathing in the musk of his bear-scent. He didn't smell like wolf, and the heavy feel of him over me didn't feel like it was trapping me; it felt like it was protecting me. It took several minutes before my heart calmed to a steady pace again, in tandem with Ramsey's slow, even beats.

After several minutes, he nodded and then sat up. "Better."

I stole a peek at my hands—normal again. My fingers went to my face, and I touched my nose. Normal, except for a nosebleed. Thank God. One time I'd been stuck with a half-monster snarl for eight hours and had been terrified I'd never change back. The nosebleed was distressing, though. It reminded me of Levi's words—that I was going to kill myself with my shifting. "Um. Got Kleenex up here?"

He stripped his shirt off and handed it to me. I

took the shirt and wadded it up, holding it to my nose. It smelled like Ramsey and sweat, an oddly pleasant combination. "Thank you."

"Who is Roy?"

I blushed in the darkness. "The asshole who changed me."

"You were screaming for him not to hurt you." Not an accusation, a statement.

How embarrassing. "I don't want to talk about this, please," I said in a small voice. I expected Ramsey to push the issue, but he remained silent, his gaze watchful on me. I reached out a hand to his big arm. "Is your shoulder okay?"

"It'll be fine by morning." He stood and crossed over to the far side of the room, made sure the door was locked, and then returned to the bed.

I watched his body as he moved. I couldn't help it. My entire body was tense with nerves. The last time I'd been in a room with a half-naked man, he'd usually beaten the crap out of me and told me I deserved it, so I was wary when it came to intimate relationships. Ramsey was massive, too. A lot of shifters were in great shape, thanks to the animal inside that loved to run and play, and most were corded with muscle, rippling with six-packs. Ramsey was just . . . mammoth. He was six and a half feet of pure, solid muscle on a massive frame. Thick and solid like a boxer. Suddenly I doubted very much that the bat had hurt him, and a quiver of fear shot through me when he sat on the other side of the bed and then lay down next to me. I clutched the shirt to my nose, waiting.

He simply closed his eyes as if I hadn't been there.

"So about this," I said, feeling the need to make excuses for my behavior. "I should have said something. It happens more often than I'd like. I'm sorry."

He looked over at me at that. "Every night?"

"Not the nosebleeds," I joked. "That's special for tonight."

He stared at me, his jaw clenched. "If you are frightened of me—"

"Oh, no, that's not it," I said hastily, surprised. He thought that was why I was having nightmares? How totally awkward. I mean, I was scared of him, but that wasn't causing me to turn in my sleep. "I have these all the time. Roy, I was scared of. You? You're just . . . big."

He snorted.

"It's true," I said, deciding to tease him a little more to defuse the situation. "It's like you're Paul Bunyan. Or since you're a shifter, maybe more like his ox."

He was silent for a moment, then said, "Bear."

"Okay, then. I'm Goldilocks, and I got stuck with the biggest bear instead of the one that's just right."

Silence again. Then he turned toward me, his eyes gleaming in the darkness. "I am big, Sara. I'm big and I don't talk much, but I would never hurt you. You understand that?"

Damn. I seemed to always say the wrong thing. I nodded. "I know. My head knows it, but my body takes a little longer to remember it."

He regarded me for a moment more, then touched my cheek again. "Sleep."

"I should probably stay up for a bit," I said, testing my nose. Good. It had stopped bleeding. "Make sure I don't shift again or attack anyone. I'll probably be a little twitchy for the next hour or two."

His hand cupped the side of my head. "Sleep. I'll watch over you."

"All right," I said softly, unsure how to take that. It was . . . sweet of him to offer, but did I trust him to have my back? He stared back at me, unflinching and solemn. I realized that if this was going to work, we needed to be a team.

And I needed to trust him.

So I lay back on the bed and tried to relax, not anticipating being able to sleep at all. Ramsey's dark eyes gleamed in the moonlight, and I knew he was watching me.

Despite my nerves and the anxiety of sharing an unfamiliar bed, for some reason I fell right back to sleep. This time my dreams were peaceful and quiet, and filled with the sounds of Ramsey's soothing voice.

The next morning I awoke warm and cozy. I blinked a few times, wondering why I felt so delicious and safe. The scent of something unfamiliar brushed my nostrils, but my sleep-drugged brain didn't seem to grasp it.

A hand slid down my back and pulled me closer,

and I realized the heavy rumble in my ear was a snore.

Blinking, I focused on the very broad, very bare chest I was curled up against. My cheek was laid against one blazingly hot pectoral, my fingers curled in blond chest hair. A massive hand rested on my back, pulling me close, and my legs were tucked close against his.

My breathing quickened and I watched his chest move up and down for a minute, trying to think of how to extricate myself from his grasp. My clothes were still on, which was a good thing. Ramsey was shirtless and, under the blankets, possibly naked. I sure hoped not.

The heavy, even breathing continued, but the snoring had stopped. Maybe I could sneak out before he was totally awake . . .

"I will not bite you," his deep voice said in my ear.

I jerked my fingers away when I realized they were still entwined in his chest hair. "Oh. Of course. I know that. I was just figuring out how to get out of bed without waking you up."

As his large hand moved off my back, I rolled away and got to my feet, straightening my clothes. My hair felt like a stiff mess and my eyes felt puffy, but the rest of me felt . . . pretty good, oddly enough. I stretched, testing my muscles. Who would have known I'd have slept so well next to a giant? Except for one small thing, of course. "I know we have this fake marriage thing going, but in the future can you not grab me when I'm sleeping?"

Ramsey swung his legs over the side of the bed, and I was relieved to see that he had slept in his jeans. He scratched his chest and my gaze was drawn to that big hand, the hard, rippling layer of muscles over his big chest . . . he was enormous. Gorgeous, but enormous.

"It was you."

"Huh?"

"You grabbed me," he said. "You had bad dreams and trembled in your sleep. Then you rolled over and grabbed me, and slept quietly. I left you there." His level gaze seemed to add, *Because I'm a nice guy.*

"Oh. Thanks. I think." Jeez, I was pretty sure I was blushing. Had I clung to him while I'd slept? My sleeping self was either a total coward or a cuddler. Neither one was optimal. I adjusted the knots on my shirt, which had held up overnight but looked ready to go. "Where did you put my bag?"

"First we will talk about this 'Roy' person."

I moved toward the door. "No, we're not talking about him."

Lightning fast, Ramsey's big form blocked my way. "We'll talk now."

Memories flashed through my mind, and I immediately began to tremble all over at the sight of the blocked exit, panic looming in my mind. "Please . . . please move."

Remorse flickered across Ramsey's face, and he immediately moved to the side and held the door open. "Not trying to frighten you."

"It's okay," I said, blinking to clear my mind of

foul memories. "Just reminded me of . . . bad things. Can we talk about stuff later? I'm hungry."

He nodded silently, and I fled down the stairs.

A cursory search of the house showed me that my bag had been left in the foyer. I rummaged through it, looking for my favorite pink T-shirt. I took it to the bathroom and yanked it over my head, tossing the other. The bathrooms were cleaner than the rest of the house, thank goodness. This one had peeling wallpaper and a broken mirror, but the tub, toilet, and sink were intact. I frowned at my reflection. Dried blood had run into my hairline on one side of my face, the black makeup had landed underneath my eyelids, and my hair stuck out in all directions. Charming. I turned on one of the faucets, and the entire wall groaned as if in pain. I quickly shut it off again and took a step backward. "Do you have water, Ramsey?" I yelled up the stairs.

"Sometimes."

"Great," I muttered. Using a clean sock from my bag, I spit-cleaned my face as best I could. At least I could use the sink at work. My wild blue hair was tamed with a shoelace headband, and I was ready to face the day. Day one as Mrs. Ramsey Bjorn. Yikes.

The kitchen proved as empty and broken down as the rest of the house, and I opened the fridge and quickly shut it again, waving a hand in front of my face to clear the smell. "Did something die in your fridge?"

"No," Ramsey said, turning the corner and entering the room to the side of me.

I glanced at him out of the corner of my eye. His shaggy blond hair was wet and slicked away from his face, curling around the dark blue collar of his security T-shirt tucked into his pants. It emphasized the breadth of his body, and I found myself oddly fascinated as those hands slipped underneath his belt, adjusting the shirt. "Where'd you get the water?" I asked.

"Well. It's outside."

That sounded . . . rustic. I frowned and gestured at the fridge. "Your cupboard's bare, dude."

"I don't eat here."

I raised my eyebrows. It shouldn't have surprised me, given that the house was falling down around our ears. But still. "But we're mated. We need a real kitchen, and a fridge if we're going to live here. Where do you normally eat?"

"With the Russells."

That didn't help much. I looked back at the ancient fridge, not daring to open it again. "That fridge croaked long ago. Do you ever stay here?"

"Rarely."

"Then why own such a dump?"

He gave me a quelling look, as if horribly insulted. "Needed a home."

"Judging by the look of this place, you still need one. I can't believe we're going to stay here for the unforeseeable future."

"It's your fault."

I stared at him. "*My* fault?"

"Your plan, wasn't it?"

He had me there. "The next time I have a brilliant plan, tell me to shut up."

Ramsey snorted. It sounded like agreement.

Chapter Six

The guesthouse turned out to be a cute little mother-in-law-type cottage on the other side of the murky pond behind the trees. It had a running air conditioner, power, and running water. And a roof, which automatically made it better than the main house. I supposed that was where Ramsey normally stayed when he had to crash here.

I knocked on Connor's door. When he opened it, I gave him my cheeriest look. "You about ready to head in to work with me, shadow?"

He gave me a wary look. "You okay this morning?"

"Of course," I said, pretending last night's embarrassing transformation hadn't occurred. "It was just a fluke accident. Never happened before." Much.

He crossed his arms over his chest. "Do you want to talk about it?"

That was the last thing I wanted. I already had Ramsey crawling all over me; I wasn't about to start confessing all my dirty werewolf secrets to Connor. "I'm going to be late to work if we don't get moving soon," I said, turning and leaving because that was the only way I could think to get him out of the guesthouse. "So we'd better get going, or Ramsey's going to be cranky."

"Wouldn't want that," Connor muttered, but I heard it anyhow.

It was decided that we'd grab breakfast on the way in. I knew Connor would be shadowing me, but I hadn't realized that Ramsey would be sticking to my side as well. I couldn't act like I didn't want Ramsey protecting me, though. That was his job in this charade. I did my best to look delighted at the thought of Ramsey at my side all day, but I'm not sure I succeeded.

The ride into town was uncomfortable. Ramsey didn't talk to me, and Connor was still giving me that skeptical look, and I knew he was thinking about my messy, involuntary shift last night. To distract him, I fired question after question about his family and the pack.

He answered them all with a lazy, casual drawl. His uncle was Levi, and the others were his cousins. His aunt Maybelle had been the mother to the Anderson pack, before she died a few years back. His parents lived in Arkansas. No, they didn't like Texas. No, he didn't miss them much. The pack kept him busy. His cousins filled out the rest of the wolf pack—Maynard, Owen, Wyatt, Buck, and Tony. The youngest was the only girl in the pack, his cousin Gracie. She was newly eighteen and a little wild, he admitted. The other wolf packs had started to sniff around her, since she was getting to about that age.

All this talk about other wolf packs and sniffing around made me highly uncomfortable, and I just shrugged when the men ordered from the McDonald's drive-thru, my appetite suddenly gone.

A coffee was shoved into my hand and a bag of food passed to me. Ramsey glared down at me. "Eat."

"I'm really not hungry," I said. Just the thought of all those wolves made my stomach lurch uncomfortably.

"To learn to be a proper shifter," Connor said as he scarfed down a breakfast sandwich in two bites, "you need fuel and a mentor, and I'm here to help you with the second part."

I could almost feel Ramsey's glare in Connor's direction. The cab of the truck suddenly felt very small, and I clutched the coffee closer. "Just a small breakfast sandwich, I guess."

Connor made a noise of approval between bites of his sandwich. "One of the first things you're going to figure out is that the wolf in you demands food— lots of it. Especially meat, the rawer the better. It's best to pay attention to what your wolf wants, or else ignoring it could have nasty side effects."

"Got it," I said in a confident voice, though I didn't feel confident. I'd been a shifter for six years now. I knew that I liked raw meat, but I avoided it for that very reason. I thought maybe if I could control my wolf urges, I could control my wolf. It seemed like everything I thought was backward. "I feel like there's so much I don't understand."

"That's why I'm here," Connor said confidently.

Ramsey's hands clenched the steering wheel a little tighter.

"You want to encourage your wolf, Sara," Connor continued. "It's an important part of you now. The better you can handle the wolf, the easier you'll fit in with the wolf pack."

And there went my appetite again. I sucked in a breath, trying to calm my stomach.

Ramsey looked over at Connor with an almost violent expression. "Fuck the wolf pack. She doesn't *want* to fit in."

"It's not about what she wants anymore, I'm afraid," Connor said evenly. "It's not my decision, you know. I'm just here to supervise and help out where I can. It's all Levi. And because he's the alpha, I can't contradict him."

Neither could I. The thought made my stomach churn even more.

We pulled up in front of the unassuming strip mall that Midnight Liaisons was housed in. I was never so relieved to get out of the car and practically leapt out behind Connor.

Ramsey was already there with his hand extended, ready to hold mine. The sight made me blush, and I handed him the bag of food. Then, coffee in one hand of mine, Ramsey's hand in the other, and Connor trailing behind us, we headed into the agency.

"Sara, there you are," my sister said with a smile and a wave from her desk. She had a phone cradled to her ear and covered the mouthpiece as she greeted me. "I was wondering if you were going to be late."

"No, I'm ready." Sorta.

"Good," she said with a smile, then held the phone out to Ramsey. "Beau wants to talk to you."

"Not right now," he said. He released my hand, moved to my desk, and pulled my chair out.

I sat down and clutched my coffee, glancing at the bear-shifter hovering over my shoulder. Connor sat across from me and proceeded to devour breakfast sandwiches, unfazed by Ramsey's glower. Ramsey stood directly to the side of my chair and waited, unyielding, his big form looming over me and my desk.

I gave my sister a *help me* look.

"Tell him that it's not a request, it's an order," Beau's laughing voice said over the phone. Every shifter in the office could hear it plain as day. Our hearing was magnified compared to a normal person's. Even in human form, I could hear a pin drop across the room. I could definitely overhear a phone call, and so could the others.

"He said—"

"I know," Ramsey growled, pulling out his own cell phone and storming out of the office.

"Hanging up now, sweet Bathsheba. Love you," Beau said to my sister, then clicked over to take Ramsey's call.

I stared at my coffee, glancing out the door.

Ramsey paced in the distance, just far enough away that shifter ears couldn't pick up his conversation. My sister resumed typing, and Connor ate. My stomach rumbled, and Connor slid a sandwich to me. "Eat. You need fuel as a shifter. You're not like a human girl anymore, and you don't have the appetite of one."

Ugh. Thanks for the reminder. I poked at the paper and then gave Connor a cross look. "I prefer Starbucks."

"Eat," Connor repeated. "Or I go and get the big guy."

Oh, fine. I picked up the sandwich and took a big, demonstrative bite. If I didn't eat, not only would I have both men hovering over me but my sister would join in next, and I had enough people fussing over me. As I ate, I typed one-handed on the keyboard, logging in and checking my work email. A message immediately popped up from my sister, dated one minute ago.

Can you ditch Connor? We need to talk and can't while he's here. Ryder's with a client in the back setting up a profile. Think we can pawn him off to her?

Gimme five minutes, I wrote back, then added, *You think it's ok to have him here at the agency?*

We don't have a choice, but I don't think he's dangerous. Beau would have never agreed for

him to be your escort if he thought he was. They
wanted to send Maynard, but Beau insisted on
Connor. Says he's run into the wolf pack before,
and Connor's the only decent one in the lot.

But what about . . . the thing with Savannah.

We asked Savannah if she wanted to press
charges against him and she said no. She said he
was a gentleman to her the entire time.

But they slept together, right?

Right. Nevertheless, she spoke really highly of
him . . . and she also told Beau that she doesn't
want to see him again. So I don't know what to
think, but I don't think he's dangerous.

I had to agree. He seemed decent enough, as far
as wolves went. Connor was polite, friendly, didn't
leer at me, didn't call me baby doll, and didn't try to
make me bow to his will like Levi did. In my book,
that counted for a lot, but I also had pretty low ex-
pectations where the wolves were concerned.

I glanced over at Connor. He was drinking his
coffee quietly, staring off into the distance. Probably thinking about Savannah. I considered him a
moment longer, then pulled up the Midnight Liaisons database to begin work.

The database was my baby. It existed on a private server, and our user interface was hosted on a

secure website that I'd scripted with the help of an Alliance programmer. In it, we kept careful tabs on all the supernaturals of all kinds that had signed up for our service, tagging profiles with jobs, statuses, activity, and carefully monitoring them. Supes were tricky creatures to matchmake—no one wanted to date a harpy, for example. Every male wanted to date were-foxes, as they were notoriously promiscuous. The profiles were monitored to ensure that the matches made were recorded, feedback given, and bad behavior noted. Since there were so many different hierarchies for every kind of supernatural, we had to be very careful not to tread on someone's toes.

My database screen immediately filled with profiles that had seen activity in the past twenty-four hours, and to my surprise, my name was at the top of the screen. I clicked on it and saw a photo of me from my driver's license, my hair brown and longer, my smile wary. When had I gotten a file? My shifting side had been a secret up until five days ago. Sure enough, my profile had been created by my sister over the weekend. A big red MATED was stamped in the Availability box, along with Ramsey's name. I clicked on it, feeling nosy.

His profile had been set up several weeks ago. My guess was that he'd set it up about the same time as Beau. Interesting. I'd never thought to look.

Curious, I clicked on his history. He'd never logged in, which didn't surprise me. What did surprise me was the lack of auto-dates.

Our system had a set of checks and balances as to what sorts of shifters would be compatible, and when they came up in the system, it automatically suggested matches. Someone in the office would approve the match, and then the invite would be sent to the female shifter first, as they were fewer in number and thus in more demand. If the female shifter accepted, the invite was then sent to the male profile.

Once Ramsey's profile had been created, he'd been added to the auto-date pool. It should have matched him up repeatedly through the database. Instead, his profile was blank. Either it hadn't been activated, or something odd was going on . . . or he was completely unattractive to other supernaturals. Strange. I looked at his picture. His hair was a little long and he wasn't smiley, but Ramsey was handsome. Not very chatty, but that was all right. Just the strong, silent type.

Why didn't anyone want to date him? I shrugged and clicked his profile away, and the computer returned to mine.

Connor touched the corner of my flatscreen monitor, turning it so he could see, too. "You get your hair done recently?"

"Just time for a change," I said lightly, then lied, "bears have a thing for blue."

He snorted. "You and Ramsey . . . it's just odd."

I scowled at Connor, insulted. "What's so odd about it?"

"Your sizes. He's a bear. He could eat you for

breakfast. You're better off with a wolf," he declared. "Most of my cousins are good guys. You'd like 'em once you got to know 'em better."

I couldn't help but notice that *"most of."* If he was here to sell me on his cousins, he was doing a pretty awful job of it. "I happen to love Ramsey," I said with a little choke on the word *love*. "And unless you want to wear your coffee, you're going to shut up about matching me up with one of your cousins."

His handsome face was somber. "Sara, I'm trying to help you. I'm here to be your friend, and as a friend, I'm trying to give you good, practical advice. Wolves don't take no for an answer. My cousins are lonely. Levi knows that they're lonely, and you're in their grasp, so he's going to be very determined to bring you to the pack, because to him, it's in the best interest of the others. And because my brothers need a mate, they're not going to give up on you so easily, either. You need to remember that, Sara." He dug into the bag and pulled out another sandwich, then offered it to me. When I declined, he began to peel off the paper. "I realize this comes across as harsh, but I'm trying to warn you. They'll play nice at first, but don't expect them to play nice forever."

A shiver ran up my spine. "It's a good thing I've got Ramsey, then." As Connor continued to study my screen, I sipped my coffee. "You interested in setting up a profile?"

"Don't know." He hesitated for a moment, as if wanting to say more, but he didn't.

That wasn't a no, I thought triumphantly and noticed my sister watching out of the corner of her eye. "There's not a lot of wolf-shifters in our database," I said. "But I know a pretty were-mink or two that you might be interested in meeting."

He seemed uninterested. "Maybe. Is Savannah in the database?"

Aha. "She wasn't as of last week, but that could have changed. Beau is making sure his family members are added to the pool. They like our service and feel it helps promote cross-species relations."

"I'll bet," he said. "Sure. Sign me up, I guess."

"I'll get Ryder," my sister said, jumping up from her desk and heading to the back part of the office. "Be right back."

Connor scowled, looking more like a thwarted young man than the vicious wolf I'd pegged him to be. I leaned over my desk. "If you want to see Savannah again, you need to make my sister happy."

His scowl darkened. "Humans? Please—"

"She's Beau's mate," I warned in a low voice, ignoring the insult to my sister. "And she carries a lot of influence with him. Just so you know."

Connor continued to scowl, even when Ryder appeared, all perky smiles, her camera in hand. She flirted outrageously with Connor, who didn't flirt back. I wasn't sure if it was because she smelled human or if it was because he was thinking of Savannah. Ryder's playful attempts to get him to open up failed miserably, however, and eventually she got the hint. Linking her arm in his, she more or less pulled him to the back conference room, where they could set up his profile and film a short video to introduce him to others. He glanced back at me once but allowed Ryder to take him away.

As soon as they were gone, Bath rushed over to my side. She touched my hair, frowning at the sight of me. "You look like Sonic the Hedgehog on a three-day bender."

"Very funny."

"How are you hanging in there?" Her eyes were concerned.

"I'm fine," I said, watching the door. "Where'd Ramsey go?"

"Beau's keeping him on the phone for a few minutes for me. He knew I wanted to talk to you privately before we launch this particular idea at you."

Uh-oh. Beau and my sister had been planning? Two busybodies were never so fearsome as when they were working together. "What's going on?"

"Clearly there's been a change in plans," she said. "The wolves didn't call off like we expected. You and Ramsey are going to have to keep pretending until Connor gets bored and goes home to the wolves. I'm so sorry, Sara. We had no idea they'd insist on an envoy to shadow you. Beau is very concerned about your ability to shift, too. He wants either Ramsey or Connor with you at all times."

"So he thinks I'm going to die if I keep shifting, too?"

To my horror, my sister's eyes filled. "Sara, we're all so worried about you. I don't think you understand—"

"I understand," I said softly. Just because I wasn't weeping about it didn't mean it didn't scare the shit out of me. Time to cheer my sister up. "Well, look on the bright side. Your wedding can still go on."

"No, it can't," she insisted. "I'm not getting married while your life's a mess. Once this stuff with the wolves is figured out, I'll be able to relax. Not until then." She thought for a moment and then added, "And after the dance."

I gave her a puzzled look. "Dance?"

Her eyes lit up. "Yes! Beau and I were brainstorming about how we could make a transition in the agency. We've had a few concerned inquiries, since we're in control of so much private information and Giselle is no longer heading the agency. Since I'm in charge now and I'm a natural, not a supernatural, people are going to worry. Marie and Ryder aren't supernatural either, and as their boss, I don't think I could ask them to have a vampire or wolf bite them and turn them." She gave a nervous laugh. "Though I guess I could ask if they're interested in dating through the agency. Maybe that would help."

"What about me?" I said, strangely hurt that I was being discounted. "This werewolf crap should be good for something."

"Well," she said as she twisted her hands. "It is and it isn't. People don't really trust werewolves since they're not normally part of the Alliance, and you're not a natural werewolf. Which kind of makes you neither here nor there. But," she said, jumping back onto her topic with enthusiasm, "we're going to start doing Alliance mixers to promote the agency and to increase everyone's comfort level with humans in charge."

"Mixers?" I echoed.

"Yes, and we're starting with a barn dance! It'll be great. People who don't normally get their profiles picked up can mingle with others, and we'll get all the supes chatting. Even our were-mongooses might find that the were-snakes aren't so bad after all if they give them half a chance."

I raised an eyebrow as she went into detail about her plans for the party. It'd be in a real live barn, provided she could find one to rent out. There'd be country music and hay bales (because what barn dance is complete without hay?), and alcohol, of course, because she wanted people to be relaxed for mingling. After a few minutes, she noticed my silence. "You're not saying much. What do you think?"

It was hard for me to muster enthusiasm for mass groups of supernaturals at the moment, but I put on a brave face for my sister. It *was* a good idea. "I like it. It'll show we're committed to the agency and that we treat things seriously. Plus it'll give us a chance to meet some of our clients out of the office environment. I think it's brilliant. And hopefully we can get the wolves out of our hair soon and I can help with planning the next few events."

My sister's smiling expression immediately changed to one of concern. "How's that going?"

"Oh, swell," I said cheerily. "Connor's going to help me figure out how to shift without the night-time nosebleeds, and everything'll be taken care of."

"You have *nosebleeds*?"

Oops. "Only every once in a while," I soothed. "Between Beau, Ramsey, and Connor, we're covered for teachers. The nosebleeds will go away when I get a handle on my shifting. There's no need to worry."

"Beau also suggested something else, and I agreed with him."

Uh-oh. I looked at her, waiting.

Her smile was a little too bright. "You need to date Ramsey."

"Haven't we passed that point? I'm mated to him, remember?"

"But Ramsey's a big, scary guy. He's Beau's muscle when stuff needs to be done. Everyone in the Alliance is afraid of him, and everyone sees you as—"

She stopped. I knew what she was going to say. *A victim*. That hurt.

"So I'm already getting a lot of calls from people asking about Ramsey and you," she continued on in a rush. "You two need to be seen in public, laughing together, smiling together, holding hands. Make people realize that you are a couple."

His face would probably break if he had to crack a full-on smile. "So you think I have to *date him* date him? Living with him isn't enough?"

Bath shook her head. "I don't think so. Beau doesn't either. He got some calls from other leaders unhappy about the arrangement. Another wolf leader, and the badger clan. Tigers, too. They're worried you're being coerced against your will."

How ironic. The fake relationship with Ramsey was to *prevent* me from being coerced into a relationship. I glanced down the hall, then back at my sister. I spoke low enough that Connor couldn't hear it. "There's a slight problem here. How am I supposed to date him when we have Connor crawling up our asses?"

She gave me a wry shrug. "We'll hook him up through the agency. It'll be like double-dating."

I groaned. This was worse than bad. "Do I even have a choice?"

"Not really."

I sighed. "Okay. I'll talk to Ramsey."

She toyed with the end of her long ponytail. "That's what Beau's doing right now. I'm guessing he'll be back any minute."

Ramsey *was* back a few moments later, and he looked ready to kill something. He stormed back into the office, sat in one of the chairs in the waiting area, and began to text feverishly. I watched him for a minute, fascinated at how fast his big hands moved on that tiny phone.

Bath returned to her desk and gave me a meaningful look.

I glanced over at Ramsey. "I hate to keep you here all day. If you want to head off to work, I'll be just fine."

His angry glare softened as he looked over at

me. "Not leaving while the wolf is sniffing around you."

Ah. "Got it. Well, we might be spending a lot of time together in the next few weeks," I said in a cheerful voice. "Hope one of you likes to play video games."

He just went back to texting furiously.

My sister looked appalled at Ramsey's unfriendliness. I almost smiled. I didn't mind his silence, and when Ramsey did speak, he was honest. I'd take that over the wolves' playful antagonism any day. I'd figured out that his silence was simply him processing his thoughts, thinking through his words. He knew he intimidated people, so he chose his words carefully.

I had to admire that. When I got nervous, I had verbal diarrhea.

Ryder and Connor came out of the back office a short time later. Ryder immediately went to her desk and began to upload the pictures she'd taken, while Connor resumed his spot on the opposite side of my desk, ignoring Ramsey's glare. He finished his breakfast without a word, then dusted off his hands. "So, tonight Uncle Levi's having a barbeque so you can spend time with the pack."

The back of my neck shivered in anxiety. Just what I needed—a night full of more wolves. "Can't," I said. "I have a date."

"Cancel it," Connor said. "It's important that you spend time with the wolves. Your alpha—"

A large shadow loomed over my desk, and Ramsey glared down at Connor. The younger shifter froze.

"You telling my mate she can't go out with me?" Ramsey's voice was barely audible, it was such a low growl.

"Nope," Connor drawled. "Maybe tomorrow night on the barbeque, then. I'll tell my uncle that there's been a change in plans."

"Maybe," Ramsey said in a dangerous voice, then cracked his knuckles. "If she's up to it."

"Got it," Connor said hoarsely and got up. "Gonna make a phone call."

I beamed at Ramsey, adopting my happily-mated-woman persona. "I know just the place, too, Huggy Bear. I'll make the reservation."

He moved to the side of my desk, touched my hair, and leaned in to kiss my forehead. As his lips brushed my skin, he murmured, "Quit calling me that stupid name."

"I'm not so sure this is a good idea," I told my sister for the tenth time as she shoved another dress through the file room door at me.

"Nonsense. I'm sure you've worn a dress once or twice in your life. Just let me know which one you like and I'll return the others to the store."

"I don't mean that the *dress* is a bad idea," I retorted, shimmying into the next dress she tossed over and adjusting the straps. It was cute, I had to admit. Spaghetti straps and a vivid orangey red, with a decorative seam just under the bust to emphasize my lack of said bust.

"Hurry up," called Bathsheba. "You and Ramsey have to go across town, and you can't be late for your reservation, or you'll lose it. And I need to get there and set up as well."

I groaned at her bossy tone and turned, checking my reflection in the mirror. Cute, but I saw a panty line. I stripped my panties off. No time to do more shopping—I'd just go commando. It's not like it was a real date, after all. "I'm hurrying," I called out, gave the dress one last glimpse, then slipped into the strappy black heels she'd bought for me. I was sure to break an ankle in these.

Bath brightened at the sight of me as I stepped out of the file room. "You look adorable." She reached over and yanked off the tag under my armpit. "I'm going to go return the others, and then I'm heading over to the restaurant. I'll text you if I need anything."

"You know you don't have to come. I'm a big girl. I can date Ramsey on my own." Heck, I'd cuddled against him in bed last night. A fake date should be easy after that.

Bath squeezed my arm with excitement. "I know, but I want to do this. I'm going to go set up in a dark booth across the room. I'll be watching you and a few other couples. The harpy has a date, and so does one of the jaguar girls, and I want to make sure neither one loses their temper."

Sounded like my sister was going to have a full

evening. Neither species was known for its calm manner. "You're going to hide behind plants and snoop. Got it."

"That's my job," she agreed, sounding way too excited about it. She loved to manage people. "Now, remember to leave your cell phone on. I'll text you if I think you guys need some help looking legit. There's going to be a lot of shifters there tonight."

Chapter Seven

*R*amsey was characteristically silent on the drive to the restaurant, which was all right with me—I didn't feel much like talking.

Connor had left earlier with my sister, anxious and a little bit fidgety. Bath had begged him to fill in on a last-minute cancellation. She had a prickly female jaguar shifter who was one of our more difficult clients. Connor hadn't been interested, but my sister had cajoled and pleaded with him. He'd be at the restaurant anyhow, right? Why not help her out with this small thing? It'd be the perfect chance to observe me with Ramsey from afar. She'd even pay for the dinner.

Connor had still balked. My sister hadn't given up, though, and in the end, the werewolf had agreed and had spent a decent amount of time poking around on the database that afternoon. I was pretty sure he'd done it so he could snoop through Savannah's profile without one of us looming over his shoulder. Either way, he was going on a date with a very different cat shifter, and he wasn't thrilled.

My sister was, though; she kept casting me satisfied looks. Bath viewed it as a favor to me—keep my wolf bodyguard out of my hair so I could relax.

The problem was that I was going to pretend in public that I adored Ramsey. Not relaxing in the slightest.

When the car stopped, I slid out of the truck and smoothed my dress, feeling out of my element, nervous and jittery, like a cat in a room full of rocking chairs.

Ramsey loomed over me like some sort of irritated god. "Come on," he growled. His hand cradled my elbow as he began to propel me forward, pulling me close to his side. I had no choice but to follow. His jaw rigid, he gave his last name to the maitre d' in an almost growl. "Bjorn. Party of two."

As the maitre d' led us into the restaurant, I stole a furtive look at my date. Ramsey cleaned up nicely—I'd give him that. His long, windblown blond waves had been tamed with a comb, and his typical three-day growth of scruff was gone, revealing a chiseled jawline. His dark eyes were vivid in his tanned face, and his brows were irritated slashes over them.

Ramsey looked sexy and fierce, perhaps a little *too* fierce. Nothing about his posture or his expression spoke of a man ridiculously in love with the woman at his side. This might be a problem.

We were led to a table right in the middle of the restaurant. I'd been hoping for something secluded, but that wouldn't fit with my sister's scheme for us to be seen. Connor was several tables away, looking awkward as he faced a chatting woman in a too-tight pink dress who waved her hands in the air as she spoke. I felt a momentary twinge of pity for him. Jayde Sommers was nice enough. She was also demanding and bossy and domineering. She was nothing like Savannah. I watched his miserable gaze flick over to my table, as if he'd been desperate to crawl over to it and escape his date.

Ramsey moved to pull out my chair. As I sat down, he pushed my chair in, leaned over, and whispered, "Smile."

Guess he wasn't the only one bad at pretending. I flashed him a wide smile as he sat down across from me, unbuttoning the front of his jacket with graceful hands, as if he'd worn a suit every day.

I laid my napkin in my lap. "I appreciate your doing this, Ramsey."

He smiled at me, but it seemed more like a baring of teeth than actual pleasure. "I didn't have a choice. Beau's orders."

Well, that made *two* men totally miserable in their dates tonight. I kept the sweet smile pasted to my face and was glad that the low murmur of the restaurant would muffle our voices from other nosy shifters. "You were quick to volunteer to be my mate, though. If you didn't want to pretend with me, you should have said something earlier."

Ramsey gave me an odd look. "This is serious, Sara."

As if I didn't know? It was my life at stake. I bit

back my reply when the waiter appeared, introducing himself to us and reciting the day's specials. Ramsey was watching me, not the waiter, and the look in his eyes was intense. Well, at least one of us was good at all this pretending.

"I'll order for you," Ramsey said, turning to the waiter.

Ordering for me? I hadn't realized that *bearshifter* was some sort of secret code word for *Neanderthal in public*. Why was Ramsey being such a jerk? If this was how shifters and their mates acted, I didn't like it. The purse in my lap began to vibrate, and I pulled out my phone. A text from my sister.

Your smile looks more like a snarl, she had sent. *Dial it back a little. The harpy is here with her date now, and they noticed the two of you. You guys need to look like you're having a great time and in love.*

I forced my mouth to relax and tried to imagine Ramsey as my real "mate." He was good looking, I'd give him that. Tall and broad and fierce. He'd make any woman's panties damp.

Not that I was wearing panties.

A movement caught my attention, and I spotted my sister talking to the maitre d' and pointing out tables. The maitre d' nodded and made notes on his clipboard. Clearly one of my sister's minions. She tended to send first dates to the same restaurants over and over again, probably because she could manipulate the situation the way she wanted it.

Typical.

"She'll have the T-bone steak, with asparagus

and potatoes," Ramsey told the waiter, drawing my attention back to him. "Extra rare on the steak. Same thing for me."

When the waiter left, I looked over at Ramsey with concern. "I'm not sure that's such a good idea." A nice bloody steak sounded good—almost too good. The wolf in me was practically salivating at the thought. And that worried me a little.

Ramsey gave me a look of disgust. "You wanted a salad?"

I laughed at that. His expression was a true shifter's reaction. "No, not a salad. I guess I should just be glad you didn't order something blatant, like lobster tail."

He snorted.

I picked up my water glass and took a sip. "Oh, come on. Isn't that what guys think? They buy the date a lobster tail and she puts out because he tossed a few dollars in her direction?"

Ramsey's gaze focused on my face, his body stiff. "This isn't about putting out."

I hadn't expected such quick, focused attention, and I blinked rapidly, then laughed, trying to defuse my words. "Aren't we supposed to put out if we're a couple? Isn't that expected?"

He grunted, the intense, searching look leaving his face, and crossed his arms over his chest. "Not everyone thinks like that."

"I work at a dating agency," I reminded him. "Trust me, everyone thinks like that." I thought for a moment, then fiddled with the napkin in my lap.

Silence fell between us, but unlike before, it wasn't laced with tension—it was a normal, awkward sort of date silence, when two people who don't know each other try to think of something to say.

My cell phone went off in my lap again.

TALK, my sister sent.

"I think we need to flirt a little more," I whispered to Ramsey.

"Right."

"So, uh, what do you do?" I blurted. Lord, this was starting to be as awkward as a real date.

"I work for Beau."

I knew that, dummy. "But what do you do for Beau? Are you a security guard?"

He looked as if he didn't know how to answer that. "I do what Beau needs done."

"Is that what's on your resumé?" I grinned. "Or does it say that you specialize in knocking heads together?" He was cute when he was flustered.

Ramsey leaned in, looking for all the world as if he'd been sharing an intimate secret with me. "I work in Alliance enforcement. I make sure they're protected."

"Don't tell me you're the local sheriff of Little Paradise?" I teased.

He shook his head, and when I laughed, he added gravely, "The sheriff is a tiger."

My laugh died. "Exactly how many supes work for the town?"

He shrugged. "A lot."

Well, that explained why things were so neatly

swept under the rugs, when they could have been front-page headlines anywhere else. "So you don't work for the city, then?"

He looked distinctly uncomfortable that I kept asking. "I volunteer. When I have time."

"You enjoy volunteering?"

Ramsey shrugged his big shoulders. "Don't get much time. Too busy cleaning up other people's messes."

My mood dimmed a little. "Like right now? I'm just another mess to clean up?"

His hot gaze focused on me, sucking the breath out of my lungs. If I hadn't known better, I'd have sworn that Ramsey was very, very interested in me. "No."

"No?"

"No," he repeated, then gave me a slow, devastating smile.

My knees went weak.

The waiter swung past and our water glasses were refilled, while a plate of artfully cut bread was left on the table for us to eat. I reached for a piece of bread at the same time he did. My hand brushed his and I jerked away.

That same wildly sexy smile curved his mouth, and he picked up the piece of bread and offered it to me. "Shifters feed their mates."

I was *not* going to blush. This flirting thing . . . boy, it was potent. I took the bread out of his hand. "So, any idea of how many of these dates we have to go on before people buy that we're an item?"

"Five," he said and pulled a piece of paper out of his pocket, reviewing it. "Next week is the Alliance barn dance. After that, we have to see a movie together, another dinner, and mini-golf."

"Are you kidding me?" I reached for the paper to see if he was pulling my leg.

He tucked it back into his pocket. "No."

"The friggin' barn dance? And mini-golf? Is my sister insane?" I yanked out my phone and began to text her. "Hang on, I have to tell her she's insane."

Ramsey's giant hand came down on the phone and curled over the screen, effectively stopping my texting. "The barn dance will have a lot of supes."

True. "And mini-golf?"

"The course is owned by the Michigos."

Damn. The Michigos were the largest family of were-otters in the South. My sister's dates were actually sounding sensible. I groaned, realizing she had us right where she wanted us. "We're going to be spending a lot of time together, aren't we?"

My phone buzzed in my lap. I didn't have to look at it to know what my sister was texting. *Smile.* I plastered a big, happy smile on my face.

"We are. Shifters are territorial. People will expect it," he pointed out.

"So when is Connor supposed to show me how to shift properly?"

"He's not," Ramsey growled, his dark eyes glittering.

He wasn't? I thought that was the point of the chaperone. Who was going to help me shift to wolf-form if it wasn't going to be Connor? The phone buzzed again. The smile on my face stretched tighter, and I forced myself to laugh like I was having a good time, then reached for my water glass, gulping down the liquid. When I could speak again, I said, "How am I supposed to learn how to control my shifting?"

Ramsey continued to glare at me. "Uncontrolled shifting is brought on by emotion. I do not want him forcing bad memories on you."

"So you want to be the one to do it?"

"There will be no bad memories with me."

I swallowed hard. Was that a command? Or just arrogance? The only way I'd have no bad memories with him would be to have good emotions involved. "Um, okay."

Ramsey then forced a smile to his face and reached over, tucking a lock of hair behind my ear. I kept still, doing my best not to pull away, my mind on fire with our conversation. If I was going to have to learn how to shift, did that mean I was going to need to get turned on? Good gravy.

"Excuse me," interrupted the waiter. He stared pointedly at Ramsey. "Might I have a moment in private with you?"

Ramsey touched my hand on the table and got up, following the waiter a few feet away. I strained to hear their conversation, but they were speaking in low voices, and the crowded restaurant hummed with scattered conversations that muffled everything.

My phone buzzed again. I clicked on the text.

U GUYS R SSOOOOOOOOOOO CUTE 2GETHR.

You're supposed to be helping, I texted back. Funny how my sister's texting got worse the faster she typed.

U don't need help right now, came the instant reply. *Doing good!!*

My face flushed with heat. That was good, right? That we looked so in love? I glanced around but couldn't see Connor's table from this angle. *Poor C looks miserable with his date,* I texted my sister. *I feel bad.*

Too bad, my sister texted back. *Him as ur chaperone is wrong. If this is what it takes 2 get him out of ur hair, so be it.*

"Excuse me," someone said and tapped me on my shoulder. My nostrils immediately filled with the scent of were-jaguar and the faint, lingering scent of Connor. I looked up at her in surprise, and Connor's date gave me an urgent look. "Can I ask you something?"

"Oh, um, I'm really busy right now," I said, glancing over at Ramsey. The waiter was gesticulating, trying to get Ramsey's attention, but he kept glancing over at me.

Jayde gave me a tight smile. "We really need to chat. It won't take long."

"Not right now," I said. "Please."

She ignored my protests, moving a step closer to my table. "You work for the agency, right?"

Clearly she wasn't going to go away. I put on the professional smile that I used for customers. "Yes, I do. Why?"

She swept up Ramsey's water glass and tossed its contents in my face.

I gave a startled yelp as the ice water poured over me. My hair fell into my eyes in icy, sopping hanks, ice cubes fell down the front of my dress, and the entire thing stuck to me like a wet napkin. My nipples hardened under the dress.

If that hadn't been enough, Jayde leaned over and tipped my water glass onto my lap. "And that one's for setting me up with a man who's in love with someone else."

I sputtered, wiping water from my face. "What? I—"

"He's been mooning over her the entire fucking date," she snarled, the sound feral. "I realize your little human crew thinks it's funny to set up a cat with a dog, but I can look past that if he's hot enough. What I can't look past is that he's already fucking *taken*."

"Taken?" I said, disbelieving. I stood up clumsily, dumping the ice cubes that had fallen into my lap. I shook out my dress and stepped backward, trying to put distance between Jayde and myself. "What are you talking about?"

"Oh, Savannah Russell is *so* amazing," she mocked, waving her hands in the air. "Savannah likes cars, too. Savannah went to A&M, too. Savannah, Savannah, Savannah." Her eyes narrowed. "If he's so in love with her, why's he out with me? You think I'm hard up for a date?"

"Why, no. I—"

"You think I can't get a date?" Her hand tapped her chest, making her jewelry jangle. "You think because I'm the apex predator in the area that men won't want me? You think I'm willing to accept just any man you *humans* toss at me—"

The words died in her throat as her gaze focused behind me.

A hand touched my back and I jerked, calming when I realized it was Ramsey. He swiftly stepped in front of me, and Jayde retreated. His massive form blocked my view, and I could hear my phone vibrating on the table, no doubt my sister texting away. Connor remained seated at his table, not looking in our direction. If anything, he looked more dejected than before. For a wolf bodyguard, he sure wasn't interested in protecting me from his date.

"There a problem?" Ramsey growled low in his throat.

"No," Jayde lied, her tone a mixture of unease and surprise. Her voice became sugary sweet. "I was just offering to help Sara with her dress."

A low, angry rumble started in Ramsey's throat. Jayde flinched.

Ramsey tugged me forward, his arm wrapping around me like a hug. His large body nearly swallowed my own. It was a possessive gesture, meant to brand me as his own. "Why is my mate wearing my drink?"

Jayde's jaw dropped and she made a startled, squeaky noise. Her eyes widened like marbles, and she stared at me in shock, then back to Ramsey. "A . . . a mate?"

"My mate," I agreed in a proprietary manner and snuggled against Ramsey's chest, ignoring the fact that I was all wet. "And he doesn't like it when other people pour drinks on me."

"No," Ramsey said, his voice so low and angry that it sounded like a growl. "I don't."

Jayde paled. "I see. I-I apologize. I did not realize . . ."

"See that you do not assault my date again," Ramsey growled menacingly.

The were-jaguar nodded and stammered apologies, backing away. It was gratifying to see how completely and utterly terrified she was. Perhaps this pretending-to-date thing wouldn't be so bad after all.

"I am so sorry," the waiter said, stepping in and handing me napkins. "I didn't realize what was going on. We'll get you a new table—"

"No," said Ramsey in the same dangerous tone. "We're leaving." He shrugged off his jacket and draped it over my shoulders. The garment nearly swallowed me whole, the hem of the jacket hanging to my knees. "She's soaked. Date's ruined."

"I understand," said the waiter. "I'll pack your dinners in a take-home box."

"Do that." Ramsey turned to Jayde. "You're paying."

"Of course," she blurted, then hurried back to her table.

Impressive. With a few scowls, Ramsey had managed to completely intimidate a crazy were-jaguar, get our meals for free, and get us out of this date. I shoved the too-long sleeves up my arms, shivering. Too bad he hadn't been able to do it before I'd had a gallon of ice water poured on me. My nipples felt like thumbtacks, and my teeth were beginning to chatter.

"We'll wait outside," he snarled to the waiter. I barely had time to stick my cell phone in my purse before Ramsey grabbed my hand and hauled me out of the restaurant.

I bit back my retort at being dragged around like an old handbag. The people lined up outside stared at us in surprise, with my wet hair plastered to my face and Ramsey's coat swallowing me. Combine that with a date well over six feet tall and looking exceedingly pissed? No wonder they were looking at us like we were certifiable.

Ramsey dragged me to his large sport-utility truck and then grabbed me at the waist, lifting me to the hood so I was almost eye level with him. To my surprise, he leaned in.

"How'd I do?" he whispered, inches from my face. His chest—scorchingly hot—pressed against my knees.

Whew, was it hot out here, or was it just me? The almost-playful look on Ramsey's face was doing funny things to my insides. I brushed a wet lock of hair off of my face and gave him a half smile. "Well, the good news is that Jayde will probably never pour a drink on another woman again."

"Good."

"Dragging me around like a caveman was a little much, though," I added dryly.

"All for show. They need to remember us."

Oh, I was pretty sure they'd remember. I glanced over at the doorway, where the waiting patrons still stared at us. Our waiter was pushing his way through them. "Here comes our meal."

"Good." Ramsey pulled me forward on the truck, and when I looked at him in surprise, he captured my mouth with his.

Surprise flared through me. His mouth, normally so hard and unsmiling, was warm against my own, his lips soft. Taking advantage of my surprise, he tugged at my lower lip, and then his tongue swept into my mouth. After that, I was lost. He kissed like a man obsessed, intent on devouring me. Over and over, his tongue stroked into my mouth, my own rising to meet it. His hand slid up my wet thigh and pulled me closer, and I wrapped my arms around his neck, encouraging the kiss.

If this was pretending, I could only imagine what really kissing Ramsey would be like.

His hand on my thigh was warm, and when his tongue swept deep into my mouth again, a soft moan rose from my throat, and I wiggled against his chest. My knees were trapped against him, so I parted my legs, allowing him to lean in even closer to me, his hand twisting into my wet hair. My legs wrapped around him in response, heels hooking together behind his broad back.

Someone coughed nearby.

Ramsey gave my mouth one last slow, sensual lick and then pulled away, turning to glare at the waiter as I panted, still clinging to Ramsey's chest. "What?" he growled.

"Sorry. Your food," the waiter stammered, setting the carryout bag down on the sidewalk and hurrying away.

Ramsey's gaze moved to the bag, then focused back on my face. His eyes were glazed with our kiss, his gaze flicking to my wet mouth repeatedly. His hand tightened on my hip. "Where are your panties?" he said hoarsely.

Oops. I'd forgotten about that. "Surprise," I said, giving my thighs a playful squeeze to distract him. Ramsey was adorable when he was flustered, and I was feeling frisky, especially after that amazing kiss. Who cared if it was pretend?

Ramsey pulled away from me as if scorched. I untangled my legs just in time for him to jerk away, and I straightened my skirts as he scooped the bag of food off the sidewalk.

Ouch. I guess I was the only one feeling that vibe.

The sound of distant wolf howls woke me from my sleep. I sat up with a gasp, my heart hammering. The room was empty, moonlight streaming in through the ceiling hole and the dirty window. Where was Ramsey? My Anderson protector? The wolf howls rose again and I shivered, the back of my neck bunching and rippling anxiously. I bit the inside of my cheek for control and crept down the stairs. Part of me wanted to hide under the bed, but the small, dreadful part in the pit of my stomach wanted to follow the howls. They almost made sense, even to my sleep-drugged mind, and I needed to know more.

I crept out on the porch in my T-shirt and sleep pants, crossing my arms over my chest. There was a chill in the air, but it wasn't supposed to bother the wolf part of me—yet another thing I was doing wrong. I stared into the trees, listening for the wolf call again. There was a faint taste of shifter on the breeze, but I smelled Ramsey's scent more than anything. He'd been here, and recently. Where had he gone?

A figure stepped out of the shadows of the porch. "Thought you'd hear them," Connor said quietly.

I smothered the wolf-snarl that rose in my throat, trying not to jump backward.

He saw my alarm and raised his hands in the air to calm me. "I don't mean anything. I just heard them and thought you might be curious."

He took a step backward, and I noticed that his scent was mixed with the light smell of . . . were-cougar? His shirt was torn and the buttons were done up wrong, and it looked like his right eye was starting to bruise.

Seemed like someone hadn't been so welcome

when he'd dropped by the Russell house to visit a certain were-cougar.

I bounced on my feet, trying not to seem wary and out of sorts. "So where's Ramsey?"

Connor squinted at the trees. "Unless I miss my guess, he's in bear-form, trying to chase the wolves off the property."

"Oh?"

Connor shrugged. "They're here to check up on you."

Because they were going to swoop in and take me back if they didn't like how he was treating me? I shivered with dislike. The wolf pack was always hovering in the background, reminding me that they were watching me. That even if I tried to cut them out of my life, they'd still show up.

The howls rose again, fainter this time.

Connor watched me. "Can you understand them? The howls?"

"No," I said. "Can you?"

He nodded. "Most wolves can. You'll eventually learn it when you become more in tune with your wolf side. Don't suppose you feel the need to transform?"

I shook my head. "I usually don't feel it coming on until it's too late."

"That's because you're waiting too long."

I looked over at him. "So when are you going to teach me?"

"I'm not," he said softly and took a step away from me.

"What do you mean, you're not going to help me? I thought my life was in danger."

"It is," he said, then took another step away from me, his gaze fixed on the dark tree line. "You know just as well as I do that he's not going to let another male near you when you're vulnerable."

"Don't be ridiculous," I scoffed. I wanted to say more, but a large shape loomed in the shadows, and my nostrils filled with the scent of bear. Ramsey. His eyes glinted in the darkness, and he hovered at the edge of the tree line, waiting.

The uncomfortable shivers started along my back again. If Ramsey wanted to hurt me in his bear-form, I'd be helpless. He was so big . . . but when Connor shifted another few feet away, I noticed that the enormous bear's gaze wasn't on me.

It was on Connor.

"So how am I supposed to learn how to shift if he won't let you near me?" I asked.

Connor gave me a lazy smile. "Don't know. You should probably ask your mate."

This was just getting silly. "I'll talk with him," I said. "This agreement between the wolf pack and our Alliance needs to work. Ramsey knows that. I can reason with him—"

"You can't," Connor said. "The mating instinct is strong and possessive. When it finds the woman it wants, it grabs ahold and won't let go. You don't think straight when she's around. When her scent's in your nostrils, she's all you can think about." A bleak look swept over his face. "And when she won't speak to you, the light in your world goes out."

I had a feeling we weren't talking about me any-more.

Connor noticed my silence and cleared his throat. "He's not going to want you anywhere near another shifter, especially one you're frightened of. It's the mating instinct."

Yeah, but we weren't really mated, so that wasn't it. "I'm sure I can reason with Ramsey."

"And I'm sure you can't. Trust me on this." Connor glanced at my neck, then headed across the overgrown yard toward the guest cabin. "See you in the morning. Don't forget we have the barbeque tomorrow. I imagine that's what they came by to re-mind you about."

Like I could forget. "How long will it take for them to forget about me?"

He studied me for a minute, and his gaze soft-ened into something that was either sympathy or pity. Then he glanced away, as if thinking. "It might take a while."

He was lying. I watched him, and he wouldn't look back at me. "*Are* they going to forget about me?" I asked in a smaller voice. "Ever?"

Connor just gave me a look of pain. "If I could get them to back off, I would. It's affecting my life, too."

"Because of Savannah?"

A flash of intense pain crossed his face, quickly masked. "They won't let me be with her. I need her, but I can't have her . . . not that she'd have me. I wasn't strong enough when she needed me." His hands clenched into fists and he stared into the woods, eyes intense. "I need to stop thinking about her, because as long as Uncle Levi is the alpha, it's *his* way. What I want doesn't matter. What you want doesn't matter. It's what Levi wants. And what he wants is for wolves to belong in a wolf pack. Not mating with cats or bears."

"If that's how your uncle Levi thinks, I'm surprised he agreed to this pact."

Connor's smile pulled up in a wry twist. "He's giving you a bit of rope."

"Just enough to hang myself with?"

He nodded. "No more, no less. If I know Uncle Levi, he's expecting this experiment to be a failure and you'll come running back to the pack soon enough. Which is why you need to tell Ramsey to hold you close and not let anyone get in the way of your love."

Before I could stammer out something appropriate, he turned and walked back to the guesthouse.

I watched him go, then turned to regard Ramsey's massive form, hulking in the woods. The scent of bear was almost overpowering, and the sight of him struck a chord of fear in my heart. What if he had the temper that Roy had? What if that helpless lack of control was what all male shifters felt around a female? I wanted to talk to him, force him to change back and discuss Connor, but I couldn't bring myself to approach the bear.

I headed back inside and slipped under the covers. It was a long time before Ramsey returned, and I heard him creak up the stairs before sliding into our room.

I feigned sleep, keeping my breathing even.

He entered and stood by the side of the bed, and the skin on the back of my nape prickled. I knew he was looking at me. After a moment he climbed into bed, his skin hot against mine, and I didn't protest when he pulled me close and tucked me under his chin. My muscles relaxed, and I leaned into the solid warmth of his broad chest.

The man Ramsey didn't frighten me. It was the beast aspect of him—and myself—that made me question everything.

Chapter Eight

The next morning, Ramsey dropped me off at work with a polite kiss on the forehead and a murmured comment that he'd be back to pick me up in time for the Anderson barbeque. He didn't like leaving me alone with Connor, and I didn't like it, either. But if we were supposed to be assuming our normal lives, he couldn't continue to hover around me. Even more than that, he wanted to show the Anderson wolves that he wasn't about to back down, and that we weren't intimidated by their threats.

But I *was* intimidated.

In fact, I was so intimidated that I wanted Ramsey to come in and spend the day shadowing me again, but he had a job to do, and Connor would suspect something if Ramsey continually hovered. So I reluctantly let him go.

Connor followed me in to the office, but he seemed bored as soon as we got there, so I gave him a stack of filing and instructions, and he got to work. He kept looking over at me, and I wondered if he expected me to spontaneously grow a tail. Exactly how often was a shifter supposed to transform, any-how? I didn't know these things, and it seemed stu-pid to ask.

My sister came in, dressed in a cheery yellow sweater and her favorite pair of jeans. Her long hair was loose around her shoulders, and she wore a beaming smile. I greeted her with a smile of my own that faded when she sat down and pushed her hair off her neck.

Her white neck proudly displayed the enormous mate mark, and a hot blush stole over my face at the sight.

Mate marks are one of those peculiar things that every shifter can see plain as day but no human can pick up. It's kind of a cross between a flush on the skin and a gleam of scent—hard to describe, but ob-vious to anyone with a tail. It declared a mate off-limits, possessed and proud of the fact.

I touched my own neck thoughtfully. Connor had stared at it, and I wondered if he was going to tell his father that I hadn't been marked. Perhaps it was time to take the pretending to a whole new level. If I had a mate mark on my neck for the dance, it'd add much more credibility to our relationship.

A shiver flashed over me at the thought, and I pictured Ramsey's big form looming over mine, his hot skin pressed against my own, mouth locked on my throat . . . jeez. I fanned myself with a file folder. It sure had gotten warm in here.

Maybe I'd bring it up to Ramsey tonight. I blushed at the thought, even as it made my pulse race. *Excuse me, do you think you could bite me on the throat a few times? I want to make sure everyone thinks that I'm your mate. Don't mind if I spontaneously orgasm. I'm doing this just for our charade.*

I hadn't had sex with a man since I was seventeen. Hadn't even wanted to consider it. But sex was like an itch that couldn't be scratched, and ever since I'd been bitten, my sex drive had been ramped up a notch. I usually took care of it myself, since the thought of a man touching me filled me with unease. What if I changed when he touched me? Sex was a solo act out of necessity.

But . . . everyone already thought Ramsey and I were doing the deed. I wondered if it'd be such a stretch. I wondered if Ramsey had ever thought about it.

As if he'd been summoned, the doorbell clanged. I looked up to see Ramsey in the doorway of the office. His big shoulders blotted out the early morning sunlight, casting a shadow over my desk, since it was the closest to the door.

I looked at him in surprise, my cheeks hot with a blush at my thoughts. Ramsey's timing was . . . eerie. "Everything okay?"

He stepped toward my desk, and I noticed what he held in his hand—a lidded Starbucks cup and a small brown paper bag. As he extended the coffee to me, I took it, surprised.

I was even more surprised when he leaned down and kissed the top of my head. "Have a good day at work."

Then he strode back out of the office.

I stared after him, watching his broad back flex in the sunlight. He squinted, put on a pair of sunglasses and a Russell Security baseball cap, and got into his truck. I looked down at the cup in my hand. The closest Starbucks was at least ten minutes away. He'd gone to get it just for me?

Had he heard my offhand comment to Connor yesterday? Or had Connor volunteered it? Surely not, if Connor's job was to entice me toward the pack. I looked at the werewolf, but he was still filing, a bored look on his face.

A small, polite cough caught my attention. I looked across to the other side of the room, and Bath pointed a finger at her monitor.

I glanced at my own screen. Bath had sent me a chat message. *Boy, he's really good at this pretending thing, isn't he?*

I'd say he was. The Starbucks was thoughtful. The kiss on my head afterward? Felt like something a real couple would have done. I didn't want to share with my sister that I was having some not-so-fake thoughts about my fake mate. I typed back, *Ramsey is very thorough. He wants to make sure this seems real.*

As I typed it, I felt my heart drop a little. Was that all it was? That he was very good at details? Surely I was reading more into a cup of coffee than I should.

Another message pinged from my sister. *Next time, tell him to bring me a coffee, too. I like decaf.*

———

As the day wore on, my anxiety grew at the thought of the Anderson barbeque. I'd tried to weasel out of it, but Connor had been insistent, and my sister was enthused on my behalf.

"Think of all the pointers they can give you," she said. "And you can tell them all about Midnight Liaisons. Maybe you can talk a few more of them into signing up with the Alliance. Think of yourself as an ambassador."

Ambassador? *Pointers?* Like they were going to swap shape-changing stories over burgers and hot dogs? My sister had a strange idea of what this barbeque would be about. The queasiness in my stomach grew. "You sure you and Beau don't want to come?"

"Can't," she said with a small grimace, typing at her desk. "We weren't invited. Beau says it's a major faux pas if we invite ourselves to a non-Alliance function."

From what I knew of shifters, he was right. More like all-out war if they decided to interfere again. I sighed. I would have felt so much better with my sister at my side.

I cast a brief look over at Connor, who continued to file diligently. I pulled up my files on the Midnight Liaisons database. On a whim, I clicked on Ramsey's profile again. He looked so surly. Big and surly. Was it a wonder the man didn't date? I pulled up an instant message window to my sister, now curious.

How long has Beau known Ramsey?

Twelve years. His family took Ramsey in when he was exiled from his clan.

Why was he exiled?

Don't know. Want me to ask Beau?

No, it's okay. I didn't want him to know I was asking questions about Ramsey. It would look like I was more interested than I should have been. I typed, *Beau ever say anything about Ramsey's dating habits?*

Just that he doesn't really date, she wrote back. *Everyone is scared of him.*

I couldn't blame them.

He hasn't threatened you, has he? my sister asked.

Of course not, I typed back. *I was just curious about him.*

I looked at his profile again. Member of the alliance for twelve years. He was twenty-seven now. He'd been in the Alliance since he was fifteen? I pictured him as a gruff teenager, hair in his face and a chip on his shoulder, hands shoved in his pockets. Why had he been exiled? He'd been so young.

I flipped around on his profile, studying it for missing clues. Something was off. The big *Mated* link still glared at the top of the profile, and I felt a flash of guilt. I clicked on the link to Ramsey's mate almost idly, waiting for it to pull my profile through, since we were linked.

The front door of the agency banged open. In

walked a fey prince, all smiles and smelling like flowers. The only way I could tell a fey from a regular human was the scent of fresh, clean, growing things. This one's glamour was of a man who looked a lot like George Clooney in glasses. Glamours were convincing, if not particularly original. They usually just copied out of the latest celebrity tabloid. All those Elvis sightings back in the day? Fey princes having a bit of fun. I was willing to bet that half the tabloid stories in Hollywood were the direct result of a fey prince's glamour-shifting. They usually didn't wear the same face for long.

Grateful for the distraction, I stood to greet him. "Hi, welcome to Midnight Liaisons. May I help you?"

He handed me his Alliance card with a smile. "I was here a few days ago. I need a dinner companion for an important banquet next week."

I ushered him to the chair in front of my desk. A fey in the office meant I didn't have to think about wolves or shifters for a while. Nice reprieve.

The fey adjusted his profile, and we discussed the kinds of people he'd like to date. He had no particular gender preference, so I suggested he consider our doppelganger. Jean always had a hard time finding dates, but the fey looked intrigued, and I passed him one of the bright orange flyers my sister had created for the upcoming barn dance. "I would suggest a glamour of someone low-key if you want to blend in," I added helpfully. "An A-list actor might be a little distracting."

He gave a long-suffering sigh. "I suppose I can

study up on my Pre-Raphaelite portraiture and pick a new face."

"Sounds wonderful," I agreed. I saved his profile on the computer and exited out.

As soon as the fey lord vacated the seat in front of my desk, Connor slid back into it and gave me a slow smile. Connor touched the edge of my monitor and nudged it back toward him again, looking at the screen. "Friend of yours?"

I looked up from the stack of paperwork I was flipping through, confused. "Huh?"

Connor nodded at the monitor. "Client?"

I had no idea what he was talking about. I stared at him, then at the computer screen. An unfamiliar profile stared back at me—a blond woman with long hair, big hoop earrings, and a colorful scarf. How did I get on that page? I turned the monitor away from Connor. "Did you want to date her?"

He shrugged and leaned back in his chair, suddenly all casual. "Nah. I was just curious why you were looking at her profile."

Had I been? I didn't remember what I'd been looking at before the fey lord had come in. I studied her profile for a moment—Nikolina Aasen—but it didn't ring a bell. I clicked the Back button, and to my surprise, the browser returned to Ramsey's profile. I studied his again, trying to remember what I'd clicked on to get to Nikolina's profile.

Then a cold, hard knot formed in my stomach. I clicked on the *Mated* link at the top of Ramsey's profile.

Nikolina's profile pulled up again.

The two profiles were linked. I studied Nikolina's information. Profile—inactive. Race—were-bear. Status—mated.

The reason why Ramsey's profile showed no activity was because my fake mate already had a real one.

I didn't know what to think.

I couldn't be angry, right? I mean, how could I be angry that he had a real mate on the side? This wasn't about feelings—this was about my safety.

So why did it bother me so very much that he'd never mentioned her to me? That when he kissed me and looked at me with smoldering eyes, that she wasn't on his mind? Were we cheating? Was it cheating if our relationship was all pretend? I felt sick.

This wasn't a real mating, but . . . I needed to know what it *was*.

By the time Ramsey arrived to pick me up, the fey lord was long gone, my sister had left for the day, and I was alone with a very bored Connor, who played solitaire on a nearby computer. I tried to ignore him as I worked, but he was always there, his scent in my nostrils.

Ramsey hadn't changed out of his work clothes to pick me up—his T-shirt had the Russell Security logo branded above one pec, and his skin looked browned from the sun. I wondered what he did all day—follow clients? Separate shifters from angry erstwhile mates? Or just throw around people that didn't do what Beau wanted? Was Russell Security just a fancy name for the Alliance version of the mafia?

The three of us piled in the truck again, and Connor gave Ramsey instructions as I tried to calm my racing heart. I didn't want to see the wolves. What if this was a trap? Roy had been sneaky like that. He'd promise me one thing and blindside me with another, to the point that anytime I smelled wolf, I immediately distrusted it. Even my own scent.

We pulled up to a sprawling ranch-style house with several acres around it. It didn't surprise me to see a half dozen trucks in front of the house and the circular gravel drive packed full. We parked on the side of the road, and Ramsey threw on the parking brake. I smelled barbeque and smoke when the wind shifted, and the overwhelming smell of wolf. Even from here I could catch breaths of conversation. Every nerve in my body sang in alarm, and I clutched Ramsey's arm.

"I don't want to go," I whispered.

Connor gave me a look of annoyance, and I knew he was revolted at my whining. "Don't be scared. No one's going to eat you."

Ramsey's big arm went around my shoulders and he pulled me against him. I heard the low growling rumble start in his chest again. "If Sara wants to leave, I'm not going to force her to stay."

"Uncle Levi wants to see how she's doing," Connor said. "He won't be happy if she doesn't show up."

"Don't care," Ramsey rumbled. "She's not his concern."

"Just because you deny it doesn't make it true." Connor's teeth bared and he slid out of the truck, slamming the door behind him.

Ramsey turned to me. "Do you want to go?"

Connor was right—Levi would be furious if I didn't show up. And then the wolves would think I was a coward. They'd eat me alive after that. My stomach twisted in an unhappy knot at the prospect of pissing off the wolves. "No, it's all right. We'll go for a bit."

Ramsey's scowling expression didn't change, and I had the strangest thought that I'd somehow let him down. "Very well."

When we got out of the truck, he pocketed his keys and then extended one massive hand toward me.

I slipped my hand in his and leaned close to him. He was warm and smelled faintly of sweat, as if he'd been out in the heat all day. I liked it, as well as the faint scent of bear that clung to his skin. It was a welcome change in the sea of dog fur that assailed my nostrils. If I lived to be a hundred years, I'd never get used to the smell of wolves.

There was a lot of conversation coming from the back of the house, so we cut through the yard. A radio played country hits, and I could hear the lazy chatter of multiple voices, Levi's laugh rising occasionally above the others.

The tables were set up in a half circle around a massive central grill. Men lounged there, and a few played football in the yard. At the grill, Levi drank a sweating beer and poked at the meat with his tongs.

Everyone quieted when Ramsey's scent touched the air, and all heads turned.

I gave an awkward wave. "Hi."

All eyes immediately went to me, and I felt my skin prickle. They couldn't have been more attuned to me if I'd shown up naked. Their eyes were ravenous as they devoured me, and I stepped closer to Ramsey, my hand clammy in his.

"Glad to see you make it," one Anderson drawled. His gaze swept over me, pausing on my flat chest. The pocket of his shirt said Maynard. "Connor told us you'd chicken out. He thinks you don't like us. Imagine that."

I flushed. "I never said that." At least not to Connor's face.

Maynard's gaze swung to Connor. "You hear that, boy? She does like us. You're just causing trouble, ain't ya? Or maybe you're trying to keep the little woman all to yourself."

Connor ignored Maynard's comments and moved to the back door of the house. "I'm gonna say hi to Gracie."

"You do that," Maynard said, his possessive gaze still on me. Once Connor left, the other men cast a few looks among themselves, and conversation picked up again.

My skin prickled. They were acting as if Ramsey hadn't even been there. I didn't know what to do, and Ramsey wasn't moving, so I simply stood there and held his hand, trying not to tremble. I didn't know what they expected of me. Mingling? Introducing myself to all seven Andersons? I'd seen them all naked and turned on at the thought of getting me away from the Russell cougars. The thought of trying to socialize with them made me cold. Maynard had already given me the creeps. I had nothing to say to them.

Levi waved at me with the tongs. "Come here, girl."

A ripple of fear brushed down my skin, stirring my wolf. The fear warred with the need to please the alpha, a disturbing feeling I didn't think I'd ever get used to. I bit the inside of my cheek hard, chasing it away. When I moved forward, Ramsey's grip tightened on my hand, but he didn't step forward, instead waiting and letting me take the lead. I wouldn't have to go to Levi alone, and I was grateful.

Levi didn't look pleased when I showed up with my mate in tow. He glared at me over his beer, then looked at Ramsey when I stood awkwardly next to the grill. "Why don't you go inside and grab your little lady a beer?" he said to Ramsey.

I froze. Was this a trick to separate us? A trap of some kind? As soon as Ramsey left, would they hold me down and kidnap me? Drag me off to some cabin in the woods like Savannah, and never let me leave?

Ramsey's hand left mine and he put a hand on my shoulders, tugging me close to him in a half hug, burying my face in his massive chest. "I'm here."

"She looks like she could use a beer to calm her nerves," Levi said. "I can hear her heart hammering a mile a minute."

"She's fine."

I curled my toes in my sneakers, flexing my feet and praying to God I wouldn't pop claws. *A fucking disgusting sight,* Levi had said at the sight of me changing. If I changed uncontrollably in front of them again, they'd do their best to separate Ramsey from me for good.

Levi gave me a narrow-eyed look. "Girl, if we wanted to kill you both, we'd have done so already. We invited you for barbeque. Ain't nothing more than that."

"We're here because you demanded it," I said, stating the obvious. "If you wanted to kill us both, we wouldn't be standing here."

He grunted. Studied the grill for a moment longer, then glanced back at the two of us. "Can't talk to you with your man hovering. He should go get you a beer," the alpha said pointedly. "There's some inside the house."

Obviously Levi wanted to talk to me without Ramsey around. That was the last thing I wanted, but the desire to please the alpha was eating away at my good sense. I pulled my cheek away from Ramsey's chest, turning to face Levi and gathering the shreds of my courage. "How do I know this isn't a trap?"

"Cause you're still breathing." He picked a hot dog off the grill and turned it.

I felt Ramsey stiffen, but oddly enough, I felt a little relaxed at that logic. Levi was right. They could have attacked us both last night when they'd howled in the woods. They could have attacked us already at the barbeque. They could have even tried to kill me at the original meeting. But they hadn't. And I knew they wanted me alive and whole . . . for obvious reasons.

So I turned and looked up at Ramsey. "Will you please get me a beer?"

He looked down at me with those inscrutable eyes, and I could almost hear the growl start in his throat.

I mouthed, *Check the inside of the house for a trap.* I didn't trust the "aw shucks," easygoing demeanor of the alpha. This barbeque had a purpose, and I wanted to know what it was.

Ramsey nodded, touched my cheek with his fingers, then disappeared inside the house.

That left me alone with the alpha. Determined not to flinch away, I clasped my hands behind my back and looked at Levi.

He took a T-bone and slapped it on the grill, the juices sizzling. "Figured you like your meat almost raw."

My mouth watered at the thought, but I said nothing.

He glanced over at me, his gaze lingering on my neck, as if looking for something. A hot blush crept over my face, and I waited for him to ask.

Instead, he only said, "That nephew of mine still mooning about the cougar girl?"

I hesitated, almost afraid to encourage the conversation. "You know about that?"

"Couldn't keep 'em apart while she was with us. Acted like it was up to him to protect her." He sneered. "From us."

He hadn't been wrong about that, I thought. "You did kidnap her," I pointed out, then quailed a little when he scowled at me.

"Just a bit of political maneuvering. You'll figure it out soon enough, girl. But I guess you know all about political maneuvering, right?" Again, his gaze fell to my neck. "Connor was supposed to woo you for Maynard this week. Bring you around to our point of view. He's doing a piss-poor job of it."

"*Woo* me?"

Levi glanced over, his gaze almost a leer. "Werewolf women belong with werewolf men. We know how to keep 'em in line. Make 'em behave. Treat 'em right. It's part of natural law that you should be with one of us."

This conversation had quickly steered into uncomfortable territory. "I have a mate."

He shrugged and looked back at my neck again. "You keep saying it, but *I* keep saying that you're gonna see our perspective, girl. Give us a few weeks, you'll be joining the pack in all ways."

"Why don't you guys just find some other girl to turn?"

Levi gave me an assessing look. "Ain't that easy. Just because you're bit doesn't mean that you'll change. Sometimes you just die." His smile grew slow and menacing. "'Sides. The boys like you.

And you'll still need a pack, no matter if we let you go or not."

Lucky me.

He swigged his beer. "Too bad Connor's fucking this up, whining about that slutty little cat. Ain't like they were mated. Bond ain't real." He sneered at me and flipped a dripping steak, barely cooked. "Ain't that right?"

Oh, God. Did he know Ramsey already had a mate? Was this some hint about our fake relationship? I gave Levi a tight smile. "Doesn't mean he can't like her, does it?"

"Yes, it does. I told him to stay the fuck away from her," Levi said, his voice harsh. "Connor been helping you change at all, girl?"

I shrugged.

Levi's sharp eyes remained on me. "And how many times have you shifted in the last few days?"

"Haven't felt the need," I said with a cheerful smile. "It's been a good week."

"That's a bad sign," Levi said with a growl. "You need to change, and change often, especially since you're trying to get it under control. The longer you wait, the stronger the shift is. You need to shift every day."

"Well, that's why you sent Connor with me."

He pulled the dripping steak off the grill. "Yeah, and it ain't doing you much good. I'll keep him here."

I blinked. Not that I wanted my wolf escort, but if he left, the implications scared me. "You're taking him back? Who's going to help me change?"

"Your lover?" He gave me a sly grin. "Unless you're not comfortable with that. I could always send Gracie with ya. Unless you think you don't need help." He dumped the dripping steak onto a paper plate and held it out to me. "Hungry?"

My stomach growled, and as I took the steak, the smell of blood wafted into my nostrils. Goose bumps prickled my skin, and I felt a sudden surge of my wolf, bile rushing into my mouth.

I shoved the steak back toward Levi. "Not hungry."

He gave me another sly look as Ramsey came out the door. "I see. Well, I'll let you sleep on it and then maybe I'll send Gracie over in the morning."

Chapter Nine

*W*e lingered at the Anderson barbeque for a little longer, but the entire situation was awkward. Levi kept looking for ways to remind me of my wolf side. The other Anderson males kept trying to approach and talk to me, only to be chased away by Ramsey's glare. Connor went inside the house and didn't reappear at all. After a half hour, we left, citing tiredness.

Levi just smiled and invited us back for Sunday dinner.

Exhausted and feeling the wolf creeping under my skin, I slumped in the passenger seat, watching the sun set into the horizon. My phone vibrated in my jeans pocket, and I pulled it out.

Call me when you get out of the barbeque, Bath texted. *I'm worried about you.*

I was worried about me, too. I'd been traded to a pack of horny, possessive wolves, and my lone protector already had a girlfriend. I glanced over at Ramsey and then texted her back. *I'm out. It was awkward, but okay.*

Did they threaten you?

If I said yes, she would only worry. So I texted back a non-answer. *Ramsey intimidates them, which is a nice benefit.*

He's not the most gentle of guys, she texted back. *Are you okay with him? If not, I can come and get you.*

I'm good, I sent back. I sneaked a look over at Ramsey. His face was unreadable, but he didn't seem tense, so I relaxed a little. *My wolf escort was sent home,* I texted.

What? Why?

They said he wasn't doing me any good.

That's bad! Who's going to show you how to shift? Sara, you need to get it under control. I don't want you to hurt yourself.

I thought for a moment, then texted, *I'm going to ask Ramsey to help me.*

A long moment passed before her next message came in. *If you're sure . . .*

I'm sure. I just hadn't told Ramsey yet.

When we returned to Ramsey's house, I hesitated in the doorway. Should I bring up the mate? Maybe Beau knew about it—maybe Bath did, too, and I was the only one in the dark. Maybe everyone assumed I already knew. I chickened out and feigned a yawn. "Jeez, I'm tired. I don't suppose I can grab a shower before heading to bed?"

"Shower's still broken," he said. "I fixed the upstairs bath for you."

I gave him a hesitant smile. "Thanks."

The blue hair dye came out of my hair as I

bathed. When I got out of the tub, my hair was a sickly grayish blue. Maybe I'd try something different. The blue hadn't had the desired effect anyhow; I still felt weak and cowardly. Idly, I wondered what color Ramsey liked.

I dressed and headed to our bedroom, ignoring my stomach's protesting growls. Ramsey had disappeared off to who knew where, and I was alone. Would he sleep somewhere else tonight, since we had no wolf chaperone? To my surprise and pleasure, I saw there was a new bed to replace the old, sagging one. It was a massive king with a nice, springy mattress and plain wooden headboard. I liked it. Grabbing my new pillow, I tucked it under my head and tried not to think about wolves and barbeques.

I woke up an hour later and bolted upright in bed. Still alone, I strained my ears to hear Ramsey. Nothing, the house was silent. I stared around the room, wondering why I'd woken up.

As I looked down, the flesh on my arm seemed to crawl and shiver. I tossed the covers aside and placed my feet on the floor, only to find my toes curling and the nails elongating.

Shit. A change. My back spasmed and I dropped to my knees, a whimper escaping my throat. A hard one, too. I needed to get outside.

I tore down the stairs and flung myself out into the yard. I began to strip off my clothing, stomach heaving with bile. I felt like I was going to throw up, but nothing was coming. Just that feeling like my skin was going to fling itself off my body as my organs rearranged themselves.

I dropped to the grass and huddled there, staring at my fingers as they shivered and curled, joints aching. Okay. Okay. I needed to calm down. I could do this. I managed it every time, and every time it was messy and ugly, but I came out the other side. This was no different. Start with the hands, I told myself. Hands and feet, work on controlling those. If I could push it down and keep my humanity in place, I'd be good. If it felt like it was going out of control, I'd force it in the other direction.

Great plan, I decided, and then promptly threw up. The scent of my own vomit made my muscles clench and I scuttled away in the grass, crouching low and shivering. I was always so cold, and never as cold as when I was trying to force a change.

After a few minutes of my hands painfully cramping, the sensation moved up my thighs, and my spine gave a wrench. I let out a low gasp of pain. Okay. This wasn't going to pass. This was going to be a wolf change. Levi had warned me that I needed to change more often or this would happen. *I could do this. I could.*

Another surge made wolf hair push through my skin, and my hips twisted painfully, my blood thundering in my ears. My hands began to burn, and I watched those nails elongate. I dug my fingertips into the grass and bit the inside of my cheek. Each change seemed to hurt worse and worse lately. Was this one going to kill me? A terrified whimper escaped my lips.

A large, warm hand touched my back. "Shh," Ramsey whispered, and I felt his large body crouch over mine. "Relax, Sara."

"I-I'm okay," I breathed. My lungs seized and I whimpered at the sharp stab of pain. "It's under control. I'll be done in . . . just a minute."

To my surprise, his hand began to rub my naked back. "Relax. No rush." His voice was low and soothing, a soft, comforting rumble. "Where's the change focused?"

"M-m-my fingers and toes," I panted, and they jerked and curled as if being seared by heat. The pain that flared up from them robbed what little breath I had. It hurt.

"That's backwards," Ramsey said in the same low, smooth voice. "Fingers are last. Don't fight it. Change in your center first. It'll spread from within. Find your core."

Another ripple of pain shot through my legs and I got to my feet, staggering. "I don't have a core! That's the problem!"

Warm hands wrapped around my body and pulled me against his warm, equally naked form. He ignored the uncontrolled twitching of my limbs and hugged me against him until my back—clenching and twisting—was pressed against his stomach. I felt the brush of his chest hair against my back and shoulders. The scent of bear was heavy in my nostrils, an oddly drugging scent.

Should I brush up against him? Should I hold myself back? My hips bucked, uncontrollable, and his hand landed on the flat of my belly, holding me still. "Shh. Calm. Relax."

"Hurts," I choked out, distracted by his nakedness and the rebellion of my body. "How do I make it stop?"

I could have sworn I heard him chuckle. "You relax." He held me against him, the warmth of his skin leeching into my own.

"But if I relax, the wolf will take over—"

"I know. Let her." His hand moved lower on my belly, pressed there. "Find your center. Change from here."

I squeezed my eyes shut, hating that I'd have to change. I didn't want to be a wolf, especially not in front of Ramsey. But when another painful wrenching twist shot through my muscles, I whimpered.

His hand brushed down my arm, caressing my prickling skin. "Let your wolf take over," he repeated.

I did. I relaxed. Stopped fighting it. Waited for the worst to happen.

For some strange reason, the twitching in my limbs began to slow down. He continued to hold me against him, and as my body became more languid and relaxed, I began to notice small things. How utterly naked he was against me. How low his hand was on my belly. The feel of him against my skin.

His thumbs moved against my skin in small, almost imperceptible tickling motions. His scent was thick in my nostrils. And when he moved against my body again, I was hit with a flush of desire.

He's taken, I reminded myself. *You can't have him.*

But I still wanted him.

It was a little alarming to think of a man in a sexual way again after all this time. I hadn't wanted a man since Roy had brutalized me so long ago. There'd been too many secrets to keep, too many things to worry about. But I didn't have to hide with Ramsey. He could handle my secrets, and he'd protect me . . .

A surge of desire flushed through my body, and my gasp was slightly different this time.

Ramsey's body stiffened against mine and I felt his fingers flex on my stomach, as if he had suddenly picked up on the change in my demeanor. Oh, no. He'd realized I was turned on and was horrified. I opened my mouth to blurt out an apology—

And doubled over as the transformation rushed to a finish.

I ran through the woods for an hour or two, until the wolf in me was so tired that I could barely think. To my shame, I ate a squirrel and rolled in some animal's crap in the woods. The human instinct was strong, but sometimes the beast overrode it. Ramsey followed behind at a distance, but he didn't crowd me. He just waited at the edges of my territory, just barely in scent range, as if to remind me that he was there and I wasn't alone. When my body began to twitch with the skin-crawling restlessness of an impending change back, I didn't fight it. I finished my run, returned home, and began to shift on Ramsey's front lawn. The transformation back to human was slow, but steady. Probably because my body was so exhausted.

By the time I changed back, I was tired as hell. I crawled into the house, my clothes clutched to my chest. I smelled of sweat and . . . other things, and I needed another bath.

When I got upstairs, to my surprise, a bath had been drawn for me, the water steaming hot. A rush of gratitude swept through me and I tossed my clothes aside, slipping into the water.

The bath awoke my mind a bit more. Maybe if Ramsey helped me, I could practice the shifting more. When he'd helped me, it had been slow but not nearly as painful. He'd been in the woods tonight as well—had he been shifted? Did he have to shift often, too? Maybe we could run together.

I re-dressed in my panties and T-shirt and tiptoed into the bedroom. Ramsey was in the bed, hands underneath his head as he stared up at the hole in the ceiling. His chest was still bare, the blankets pooled around his waist.

He looked . . . impressive. I twitched my fingers, wanting to place them against that impossibly broad chest again, dig my fingers into his chest hair.

"Hi again," I said softly.

He glanced over at me. "Feel better?"

I nodded awkwardly.

"Gets easier with practice," he said. His gaze skimmed my form in the darkness, and then he turned to glance back at the ceiling.

"That's what everyone keeps telling me," I said

lightly. I moved to the bed and, after a moment's hesitation, got under the covers. Ramsey's new bed was big enough that we didn't touch.

I lay stiffly for a few minutes, wondering if I should continue the conversation about shifting. Or was now the time to bring up Nikolina? I could tell he wasn't asleep. He didn't seem relaxed either, and his breathing was erratic. The scent of him filled my nostrils, warm and delicious and comforting, and after a few minutes of drinking it in, I rolled over to face him. His eyes were closed, but he hadn't moved a muscle.

"Ramsey," I whispered.

"What?" He didn't look over at me.

"When were you going to tell me about your mate?"

He stiffened in the big bed next to me, and his frown was dark. "My . . . mate?" He said the word slowly, as if it had been foreign to him.

I rolled on my side to face him, propping my chin up with my hand and resting on an elbow. "Nikolina Aasen," I told him. "I was doing some maintenance in the Midnight Liaisons database and noticed you both had profiles. *Linked* profiles. Linked, mated profiles."

He sighed heavily.

My heart sank. "So it's true?" Damn. "Is she going to be mad about this?" I sat upright, scooting away a bit. "Should we even be in the same bed together?"

Ramsey scowled. "Lie down and I'll explain."

I relaxed again but kept my gaze on him.

He didn't look at me as he spoke, as if it was difficult for him to share. "You have to understand where I come from to understand my relationship with Nikolina. My family is bear clan. I was born into the Bjorns of the Ozarks. The bear clans keep to themselves. They do not mix with other shifters, nor do other shifters harass them. They exist outside of most circles, because no one wants to enrage a bear. The bear clans have several long-standing customs that ensure that the bloodlines remain strong and the clan is protected."

"What kind of rules?" I remembered his statement when he'd claimed me. *In accordance with the bear clan and the laws of the Bjorn . . .*

"You do not talk to outsiders. You are not friends with outsiders. You do not mate outside the bear clans. And always, *always,* the bear clan comes first." There was the barest hint of bitterness in his deep voice. "Children of the bear clan are betrothed at an extremely young age so we can grow up knowing we are to be mated and grow into the idea. Nikolina was betrothed to me when she was born. I was two. It was intended that we should marry when we reached an age, and bear more children for the clan."

My breath caught. "So it's a . . . childhood betrothal?"

He looked over at me, his dark eyes so serious. "I have not seen her since the day I was exiled."

My burst of relief and elation dimmed at the

weight of that word and the lines of unhappiness that creased Ramsey's face. "Really? Is she why you were exiled?"

He was silent. I touched his arm and he sighed heavily, then began to speak again. "Twelve years ago, Beau's father demanded that the bear clan meet with the cougar clan to speak of joining his new alliance. My father was not interested, and it took them many days of arguing and fighting to come to this agreement. While they met, Beau and I became friends despite the warring of our fathers. I was younger than Beau and he looked out for me as if he would a brother. It was a . . . unique situation for me. I did not know what to make of it. Being teenage boys, we stayed out too late one night and were discovered by my cousin. He attacked Beau, and when I stepped in, he attacked me as well." He gave me a grave look and added, "Bears are very territorial, and we were on what he deemed bear territory."

I licked my dry lips. "I see."

"When my father discovered me standing over my beaten and bloody cousin, and learned I had fought to save a friend that was not of the bear clan . . . " He shrugged. "I was exiled."

I gasped and leaned in, unable to stop myself from brushing my hand on his arm. "What? Just like that?"

"I broke the rules," he said simply. "I am exiled until I petition to return. To do so, I will have to leave the Alliance behind and take up life as one of the bear clan again."

I knew what that meant. No outsiders. No Alliance mate. I felt a little sick to my stomach. "When will you go back?"

"When I am ready."

Such a simple statement, yet such a wealth of information. No wonder his house was falling down. Why fix it up if he was just going to leave again? He didn't date. He kept to himself, except for his friendship with Beau and Beau's family. His role in the Alliance was protector. Aloof, fearsome, and remote. I wondered if he was ever lonely.

And I wondered . . . if he thought about Nikolina. "What do you think happened to Nikolina?"

He gave me an odd look. "I am exiled, not dead."

"So she's still waiting for you to return? Engaged?"

"That is how the bear clan works. For her to approach another would be to shame her family. There are no other unattached males my age."

I felt a surge of pity for her, an outcast through no fault of her own, cursed to spinsterhood simply because her betrothed had chosen a different path.

He looked over at me. "What are you thinking?"

"I'm thinking those are stupid rules."

He grunted in agreement. "The bear clan is not the most forward-thinking clan."

And you want to go back? Why?

I lay back in the bed and stared up at the ceiling. Bears mated to bears to keep the bloodlines strong and pure. It sounded so archaic, and yet, from a shifter standpoint, sensible. Bears were probably all tall, strong, and sturdy. Ramsey would be with a big, strapping woman who was a match to him in all ways, instead of tiny little me, who he was probably afraid to crush if he rolled over at night.

I thought about babies and bloodlines for a bit longer, then looked over at Ramsey again. "If Savannah was dating Connor and he bit her, would she start to turn into a wolf?"

"No."

"Why not?"

"Doesn't work that way."

"Well then, how does it work?" I felt stupid that I had to ask.

"You can only be one kind of shifter. It changes something inside you."

That was good to know. "Are you sure? If we had kids, they wouldn't be wolf-man-bears? Lots of claws and like to fetch sticks?"

He gave me a quelling look. "No."

The man just did not have a sense of humor. I played with the blankets, thinking. "So would Savannah and Connor's children be dog or cat?"

"Depends on the blood. They'll be one or the other. When she goes into heat, it only calls others of her kind to mate with her while she is fertile. It is nature's way of trying to keep the bloodlines going." He glanced over at me after a long moment, his gaze wary. "Why?"

I hoped I didn't have to experience going into heat for a really long time. "No reason."

He continued to watch me, wary. "Why?"

I sighed. "Well, I think you should bite me."

His eyes narrowed at me and he leaned up on one elbow. I tried not to shiver as his large form loomed over mine. I wasn't scared of him, but the way he looked at me, I knew we'd left the safe part of our relationship.

"Why," he repeated again.

"I need a mate mark on my neck. Bathsheba has one. I don't, and everyone's looking for it. You saw how both Connor and Levi stared at my neck. They were expecting to see a mark. No one's going to buy us as a mated couple if I'm unmarked."

"You don't know what you're asking. Those marks take months—maybe years—to go away. A mate replenishes the mark when it begins to fade."

"So?"

"You might find someone you like better. No shifter will touch you if my mark is on you."

A wry smile curved my mouth. "I haven't had sex in six years. I think I'll be all right if I wait another year or two." I touched his arm. "And I'm not the only one giving up my dating life for this little escapade. You had to give up yours, too."

Of course, his dating life had all kinds of complications that mine didn't. I couldn't help but think of Nikolina, waiting patiently for Ramsey to return to her. Had she been in love with him when he'd left twelve years ago? Was he in love with the memories of them as teenagers?

I couldn't let my thoughts go down that path or I'd go crazy. I gave him my brightest smile and kept on track. "Anyhow, I just wanted to say I appreciate what you're doing for me. But if you're uncomfortable giving me a mate mark because you have someone else in mind, I totally understand." I turned away and pulled the covers up.

"I will give you the mark," he said after a moment, his voice low and almost grudging. "If you want."

Jeez. He didn't have to sound so enthusiastic. I rolled back over and looked at him. "It's not that I want one. It's that I think it's what's best."

Ramsey nodded. "Very well."

"You sure? I don't want you to feel like you're stuck in a fake relationship with me." Well, he was, but I didn't want him to *feel* like it.

He scowled. "If you're sure."

"I think it'll be good." I shifted in the bed, lying flat on my back and tugging down the neck of my T-shirt, trying to ignore the pulsing of my blood. "Very convincing. No one will question a woman with a mate mark on her throat." I touched my neck and frowned. "I'm kind of new at this. How much skin do you need?"

He leaned over me and his large form suddenly blotted out the moon overhead. His dark eyes gleamed in the moonlight, and I felt his hand hesitantly touch my neck.

A surge of longing flashed through me but I quelled it, staring up at Ramsey. He seemed . . . almost skittish. I didn't want him to change his mind.

It felt incredibly intimate as his chest leaned over mine as he maneuvered closer to my neck. I kept one hand tugging down the neck of my shirt; the other lay on the pillow, as I wasn't quite sure where to put it. Touch Ramsey? Keep it to myself?

He studied my neck for a moment, then glanced back up at me. "The man that changed you . . ."

"He never marked me. Humans weren't worthy of being a shifter's mate. He didn't want to claim me as his in public."

"Many shifters think that way," Ramsey said after a minute, and I felt his large fingers brush the soft skin of my neck again. "A mate mark is a public signal, but it is a very . . . personal thing."

I shivered. That sounded intense.

He froze.

"Not scared," I quickly told him. "Just a little . . . nervous. That's all." I had a feeling if I told him that his touch was making my pulse quicken, he'd bolt out of the room. Maybe he found humans—or once-humans—distasteful, too.

Ramsey's knee slid between mine as he adjusted his weight. His mouth dipped in low to my throat and I felt his warm breath there. My nipples immediately hardened. I ignored them, hoping he wouldn't notice. He was doing me a favor; it'd be a bad time to get turned on.

"I . . . need to touch you first," he said, his voice low. "On your skin. The spot to mark."

"That's okay," I said softly. My fingers curled harder in my shirt. "You can touch me. I don't mind."

His lips brushed the skin of my throat and my

pulse fluttered in response. He skimmed his mouth along the length of my throat, as if trying to judge the best place to put the mark. The sensation was ticklish and pleasant; my neck was a strong erogenous zone.

His mouth moved down toward my collarbone, and I felt his tongue touch the skin there, tasting it.

"Oh," I breathed softly.

"Sorry," he said gruffly. "Part of the bite. I should probably lick the skin first."

"It's okay." My breathing had quickened, and I was pretty sure his had, too. "You can lick me."

His tongue brushed against my skin and I felt a pulse low in my hips. Oh, jeez. This was . . . way more erotic than I had imagined. Luckily, my hips were pinned under his or they might have lifted in response. His leg shifted between mine again and I realized he was nearly naked, wearing just a thin pair of boxers. Well, that was only fair. I was in just a pair of panties and a T-shirt.

His tongue rasped against my skin and I felt that sensation all the way down to my core, my nipples tight against my T-shirt. I bit my lip to keep from making any noise.

"Still okay?"

"Still okay," I breathed.

"Your hands are clenched," he said. "Put them on me if you don't know what to do. Relax."

I placed my hands on his big shoulders. It felt curiously like I was pulling him into my embrace, like I would a lover. That did crazy things to my already overacting imagination. I felt his mouth nuzzle one particular spot on my neck again . . . and then he bit.

A gasp escaped my throat and my fingers clenched on his shoulders. Oh, wow. That was deliciously close to orgasmic.

His breath fanned the sensitive spot. "Still . . . okay?" His breathing sounded as harsh as my own.

"Good. You should mark me again," I said in a soft voice. "Just to . . . you know, make it convincing."

I'd expected him to need to be talked into that, but to my surprise, his teeth immediately sank down on a spot just slightly lower than the last one. Another gasping cry escaped my throat. Then he bit me again, the motion lingering and the bite more intense than the last. Oh, God. I needed his hands on my breasts, my sex . . . "Please . . ."

He stiffened in shock against me. Before I could blurt an apology, he released me with a growled oath and vaulted out of the bed.

Surprised, I watched him slam out of the room, the door thundering shut behind him. Plaster rained from the ceiling as the house shook.

Well . . . shit.

I sat up, trying not to feel terribly humiliated. He'd figured out that I'd been turned on and it had grossed him out. I sighed and flopped back down on the bed, my hands going to my shirt. Maybe I'd take care of myself tonight and just picture him on top of me, biting my throat . . .

My hand slid down my shirt and then I stopped.

Something warm, sticky, and wet touched my fingertips just before the smell of semen reached my nostrils.

Ramsey had . . . come? On me?

What the fuck? I sat up and ripped my shirt off. Sure enough, he'd come on my side when he'd been biting me. Dazed, I stared at the shirt, and then at the door. He'd cussed under his breath and then jumped up like he'd been on fire.

I hadn't noticed how raspy his breathing had gotten or how his body had jerked against mine; I'd been too caught up in fighting my own pleasure.

I tugged on another shirt from my suitcase and lay back down again, thinking hard. Ramsey had been in the Alliance since he was fifteen. He never dated. Everyone was scared of him. He'd left the bear clan and Nikolina at fifteen. And he came from a clan that didn't date outsiders.

He'd come on my shirt, unable to stop himself. And then he'd bolted away, angry and probably embarrassed.

Holy crap. Was Ramsey a . . . virgin?

Chapter Ten

*H*e didn't return to bed that night. I fell into an exhausted sleep after a time and woke up when the sun was shining through the windows and ceiling. I dressed, ran a comb through my short, messy hair, and padded downstairs.

To my surprise, the kitchen had been scrubbed clean. Sure, the counters were still demolished and the cupboards had missing doors, but they'd been cleaned and food was placed in them. A shiny new fridge sat in place. When I opened it, there was no hum of electricity, but bags of ice had been stuffed into the compartments, with drinks sandwiched between them. Bread and cinnamon rolls lay on the counter. I grabbed a soda and a cinnamon roll and went outside, looking for Ramsey. We needed to talk.

I went outside and found his legs sticking out from under the house. He'd half crawled under the floors, and judging by his toolbox, was fixing . . . something.

"Hey, Ramsey," I said brightly. "Thanks for breakfast."

No response.

"Can you hear me under there?"

"Yes," he said after a long moment. "I'm busy."

Okay, so it was going to be like that. "Are you going into town today? I have work at eight."

"Off today," he said brusquely, then stuck a hand out from under the house. "Pliers, please."

I shoved the last of my cinnamon roll into my mouth and handed him the pliers. Then I wiped my hands on my jeans and squatted down by his legs. "What are you doing?"

"Fixing the wiring."

I smiled. "Awesome. What about the plumbing?"

"Not a plumber."

"Can we call a handyman? I bet there's one in the database at work."

"Whatever you want."

Excellent. "So how am I getting to work?"

"Austin's going to come by and pick you up."

Jeez. So much for the protective mate. "Guess I'll see you later."

He said nothing as I walked back into the house.

Man. A guy accidentally comes all over his fake spouse's side, and he won't even talk to her the next day.

"You look like you're in a bad mood," my sister observed as I came into the office. "Honeymoon over?"

I stuck my tongue out at her.

She grinned. "Looks like there's a little bump in the road of true love."

I said nothing and slid into my chair. You never knew what sorts of ears were listening in the next room.

"Anything I can help with?"

I gave her a look. "Probably not."

"Come on. That's what sisters are for."

When it came to men, I had way more experience than she did. Still, dealing with a massive adult virgin was probably new territory for both of us. I played with a pencil on my desk as my computer booted up. "What do you know of Ramsey? From Beau?"

"Well, there's some stuff Beau has asked me not to talk about."

I stared up at her, hurt. My sister was keeping secrets from me? *Me?* We'd shared everything up until she'd met Beau. And while I didn't resent her happiness, a little part of me felt . . . lost. Had she known about Ramsey's mate and had decided not to tell me? "Is there anything you *can* tell me?"

She shrugged. "He's a good guy. Beau trusts him with his life. He's quiet. Doesn't really socialize much."

"He ever date around?" I asked casually. I didn't want to tell her that I already knew he had a *real* mate. "I'm sure Beau has a string of ex-girlfriends. Most shifters are good-looking."

She rubbed her neck, right where the mate marking was. I felt the oddest urge to rub my own neck. "I've never heard of him dating at all, actually. Why?"

"I was just curious." So Ramsey was definitely a virgin. Dear Lord, no wonder he'd freaked out on me. Did this mean he was never going to talk to me face-to-face ever again? The thought made me incredibly anxious. And then I thought of him leaning over me, his mouth pressed against my neck, and a flush crept over my skin.

The door to the agency opened, the bell clanging. I glanced up and my nostrils immediately filled with the scent of wolf. Anderson wolf.

"Welcome to Midnight Liaisons," my sister called out as the girl sauntered past the waiting area. "Can we help you?"

The girl grinned and sat down across from me, ignoring my sister. Her hair was long, dark, and curly, a wild nimbus that probably didn't see a hairbrush often. Her eyes were bright blue against her tanned skin, and she wore a spaghetti-strapped denim sundress that was so tight on her lean body that it left nothing to the imagination. Her legs— and feet—were bare.

The woman's gaze rested on my neck and the mate mark for a long moment, and then she raised a hand in the air to high-five me. "Get some, girl!"

Oh, jeez. "You must be Gracie."

She winked at me and wiggled her fingers, still waiting for the slap.

I sighed and reached up and gave her hand a halfhearted smack. At my sister's inquiring gaze,

I explained, "My new wolf escort. Connor wasn't doing the job, so Levi sent someone new."

Gracie tossed her curly hair and gave me a smug look, then propped her feet up on the corner of my desk. "Gimme just a sec. I gotta text Daddy something."

She glanced over at my neck again as her fingers flew on the keyboard, and she grinned. Her gaze moved to my neck again, and then she typed even more.

I flushed under her scrutiny.

My sister gave me a curious look and I gave a subtle shake of my head. I'd tell her later. Well, at least I'd tell her all she needed to know.

"Soooo," Gracie said, dropping her phone back in her purse and swinging her feet back down to the floor. They were immediately replaced by her elbows on the corner of my desk as she leaned in and gave me an interested look. "Daddy wants me to show you how to shift. You any good at Kegels?"

Behind me, my sister spit out her coffee.

"Um?"

Gracie grinned. "What no guy will be able to tell you is that the concept behind shifting and Kegels is pretty much the same. There's that inner muscle deep inside that needs a good workout in order for it to perform. Once you find it, you gotta exercise it." She leaned forward and gave me a feral look that was supposed to be playful but struck me as vaguely menacing. "Go on, give it a try."

"M-my Kegels?" I stammered.

"Sara, can I talk to you for a minute?" My sister went over to the coffeemaker.

Gracie rolled her eyes and whipped out her cell phone again, beginning to text once more. I wondered if she was going to report everything back to her father. No wonder he'd wanted to send her.

I hurried over to my sister, who whispered, "Can you get rid of her? At least for an hour? I have a very shy were-lion coming in at nine, and I don't know how he's going to react to her."

Behind me, I could hear Gracie's fingers clicking away as she texted. I nodded. "I'll handle it."

I returned to my seat and Gracie winked at me. "I'll be on my best behavior, promise."

Somehow I doubted a wolf's best behavior was any shade of appropriate, but I nodded. "Thank you."

Bath gave me a long, meaningful look. "I need to make sure today's cases get wrapped up early. We don't have any appointments tomorrow if we clear the books today, and I'd like you to go wedding dress shopping with me." Her smile grew even wider. "The maid of honor has to pick out a dress, too."

Ugh. Not my idea of a fun time. I'd rather go computer shopping than dress shopping.

"Can I be your flower girl in the wedding?" Gracie asked. "I got some daisies in the backyard."

My sister froze. "Um, well, I really don't know—"

Gracie giggled. "I'm just shitting ya." She turned back to me. "Now, about those Kegels—"

The office door opened and a man walked in, tall, lean enough to almost be skinny, with fine cheekbones, tawny hair, and a leonine look to his face. His gaze immediately moved to the she-wolf. Gracie sat up, adjusted the hem of her skimpy dress, and gave him a too-sweet smile.

"Toby," Bathsheba said with a smile. "Come sit down. Would you like a coffee?"

He moved to my sister's desk, his gaze flicking to Gracie. The sweet smile remained curved on Gracie's mouth.

"What can I help you with today?" my sister said in a calm, easy voice, drawing his attention back to her.

He gave another uneasy look back at Gracie, then my sister, and swallowed hard. "Elma didn't work out. We're too different. I'm looking to date someone new."

No surprise there. Elma was our resident harpy, and she struck out more than she scored. My sister must have been desperate to pair a cat with a bird shifter; those types didn't mix well at all. Poor Elma was totally scraping the bottom of the barrel.

"I see." My sister began to type. "And what are you looking for in a companion? Do we need to update anything?"

"I'll do it," Gracie said.

All eyes turned to her.

She gave us a coy, playful smile. "I've never dated a lion before. I'd love to try one on for size."

Toby blushed. I'm pretty sure my sister did, too.

I rolled my eyes. "What's your father going to think about that, Gracie?"

"Daddy says I'm going wherever you're going for the next month." She continued to smile sweetly at Toby. "So if you're at a dating agency all day long, I don't see why I can't date the clients if you're my chaperone."

"You don't even have a profile yet," I pointed out. "I'm not sure that Toby wants to date someone he doesn't know anything about—"

"Sure," Toby said in a slightly hoarse voice. "You wanna do lunch? Chili's?"

Ouch. Not the smoothest choice for a first date.

But Gracie exclaimed, "Oh, mercy. That sounds delightful." And she turned and gave me a wink. "Guess you should set up my profile right about now so we can get this logged in the system."

"Guess so," I muttered. "So what kind of date preference should I put on your profile?"

"All of them," she said promptly.

"All?"

"You can even put a vampire or whatever else you've got on there." Her blue eyes sparkled. "I'm open to everything as long as it's a good time."

Oh, boy. "Reservations at Chili's, coming right up."

The she-wolf took to shy Toby as if she'd been born to be at his side, and she laughed and flirted all the way through their lunch. I sat at a nearby booth, chaperoning.

Gracie didn't have a shy bone in her body. She also had the charming ability to make whatever she was talking about sound fascinating to the male sex, I realized, as Toby leaned in, entranced by her description of going shopping for new dishes because her wild brothers had broken the others. Her bare feet wiggled on the floor as she chatted, clearly enjoying herself.

Meanwhile, I curled up with my BlackBerry and did a little remote work. I found a handyman in the database and immediately requested that he come out to Ramsey's place for a quote the next day. He was a wolf, but between Ramsey and Gracie, I figured I could handle it. And with the mark on my neck, I felt a little more secure in my spot as Ramsey's alleged mate.

The waiter gave me an odd stare as he refilled my glass, and I subconsciously touched my neck. His human scent hit my nostrils and I frowned. What was he staring at? I checked my reflection in my knife and winced. My hair looked like shit. Tangled and dry thanks to the hair color, it resembled a sickly gray-blue tumbleweed. It was a wonder Ramsey had wanted to bite me at all.

Thinking about Ramsey, I decided to message him. *Hey,* I texted. *I'm changing my hair color. You got a preference?*

After a minute, he sent back: *You look fine.*

Thanks for the compliment, but I'm still changing my hair color.

I liked it when it was brown.

Sweet man. I wanted to pinch his cheeks. Actually, thinking about last night, I wanted to do rather dirty things to him. How would he react if I kissed him again? Crawled all over that big body and let him know I was interested in fixing that virginity problem for him?

I shivered at the thought and texted again. *How about red?*

I like red.

Red it was.

By the time five o'clock rolled around, I was more than ready to leave. After we'd gotten Gracie back from her date (and she'd gotten Toby's number), she'd insisted on tweaking her profile and going through the database, picking out a long list of candidates that she was interested in. Then she began to critique the sorts of questions asked on the profiles.

"Eye color?" She snorted. "Who cares about his eye color? All I want to know is if he's still got both of 'em."

When Gracie began to surf the database for eligible women for her brothers, I let her take over the computer and went to Marie's empty desk. If Gracie wanted to set up her brothers, I certainly wasn't going to stand in the way. By the time my ride showed up, I'd never been so glad to see Austin. Gracie was exhausting, a whirling dervish of ideas—most of them centered around men and how she could date them. She'd given Austin some rather heated looks that he'd returned with a scowl.

The scowl only seemed to make her even more interested, as if he'd been a strange creature she was determined to figure out.

He stopped at the grocery store so I could run in for a few things. When Gracie offered to wait with him, Austin shot me a panicked look. I made her come with me, saying that I needed help carrying the groceries. I didn't miss Austin's look of relief. He totally owed me.

Once inside the store, Gracie wandered off, which I didn't mind. Heck, if she wandered off for good, I'd be just fine with that. I grabbed a cart and pushed it down the beer aisle, staring into the rows of freezer cases. An ice-cold beer sounded really damn good right about now.

I opened the cooler door to pull out a six-pack, then hesitated. My "mate" probably wanted beer, too. It was going to be odd thinking about having a partner. I pulled out a case instead.

The glass door swung shut, blowing a puff of cold air into my face . . . and I caught the scent of wolf. I froze, momentarily confused. Was that my scent? Gracie's? But it didn't smell like either one of us. Wary, I glanced around. The supermarket was full of the scents of shoppers, the squeaking of carts, and the low murmur of voices. Was there another wolf here other than myself and Gracie? I guessed they could have been grocery shopping. I stared down the empty aisle, then turned my cart down the next one.

A man disappeared around the corner just as I

turned, and I caught the scent of wolf again. My nape prickled with alarm. I forced myself to head down the next aisle, grab a box of red hair dye, and then keep going.

The smell of fresh, bloody meat wafted in my direction, and I automatically veered that way. Maybe a steak for dinner to go with the beer. I stared at the rows of steaks, the smell of blood heavy in my nostrils, and grabbed a package. Maybe two steaks. It smelled so good that I was tempted to rip off the cellophane and eat them in the middle of the store.

The smell of wolf hit me again, and I turned.

Gracie sauntered toward me, a wine bottle in her hand. "Buy me a drink, Sailor?"

Relieved, I took the bottle from her hand, ignoring the dirty looks a nearby customer was giving Gracie's bare feet. "I'm pretty sure you're not old enough to drink?"

"Of course I am," she said smoothly. "I must have left my ID at home."

Likely story. But I took the bottle and placed it in the cart anyhow. And then glanced around one more time. "Are there any others here?"

Gracie wrinkled her nose at me. "Any other whats?"

"You know," I said, giving her a pointed look as an old woman stopped to browse the meat not too far away. "*Others*."

"Other . . . shoppers?" Gracie said innocently.

I gritted my teeth. She was going to be like that, was she? I plucked the wine back out of the cart and handed it back. "You know what? You can just buy that yourself."

"Of course no one else is here. You're paranoid, you know that?" Gracie said and put the wine back in the cart.

Maybe I was. Still, I couldn't trust her to tell the truth. She wasn't trustworthy in the slightest. "Come on," I said, turning my buggy toward the front. "Austin's going to be tired of waiting for us."

We checked out quickly and headed back out to the truck. When we pulled up to Ramsey's house I saw a single light on inside, and it was sad how much it thrilled me. "Hey, we have electricity!"

Gracie wrinkled her nose. "I get the guesthouse, right?"

"Yeah. It's on the far side of the yard. Let me show it to you."

I showed her in to Connor's old quarters, and Gracie dumped her bag on the bed. "You wanna color your hair now? Surprise your man?"

The thought of surprising Ramsey gave me unexpected pleasure, and I agreed. We slapped the steaks into the mini-fridge, then I stripped out of my T-shirt and borrowed an old one from her. Thirty minutes later, my hair was a vibrant shade of maroon.

"Wow, that color really took," Gracie said with a grin. "I have a yellow sundress that would go awesome with that. You should try it on. Impress your man. It'll show off those love bites really nicely."

"I doubt it'll fit. I'm kinda small in some areas."

She was already pulling it out of her bag. "That's okay, I buy 'em small."

I slipped out of my bra and jeans and into Gracie's sundress. It was too loose in the front, but Gracie tightened the laces in the front and the back so it emphasized my lean figure and downplayed my lack of curves.

As I changed, I noticed Gracie watching me, which made my hackles go up a little. Was she checking me out for her brothers? How creepy was that? But when I straightened, she came over to my side and adjusted one of the spaghetti straps.

She smiled. "Looks good. Shows off your mate marks."

I exhaled. Maybe I *was* being paranoid. Gracie was a bit weird, and her smiles a little too toothy for my liking, but she seemed decent enough. Not like some of the other wolves. I gathered up my things and gave her a hesitant smile. "Thanks."

She put her hands on my shoulders. "Now. About tonight."

"Tonight?"

"You need to shift. Daddy says that you need to shift every night. You gonna shift with that man of yours?"

Awkward. "Um. I think so."

"Okay. Remember what I said. Kegels. Find that muscle and flex it."

"Got it," I said in a small voice. "Kegels."

"Attagirl. Now, go get some." She swatted me on the ass when I turned to leave.

I headed back to the house, steaks and clothes clutched in hand, my damp red hair swinging against my cheeks. Would Ramsey see my new hair color and light up with lust? Or would he scowl at my frivolousness? Or worse, would he just ignore me like he had earlier?

I crept up the front porch steps and hesitated, bolstering my courage. I had to approach this the right way. One wrong move and I'd freak him out, or make him run away.

A hand dropped onto my shoulder from behind. "Hey, miss," a voice drawled, and the scent of male wolf flooded my nostrils.

Roy grabbed me by the shoulder and forced me against a wall. "You need to show me if you're strong enough to be my mate, girl. All I see here is a coward. I need to beat some toughness into you again, don't I?"

I screamed.

Chapter Eleven

A low roar broke through the blood pounding in my ears. I stood up—didn't realize I was crouching—and stared dazedly at the front yard. The stench of wolves was heavy in the air.

Ramsey had a smaller man pinned to the ground. I could hear Ramsey's snarls from where I stood, trembling, on the porch. Thick brown hair coated his limbs, clearly on the verge of a change. Beneath him, the man struggled.

"I didn't hurt her," the man choked out.

A horn honked in the driveway and I swung around, staring. The side of the white van parked there read Jackson Wilder, Plumber and Handyman. Inside the van a teenage boy hammered on the horn, clearly terrified.

Oh . . . shit. I'd smelled wolf and thought it had been one of the Andersons come to kidnap me, but it was just the handyman. I inhaled sharply, and I smelled wolf, but . . . not what I'd smelled at the store earlier. This man was a stranger. His scent was new to me.

"Ramsey," I cried out, tearing down the steps. "Ramsey, let him go. I made a mistake."

He rolled off to one side immediately, crouching low on his hind legs. The other man rolled in the opposite direction, then raced for his van.

I watched the muscles in Ramsey's legs tremble, his clothing straining at the seams, his face contorted in a snarl. After a moment, he shook off the change and got to his feet, muscles flexing. He looked over at me and held his hand out, calmly, deliberately, as if trying not to terrify me.

I extended my hand toward him slowly, realizing how much it shook. My entire body was quivering like a leaf.

"Hey," Gracie called from the side of the house, running forward. "What's goin' on?"

"Misunderstanding," Ramsey said, tugging me forward with gentle eyes and pulling me against him. My entire body trembled, my teeth chattering even as I tried to stammer and explain that I was just fine, and terribly sorry that I'd caused such a mess. Ramsey placed a hand along my jaw, shushing me, and pulled me close. I felt him press a kiss to the top of my head.

"It's all right," the handyman said, his voice low and soothing and almost hypnotic. "Don't be alarmed. I didn't mean to scare you."

"My mate has a bad past. Do *not* touch her or sneak up on her." The words were said in a steady voice, but I could almost hear the snarl in Ramsey's throat, and I placed a calming hand on his chest. My fingers had stopped shaking at least, but I felt no desire to leave Ramsey's comforting embrace.

"My apologies," the man said, his voice pleasant and unruffled. I wasn't sure if he was deliberately trying to be soothing or if that was his normal demeanor, but it was already calming me down. "I was supposed to come by tomorrow for the job," he said, "but we were in town tonight and I thought I'd stop by the place and give it a quick look-over."

"It's okay, Ramsey," I said. "I called a handyman through the agency."

The man scratched his head, his curly hair messy. "We'll come back in the morning." He flashed an awkward smile in my direction. "Didn't mean to scare you."

"You want to come over to my cabin?" Gracie said to the man. "You can clean up the cuts on your face."

I hadn't even realized that Ramsey must have hit him.

The man shook his head. "I'm good. Thanks." He put his baseball cap back on, tipped his hat, and got back in the van.

Gracie gave us an odd look and returned to her cabin, fishing her phone out of her pocket, no doubt to tell her father what a mess I was.

Ramsey rubbed my bare arm. "You okay?"

"Just a little shaken," I said breathlessly. I took another deep breath to reassure myself. The scent of the handyman wasn't what I had smelled at the store. Had I just been imagining the scent from earlier? Was I paranoid, like Gracie had said? I shuddered. "Let's just go inside and forget it."

Ramsey picked me up and, cradling me against his chest, went into the house. He set me down carefully in the center of the nearly empty living room and then began to run a big hand over my shoulders. "You sure you're all right?"

I nodded. "I just had a fright. Bad memories."

"Tell me."

"No." Reliving them once was enough. I didn't want to go through it again.

His hand slid over my shoulder and across my collarbone, and I watched his gaze move to the mate mark on my neck, his eyes intense.

"I brought steaks," I said suddenly. "For dinner."

He quirked an eyebrow at me, and for the oddest moment, I had a feeling that Ramsey wanted to smile at me.

"I'll get the steaks," he said. "You sit here. Relax."

I sat down on the old sofa and waited, smoothing the skirt of my borrowed dress. I felt like an idiot all around. I'd nearly gotten the handyman killed. I'd dressed up for a man who ran away at the thought of touching me. And I'd shown everyone that I was still the weak, fragile creature they thought me to be. I *hated* that.

I heard Ramsey toss the steaks in the fridge and then his big heavy feet move across the wood floors toward me. I straightened the spaghetti straps of my sundress and looked up at him.

"I need to change tonight," I told him. "I need to change every night. To practice."

He nodded.

"Will you help me?"

"Yes."

It felt awkward to be around Ramsey while I was naked and waiting for my muscles to shift. I kept thinking of last night, and I guessed that he was, too, judging from the way he absolutely refused to look at my naked body. That was all right; it gave me a chance to look at his.

His chest was covered in a dusting of hair. His arms were impressively thick and his waist long and lean. A thick line of darker hair started at his navel and trailed down to the largest piece of male equipment I'd ever seen. I swallowed hard. I'd expected him to be big. I just hadn't thought about *how* big. It distracted me, especially when Ramsey pulled my body tight against his again, his hands on my shoulders.

"Relax," he told me in that deep, rumbling voice that reverberated through my muscles. "Look for that place in your mind. The shifting starts in your head, not in your body. If you think it through, you can encourage the shift. It's hardest when you don't anticipate it."

I felt the warmth of his body, the slow thrum of his pulse. I stretched an arm out into the air, watching my skin tremble as it sprouted fur. To my surprise, Ramsey's hand reached out and caught mine, grasping it tight.

I will always catch you, it seemed to say.

The change was not swift that night, but it was far less painful, which was encouraging. When I was in my wolf form, Ramsey's large body shifted to bear, and he crouched low on all four of his massive legs. Immediately, his scent changed and my senses went on alert. A wolf always noticed when there was another predator in the area, and a much larger predator was standing right in front of me. The wolf-mind couldn't handle it.

But Ramsey only moved forward and licked one of my ears, and then his scent became familiar all over again. He was still Ramsey underneath, and Ramsey would die before harming a hair on my head. My wolf-body relaxed and I danced away. When I dashed into the woods on the scent of a rabbit, he followed a fair distance behind, giving me room to breathe but still close enough to keep me safe.

I was hot on the tail of a rabbit, deep in the underbrush, when my body trembled and my legs seized. I collapsed onto the ground, startled to realize my body was changing back. That hadn't happened before. It didn't feel painful, though, only urgent, so I crouched low and let it happen.

When the transforming was done, I flung myself backward in the dirt and stared up at the night sky, sprawling and utterly naked, and utterly winded.

A large, naked male body thumped down on the

ground next to me, and I looked over to see Ramsey staring up at the skies as well.

"I've never had that happen before," I said, looking over at him. "Changing back so fast."

"Shifting is a muscle," he explained without looking over at me. "If you use yours every day, it will get tired. But you will build up stamina, and that is when true control comes. Nothing to be worried over."

Like Kegels.

I looked over at Ramsey, a hot flush on my cheeks. He continued to stare pointedly at the sky. Was it because of me, or because he was thinking about Nikolina? Did he want to be running naked with her?

"Can we talk about last night?" I ventured.

"No."

I rolled over on my side and propped up on one elbow. "Let me rephrase. I really need to talk about last night."

He started to get up. I placed a hand on his shoulder. He glanced over at me, then seemed to realize how naked I was, and immediately flicked his gaze away again.

My hand remained on his arm. He was so warm, his skin so vibrant under my touch. I loved touching him. "I wanted to tell you that . . . I really liked it when you bit me. It made me feel things I haven't felt in a long, long time. And I was wondering . . ." I trailed a finger along a thick muscle. "If you wanted to continue . . ."

He looked over and glared at me. "No." He sat up in a rush of leaves.

I grabbed him before he could leave. "Ramsey, I know you're a virgin." He gave me a glare of such anger that I rushed to continue. "That's why I think this would be good for both of us. You need someone to teach you, and I need someone to show me that sex doesn't have to come with fear."

He leaned in close, seething with anger. "I am not a charity case—"

"No charity," I said, and leaned in and kissed him lightly, my tongue grazing his lips. "I want you."

His face remained stony, unconvinced.

"It's true," I whispered. At least he wasn't running away. This was good. "Do you want to feel how wet you make me?"

His eyes flared with hunger.

Excitement trembled through my body, and I got to my knees and crawled toward him. "Put your hands on me, Ramsey."

He glanced down at my naked body for the first time, and I felt a shudder pass through his big frame. "I don't . . . I'm not . . . ."

"I know," I said softly. I took his big hand in mine. "It's fine."

He gazed on me as if he'd been starving. "You're so small and fragile and I'm . . . ."

"Big," I breathed. "I know. You won't hurt me. I trust you." When he still hesitated, I placed his hand at the vee of my thighs.

He groaned with need, and I felt his hand cup the hot flesh there. A finger slid between the lips of my sex and he stroked, feeling the warmth there. "So wet," he groaned.

"Wet for you," I encouraged, rocking my hips on his hand. "Touch me."

His finger slid through the wetness, soft at first, then stroking harder. When I moaned in encouragement, he tugged me into his lap. I straddled him and felt just how enormous and hard his cock was against my smaller frame. A quiver ran through my body.

He noticed it, and when I leaned in to kiss him, the kiss he gave me in response had a hint of hesitance.

"We'll take it slow," I said. "Just kissing tonight."

"And if I . . ." His words broke off with a groan when my hips flexed over his.

"Then we'll learn stamina together." When he didn't smile, I leaned forward and bit his lower lip. "But if you get to come, I get to, too."

I'd been enjoying just kissing him when exhaustion had hit me like a ton of bricks, so Ramsey had picked me up in his arms and carried me back to the house. The exhaustion was to be expected if I was learning how to control my wolf, he'd explained.

All I knew was that I woke up to see late morning sunlight streaming through the window. I was sprawled in the bed, alone, still naked. Guess I'd slept all the way through the night. How disappointing.

I took a quick bath, dressed in a T-shirt and jeans, and headed down the stairs. The kitchen was empty, but there was bread and jelly, and I decided to make myself a few slices of toast.

Until I realized there was no toaster. It was probably just as well, since plugging in a toaster was probably tantamount to a death wish in this house. I found a tarnished silver knife in one of the drawers and spread jam on plain white bread instead. I was ravenous.

As I ate my fourth slice standing up, Ramsey entered the house. He was already sweaty, his dark shirt plastered to his big body, a baseball cap tugged low over his brow. He had streaks of dirt on his forearms and mud on the knees of his jeans.

"You shouldn't have let me sleep so late," I said around a mouthful of bread, and swallowed. "Makes me feel lazy."

He moved over to my side and grabbed me by the hips, lifting me onto the counter.

I looked at him in surprise, then his mouth brushed against mine in a soft kiss. It was greeting and subtle request all in one, and I melted underneath it. I didn't care if he was sweaty or dirty—he was delicious. I dug my fingers into his shirt and leaned in to his kiss, my tongue stroking into his mouth.

He groaned, his big hands clenching my bottom

so hard he nearly pulled me back off the counter. I felt a shudder go through him, just before his tongue licked into my mouth in a deep, claiming surge.

I broke the kiss off with a gasp, feeling that stroke all the way through my body. "Wow."

"Hi," he said, and pressed another hard, fierce kiss on my mouth.

"What are you doing that has you all dirty this morning?" I asked, running a hand down his chest. The smell of sweaty, sexy skin filled my nostrils, mingled with Ramsey's warm scent. It was so unfair for a man to smell that good.

"Fixing the steps on the front porch. How are you feeling?"

I ran a hand down his sweaty chest. "Turned on?"

His dark eyes flared with need. "Tired? Muscles hurt?"

I shook my head.

He leaned in and kissed my nose. "Good." His gaze searched my face for a moment, then he asked, gruffly, "Second thoughts?"

"God no," I said, my fingers brushing over his nipple through the sweaty shirt. "I just wasn't sure if now was an appropriate time—"

"Fuck appropriate," he rumbled and leaned in to kiss me again. He stopped just before his lips touched mine, and I watched him, entranced. "Your hair's pretty."

Was that his way of flirting with me? I grinned, entranced by this new side of Ramsey. "You said you liked red."

"I like you," he said, his gaze intent on my face. "I just don't know . . ."

Oh, no. He wasn't getting second thoughts on me. I began to wrap my legs around his torso to hold him into place, but a sharp knock at the front door made both of us jump.

A low growl of dislike rumbled in Ramsey's throat. For some reason, that made me giggle. The man did not like to be interrupted. I liked that about him. I patted his shoulder. "That's probably the handyman again."

He offered me his hand immediately, and I felt warm. So thoughtful. I slipped my hand in his, and we went to open the front door together.

Gracie stood on the doorstep, chewing gum. "You got breakfast over here? This big bad wolf's cupboard is bare."

I let her in. "Just bread. I should go into town and grab some stuff."

"I'll do that," Ramsey said. "You stay here. Rest."

Gracie wrinkled her nose but said nothing, spreading jam on a slice of bread.

"I'm not an invalid," I said crossly.

Ramsey scowled down at me. "You need to rest."

"I'm fine." I put my hands on my hips and glared back, ignoring his frown. "I just spent the last eight hours resting."

There was another knock at the door.

"That's going to be the handyman," I said.

"I'll get rid of him," Ramsey said.

"You will not," I said. "There's a hole in the ceiling the size of a cannonball, and I don't want it raining on me."

He continued to scowl down at me.

I ran a finger down his chest. "Please?"

His scowl didn't change, but he pulled me close and lifted me for another hard kiss, then set me down on the ground and answered the door.

The handyman gave Ramsey a perplexed look when he answered the door. "This a good time?"

"No," Ramsey said, but he gestured for him to enter the house anyhow.

The handyman smiled at the sight of me, slow and easy. He held out his hand for me to shake, and I felt a weird sort of compulsion. I liked this man. I trusted him. I placed my hand in his and smiled.

"Name's Jackson," he said. "Now, show me what you need done to this place and I can give you a quote."

"Let go of her," Ramsey growled.

Jackson let go of my hand easily, but he didn't look frightened. "Not trying to steal your mate, friend. Just trying to hear about the job."

I felt the absurd need to please Jackson and then realized what it was. The handyman was not only a wolf but he was also an alpha. That was weird. I looked over at Gracie, who was specifically avoiding eye contact with him. With Ramsey here, though, I wasn't scared. Jackson's demeanor was calm and relaxed—not vicious like the Andersons. "There's a lot we need to get done around here. I'll show you the most urgent ones, and then Ramsey can supervise."

"Aren't we going into town?" Gracie asked suddenly. "Your sister wanted to go wedding dress shopping, remember?"

Oh, jeez. I'd totally forgotten. Poor Bath. I grabbed my purse off the counter. "Ramsey, can I take your truck?"

"You can. Just be safe and call me if you're going to be late." He leaned in and gave me another kiss, which made me flush. It was like he couldn't stop kissing me now that he had permission.

"Show him the shower and the ceiling and the—"

"Go on," he said gruffly, touching my chin. And then he leaned in. "And take Gracie with you. Please."

"Got it," I said and dashed out the door. Bath wouldn't be thrilled, but as long as Gracie didn't try to invite herself into the wedding party again, we'd be just fine. As we got in the truck, I looked over at Gracie. "You sure you don't want to stay? Dress shopping's not all that fun," I said. "And Jackson's kind of cute."

She rolled her eyes. "The last thing I want in my life is another alpha wolf. I'm looking for a little variety, thank you." She grinned and twirled a lock of her hair. "That's why I think I'm going to like your dating agency."

———

Several hours later, Gracie and I pulled up in front of the house. Jackson's van was still there, and when we got out of the car, I could hear hammering.

Gracie flounced out of the truck and immediately flipped open her phone. "I'll catch ya later."

I watched her saunter through the yard. "Shouldn't we, uh, be spending wolf time together?" I asked her.

She waved a hand at me, not looking up from her phone. The woman got a constant stream of text messages, no doubt from all the profiles she'd signed herself up for. "Just remember the Kegels."

"Right," I said, picking up my pink bag and heading into the house. I yawned as I went inside. It had been a long afternoon, and I was exhausted. Between Bath's insistence on checking out every store in the Metroplex area that even smelled of weddings, and Gracie's constant smirky needling of her, I was worn out.

Plus, I kept smelling wolves wherever we went. I never saw anyone, but the scent of unfamiliar male wolves lingered whenever I turned a corner. Gracie always said she smelled nothing. My sister was human and couldn't scent wolves, so that left only me.

Hell, I smelled wolves even now. The scent of male sweat and werewolf was all over the house, making my hackles rise. The scent was to be expected, since the handyman was here, but it still made me uneasy. "Ramsey?" I said softly. "You in here?"

Something crashed in one of the rooms down the hall, and I opened the door to see a tall, awkward teenage boy with a tool belt slung low around his waist and a plumber's cap on his head. He held a hammer in one hand and stared at me, frozen.

His scent hit my nostrils—wolf. I froze in place, but the scent wasn't Anderson. The boy quickly averted his eyes, as if not wishing to alarm me. "Mr. Bjorn said if you came looking for him that I wasn't to scare you," the boy said in low, even tones. "Want me to call him?"

"No, I'm fine." I gave him an awkward smile and took a step or two backward, not letting him out of my sight. Roy liked to pounce on me when I had my back turned. . . .

"Sara," said Ramsey's low, delicious voice. "Come here."

I turned and saw him down the hall. I knew his voice was low and calm because he was worried I'd become all skittish again. I moved toward him, placed my hand in his, and tilted my face up for a kiss, mostly just to see how he'd respond.

Ramsey leaned in and brushed his lips on my forehead. Which was a little disappointing. "We're still working on the roof," he explained. "Will you be all right with the Wilders here?"

I nodded and yawned.

"Tired? You should sleep." He laced his fingers through mine, and when he stepped closer, I knew he was one inch away from swinging me into his arms and carrying me upstairs to force a nap on me.

"Just tired from watching Bath try on all those dresses. I think she tried on a hundred before she found one she liked."

"When's the wedding?"

"I don't know. They postponed it because of . . . you and me. Bath says she doesn't want to get married until we're settled, and Beau agreed." I guarded my words carefully, sure that the boy was still nearby, and moved in close to Ramsey so I could whisper the next part. "Jackson . . . he's an alpha."

Ramsey brushed a hand over my cheek. "I know."

I bit my lip and tugged him down so I could whisper in his ear. "He . . . he's not looking for a mate like the Andersons, is he?"

Ramsey's face turned toward mine, so close that our mouths were nearly touching. "He knows you are mine, and that if he touches you, I'm going to remove his spine through his throat."

Well, that explained why the boy had looked utterly terrified when I'd run into him. I leaned in and gave Ramsey a quick kiss, grinning. "Good."

He nodded at my bag. "What's that?"

"Nothing," I said, hiding the small pink bag behind my back. After finding a bridal gown, we'd headed to a lingerie store, and I hadn't been able to resist getting something a little naughty for myself. Just the thought of blowing Ramsey's virgin mind had been enough to make me giddy with excitement, and I'd forked over far too much money for far too little fabric, but it was worth it.

When Ramsey caught me yawning again, his

mouth turned down in a frown. "You're exhausted. Go upstairs and take a nap. Learning to shift takes a lot of energy. Energy that you're going to need for later tonight." His face abruptly turned beet red, and he added, "So you can shift again."

I yawned once more, exhaustion suddenly crashing on me. "Okay," I said, pulling my fingers from his. "You'll come get me later, won't you?"

"Promise," he said in a low, rumbling voice that sent a shiver all the way through my body.

Chapter Twelve

*W*hen I awoke, it was dark outside. Something radiated heat next to my side, and I rolled over to see Ramsey's large form next to mine, his chest bare.

I gave him a sleepy smile. "Hi. Did I miss anything exciting?"

He pointed at the ceiling.

I blinked and looked up, tugging the sheets close as I did. Huh. "My skylight's gone. How'd I sleep through that?"

"It's just patched with a tarp for now," Ramsey said. "I thought you'd prefer a roof. It's supposed to rain tomorrow."

I gave him a shy smile. "Thank you."

He said nothing, simply watched me.

Well, okay, this could get a little awkward. Was he waiting for me to make the first move? I toyed with the sheets, noticing that I'd fallen asleep in my T-shirt and jeans. "And here I thought I'd wake up and find you pouncing on me," I teased.

He stiffened, and the hint of a smile on his face

disappeared. "I would never touch you against your will."

"I didn't mean it like that," I said quickly. I never thought of Ramsey like Roy. Surely he knew that? When he continued to stew in the darkness, I leaned forward and placed a hand on his chest. He felt large and warm underneath my fingers. "I know you wouldn't. I was just . . . hoping for more of a reaction from you. After, you know, our talk earlier."

"Sara," he said softly, and I felt a thrill of delight at the sound of my name on his lips. "If you move your hand lower, you'll know my reaction."

A smile curved my lips and I did just that, feeling a little pleased when he jerked in surprise, then sharply inhaled.

I'd seen his equipment earlier, but feeling the massive length under my hand drove home the size difference between us. "Well, I'm glad it's not just me that's interested," I said, keeping my voice playful despite the pounding of my pulse. I felt nervous now that the moment had arrived. Did he want me, or did he just want to have sex? Or was that just my shattered self-esteem talking?

He was still quiet.

I took a deep breath. "I know you're not the most . . . verbal of guys, Ramsey, but I'm feeling a little nervous right now, and I'd really like to hear what you're thinking. Please."

He sat up and moved oh so close to me, his body leaning in against where I sat huddled in the sheets. "I want to touch you, Sara."

"That's a good start," I said softly, unable to look away from his mouth. "Keep going."

"I . . . keep thinking about your mouth on mine. Thought about it all day." His breathing became quicker, the scent of his familiar musk stronger. "How it would feel on my body. What you would look like if I touched your . . . breasts. What you look like naked."

My breath caught in my throat at his scorching words. "You've seen me naked," I said softly.

"Not while you're under me," he said softly.

A shudder of lust ripped through my body, and I grew instantly wet. "That sounds . . . sexy as hell, Ramsey."

He growled low in his throat, sending a ripple of anticipation through my body.

I dropped the sheets and put a hand to his cheek—smooth shaven, just for me—and leaned in for another kiss.

His mouth met mine in a hot, wet, open slicking of tongues that immediately made me moan. Ramsey was an incredible kisser; his tongue did amazing things to my insides. It stroked deep into my mouth, and I rubbed my tongue against his in response.

When we broke the kiss, he pressed his forehead to mine. "Tell me what to do . . . to please you."

I skimmed a hand down his front and brushed my fingers against the thick length of his cock.

He hissed and immediately pulled my hand away. "I want to touch *you*. Explore you."

"Can't I touch you?" I protested, sliding my hand back up the wall of muscle that was his chest.

"I'll come," he growled.

"That's kind of the point of this," I said softly, moving my mouth against his in a light, fluttery, almost-kiss.

"Want you to come first," he gritted. "Want to make you come."

My hips rose in response and my breath sucked in. Perhaps he wanted to explore my body before moving to the good stuff. I could get behind that. I lay back and let my hands fall to the pillow. "I am yours to play with."

He stared down at me for a minute, and then his big hand hesitated, hovering over my body.

I wiggled to coax him. "It's okay. You can't break me with just a touch."

His hand landed reverently on my shoulder, brushing against my shirt and flexing there. Nice and safe. "Where do you like to be touched?"

"Everywhere."

He scowled down at me as if I was being supremely unhelpful.

"Everywhere," I reiterated. "Anywhere you kiss me, anywhere your fingers touch, or your mouth touches, it'll give me pleasure. I promise."

His fingers flexed on my shoulder again, brushing lightly over my arm, and then stopped. He looked down at me again.

Clearly he was going to need encouragement to get to the good parts. I grabbed the hem of my shirt and tugged it over my head, shimmying out and dropping it to the floor. I did the same with my pants, leaving only my panties on, and lay back down in the bed. My breasts were so small that I normally didn't wear a bra, and my nipples were already hard, pointing at the ceiling.

Ramsey stilled, his breath rasping in his throat. His gaze moved to my breasts, but he still hesitated.

"Please," I said and took his big hand in mine. I slid it to my breast and let him cup me there. "Touch me, Ramsey."

His hand flexed against my torso. "You're so small."

"Probably not what you want to tell a girl when you're feeling her tits," I observed dryly.

His gaze slid to me, startled. "No. *You*. You are so small." His hand slid to my waist and was joined by the other. His thumbs touched just over my belly button. "I could snap you in my hands."

"Is this your idea of bedroom talk?" I asked irritably. "I want you to make me wild with desire, not harp about how you fear you're going to hurt me."

Another thought flashed through my mind and I sat up, nearly knocking my forehead against his. Maybe he thought my small, lean body wasn't feminine enough. Maybe he thought I smelled like wolf—a foul odor in my own mind. "Is it me? Am I unattractive?"

His gaze darkened and he lifted one of those big hands and pressed my shoulder until I fell backward in the bed. "Don't be stupid."

"Well, it has to be something," I snapped back, trying to shove him away. "Here I am, shoving my breasts in your hand, and you're acting like you're about to go to a funeral. So I kinda have to think it's *me*."

He kissed me, hard. "You're perfect. Perfect all over." His hand dipped to touch my breastbone, his fingertips grazing the soft, pale skin there.

I made a soft noise of pleasure and arched against his hand, letting him know that his touch was pleasing. "Then show me."

"Perfect," he said, and grazed his fingertips over a hard nipple, brushing the tip.

I gasped at the lightning bolt of sensation and arched against his fingertips, encouraging more.

His fingers brushed the slight curve of my breast and then his thumb grazed the peak, teasing it. His gaze flicked back to mine.

"Oh, God," I breathed, aching at the touch.

He stilled.

"No, no," I said, pulling his face back toward mine. I kissed him hard and fierce. "That's good. I'm going to say a lot when you touch me. The more I say, the better it is. Got that?"

Experimentally, his fingertips closed over the nipple, and he pinched lightly. My kiss turned into a gasp and I fiercely bit his lower lip, then licked away the hurt. A growl started low in his throat, and I felt the oddest desire to do the same. It had been six years since a man had touched me, and even longer since I'd wanted it. This was making me crazy with need.

"Please don't stop touching me," I said. "Use your fingers, your mouth, everything."

His mouth broke away from mine as he continued to brush his thumb over my nipple, and I saw his gaze slide to my other straining breast.

"Yes," I agreed, my breath coming in sharp little pants. "Put your mouth there."

He slid down my body, his mouth hovering close to my aching, needy breast. He hovered for a moment, and then I watched his tongue move out and ever so lightly graze my nipple.

I cried out in pleasure.

When he stiffened, I dug my fingers in his hair and pulled him closer. He didn't need much more than that—his mouth latched onto my nipple and he began to lick it slowly, swirling his tongue around the sensitive skin. Every time he moved his tongue, it sent a bolt of pure pleasure through my body, and, with words and soft cries of pleasure, I let him know how much it pleased me. His mouth was incredible, and before long I was arching my hips, bucking slightly in response to each stroke of his tongue.

"Sara," he growled, staring up at me, his eyes gleaming feral.

"What?" I panted, my hands tangled in his hair. God, his fingers were still rolling my nipple, teasing the peak and driving me wild. "What is it?"

"I can smell your need." His hand went to my panties and I could hear the low growl in his throat again. "Smells . . . amazing," he said with a hard rasp, and ripped them off. "I need to taste you."

He got off the bed, grabbed my hips, and tugged me forward to the edge of the bed, my legs dangling over the side. Ramsey knelt on the floor, the boards creaking.

"Your perfume's . . . incredible," he growled low against my belly, and then his mouth was on me.

"I . . . oh . . . ," I breathed, falling backward on the bed as the sensations flashed through my body. His big hands held my hips, my legs wide open, and I felt his tongue brush my folds, sliding over their slick heat, tasting me. A rippling shudder of desire cascaded over me. "Oh . . . that's really good," I said, my voice dreamy as his tongue lapped at the wetness. God, he had a big, wonderful tongue. And oh wow, he was using it in ways that made my toes curl with desire. "Oh . . . oh, Ramsey. Really good."

He licked the sides of my sex, exploring each soft fold. His tongue found my core, and when he pressed into me, I nearly came off the bed. My fingers went to his hair and twisted there. "That's *really* good," I panted as he thrust with his tongue. "Really, really good. Oh . . . oh . . . oh yes."

His tongue stroked out of my core and back in again.

I screamed as his tongue found my clit and my hips rose off the bed. When he growled low in his throat with pleasure, I felt it against my sex. The rippling shock waves of pleasure became a tidal wave, and I twisted my hands in his hair, pulling his face against my sex. "Oh, right there," I moaned when he flicked his tongue against the nub of my clit. "That feels so amazing. Oh, yes. Oh . . . keep doing that with your tongue. Oh, Ramsey."

The more I moaned and demanded, the faster his tongue worked. Flicking against my clit, then rubbing in circles and swiping hard with his tongue when my hips jerked in response. The steady stream of words died. I needed him. Needed *more*. Needed him to lick faster, harder—

He growled low against my clit, swiped hard with his tongue, and I shattered in a keening wave of pleasure. Every muscle in my body locked tight, vibrating, and he still continued to lick, instinctively drawing out my orgasm. It seemed to last for endless minutes. My body was quivering like jelly, and I'd lost all ability to speak. When my muscles finally unlocked, I realized that I'd wrapped my legs around Ramsey's shoulders and my fingers were still dug in his hair, still holding his face to the cradle of my hips. He was giving me slow, languid licks now, as if he couldn't get enough of my taste. Like a favorite treat.

"Oh . . . oh, Ramsey," I breathed, rubbing his scalp with my fingers. "You have an amazing mouth. Really, *really* amazing. Especially for a virgin."

He leaned over and kissed the inside of my thigh. "I came," he said in a low, husky voice.

"Oh, good," I said with a dreamy smile.

"Three times."

I giggled.

He stiffened against my legs.

I wrapped them around him again and continued

to massage his head. "That was flat-out incredible. I'm going to be greedy for that tongue of yours."

The stiffness disappeared and he kissed the soft inside of my thigh again. "First, we shower," he said. "Then, you need to shift."

I groaned. "My legs feel like noodles. I won't even be able to walk to the shower, much less run in the woods."

"Then I will ask Gracie to wash my back." He began to pull my legs off his shoulders.

I stared at the half smile tugging at his lips. "Did you just make a joke?"

He bit my thigh in response, eliciting a squeal from me.

Wow. An orgasm—or three—really mellowed the man. I couldn't wait to find out what he'd be like after full-on sex.

After a shower and a run through the woods, I was falling asleep on my feet. I vaguely remembered curling up next to him in bed, but when I woke up the next morning, he was already up, and the sound of hammers on the far side of the house told me that we had visitors.

I spent the day helping renovate the house. While Ramsey and Jackson worked on the roof, Dan—the teenage werewolf assistant—had been assigned to give the outside of the house a fresh coat of paint. While he ran the power-gun painter, I used a brush to get the spots he missed, and we chatted.

It turned out that he and Jackson were looking for a new pack. Their old pack had died in a fire, and I didn't pry when I saw how choked up Dan got. They were alone right now because Jackson was an alpha, and no pack would accept him for fear that he'd challenge the existing alpha. A few packs had offered to take in Dan, but he wouldn't leave Jackson's side.

I felt a surge of affection for the kid, and Ramsey seemed to get along with Jackson pretty well. A few times I caught the sound of male laughter coming from the roof.

Gracie came out of her guesthouse, texting away, and when she found out our day was going to be spent doing manual labor, she went right back in, chiding me for wasting my strength.

By the time the sun was setting, Dan and I had painted the first level of the exterior of the house, the roof was patched, and my nose was sunburned.

"It's looking good, Miss Sara," Dan said shyly, lifting his baseball cap to wipe the sweat off his brow. "Pretty soon it'll be a real home for you and Ramsey, and then you can start on a family."

It was a good thing my cheeks were already flushed with exertion. "I'm still not entirely convinced that our species should be interbreeding," I said with a laugh. "Our children would be big and snarly, with a weakness for honey."

The wind shifted, carrying Ramsey's scent just as a shadow fell over me. "He's standing right behind me, isn't he?"

Dan nodded, grinning.

A hand slid around my waist, and for once, I didn't jump. My hands moved to it and caressed his big fingers.

Ramsey pulled me close to him and leaned in and murmured, "Pretty sure you're bad at fetch."

"Throw me a stick and see what happens," I teased, then squealed when he kissed my neck. "You're sweaty."

"So are you."

Jackson appeared from the side of the house, mopping his brow and drinking from a water bottle. "We'd better get going, Dan."

I immediately felt bad that he was staying so far away from me. "Do you guys want to stay for a bit? The shower's fixed, and we could order a pizza."

Jackson gave me a smile but shook his head. "Thank you, but we've got a hotel room that'll do just fine. You two need some alone time."

I blushed, because he wasn't entirely wrong about that. Ramsey's arms were still wrapped around me, and I was content to lean against him and soak up his strength, sweat and all. It felt good to be in his arms.

When Dan and Jackson had packed their things and the van crunched down the gravel road, Ramsey leaned in and nipped my ear. "Shower?"

"Only if you promise to towel me off with extra-special care," I teased.

His eyes gleamed.

We raced to the shower and got in together. I

scrubbed his back, then he scrubbed mine. When his big hand slid to my front and cupped one of my breasts, I knew shower-time was over. I turned around and looked up at him, wishing our heights weren't so different—I didn't reach higher than Ramsey's pectoral, and his massive erection was stabbing me in the stomach. Not that I minded, but I really wanted to kiss him at that moment and told him so.

Ramsey reached past me, flipped the shower off, then lifted me as if I'd weighed nothing. There were benefits to dating a ridiculously strong man, I decided as I leaned in toward his mouth.

He sucked on my lower lip in response, and I moaned low in my throat. Still kissing, I wrapped my legs around his waist, and Ramsey moved us to the bedroom. He dumped my wet body on the bed, and then his hot, sleek, wet one slid over mine. I gave a shiver of delight and rubbed up against him.

"I want to lick you again," he said between kisses. "Over and over again. Love your smell. Love your taste even more."

My innards clenched with need at the thought, and my kiss grew fiercer. His hand slid between us, and I bucked when his fingers brushed against the slippery heat of my sex. I'd waited all day for this, wanted his thick, enormous length deep inside me, to fill the ache that had been rising each time I thought of last night and his head between my legs.

A horn honked somewhere below.

Ramsey's head lifted.

"Ignore it," I said, wrapping my fingers in his hair and tugging his face back down to mine. My hips rose against his hand, waiting and hoping for his fingers to explore me. "I need you."

A haze of desire moved over his face and he leaned down, nipping at one of my wet nipples. I gasped and arched, encouraging his mouth.

The horn honked again. Three times in a row, repeatedly. From down below, I heard the sound of raucous male laughter.

Ramsey swore and detangled himself from my body. "Get dressed," he said, and in a flash he'd grabbed a pair of jeans and was out of the room.

I sat up on my elbows and scowled at the door. Damn. That was some crappy timing.

"Sara," a voice bellowed downstairs. "Where are ya, girl? We brought you a present!"

I recognized that voice, and it made my heart pound with delight. "Joshua?" I jumped to my feet and hastily dug underwear and pants out of my overnight bag. The only pants I grabbed were pajama bottoms, but I didn't care—I slid them on, grabbed one of Ramsey's shirts, and pulled it over my head. Then I tore down the stairs and gave a happy squeal at the sight below. The Russell clan sat in Ramsey's shoddy living room, minus Beau. Joshua, Jeremiah, Everett, Ellis, and Austin grinned up at me. Everett held up a case of beer. Austin and Joshua were setting up a flatscreen on a folding table against the wall. Ellis held up the Xbox he'd brought. "Saturday nights are gaming night, remember?"

I gave a happy little jump and pounced on Joshua. "You guys are the best," I said happily. "I totally forgot about game night!"

"We didn't forget," Everett said with a grin, setting down the beer so I could bound over and hug him, too.

"Figured it'd be a good time to come check up on you," Jeremiah said. "Make sure everything's all right over here."

"We're great," I said enthusiastically, ignoring the glances that lingered on my neck. "It's sweet of y'all to come by."

The boys popped open a few beers and began to set up the Xbox, and someone was always appearing to hug me, tickle me, or tease me about my appearance. It was like being back in the Russell house on Saturday nights. We'd all gather around the gaming consoles, drink beer, and talk shit. It was like having a pack of brothers, and I'd loved every moment of it while I'd lived there.

Smiling, I glanced around. "Where'd Ramsey go?"

"Went to get something," Ellis said. He sat on the floor and grabbed his beer. "I can't believe there's no internet out here. That's criminal. Do you know what year it is?"

"Sorry," I said with a grin, flopping down on the couch between Joshua and Everett. "Ramsey's fixing the place up. Maybe we'll have it next weekend. Electricity was kind of a priority this week. Savannah's not with you?"

"She's staying home tonight." Jeremiah, the quiet, perceptive one, nodded at me. "Are we bothering you guys?"

"Not at all," I said with a grin, reaching for the control passed to me. I looked to Ramsey, and then realized he wasn't in the room. "What exactly was Ramsey getting?"

Ellis shrugged and nudged my arm. "You gonna play?"

I stared down at the control in my hands. The Russells were overwhelming and boisterous, and I didn't mind their teasing. But maybe Ramsey was feeling excluded? Even when he'd been at the Russell compound, he'd never participated in the Saturday night gaming sessions. "I want Ramsey here."

Austin grinned and offered me a beer. "I scared him off. Told him that if he hurt you, I'd skin him and use him as a fireplace rug."

I rolled my eyes. "You do *not* scare him, Austin. He'd eat you for lunch and you know it."

"I know. But I just couldn't pass up the bearskin rug joke."

I handed my control to Joshua. "Let me go find Ramsey. Be right back." I stood and sniffed the air, looking for Ramsey's unique scent—so warm and different from the now-overwhelming scent of were-cougar in the house—and followed it.

I found him out on the back porch, sitting on the top step and staring off into the woods. I sat next to him, tucking my bare feet close, and slid a hand through the crook of his arm.

"What is it?"

He shook his head, not looking at me.

I took his hand, linking my fingers through his. The breeze carried the scent of paint on it, and then Gracie's light wolf scent. I heard her laughter as she joined the others in the living room, and I was glad she'd come out to play. The only thing marring my happiness was Ramsey's obvious discomfort. "It wasn't Austin, was it?"

He snorted. "Not likely."

I had figured as much. "Then what is it? Talk to me. I'd really like to know."

He looked over at me, then glanced back at the house. "You're . . . easy with them."

And . . . not with him? Was that where this was going? I smiled at him, stroking my other hand over the corded muscle of his arm. I just liked touching him, and I suspected he liked it, too. "I'm easy with them because they're easy to be around. It's like having older brothers."

"Am I like your brother?" His dark eyes narrowed.

"Not in the slightest," I said and gave his hand a squeeze.

"You didn't jump when they touched you," he noted. "You still jump when I touch you sometimes."

So *that* was what was bothering him. "I'm a jumpy person," I said softly. "But I'm getting better every day. And if I jump when you touch me, it's because I'm thinking about you touching me everywhere." His eyes darkened as they met mine, and I watched that possessive, sexy look cross his face and reveled in it. "And I've *never* entertained thoughts like that with them."

He seemed to struggle with saying something. "I . . . don't want to be like them . . . to you."

"You're not," I said and leaned in to kiss him. His mouth grazed mine in the lightest of kisses. "I certainly wasn't thinking anything brotherly last night."

"Good." He kissed me back, this time harder, more possessive.

"You guys going to make out all night?" someone called from the living room.

"Tell him yes," Ramsey said against my lips.

I laughed. "We should probably go in before they drink all the beer." I tugged at his arm. "Come with? It'd be fun if you played, too."

He seemed hesitant but allowed me to pull him along, and I knew this was part of Ramsey's discomfort around people. Close but not too close. I'd been able to get closer to the Russell brothers in a few weeks than Ramsey had in the twelve years he'd known Beau. He kept to himself, always. Perhaps his bear clan upbringing instinctively made him hold back.

When we returned to the living room, I noticed Gracie curled up on one corner of the sofa, chatting with an admiring Ellis. She texted even as she talked, and I wondered how many men she was determined to wrap around her little finger. A few others lounged on the floor since we were light on furniture, and I dragged Ramsey to the front, toward the TV. "Give Ramsey a turn," I said. "He wants to play."

A control was handed to Ramsey, and he held it awkwardly. It looked ridiculously tiny in his big hands, and he looked over at me as if pained.

"It's not hard," I declared, tugging on his arm and sitting on the floor in front of the TV. "Here. I'll show you how to aim and shoot."

He sat down cross-legged next to me, his shoulders nearly blocking out the TV screen. I was amazed anew at his size and, oddly, possessively proud. I liked that he was the biggest man in the room.

He gave me a helpless look when his turn started, then he stabbed at the wrong button.

"The A button," I said, reaching over his lap to point it out to him. "Hold down the right trigger and tap the A button—"

He dragged me into his lap. "Sit here."

I blushed, expecting someone to tease us, but Ramsey was apparently tease-free. When Ramsey handed me the control, I took it and began to play while Ramsey's big hands brushed along my skin.

The conversation started up again as I played, and when my turn was over, I handed the controller to Everett. "So where's your brother and my sister tonight?"

"They're at the cabin," Everett said with a grin, and his comment was met by a chorus of kissing sounds. "Someone's getting lucky tonight."

I snorted. "You guys are so juvenile."

"I think Bath finally figured out how far our

hearing stretches," Ellis said with a grin. "It's been a long, dry spell for poor Beau this week. I think it was getting to him. He bought her five dozen roses earlier today, and the next thing we knew, they were headed up to the cabin for the weekend."

"That's so cute," I said, glad for my sister. "You guys need to give them their privacy more often."

"We give them lots of privacy, but some people are just really, really noisy in bed," Joshua said.

"Ugh. I think I could have gone the rest of my life without knowing that about my sister."

"Me, too," agreed Joshua, still grinning.

Chapter Thirteen

*S*unday was a lazy, wonderful day. Ramsey had me shift early in the morning to exercise my muscles. With his calming help, the shifts were coming less painfully, if not any faster. Still, progress was progress, and I'd take it.

He had to check in on a job that morning, so I accompanied him to a small house in the suburbs. I waited in the truck as he knocked on the door. He met a middle-aged woman there, a child perched on her hip. They stood on the doorstep talking, far enough away that I couldn't hear the conversation, but Ramsey's expression was grave.

He circled the house and checked the locks on the windows. Next he tested the security settings of the alarm, then he examined the bars on her windows thoroughly, testing them for strength. He didn't seem satisfied, so he went back over them with a screwdriver. After the house was checked out, Ramsey asked her a few more questions, taking notes on a clipboard. He eventually nodded at her and headed back to the truck, and I watched the woman go inside again.

When Ramsey returned to the truck, I picked up the clipboard and flipped through the notes written. "No sightings in seven days? No attempts at a break-in? What's all this?"

He started the truck and put it in reverse. "Mrs. Pierce is being stalked. I check on her regularly to ensure her safety."

"Stalked? By who?"

Ramsey glanced over at me, then back at the road. "A rival clan. Her husband died last year, and another lynx clan is trying to move into the area. They're encouraging her to cede her territory, but she's not ready yet, so we're keeping a close eye on her."

"That poor woman," I said softly. "And that's your job? Protecting her? And others like her?"

"Among other things," he said. "I serve the Alliance, and she is a member of the Alliance. I'd protect anyone being hunted by others."

Just like he was protecting me. Was I a job to him as well? Just one with benefits? I didn't like the thought. We drove home in subdued silence. When we arrived back at his house, he extended a hand toward me.

I placed mine in his quietly.

He pulled me close. "I won't let anything happen to you, Sara. You don't have to worry."

"I know you won't."

It was nice to just spend the rest of the afternoon together and relax, and my anxiety soon ebbed. When he sat on the couch and watched TV, I threw my legs over his and stretched out on the sofa, reading a gaming magazine.

Ramsey grilled the steaks I kept bringing home—nice and rare. While he didn't have the same cravings for raw meat that I did, he understood it. And when I grumbled about my weird tastes as a wolf and how he didn't have the same, he leaned in and kissed my brow. "Bears like a taste of everything."

The naughty gleam in his eyes made me blush.

Ramsey's playful side was buried, but it was there. I was pretty sure he didn't show it to many people, and it pleased me that he'd shown it to me. When we got tired of watching TV, we played cards. I didn't know poker, so we played slapjack instead. I lost every time.

"It's because you have Godzilla hands," I grumbled, picking up the cards. "We need to play something else."

He simply gave me a lazy, slow smile that made my heart flutter. "Pick a game, then."

We moved to hearts next, but I lost that one, too. We spent the afternoon trying different card games and alternately arguing and laughing over them. He touched my skin frequently, his hands brushing over me as if he couldn't help himself, and I leaned in to each touch. I'd hated being touched before my secret had been let out; now I was starved for it.

Ramsey made me shift one more time that evening, and though I grumbled, I did so. Gracie showed up to supervise but quickly lost interest and returned to texting, wandering back to her cabin. I guess she felt like if I wasn't going anywhere, she didn't really have to supervise me. That was fine with me—I shifted into my wolf form and ran through the woods with Ramsey at my side.

When the second shift was done, I collapsed in the front yard, panting, and then rolled in the grass. "Mercy on me. I can't take any more shifting."

Ramsey squatted next to my naked body, where I dramatically put a hand to my forehead as if in a swoon. He studied me with a critical eye. "You're sweating less. Did it hurt?"

"It always hurts," I said irritably, but I accepted the hand he held out and hoisted myself up. "But it wasn't as bad that time."

"You're getting better," Ramsey said. "That's good."

I still hated the shifting, but it didn't seem as terrible a punishment when Ramsey shifted to bear form and ran with me. I didn't feel quite so alone then. "Guess this means I won't die as early as everyone thinks."

Ramsey's hands clamped down on my shoulders, and he turned me to face him. "You won't die," he said, the low growl edging into his voice. "I won't let you."

He pulled me into his arms, and the next thing I knew, he was kissing me hard, fierce. My naked legs wrapped around his torso and I clung to him, exhaustion forgotten in a surge of lust. Ramsey's tongue thrust into my mouth, stroking deep. I moaned in response.

He carried me up the steps of the front porch,

then into the house and up the stairs, toward our room. Our mouths were still locked as he thrust the bedroom door open, stepped in, and then slammed it behind him.

Then we were on the bed, kissing hotly, and I tugged at the shirt covering his muscles. I wanted his hot skin against me, his body deep within mine. I lifted my hips. "Please, Ramsey. I need you."

His tongue licked at mine, then lightly down my throat, down my naked breasts and my flat stomach. I quivered with anticipation as he tasted my belly button, then pushed my thighs apart. "Ramsey," I breathed as his fingers parted my folds for his gaze. "You don't have to—"

He gave me such a fierce look that the words died in my throat. "I want to taste you again."

"Can't argue with that," I said shakily, then keened when his mouth went immediately to me and began to suck. "Oh. Oh, God. Oh, Ramsey," I moaned. He'd gone straight for the gold this time. My hands fisted in the blankets and my hips raised against his mouth. A string of needy words fell from my lips as he continued to lick and suck at my slick flesh. I heard the low rumble of pleasure deep in his throat and knew he enjoyed tasting me as much as I was enjoying it.

An orgasm ripped through my body and I cried out, raising my hips even higher. I needed him deep within me and told him so.

Something hard and thick nudged at my core. His mouth continued to suck and lick at my clit, and then his fingers thrust into my body. Once, twice. I keened and nearly came off the bed with the force of the second orgasm, building high on the first one. My body was wracked with shudders for long moments, until Ramsey lifted his head and brushed his fingers over my leg.

I held my arms out for him, waiting for his big body to cover mine, to sink over me, sink into me. Waited for him to take control of the situation—and of me.

But he kissed my knee one last time and then stood. "Thank you, Sara."

I sat up, trying to tug him down on top of me. For heaven's sake, he was still fully dressed. "Don't thank me until you're deep inside me."

He shook his head and then leaned in to kiss me, his mouth tasting like . . . well, like me. "Not tonight," he said softly. "You're tired."

"Not that tired," I pointed out, but he shook his head.

"Rest. I'll be back later."

And he got up and left the room.

Well, damn. I threw a pillow at the door, confused and hurt. Ramsey loved kissing. He loved touching me, licking me—but when it came to actual sex, he stopped and left.

Or . . . was it loyalty to Nikolina? I didn't know.

The next morning, Ramsey dropped us off at work with a kiss for me and a scowl for Gracie. "I want to stay with you, but I have a few cases to check in on. Pick you up at five."

"I'll be fine," I said softly, then waved as he drove away.

When we entered the agency, Gracie propped herself up in a chair and began to text. I rolled my eyes.

My sister sat at her desk, humming softly to herself as she worked. She wore a bright pink scarf over her white sweater, and I could just guess what it was hiding.

"Nice scarf," I teased. "You have a good weekend?"

My sister nodded and didn't look up from her screen. "Very refreshing, and I'm ready to tackle the week. Going to be a busy one. We have a lot planned."

I knew she was referring to the dance. It'd definitely be a boon to our business if it took off. I sincerely hoped that it'd go well; Bath would be devastated if no one showed up because the agency was headed by a human and not a supe.

"You guys should hire me," Gracie volunteered, not looking up from her cell phone, her thumbs flying across the keys as she texted.

Bath shot me an appalled look. "That's nice of you to volunteer, Gracie, but we're good on staffing."

"I'm just saying," Gracie said, swinging a foot over one side of the chair she lounged in, the sundress sliding up her thigh. "I wouldn't trust a vegetarian to tell me the best cut of steak, if you know what I mean."

Bath ground her teeth a little.

I grabbed a stack of mail on the corner of my desk and smiled at Gracie. "So who are you dating today?"

Gracie shrugged. "I threw something on the calendar. Can you make me reservations someplace?"

Oh, boy. The fun of a wolf escort. Or spy, I thought with a grumble, since her primary job seemed to be to keep an eye on me and report back.

"Ah, here we go," Gracie said, peering at her phone. "I'm dating a coyote at three, and a vampire at eight tonight." She looked over at me and winked. "Be ready for some hot action tonight. We're going to a movie, and I hear there's going to be some necking, wink wink."

"Your father would not approve."

"Nope," she agreed. "You don't tell him about who I'm dating, and I don't tell anyone how you were screaming for God last night. Sound carries, you know."

I froze, then forced myself to relax. Gracie was just trying to rattle me. "Cancel the vampire. I'm not staying out that late just to watch you make out with a dead guy."

Gracie pouted. "Fine. I'll switch him out for a satyr at four thirty."

I pulled up a restaurant list online and made reservations for Gracie . . . and then spent a little time surfing the internet for how to make a man stop ejaculating early. I was pretty sure a lot of women didn't have to deal with enormous, twenty-seven-year-old virginal bear shifters, but you could pretty much find anything on the internet if you looked hard enough. And as I clicked through a page of techniques, I began to take mental notes.

Just in case.

Gracie grinned over at me. "By the way. My brothers will like it that you're noisy in bed."

And there went my good mood.

"Wow, I've never dated a satyr before," Gracie said in a cooing voice, her chin propped on her fists as she leaned over the table at the diner. "What's it like being you?"

From across the room, I rolled my eyes and unfurled my napkin in my lap. "Sorry we had to come here," I told my sister. "But it's best I don't leave Gracie alone with anyone."

"You really should have warned her about the satyrs," Bathsheba said in a mild voice. "You know they only want one thing."

"Oh, I know." I deliberately kept my voice low so it wouldn't carry across the busy diner to Gracie's wolf ears. "But if you try talking Gracie out of something, that just makes her want it more."

"Point taken. So how are things going?"

I played with my fork, desperately wanting to unload on her. *The wolves won't leave me alone. Gracie's psycho. Ramsey has a childhood fiancée that he hasn't seen in years and wants to go back to her when we're done. And I think I'm falling for him, and that's probably the worst thing that could happen because nothing in my life is stable right now. And it terrifies me and I don't know what to do.*

But I couldn't unload all my problems on her—she'd take over, pushing aside her wants and needs for mine, like she always did. I needed to handle things myself.

Bathsheba chatted with the waiter as she ordered, and as she looked up at him, I caught another glimpse of the love-bites all over her neck. I watched her face, so animated. When the waiter flirted with her, she blushed but deflected his teasing with an easy grin.

My sister was happy. Really, truly happy. And it was all because of Beau.

I'd seen my sister at her worst, digging a grave in the pouring rain in the middle of the desert after she'd killed a man to save me. I'd seen my sister at her most stressed—trying to hold her job, my life, and her relationship together just a short time ago. It was rare that I saw her totally content.

I couldn't ruin it. I just couldn't.

Bathsheba snapped a finger in front of my face. "Earth to Sara, come in, please."

"Sorry," I blurted. "Burger. Rare enough to moo. Thanks." I shoved the menu at the waiter. When he wandered away, Bath gave me a curious look. "What's this about?"

I was trying to think of a way to deflect her when Gracie's boisterous laugh rang across the restaurant. Bath turned her head to see, and inspiration struck.

"How do you feel about hiring Gracie to work at the agency?" I asked.

Bath's pale brows wrinkled. "I hate the thought. Why?"

I didn't like it either, but it was the only thing I'd come up with off the top of my head. I fiddled with my cutlery. "I thought it might be a good idea to add a supe."

Bath dropped her voice. "She's horribly obnoxious."

"But it'll seem less weird to new clients if we have at least one supe on the payroll," I said reasonably. "Like she said—people will trust us more if we're not all human."

"You're not human, remember?"

"It's not the same, though. You said so yourself."

Bath chewed on her lip, staring at Gracie as she thought. "I don't know. I just don't think we can trust her."

"You're probably right," I said, dropping the subject. "So what color did you pick out for the bridesmaid dresses?"

Her eyes lit up and she pulled a bridal magazine out of her purse. "I was thinking maybe peacock green, but you have to promise not to have the same color hair for the wedding."

I grinned back at my sister. "Can't promise anything."

"Oh, and I meant to remind you," Bath said, snapping her fingers. "You and Ramsey."

"Me and Ramsey what?"

"You guys need to go out on another date. Have you gone to a movie yet?"

I groaned.

"Don't groan at me," my sister said cheerfully. "You know it won't work. Just make sure and see something popular. You'll need to go to this theater." She wrote the address down and handed me the slip of paper. "The owner is were-friendly, and he hires a lot of teen supes."

"Yippee. I'm sure Ramsey will be thrilled. You know I have to bring Gracie, right?"

Bath gave me a prim look. "Then don't go see a romantic movie. Go see something with a lot of guns."

"Yeah, but then I'm stuck there, too."

"Yes, but you'll have a man to make out with. That's what a nice, dark movie theater is for. And I think you will need to do some serious making out. Think you can handle that?"

My face felt bright red. The expression on my sister's face was totally innocent. Had someone told her that Ramsey and I were getting flirty? Had Ramsey told Beau, and Beau passed it along to my sister?

"Well?" Bathsheba prompted at my silence.

"I'm sure I can manage something," I mumbled.

I called Ramsey to tell him we'd be late that night. Gracie's date ran over, and then there was a small crisis back at the agency where we had to redesign the invitations to the barn dance. Bath deemed Ryder's slogan "Who wants to meet up with a little tail?" potentially offensive, and we spent two hours arguing over the layout and fonts of the redesigned digital invitations that said simply Barn Dance across the top.

"You guys are driving me crazy," Ryder said, adjusting the font. "You're going to give me a permanent twitch with all these changes." As if to prove us right, her fingers spasmed on the mouse and she reached back and rubbed her neck.

"Har har," my sister said. "I'm paying you overtime to fix those. You said you wanted the extra hours."

"Not with you hovering over my shoulder." If anyone stood up to my sister's bossiness, it was Ryder. "Don't you guys have some men to go make sweet, sweet love to?"

My sister blushed. I rolled my eyes.

Ryder made a shooing motion with her hands. "I'm serious. You'll have the new invite in the morning, *without* any lurid catchphrases. I promise."

Sitting at my desk, her dirty feet propped up on my keyboard—gross—Gracie yawned. "Seriously. Can we go already? It's getting late, and I've got to choose the lucky man I'm going to date tomorrow."

I snagged my purse and made a mental note to spray down my keyboard in the morning with antibacterial soap. "Why don't you just pick whoever's the most appealing?"

Gracie laughed boisterously. "I come from a

wolf pack, dummy. I know exactly who the alphas are for the next three closest packs. It's practically like being stuck in an arranged marriage." Her eyes gleamed. "I have choices now, and I like it. They're *all* appealing."

Her choice of words had stopped me cold. Arranged marriage? That immediately made me think of Ramsey and Nikolina. We'd gone past "flirty" and moved straight into hot and heavy petting, but nothing more. Was he saving himself for her?

I suddenly felt very guilty. Was it wrong of me to want Ramsey? I was just a mongrel. What could I possibly offer him except a never-ending feud with the wolf pack and a bunch of stalkers that might never get the hint?

Just thinking about it depressed me. When we got home, Ramsey met me at the door, his face lined with concern. "What's wrong?"

I hesitated, unable to tell him I was jealous of a woman I'd never met. I doubted he would understand; I didn't understand it myself. "Just a long day at the office."

Mistaking my sadness for exhaustion, Ramsey lifted me into his arms and began to carry me toward the stairs.

"Wait," I protested. "My sister wants us to go to a movie."

A low growl rumbled out of Ramsey's throat. "Your sister can wait. You're tired."

"No, I'm okay," I told him and slithered out of his arms until my feet were on the floor. At his skeptical look, I said, "Really, I'm fine. Let's go and get this over with so my sister will leave us alone."

"A movie," Ramsey repeated.

"Just like on your list," I agreed. "What kind of movies do you like?"

"The ones where the monster eats everyone."

Not my kind of movie. I grinned and reached up to smooth the front of his flannel shirt. "How about I pick instead? I promise it'll be something that'll allow us plenty of make-out time."

He grunted, his hand sliding around my waist and pulling me closer.

I'd take that as a yes. "Great. Give me five minutes and I'll go round up Gracie."

That brought a fresh scowl to his face. "Gracie can get her own ride."

The movie theater was crowded, and I remembered my sister's suggestion that we see something popular, the better to be seen out in public. The scents in the air were thick—teenagers, perfume, popcorn, and I thought I even caught a whiff of shifter. Gracie wandered inside to flirt at the refreshment counter in the hopes of free food while we got the tickets. Ramsey held my hand as we waited in line, and people moved carefully around him, as if they were afraid of incurring his wrath. I had to admit, I found it kind of funny. This was his *good* mood expression.

As I reached the ticket window, I looked up at

the list of movies. Over half the theaters were a very popular teen movie that I knew Ramsey would hate. I purchased the tickets anyhow, giving him an innocent smile when he frowned. "I've been waiting all year to see this one," I told him.

He gave me a suffering look but said nothing, holding his hand out so I could take it again. I slipped mine in his and we headed inside.

I smelled wolf as soon as we entered. Wolf, and buttered popcorn, and nacho cheese. The roar of voices was nearly overwhelming in the small area, along with the thick scent of human upon human. I looked around, my hand tightening in Ramsey's. "Do you smell that?"

"I smell teenagers."

Gracie sauntered over, a tub of popcorn cradled in each arm. "Ready when y'all are."

Well, that was surprisingly thoughtful of Gracie to get us popcorn. I reached out for a bucket.

She drew back, shaking her head. "Get your own. I had to flirt hard for this."

"You're going to eat two buckets of popcorn?"

"No," she said, juggling them on her hip. "One is for eating. The other is for throwing at everyone else in the theater."

"Gracie," I scolded. "If you get thrown out, we're not driving you back until the movie's over."

Ramsey leaned down to my ear. "Wishful thinking," he said. At my laugh, he slid his hand from mine and added, "I'll get us something to eat."

"Just a drink for me," I told him and gave Gracie

her ticket while we waited for Ramsey to endure the snack bar line.

She giggled with laughter at the title of the movie. "Is this what I think it is? The one with the teen werewolf in love with the vampire?"

"That's the one."

"Oh maaaaaan," Gracie drawled. "This is gonna be fun."

I shrugged.

She gave me a speculative look. "So, things heating up between you two?"

That was direct of her. "None of your business."

"Of course it's my business," she said, glancing down and wiggling one flip-flop against the floor. "You're in my pack. What you do is my business."

I'm not in your pack. I bit back the words and replied only, "None of your business."

She leaned closer, grinning that half-wild smile. "He a good kisser?"

"None of your business," I repeated again.

Gracie shrugged her thin shoulders. "Just curious. He just looks like a nervous sort, is all. Like he'd flip out the moment you touched his dick."

She had no idea how close to the truth that was. She was watching me like a hawk, so I said, "Ramsey doesn't like wolves. Something about the popping sound their necks make when they break, he told me."

Gracie stared at me. And then gave a nervous laugh. "Quit shittin' me."

I simply studied my nails.

She snorted and stomped away. "Whatever. I'm gonna go get a seat."

I smirked with satisfaction as she left. It felt good to finally get a leg up on Gracie. As Ramsey returned to my side, I smiled up at him and took the soda he offered. "Come on. Let's go get our seats."

Once in the movie theater, we sat at the back. Gracie had a seat off to one side. I heard the slap of her flip-flops hit the floor, and a moment later, her bare feet were planted on the back of the chair in front of her. Ramsey moved the armrest between us out of the way and tugged me close, and I was only too happy to snuggle against his side. This was nice. Romantic, even if Gracie's presence was unavoidable. I leaned my head against his arm, and we watched the previews as people filed into the movie theater. We didn't chat, but I didn't mind. That was one of the things I liked about Ramsey. I didn't have to talk and talk to get my point across.

After a while, the lights went down and the movie began. A shirtless teenage boy came on-screen, and the girls in the theater gasped in delight.

Ramsey snorted.

Peeking over at my date, I stifled the giggle rising from my throat. He was watching the screen, a half-incredulous-half-disgusted look on his face as the teenage boy changed into a werewolf and began to race through the woods.

"Everything okay?" I asked, leaning in.

He gave me an odd look and leaned down to

whisper back to me. "Why did you wish to see this movie?"

Ramsey's warm breath tickled my ear, and I did laugh then, earning a few hateful looks from the rest of the audience, since the scene unfolding was a dramatic one between the werewolf and his vampire girlfriend. "I thought I could pick up some shifting pointers," I whispered back to Ramsey.

He leaned down to me and whispered, "He shifted in two seconds. That's not normal."

No, it wasn't. But I feigned ignorance. "No?"

He nodded. "His pants also disappeared with him. Also bullshit."

I grinned as Ramsey turned back to the screen. The story continued, the wolf hero being chased by evil vampires despite his girlfriend's pleading. When the wolf jumped off a cliff and disappeared into the raging river below, Ramsey gave me a quiet thumbs-up, as if he approved of the untimely death of the hero.

I laughed again, sliding my hand down his thigh.

His attention was instantly riveted on my hand.

Deliberately, I flexed my fingers against his muscles and turned my attention back to the screen. The muscled wolf boyfriend was rising from the river, the scene no doubt added to show off the young actor's incredibly buff body. His tanned skin gleamed as he pulled himself to shore. The women in the audience sighed with appreciation as he flexed and began to change back to a werewolf. As I glanced over to Ramsey, he rolled his eyes. I laughed at that, enjoying myself far more than I had expected to.

The scene cut back to the vampire, and, startled, I realized I smelled wolf. My brain had been so focused on the wolf on the screen that I hadn't noticed the heavy scent of it until now. I stiffened in my chair.

Ramsey's arm looped over my shoulders, and he pulled me in tighter. "Shh."

"Do you—"

"I smell it." His voice was quiet and low, barely audible through the noise of the theater. "Near Gracie."

I scanned the theater, looking for Gracie's curly head. One of her brothers sat in the seat next to her, his hand in her popcorn. He glanced back at me, grinned, then turned back to the movie.

My body went cold with fear.

Ramsey's hand rubbed my arm. "I'm here."

"Why are they following me?" I whispered to him. "They sent Gracie. What more do they need?"

"They're reminding you that you're theirs," Ramsey said quietly.

Reminding me who I belonged to, just in case I forgot. Irritation flashed through me. Is that what this was? The constant tailing was to remind me that I could never escape the wolf pack? That they'd persistently be on the fringes, waiting for me?

I hated that. And I hated them. Well, if they wanted to remind me? I'd remind *them* that I'd chosen someone else. "If they're going to watch," I said, "let's give them something to watch."

I tugged on Ramsey's shirt. When he leaned in closer to me, I pressed my lips to his and kissed him. His arms went around my waist and he pulled me into his lap. I heard the muffled giggles of people sitting near us, but I didn't care. I twined my fingers behind Ramsey's head, his long, shaggy hair brushing against my arm. My lips locked to his, and I didn't have to fake my gasp of delight when his tongue licked into my mouth.

His kiss was intense and possessive. When I tried to pull away to check on the wolf, his fingers gently tugged my face back toward his, and his mouth caught mine once more. Not a hard claiming—a tender, soft kiss that melted my insides and made my pulse race with desire. He settled me in his lap, his hands stroking down my back, and I realized this was part comfort, part desire. Even as he showed to the others that I belonged to him, he pulled me close to protect me.

And I went, all too willingly.

Ramsey's mouth pulled from mine an eternity later. "He's gone," he whispered, his lips brushing against mine, sending shivers down my spine.

"Mmm," I said softly, dazed by his kiss.

He brushed his lips against mine again, then nuzzled my neck. "Smell the air. Tell me if you scent anything."

I inhaled, but all I smelled was Ramsey's intoxicating scent. "Nothing." Nothing but him.

His enormous hand skimmed down my back, and Ramsey pressed a kiss to my neck. "Do you want to get off my lap now?"

I didn't want to go anywhere. When I hesitated, his low chuckle sent longing through my body.

"You'll miss the rest of the movie if you stay in my arms."

"Oh, darn," I said lightly, skimming a finger down his front and snuggling close.

"Think of all those shifting tips you could be missing out on," he murmured, and his hand slid to my ass, cupping it and tucking me closer to his body. "Besides, you picked the movie."

"There's a movie?" I teased, even as I moved in for another kiss. When his mouth moved to mine again, I forgot about the wolves, the movie, and everything but the feel of Ramsey's body against mine.

When we left the movie, Gracie was alone again. She bounded up to us as if nothing had happened. "Shitty movie, huh? Man, I was totally rooting for the wolves and not the vampires."

I shrugged. I'd stopped paying attention to the movie a long time ago. Ramsey kept a casual arm looped over my shoulders, the gesture possessive. He scanned the parking lot as we walked out to the truck, and I knew he was checking to make sure we weren't going to run into any surprises. With his arm around my shoulders and his big form standing tall next to me, I wasn't worried about the wolves. Let them follow me around. I'd show them that Ramsey and I were the real deal.

Except you're not, a small voice whispered in my head. *What about Nikolina?*

The drive home was quiet. At least I was quiet. Gracie went on and on about the movie, clearly enthusiastic about it despite declaring it to be "crap." Lost in my own thoughts, I let her chatter. When we got home, Ramsey looked at me gravely, touched my cheek. "When we get inside, go upstairs and head to bed. I'll lock the house up."

Suddenly bed seemed like a great idea. I yawned. "Shouldn't I shift?"

"It can wait until morning." He leaned down and kissed my forehead, then nodded as he opened the front door. "Go on."

I was relieved to hear that—I was so tired I didn't think I could hold animal form for longer than a minute before shifting back and curling into a tired ball. I made it to the bedroom, slipped out of my jeans and shoes, and fell into the bed. I sniffed, noticing a clean, fresh scent—he'd bought new blankets. I snuggled in them, enjoying the feel of the fabric against my skin, and fell asleep in moments.

I woke up a short time later to hands sliding over my hips and a warm mouth brushing over my belly. For a moment terror locked my body as I remembered Roy, but another scent was thick in my nostrils, driving the memories away immediately. "Ramsey?" I gasped.

His dark eyes flared above mine, a feral gleam in them as he bent low to kiss my stomach again. "Sorry I woke you," he said gruffly, not sounding sorry in the slightest. "Just wanted to touch you a little."

"Oh," I breathed, my hips arching when his fingers teased the sensitive curve of one knee. I thought back to my earlier worries about Nikolina, and hesitated. "Maybe we shouldn't . . ."

He paused. Sat up. Stared down at me. "Am I forcing you? Are you wanting out of this?"

"Out of what? Our fake relationship?" I laughed weakly. My heart beat like a hummingbird in my breast.

He looked stung at my laugh, his face growing stony.

Oh. I hadn't realized I was hurting his feelings. My fingers went to his big arm. "I'm trying to let *you* out of it, silly. I don't want to steal another woman's mate."

"She's not my mate," he murmured, his hands tugging my T-shirt up to expose my breasts.

"She's pretty," I admitted and thought of the female bear-shifter's tall and sturdy form. "And strong. And she doesn't smell like wet dog."

"You don't smell like wet dog," he murmured against my belly, kissing the pale flesh there.

"Then what do I smell like?"

"Like you belong to me."

My breath caught in my throat at the possessive look in his eyes. "And do I? Belong to you?"

"Only if you want to."

"Ramsey Bjorn," I said in a soft, scolding voice. "That is such a pussy answer."

"I won't force you into anything, Sara. Your life is your own. It doesn't belong to wolf or mate. Just to you."

So sweet. I brushed my fingertips over his lips. "I'm wearing your mark. I'm aching for you to take me as yours in all ways. It's not pretending for me anymore." My hands moved down his chest. "I want you."

His eyes flared, reflecting the light the way all shifters did, and I shivered with pleasure. "I want you to mark me," he said in a rasping voice.

"What? Can we . . . is that allowed? Can we do that?"

"I don't care," he said, his voice a low rumble in his chest. "I want everyone to see your mark on me."

Scandalous excitement shivered over me, and I touched his neck. Everyone would see that I'd claimed him as my own. The wolves would hate it, too.

I'd freaking love every minute of it.

I licked my lips, suddenly overcome with the craving to sink my teeth into his skin and taste him. "Are you sure?" I asked one last time.

"I want it more than anything."

I wrapped my fists in his shirt and tugged him to the side, encouraging him to roll over. He did, and I straddled his chest. "Can I touch you everywhere?"

"If you like," he said hoarsely.

"Oh, I like," I said with a grin. My hands slid his shirt up his body, and he reached down and grasped it, ripping the fabric off his chest. A sigh of pleasure escaped me at the sight. He was all thick, hard muscle lightly dusted with golden hair. I sat back and ran my fingertips along his chest, feeling the twitch of his muscles under my hands. I curled my fingers in his chest hair and suddenly wanted to feel it against my own naked skin. I ripped off my own T-shirt, my small breasts bouncing with the motion.

He gave a groan of need, one big hand reaching up to brush a peak. I arched against his touch, then leaned over him and brushed my nipples against his chest, enjoying the shock waves that rocketed through my body—and his sharp inhalation of breath.

He reached for me again, and I caught his hand and forced it to my jeans-clad hip. "Let me touch you," I scolded with a smile, then leaned in and licked one of his hard, flat nipples.

He groaned again and his hands cupped my ass, kneading the muscle there. I wiggled against his grasp, enjoying the sensation, and swirled my tongue around the areola of his nipple, then lightly bit the tip. A rumble began low in his throat as I teased the other one with my fingertips.

I felt his fingertips skim along the seam of my jeans, brushing against my sex. I gasped in response. "Not fair."

"Don't talk to me of fair," he said in a low rasp. "I'm about to spill in my jeans."

"Let me help you with that," I said, sliding off him and reaching for his belt. His hands beat mine, and within seconds he had his jeans and boxers down around his knees. I tugged them the rest of the way off and he kicked them onto the floor, his gaze raptly focused on my body. It was a heady, delicious feeling, that I had this big, naked man so utterly captivated by my simple touches. My hand feathered down his torso, grazed his abdomen, and then paused.

I'd seen his cock plenty of times before, but this was my chance to truly explore him and touch him. And what I saw made my mouth a little dry even as it made my sex wet. I wrapped my fingertips around the girth. He groaned in response, and as I watched, another drop of pre-cum slid down the head, the tip already wet.

"Sara . . . please," he groaned. "I'm going to—"

"Shhh," I said and quickly grasped the head in my palm, a trick I'd just learned on the internet. Either this would go over really, really well, or it would be a disaster.

His entire body shuddered.

I squeezed the head of his cock and kept squeezing.

He nearly came off the bed, his hips bucking, his breath escaping in a massive gasp. But he didn't come. I kept my grip firm and continued to squeeze for a moment longer, and then released.

He panted and stared down at me in shock.

"Speechless?" Jeez, I hoped he wasn't in pain.

Ramsey shook his head at me. "Where did you learn that?"

"Internet," I said proudly, then licked my wet hand, slick with his pre-cum. It tasted of salt and Ramsey, and was utterly delicious.

He groaned again at the sight, reaching for me,

but I slid out of his reach and straddled his knees this time, the better to concentrate my efforts. "Lie down," I told him in a kittenish voice. "I'm playing and I don't want to be interrupted."

He dropped back to the pillows with another groan, his cock jerking slightly against my hand.

"Tell me if you're going to come," I said, "and I can squeeze again."

"I'm not sure I want you to," he growled.

"You'd deprive me of getting to touch you?" I said lightly, brushing my fingers through the thick blond curls that surrounded his sex. "Cruel man."

"Sara—"

Recognizing the desperate tone in his voice, I immediately put my hand back on the crown of his cock and squeezed. "I'll never get to explore you if you don't last a few minutes longer," I teased. "Lie back and think of math equations."

I kept one hand grasping the head of his cock tightly, and with my other, I touched his heavy sac. He made a choking noise as I touched the soft skin, and his hips bucked as I rubbed the seam, then reached down to taste it with my tongue.

"Sara," he growled hard, and I felt his hand close over mine, forcing it down and over his thick shaft, pumping into my hand.

"No, Ramsey," I said, squeezing hard again.

"Want. To. Come."

"I know," I said softly. "But I want to bite you first, and I haven't finished playing yet—"

Before I could finish my teasing statement, he

hauled me up his body and pulled my mouth close to his neck. His other hand went to the fly of my jeans, popping the buttons apart. I arched against his hand, suddenly wanting that big, warm hand in my panties, and I leaned in and licked the base of his neck, encouraging him. "Just like that," I breathed when he slid his hand into my pants and his fingers encountered my hot, slick sex.

His breath came in sharp, ragged pants as his fingers slipped through my folds, gliding over my clit and dipping deeper. I cried out and lifted my hips against his hand as he sank a thick finger deep inside me. My cry erupted as a hiss and my nails dug into his shoulders.

"Bite me," he growled low, the rumble building in his throat. "Mark me, Sara." His finger thrust again into my wet heat.

I swirled my tongue against the hot, smooth skin of his neck and then bit down, scoring my teeth over the skin. His body bucked under mine, his hand jerking in my pants, causing me to rock hard against his hand with a whimper. His big body stiffened and he thrust his finger inside me again, hard, and I bit him again. And then a third time when he thrust his finger deep into me again and I shattered, my cry of ecstasy coming out as a moan as I bit down on his neck once more, my hips rocking against his hand over and over again, my body shuddering.

When I finally stopped shuddering, I remained sprawled over him, my mouth buried against his neck. I licked his skin in apology. "I think I bit you too hard."

"No such thing," he said softly, and I felt his hand slide out of my panties, and he hugged me close. I didn't need to look down to see if he'd come or not; I felt the wetness.

He sighed and turned his head toward mine, and I impulsively kissed him. "That was nice."

"Very nice," he agreed gruffly, and I would have bet that he was blushing in the dark.

I trailed a finger over his naked chest. "But not as nice as full-on sex," I said softly.

"No," he agreed after a moment.

Then why wouldn't he have sex with me? I stared down at him, waiting for him to say more. When he didn't, I brushed a fingertip over his chest. "Ramsey?"

"Hm?" He pulled me close, cuddling me.

I needed to ask him why we stopped every time before we sealed the deal, but . . . I was suddenly afraid of the answer. What if he was holding back because of the bear clan? Did I want to hear that? Then what would happen? Would our semi-relationship die?

I laid my cheek against his chest. "Nothing."

Chapter Fourteen

*R*amsey drove us to work the next morning. Gracie hopped out as soon as the truck stopped, but when I moved to follow, Ramsey grasped my hand. He pulled me close and kissed my forehead. "Don't leave the agency today, Sara. If anything happens, call me immediately. I'll be there as fast as I can. Understand?"

I nodded. He seemed tense and unhappy at leaving me. "I'll be perfectly fine," I told him. "Nothing ever happens. What's going on?"

"Just rumors," Ramsey said. "I'm taking two of the Russells to check it out."

If it had been just rumors, he wouldn't have been practically vibrating with tension. I squeezed his hand. "Be careful."

He pulled me back to him and then kissed me, hard. I was surprised, but I returned it with equal passion.

"You be careful today," he said against my mouth, gave me one last, light kiss, and then released me. Breathless, I wobbled out of the truck.

Like I was going to be able to concentrate on work after that kiss?

As I reached the office, Bathsheba came to the door. "Oh, good. I thought you'd never get here," she exclaimed in a rush.

I looked at my watch. Ten minutes early.

"I have to run," Bath said, handing me the office keys. "The community center double-booked the location for the barn dance tonight, and I have to go down there and make sure that we get the place and not the Boy Scout troop. Ryder's already there waiting, and she said the hay guy is on his way."

"Tonight?" I echoed.

She gave me an odd look. "Don't you remember?"

"I remember. I just thought it was next week," I said. Guess I'd been distracted. "I'll call you if I need anything."

She nodded, her phone already to her ear.

I looked over at Gracie. "Guess it's just you and me."

"Goody," she drawled, went to Bath's desk, and sat in her chair. She propped her bare feet on the edge of the desk, pulled out her phone, and began to text with one hand. "So what's this about a barn dance?"

"It's an Alliance get-together put on by the agency."

She didn't look up from her texting. "So can I go?"

I sat down at my desk. "I don't know. Are you Alliance?"

"Nope," she said with a wolflike grin. "But I'm

supposed to follow you everywhere. Daddy says so."

I ignored that. Gracie's version of "following me everywhere" was only when it suited her. She was a more lackadaisical guard than Connor.

" 'Sides, your business isn't all Alliance, is it? You have vampires and fairies and some wolves, and I bet they aren't Alliance."

"They're not," I agreed. The ones that weren't in the Alliance were definitely being worked in that direction, though. "But this dance *is* Alliance."

"Too bad," she said. "Wolves are good dancers. Guess you'll have to represent our pack on the dance floor."

Like I wanted to represent the pack in any shape or manner.

Gracie continued to text while I went through my email. The office was quiet, and I hoped Bath was doing all right. I'd just picked up the phone to check in with her when the front doorbell clanged against the glass. I looked up . . . and my blood ran cold.

Three men had entered, one wiping his hands on an oily rag. All three wore dirty jeans, dirty baseball caps, and stained blue uniform shirts. The hot, pungent smell of sweat and wolf hit my nostrils, and I instinctively recoiled.

The Anderson pack was here and I was alone, with Gracie.

She swung her feet off my sister's desk and stood up, crossing her arms over her chest. " 'Bout time y'all got here."

She'd invited them? I eyed Gracie uneasily. Had she waited deliberately for my sister to leave? Was she going to hand me over to the wolf pack?

"Had to leave work," said the first, wiping his hands with the greasy rag. He looked over at me and winked. "Hey, baby doll."

"My name is Sara," I said stiffly, eyeing them. Maynard was the one with the rag. The patches on their shirts said that the other two were Buck and Wyatt. They were watching me with far too much interest, and the skin on the back of my neck prickled a warning. "What do you want?"

Buck sat down across from me and crossed his arms, grinning. His teeth were crooked and his breath smelled. "Want you to set us up with your agency. Find us some girls, like you been finding Gracie some men."

I looked over at her in surprise.

She beamed at me. "Just drumming you up some business." She moved to her brother Wyatt and wrapped an arm around his neck in a wrestling hold, even though he was twice the size of her. "These idiots don't get a lot of action 'cause there ain't a lot of wolves in the area."

"There's a few in the Savage pack out in East Texas," Buck said, "but Dylan's done put his claim on them."

Poor women.

"Figured if we wanted to get us some tail, this was the place," Maynard said, leering at me. "But I'm up for dating just about anything."

"I'm not sure—," I began.

"Now's the best time to do this," Gracie interrupted. "No humans around. Just wolves."

"I don't mind humans," Maynard said. "Long
as they're pretty."

Ugh. I hesitated, torn. Everything in my body
told me that this was a bad idea, but what choice did
I have? I had four wolves sitting right across from
me, and I didn't want to piss them off. Any of them
could take me in a fight. Plus, I knew my sister and
Beau wanted the pack to join the Alliance. Beau had
a dream that if all supes were under the same um-
brella, the harassment from those outside the Alliance would end.

So I gave them a polite smile and turned to my
computer, opening up a blank profile document.
"All right. Who should we start with?"

"You can start with me," Maynard said. "After
all, it's only right."

"Why is that?"

His eyes glittered. "Because you were supposed
to be my mate. I'm the oldest. Second only to the
alpha."

I swallowed hard and feigned cheerfulness. "Too
bad for you that I'm taken. Let's work on your profile a bit. Name?"

"Maynard Anderson," he said, then drawled,
"You know that."

I did know that. "It's just a formality," I said
stiffly.

"I'm interested in names, though. Like the name

of the fella that turned you, and why he ain't hovering over your shoulder right now. Wolves watch their women closely."

I stiffened in fear. What did they think they knew?

Gracie rolled her eyes, oblivious to my reaction. "They only watch the ones that look like they're gonna bolt."

"True enough," Maynard said with a chilling grin.

I found my voice. "We're not here to talk about me. We're here to set up a profile for you. If not, I'm going to have to ask you to leave. I'm too busy to waste time. Now," I said firmly. "Age?"

Maynard's gaze remained focused on me. "Thirty-six."

As I typed, I asked the next question, and he gave me his stats and we continued on like normal, civilized people.

"All right," I said. "This next part is about your preferences in a mate, and what you're looking for. Let's start with species. What is your dating preference?"

"Wolf," he said with another leer at me.

The shiver on the back of my neck started again, and my mouth filled with saliva. "I see," I said evenly. "You are aware that we don't have many wolves that use our agency, Mr. Maynard? I'm afraid you'll be limiting your dating pool. We have lots of lovely women from all supernatural races—"

"Fine." His eyes glittered as he watched me. "Put whatever down."

I checkmarked the box for Any. "Any physical build you prefer?"

Again, his gaze went over me. "Small. Flat-chested's fine, too."

Quelling the anxious flash that shot through me, I continued on as if nothing had been wrong. I was going to keep this professional, damn it. "Any other preferences for your dates?"

"Red hair," he said, and when I turned to look at him, that nasty, leering smile was back. "Short red hair," he amended. "I like it a little bit wild."

"I like red hair, too," Wyatt said, his wolfish grin as revolting as his brother's.

"I'm partial to blue," said Buck with a drawl. "A nice, slutty blue to go with her big brown eyes."

My skin crawled. It was obvious this was the next stage of their harassment—show up and demand to date someone just like me and make me realize that they weren't giving up. I ignored their pointed looks and continued filling out the dating questionnaire, skipping the personality profile. That would take too long, and I wanted them out of here ASAP. So I defaulted on the rest of the fields, saved it, printed up his confirmation, and then held it out to Maynard. "You're all set up. You'll need to fill out a few more fields in the privacy of your home, and then you can contact other profiles."

Maynard took the paper, smirking down at me. "Where's that mate of yours? I don't see him around here."

"He's out for the day," Gracie said helpfully,

and I could have kicked her. "The human gal, too. There's a big dance tonight. An *Alliance* dance," she said meaningfully.

"Oh?" Maynard said, looking interested. He didn't even glance at the profile, just folded it up and stuck it in his pocket. "You in that Alliance? Levi ain't gonna like that."

"I didn't ask him if he liked it or not," I said stiffly and turned to Buck. "Did you want to start your profile?"

All three men stood, and Gracie moved back to Bathsheba's desk, putting her feet back up again. "Don't need one," Buck said, grinning down at me.

"Changed your mind?" I asked, but I couldn't say I was sad to hear that. The dating pool would be better without them in it.

"Didn't say that." He thumbed a gesture at Maynard. "You got him in the system, so Wyatt and I don't need a profile. Everybody knows that Maynard shares with his brothers."

Buck leered at me and elbowed Wyatt. "Can't wait until you're Maynard's woman."

Maynard winked at me, and then the three turned and left, grinning back at me.

I was going to throw up. I stood, my desk reeking of their wolf scent, and seized one of the files on my desk. "I'm going to do some filing," I said in a tight voice, the muscles in my calves rippling.

"Whatever you want," Gracie said lazily, picking up her phone and texting again.

I walked tightly back to the filing room, shut the

door, and fell to the ground in a shuddering heap. The urge to change fought hard within me, and it took long, long minutes of trying to control it before I could breathe easy again.

They had come to the agency specifically to threaten me. When would they stop? Would they ever stop?

The afternoon was excruciatingly slow. "Any dates lined up today?" I asked Gracie hopefully.

"Nope," she said. "I'm all yours."

Lucky me. I worked absently until Marie showed up to take over the late shift. She'd come in early, since the rest of us would be helping with the barn dance. Marie looked a bit tired, her normally beautifully curled dark hair pulled into a tight bun. She wore no makeup, and I could see dark circles under her eyes.

As she sat down at one of the desks, I asked, "You okay? You don't look so well."

"Just having trouble sleeping," Marie said and gave me a faint smile. "Don't worry about it. I'll be fine once I get a cup of coffee in me."

I noticed that she didn't move toward the coffee machine, though. She just sat at the desk, as if all her energy was gone. "Do you need to go home?" I asked.

"I'm fine," she stressed, and I heard a bit of annoyance in her tone. "I've just been working more overtime than I'm used to. It's okay." When I still hesitated, she laughed. "If it'll make you feel better, I'll turn the phone's ringer up and take a nap in the back if it's slow. Okay?"

Guilt flashed through me. Marie had been working extra hours since Bathsheba and I had taken over. I hadn't realized just how many. "Since I'm your manager when Bath's not here, I should tell you no. But you look like you could use a nap. Just don't work too hard, and if you have to leave, call me, okay?"

"Will do," she promised.

"I'm out of here," I told her, getting my purse out from under my desk. The dance wouldn't start for a few hours and I was scheduled to work a little longer, but the phones were dead and I was a nervous wreck. "I just called Jeremiah, and he's swinging by to pick us up."

"Have fun at the dance. If someone gets drunk and does something embarrassing, I want pictures." After a moment more, Marie added, "Especially Joshua Russell."

I laughed and held the front door open for Gracie, who sauntered out at a much slower pace. "We'll drop you off at the house first—"

Gracie blinked her eyes at me. "What do you mean? I'm goin'."

"No wolves allowed," I told her. No Anderson wolves, anyhow. "This is an Alliance dance."

"You're going," she pointed out.

"I'm Alliance."

"But you're letting me date Alliance men," she

pointed out. "I can date them but I can't go to your dance?"

She had a point.

"This is so unfair," she said in a pouty voice, pulling her phone out and beginning to text again. "I'd hate to have to tell my father that you're going to be out tonight and I can't be at your side."

I snatched the phone out of her hand, my temper snapping. "Fine," I said sharply, and tossed her phone into my purse. "You can go to the dance, but I have a few rules."

Gracie crossed her arms over her chest and waited.

"One," I said. "You do not text your dad or your brothers or *anyone* that you're at the dance. Understand?"

She nodded.

"And two. Be on your best behavior. This is very important to our clients and our Alliance."

She looked hurt. "You don't trust me?"

Gracie herself wasn't bad, but I didn't trust her family a lick. "I'm just saying in general," I explained. "And three. Put some damn shoes on."

Gracie grinned at me, delighted. "I can buy flip-flops at the gas station."

When we pulled up to the Little Paradise community center, I was impressed. Decorative bales of hay had been placed near the front doors, and Ryder and Ellis Russell stood atop them, hanging a sign that proudly proclaimed BARN DANCE. Ryder even wore a cowboy hat and a red checked shirt.

I was still in my work uniform of jeans and a T-shirt. Today's shirt said Be Careful, I Byte, an ode to my geek sense of humor.

When we got out of Jeremiah's car, Gracie shielded her eyes from the setting sun and stared up at the sign. "Looking good," she called out. Then she added, "The sign, too."

Ellis Russell turned around, and I could have sworn that he blushed a little. "Hey, Sara," he said. "Bath's inside if you're looking for her."

I gave him a little wave and tugged at Gracie's arm, dragging her inside the community center. Her flip-flops slapped with every step, but she was grinning as if amused.

"Didn't realize there was a dress code," she said. "I'da worn something pretty."

"A sundress?" I quipped. Her entire wardrobe was sundresses. The shorter, the better.

"However did you guess?"

"Just a hunch," I said dryly. Men were moving hay bales to the corners of the room, and a few folding tables had been set up along one wall for refreshments. The heavy scent of hay and were-cougar touched my nostrils. Smart of Bath to recruit the Russells to do the heavy lifting.

Joshua Russell tossed aside his hay bale and came over to us, lifting his cap and wiping his brow underneath. I noticed his gaze went to Gracie and her skimpy dress and long, tanned legs. "You guys are here early."

"Work was slow," I said with a shrug. "We decided to come see if we could help."

He tilted his head, flashing a grin at Gracie. "Your sister's in the kitchen, trying to make everything herself."

"I'll go help her out, then. Gracie, you coming?"

"I think I'll stay out here and . . . supervise the hay," she said in a low, husky voice.

Joshua gave her another appraising look, then winked at me. His thumbs hitched in his belt loops. "Come on, Miss Gracie. I'll make you up a seat."

He was deliberately flirting to get Gracie off my back. Good man. I waved at a few more of the Russells and slipped into the kitchen.

Bath was alone, slicing toothpicked sandwiches into triangle quarters. She looked up briefly and then kept on slicing. "You're here early. Something wrong?"

I didn't miss the note of stress in her voice—Bath very badly wanted this to go well tonight. I lifted a slice of bacon from the enormous tray next to the sandwich assembly line. "So do you want the good news or the bad news?"

She looked up again and thought for a second. "Good news?"

I tilted my head and gave her a little grin. "I'm here two hours early?"

One eyebrow rose. "And the bad news?"

"I brought Gracie."

"Oh, Sara," she exclaimed, setting aside the four perfect triangles and reaching for the next sandwich. "You couldn't ditch her for the afternoon? Set her up with another satyr?"

"I thought it would be a good idea to keep her close," I said. "Because the wolf pack stopped by the agency earlier and signed up for the service."

My sister's downward slice stuttered and she yelped, nicking her thumb. Bath dropped the knife, staring at me with wide eyes.

I took a clean knife and pushed her aside, and began to cut as she sucked the blood from her thumb. As I cut, I told her about the wolves and what they'd said.

"What are you going to do?" my sister asked quietly.

I shrugged with more calmness than I felt. "What can I do?"

Bath frowned and reached to tug her ponytail out of habit. Her hand fluttered, finding nothing, as her hair was put up in a bun. "I'm not so sure that it's wise to invite the wolf pack into the service and let them date Alliance clients."

"It's not. I don't trust them, but what can we do? If we refuse to serve them at the agency, it'll cause a huge stink. You know Beau wants the wolves to join. One wolf pack leads and the others will follow. If we piss one off, we kiss them all good-bye. All we can do is put their profiles in the system and hope that no one shows interest."

I didn't tell my sister about the three-for-one deal that they'd mentioned to me. Some things just weren't for sharing. I planned on curling up in Ramsey's arms and telling him, though.

Speaking of . . . "Have you seen Ramsey today?" I set aside the plate of sandwiches.

Bath moved to the far counter, digging out plastic wineglasses. They were the kind you had to assemble, and she grabbed a stack and began to snap them together. "I haven't. He's off with Beau on a job, and I've been busy buying up all the wine in the county. I got a variety, because I'm not sure what the various breeds like to drink. Do you think this stuff is okay?" She gestured at the rows and rows of bottles.

I leaned against the counter, wondering exactly what kind of job Ramsey and Beau were up to. I didn't ask, though; it'd just make my sister more anxious. So I looked at the varieties of wine. "If it's free, no one's going to care if it comes from a barrel, a box, or a bottle."

"You have a point," she said, chewing on her lip. "I just want tonight to go perfectly. To show Beau that I'm a good mate for him, and that I don't have to have fur to be able to hang with the Alliance or run an Alliance business."

Jeez. My sister really *was* nervous. "So what else is on the menu tonight?"

"Peach cobbler," my sister announced. "And the brisket is going to be delivered half an hour before the dance officially begins. Austin's out on a beer run, since a lot of guests are going to want that."

"Good call," I said. "So what else needs to be done?"

My sister sagged against the counter for a minute, looking exhausted. "Everything."

I gave her a cheerful smile. "Then I guess it's a good thing I showed up early."

———

We worked companionably through the afternoon. As the Russells and Gracie set up the dance area, my sister and I prepared food. Cookies, cupcakes, and appetizers were also on the menu. When she started to pull out ingredients for homemade chili, I stopped her. At this rate, we'd have enough food to feed an army.

Austin returned with beer and bags of ice, his cousin Savannah tagging along. She gave me a faint smile as she entered with two bags of ice in her arms, while Austin reached over and tousled my hair.

"Hi, Savannah," I said cheerfully. "Nice to see you out and about."

She blushed and nodded at me, then disappeared into the kitchen. My sister recruited Joshua and Gracie to fill some of the barrels with ice for the beer. As she did, I moved to Austin's side. "She doing okay? Your cousin?"

Austin nodded. "Got a sad look on her face every now and then, but she seems to be all right. We try not to leave her alone at all times. I heard that wolf guy can't take a hint."

I nodded, thinking of Connor's desperate longing for Savannah.

Austin suddenly stiffened, and I lifted my head as a familiar scent caught my nostrils. Not Gracie, but close. It was odd to smell wolf just when we'd been talking about them. . . .

And then I realized that things were about to get really bad. Because Connor had clearly followed Savannah here.

Three of the Russells dropped what they were holding, their bodies stiffening with anger.

Then the door of the kitchen opened. "Savannah?" a man called out.

Oh, shit.

Joshua and Ellis rushed past me, Austin a few steps behind. The door hadn't even closed behind Connor before he was tackled and flung to the floor. The Russells piled atop him, and the human sounds of anger gave way to animal snarls. Ellis's back rose, a sure sign that he was going to shift.

"Savannah," Connor howled, the sound then muffled by the smack of a fist into his jaw. "I want to see her!"

"Get Savannah out of here," shouted Joshua from the pile.

I saw Savannah hesitate, but she didn't leave. Her face seemed agonized.

A cry of pain erupted from Connor, and the snarls intensified. I rushed forward, shoving my way through the thrashing limbs.

"Stop it," I shouted, grabbing hands and arms and trying to wedge my way through the seething mass of bodies. "Joshua! Jeremiah! Ellis! Stop this right now!"

They ignored me. Austin tried to pick me up but I clung to Ellis's shirt, unwilling to be removed from the fight.

Connor continued to struggle, and as I watched, his face seemed to grow more canine, a slight shift occurring even as he struggled against Ellis and Jacob. "I just want to talk to her," he snarled.

"No wolves allowed," Ellis said, leaning over Connor's prone form with a feral snarl curling his lip. "No one wants your filthy kind 'round here."

I flinched and moved forward, just in time to catch a flying fist. It hit me in the mouth, and I wrapped my hands around that big arm and bit down.

"Ow," Joshua yelped, and all eyes turned to stare at me. "What the fuck, Sara?"

I released him, my lip curling into my own snarl. Connor's mouth was bloody, his face defiant, nose crunched like a snarling wolf's. He looked ready to take on all the Russells, his nostrils flaring. It didn't matter to him if he won or not, I realized. He simply had to see Savannah or go insane.

And suddenly, I understood that.

"Let him go," I said and released Joshua's arm. "He just wants to talk to her."

Austin stepped between Connor and me. His hands raised in a placating gesture. "Sara, you need to let us handle—"

Someone moved to my side, and I caught a whiff of Gracie's scent. I knew what she was feeling— anger and outrage. I felt a little of it myself at the sight of the three Russells beating up Connor.

The wolf side of me grew agitated. "Handle it?" I finished for him. "You mean, you want to beat him to a pulp just because he's a wolf? *I'm* a wolf, too."

Jeremiah shook his head. "Not like them."

"She's just like us," Gracie snapped. "That's why Maynard and Daddy want her so bad, you big idiot."

"Connor isn't like the others," I said quietly. "I know him." I pushed between them, putting my hands on my hips to increase my mass. "Connor signed up to be in the Alliance. He's as welcome here as any Russell."

"Or me." Gracie's normally playful voice was cold and unfriendly.

Joshua's expression darkened. "That so?"

"I just want to talk to Savannah," Connor panted. "Then I promise I'll go."

We all looked to Savannah, hovering at the far side of the room. Her face was deathly white as she stared at the scene.

"Do you want to talk to this low-life wolf?" Joshua said, and I wanted to kick him.

Savannah hesitated. After a long, long moment, she shook her head. "No." Then she turned away and walked back into the kitchen.

I looked at Connor. Anguish was etched on his handsome face. Ellis slowly got off of him, and Connor hauled himself up and headed for the door, his stride angry. Joshua elbowed Austin, grinning.

Irritated with the two of them, I gave them both a shove and raced after Connor.

"Connor, wait," I said, chasing him through the parking lot. He wouldn't turn to look at me, but I eventually caught up to him and touched his arm. "Are you all right?"

He turned dark, agonized eyes on me. "Do I look all right? I love her. I can think of no one but her. I don't care that she's not a werewolf. I want to take her at my side and keep her safe. But she won't even talk to me."

"I'll talk to her," I said, helpless at his pain. "See if I can find out what's bothering her."

"I know what's bothering her," he bit out. "I fucked her. She begged me to let her go when we found out she was in heat, but my father wouldn't agree. And so we slept together, and now she hates me because it wasn't her choice."

Savannah had every right to be upset. What could I say?

"I just . . . I just want to talk to her. Hold her in my arms and let her know that I care for her. That she's the one for me, and I love her and our child."

Child? Well, hell. Of course she was pregnant after being in heat. That was how nature worked. The human part of me just hadn't put two and two together. "I'll talk to her and see how she's feeling. I'll call you in the morning, okay?"

Behind us, I heard the door to the community center slam, and we turned to see Gracie stomping across the parking lot, flip-flops slapping the pavement. She was furious, her curly hair flying.

"Let's go, Connor," she said, glancing over at me. "We're going to tell Daddy just what the Alliance thinks of wolves, and see what he has to say about things."

"Gracie," I began, a note of alarm in my voice.

Gracie bared her teeth at me. "You heard them. Wolves are shit and good for nothing. Ain't all wolves like that, just like I'm sure all were-cats ain't assholes," she snapped. "You're better off with our kind, and the sooner you realize that, the better off you'll be. You're always going to be trash to them, just because of the kind of fur you grow. And don't you forget that."

With that, she got into Connor's car and didn't look back at me. Connor, his shoulders slumping, took one last dejected look at the community center and then got in, too.

I watched them drive off, my arms crossed tightly over my chest. I didn't know what to do. I liked Connor. I liked Jackson and Dan. I even liked Gracie in a roundabout way—but I hated the rest of the wolves. But what had just happened in the community center alarmed me. The wolves were the enemies of the Alliance. They'd bullied other supes for so long that they weren't familiar with being outnumbered, and it was clear they didn't like it. Would there always be a war between our breeds?

And of course there was Savannah to think about. If Connor was right, she was carrying his baby. A cat-dog-human.

I really, really wanted to talk to Ramsey in that moment, to share my confusion and have him rub my back and tell me that it'd be all right. To remind me that I was welcomed, not the enemy. He'd be here soon, and I looked anxiously at my watch.

Rubbing my arms, I returned to the community center. The three Russells were parked next to the beer, each with a bottle in hand, pressing it to their jaws where Connor had gotten a wallop in.

Joshua looked over at me and adjusted his baseball cap with a frown. "He hit you, too, eh?"

I touched my throbbing cheek and raised an eyebrow at him. "Actually, *you* did."

His look of shame was almost worth the pain.

Chapter Fifteen

A few hours later the dance began to fill up, and my sister's nervousness was in full bloom. She twisted the long, silky fall of her blond hair. "Are you sure I look all right?"

"You look beautiful," I said for the fourteenth time. She wore a pale yellow sheath made of eyelet, and due to the chilly weather she'd put a white cardigan over it. She was golden and beautiful, and I knew Beau would love the sight of her.

"I don't look like a supe," she said with a rueful smile.

"And that's perfectly okay," I said, reaching over and giving her a squeeze around the waist, happy I could do so for once. Before my secret had gotten out, I'd been afraid to touch anyone for fear of my scent lingering. Now I didn't have to worry about that, and I enjoyed touching.

I especially enjoyed it when Ramsey touched me.

Bath gave me a critical look. "I think you need more makeup on your cheek."

I touched the bruise. "That bad?"

"It's not good," she agreed, pulling out a compact of powder and offering it to me. "Downplay it a bit more so Ramsey isn't upset. Trust me."

I felt a blush creeping over my cheeks and adjusted my own dress. My sister—who likes to think of everything—had brought me a short, swingy little green number with spaghetti straps. I liked the color and was glad I'd dyed my hair red to match.

The music changed to a slow song and my sister smiled when the floor filled with supes of all kinds and their partners. I knew she was mentally cataloging which ones seemed to be getting along well and making notes for when she got back into the office. I'd seen badgers dancing with tigers, jaguars dancing with cougars, and even the harpy had gotten a dance or two in—no small feat. The scent of the different supernaturals filled my nostrils, but not in a bad way. As I watched, a tiny female were-fox led Jeremiah and another man out on the dance floor and slipped between them, her hips cradled between both men.

I'd heard that sort of thing about were-foxes.

Savannah had disappeared, citing a headache. Austin had driven her home and offered to stay with her.

Speaking of Russells—the scent of one in particular touched my nostrils and I turned to see Beau working his way through the crowd. My sister hadn't noticed yet, and I shared a conspiratorial smile with him as he snuck up on her, a bouquet of roses in his hand. I put a hand over my bruised cheek and played with my hair, pulling it forward so it wouldn't ruin the adorably frisky mood he seemed to be in. He was so cute with her.

He was dressed in a casual gray suit and looked rather dashing. Beau slid behind my sister and I gave her a sideways glance, waiting.

Sure enough, she yelped in surprise when one arm snaked around her waist and the other presented the roses. At the sight of those, she relaxed backward. "Hey, baby."

"Hey, sweet Bathsheba," I heard him whisper in her ear. "Miss me?"

My sister's blush told him everything.

"I'm going to check on our supplies." I turned and left, allowing them a few minutes of privacy. As I crossed the room, I scanned it for Ramsey. I missed him, which worried me. Did he miss me like I missed him? Or was he enjoying a few minutes away from me?

I uncorked a few bottles of wine and smiled at those who stopped at the table for refills. Not surprisingly, people were filling up on the free booze and ignoring the sandwiches and barbeque. That was okay. As far as dances went, this one was firmly in the "win column." The dance floor was packed, people were smiling, and I could have sworn I'd just seen a fey lord dance with a were-otter. Those who weren't dancing seemed to be having a good time anyhow. Every woman was surrounded by a bevy of admirers; Alliance men outnumbered Alliance women over three to one. Every woman but my sister—who was human and taken—and myself, who was wolf and only sorta-kinda taken. No one approached to chat with me, but I understood their reactions. Most of the Alliance had a big question mark as far as I was concerned. If Levi and Maynard were the kind of wolves they ran into, I didn't blame them. So I smiled and filled glasses and asked people how they were enjoying the dance.

I watched Beau lead Bath around the dance floor, his arms around her waist. My sister's cheek lay against his shoulder, and Beau's eyes were closed as they swayed to the music, simply enjoying being in each other's arms. I felt a sweet piercing in my chest and realized it was happiness for my sister. That she'd found someone to lean on. That she was so content. I loved her happiness . . . and I envied it, a little. What would it be like to be able to relax in your man's arms and not have to worry if the next change was going to make you vomit your spleen, or if the wolves were going to show up and demand a threesome?

I was so very tired of wolves.

A throat cleared and a wobbly, long-stemmed daisy appeared before my eyes.

I looked up into Ramsey's face, a smile curving my mouth. He'd put a suit jacket on over his Russell Security T-shirt, and his hair was wet and slicked away from his face, as if he'd just jumped out of the shower minutes before. "I'm late," he said as the music switched into another slow song.

I put down the wine bottle. "That's okay," I said

with a smile, moving around the table toward him. "Busy night?"

"Yes."

"Anything you want to tell me about?"

"No."

I took the flower he held out to me and smiled up at him. "Did you forget the rest of the bouquet?"

"You're not a bouquet kind of girl."

I laughed. "I'm not. I'm glad you got me this." I twirled the flower. "I like daisies."

"I wanted something for your hair," he said in a gruff voice and took the flower from me. He snapped the stem and tucked it behind my ear, his fingers trailing along my jaw once the flower was in place.

A soft warmth swept over me and I stepped closer to him, tugging the lapels of his jacket. "You're a good man, Ramsey Bjorn."

His fingers stopped tracing my jaw. "Why are you bruised?" The rage in his voice was palpable.

"Broke up a fight earlier. It's no big deal." When he looked skeptical, I wrapped an arm around his waist and leaned in. "Want to dance?"

"No?" he said with a hopeful note.

I slipped my hand into his and tugged him closer so I could whisper in his ear. "I'm not much of a dancer either, but my sister wants us to try. For show."

He gave me a resigned look and led me onto the dance floor.

Okay, so my sister really hadn't said anything

about the dancing, but I knew it'd be good for the relationship. Plus, it gave me an excuse to snuggle deep into Ramsey's arms and forget about all my worries.

When we made it to the dance floor, he placed a large hand on my shoulder and the other hesitated, as if he was unsure where to put it. I guided his hand to my waist and then slid my arms around his back, pressing my cheek to his jacket. Ramsey's scent and warmth immediately enveloped me, and I closed my eyes with pure pleasure. I desperately wanted to tell him about the wolves at the agency earlier, or Connor, but it was too crowded. I'd have to tell him later.

We swayed to the music, Ramsey's steps halting. He was clearly uncomfortable but trying for my sake, and I appreciated it all the more. When the song ended, I smiled up at him and tugged his hand. "One song is enough to prove your devotion. I won't torture you with more."

He flashed into one of his rare smiles, clearly grateful for the reprieve. My heart stuttered at the sight of it. Ramsey was rough around the edges, but when he smiled at me . . . My skin heated with my thoughts, and I forced them back to more polite channels.

"I'm glad you're here," I said softly, knowing he'd be able to pick up the words with his shifter hearing.

"Why?" His brows furrowed and the scowl retook his face. "What's wrong?"

Couldn't a girl just be glad to see him? But he was right—something *was* bothering me. I thought of Maynard and the others from earlier today and shuddered. "Can't tell you about it here."

His big hand clasped the back of my neck and he pulled me close—the Ramsey version of a comforting hug. It was a gesture that made me feel totally owned and overwhelmed by his strength, but in a pleasant way. His light clasp said that he was there for me, that he'd protect me. Not that he would force me to bend to his will.

Yet another thing I liked about Ramsey—he knew what frightened me and strove to make me comfortable around him at all times. I had the lead in the relationship. A girl could get used to that.

Provided the wolves would ever let me.

I took his big hand in mine and tugged. "Let's go outside?"

I led him through the crowds of shifters and gorgons and lord knew what else. I thought I might have seen a vampire, but their lack of socialness didn't surprise me—vampires were about as comfortable around shifters as shifters were around them; which was not at all. Plus, I imagined that being around a bunch of sweaty, delicious people made it difficult. It'd be like taking a starving man to an all-you-can-eat buffet and then telling him he could only taste if the dinner allowed him to.

We made it to the doors and escaped into the cool night air. The parking lot was cram-packed with vehicles of every make, with a very large percentage of trucks. Cars were double-parked behind one another, and a few people hung out on the hay bales near the entrance, drinking beers and chatting. I continued past them to the far side of the parking lot, where others wouldn't be able to hear us over the music and chatter closer nearby.

When I stopped, I dropped his hand and raised my chin, sniffing the air for any lurkers. The parking lot for the community center was too small for the crowd, and like any Texans worth their salt, people had parked in the open field next door. Trees dotted the distance, and farther away, I saw the occasional flash of headlights from the highway. This was about as private as we'd get.

"What is it?" said Ramsey. His tone was disapproving, but I knew him now, and I knew that he was disapproving not of me but of the things that made me anxious.

I crossed my arms over my chest, uncertain how to begin. He wouldn't like what I was about to say.

He mistook my crossed arms for human chills and shrugged off his jacket, then pulled me close, wrapping me in it. I was going to protest that I no longer suffered from the weird chills now that I shifted on a regular basis, but the scent and warmth of his jacket were intoxicating. I snuggled deep, and when he leaned against a nearby truck, I let him pull me into his arms and rub my back.

If wolves could purr, I'd have definitely been purring at the moment.

"What did you want to tell me?" Ramsey asked in his rumbly low voice.

"The wolves showed up at the agency today."

He stiffened, his hands stopping on my back. "Yeah, it's exactly as bad as you're thinking it is. Maynard and Wyatt and Buck showed up and did the wolf equivalent of flirting. They reminded me that they wanted me for their wife and I wasn't going to get away so easily."

"They?" he said, his voice a low, angry growl.

I nodded, shivering at the memory. "Maynard made it quite clear that he likes to share his toys. They creeped me out."

"Where was your sister? Where was Gracie?"

"Bath was here getting ready for the dance," I explained. "As for Gracie, I'm pretty sure she invited them." When the growl formed low in his throat, I placed a hand on his chest. "Gracie is Gracie. She's harmless herself, and I think she likes me, but her allegiance is never going to be to anyone but the pack. We just have to keep that in mind."

"You are not going to be alone with her anymore," Ramsey said in a voice hard as iron. "If I'm not with you, one of the Russells must be."

There'd be no complaints from me. It sounded like a pretty good plan. I nodded.

Ramsey's big hands rubbed my back again, as if he could soothe away the fear. "I should have been there at your side."

"You have things to do, too," I said softly. "Your job. People you protect. Helping Beau. You can't babysit me the rest of my life."

"I can if it'll keep you safe," he growled.

But what if this takes ten years? Or twenty? What

*about when you decide that you want to rejoin the bear
clan and leave me to go back to your bear bride?*

A wolf howl pierced the air in the distance.

I stiffened and Ramsey sprang to his feet, pushing me behind him so I was between his big body
and the truck. I tried to peer over his shoulder. The
wind was high tonight, and in the wrong direction
for me to get a scent.

"The pack is back," he said with a growl.

"Not all the pack," I said, listening to the howl.
"Just one. Connor was here earlier."

"Is it him?"

The tone changed and I suddenly realized that I
could tell who it was. "It's not him," I said. "It's one
of the others. Owen."

Ramsey began to strip his clothes off. "I'm going
to teach that fucker a lesson," he said with a snarl.
"He won't touch you, because I'm going to rip his
arms off."

He stripped off his clothes and I gathered them,
tucking his shoes in my arms. "Go back inside," he
said, then his skin rippled with fur, and he crouched
to change. A few moments later, I was staring at the
massive brown-furred form of an enormous brown
bear.

I gave him a worried look. "Be careful, all right?"

His nose touched my arm and then he swung his
head, indicating that I should return inside. Then
he turned and began to lope toward the trees. The
howl broke off, then continued again, retreating.

I stacked Ramsey's clothes neatly, something

about this bothering me. I took his jacket off and placed it over the clothes, then headed back toward the center. There was definitely something wrong about the situation. All the times I'd met the wolves, they'd never gone anywhere alone. And that howl hadn't been anything specific, it had just been a . . . greeting?

I stiffened as a thought occurred to me, and I raised my head to sniff the wind. I caught the faint scent of hay and . . . wolves.

My senses immediately went on alert.

My breath ripped from my throat, panting fast. I could hear them now, the soft crunch of boots on gravel, the scent of man mixed with wolf. I assessed my surroundings—barely a few feet between each car in the packed lot. Plenty of room to hide and sneak up on someone. I looked back at the entrance to the dance. A hundred feet away, but I might be able to make it . . .

A shadow fell in front of me and I looked up in dismay as Buck Anderson rose from the back of a nearby truck and hopped down to the ground. He grinned at me, then spat a wad of tobacco off to the side. "Looks like we're just in time for the party, ain't we?"

Someone came up behind me, and I turned just as Maynard grasped the lacy edge of my skirt. I jerked the material away from him as he whistled.

"Well," he drawled. "We're shittin' in high cotton now, ain't we, boys? Our little woman looks mighty delicious."

The skin on my body crawled fiercely, and I knew I'd start sprouting fur if I wasn't careful. I bit the inside of my cheek hard and edged backward. "I'm not yours. I'm taken."

"You keep sayin' that, but I ain't seeing an alpha here with his arm around you, am I?"

As I took another step backward, I smelled someone else coming up alongside of me on the opposite side, blocking my way out from around the large black truck.

I was trapped.

"My mate is a bear," I said calmly. "And he's going to have you for breakfast if he finds out you're harassing me."

One of them—Wyatt—reached out to touch my hair. "Just a friendly pack greeting, is all. Heard we weren't allowed at the dance. Gracie was quite upset."

"That's not true," I protested.

Maynard seized my arm and I let out a wolflike yelp. He wrapped an arm around my waist, holding me against him as if he wanted to dance. His eyes were gleaming with menace. "Does that mean we get to dance, then?"

I felt another walk up behind me, press his hips against my own from behind, and I was sandwiched between Maynard and Wyatt, their scents choking me. "She can dance with both of us."

I struggled against their grasp, my breath coming in short, terrified rasps. Memories of Roy flashed through my mind, fast and hard, and I tried not to think about them, even when Maynard began to hum and swivel his hips against mine.

"Let me *go*," I repeated, the sound more of an angry, wolfen growl now. Oh, no—it sounded like I was about to change.

"Ain't never gonna let you go, baby doll," Wyatt drawled from behind me, toying with the flimsy straps of my dress as if he wanted to move them down my shoulders. "Wolves don't like being told no. 'Bout anything."

I thrashed in their grasp, and when one reached for my skirt again, the snarl that arose in my throat was definitely wolfen. Fur sprouted on my arms, and my muscles seized and clenched.

"Looks like our girlfriend still can't control her inner puppy," Maynard drawled, and when I jerked away again, they let me stagger backward, but I couldn't go far—my legs were cramping and shifting, and I dropped to all fours, heaving blood. A flash sounded and I looked up to see Wyatt holding his phone out, taking a picture of me mid-change.

"Dad ain't gonna be happy that your boyfriend doesn't seem to be doing a good job with your changing."

"I'm thinking she needs some extra tutoring from her pack mates," said the other with a grin.

Then they left me there, vomiting down my party dress and changing to a huddled, miserable lump of werewolf.

————

When Ramsey found me a short time later, I was weakly changing back to my human form. I said nothing, even when he quietly wiped the blood from my mouth and pulled his jacket back over my shoulders.

Beau arrived a few minutes later. "You all right?" he asked, concern in his eyes.

"Sure," I said dully.

"Why do you think they attacked you?" Beau asked, his tone easy in order to keep me calm.

I gave him a flat look. "They're reminding me that I belong to them. They're not going to forget about me. Ever. We thought they'd give up on this, but we were wrong. They're just toying with us. They've never had any intention of letting me go."

Beau's mouth tightened and he looked over at Ramsey.

"A lure," Ramsey said harshly. "I heard the howling and didn't realize they were setting up a trap. One kept me on a chase through the woods, and it left Sara vulnerable. By the time I realized . . . it was too late." His big, square jaw set and I could almost hear his teeth grind in frustration. "I'm going to kill them."

"You're not," Beau said in a firm voice. "Sara needs you at her side."

His hand tugged me closer, pulling me against his side. "It won't happen again. She's not leaving my sight."

Instead of making me feel better, I felt worse. Now Ramsey was stuck at my side until my fate was decided. "Can we not tell my sister about this, please?"

Beau gave me a flat look, his mouth firm with distaste. "I don't like keeping secrets from your sister."

"She'll just worry, and I don't want her getting hurt by the wolf pack," I said, appealing to his protective side. "And I'm fine," I lied. "Just a little shaken."

He looked skeptical, but after a moment, he stood and clapped Ramsey on the back. "I'll go tell Bathsheba that Sara went home with you."

Ramsey leaned down and picked me up. I should have protested being babied, but all the energy had gone out of me, along with all hope.

The wolves weren't ever going to let me go.

Ever.

Ramsey washed my hair as I sat in the bathtub, numb with misery.

He'd taken me home from the dance, undressed me, and then helped me slide into a hot bath. When that hadn't snapped me out of my funk, he'd calmly begun to soap my body. All I'd felt had been terribly numb. In my mind, I kept hearing Maynard's words.

"You think we're going to let you go that easily?"

Ramsey's fingers brushed my jaw. "Sara?"

"Did you check on Gracie?" I asked. "Is she at the guest cottage?"

He paused for a minute. When I glanced over at him, he frowned powerfully. "It's empty. She's gone."

That was it, then. They'd pulled their ambassador. Next they'd come for me, and they wouldn't take no for an answer. It was simply a matter of time.

I stared at the faucet, unable to muster panic or dread. All I felt inside was cold.

"Sara." Ramsey's big hand touched my jaw, forced me to turn my face toward his. "Talk to me."

I'd been living the past six years under a carefully constructed pretense, and the jig was up. I felt shredded on the inside. "You know they're not going to give up, Ramsey," I said softly. "They've made it very clear."

The low, protective rumble started in his throat. "If they ever touch you again—"

"They will. They'll wait until I'm alone, and they'll strike."

"Not if I'm with you all the time." He reached under the water to grasp my small hand in his large one and give it a gentle squeeze. "I'm not leaving your side."

"Until when, Ramsey?" I looked at him, tears dangerously close to brimming in my eyes. "Until six months have passed? A year? Three? You have to get on with your life, too. You were planning on returning to the bear clan. To Nikolina. I'm just holding you back."

He said nothing.

A little part of me withered inside. "Being my

protector isn't a short-term job, Ramsey. Bath had to put her life on hold for six years to be my watchdog. Six years of waiting and worrying. Of knowing that I was ruining her life and being too scared to do anything about it. And I'm just . . ." I slumped in the water. "I'm just so tired of it. I'm a prisoner no matter what I do, and you're forced to be my jailer and bodyguard until either they give in or I do. And I know they won't give in."

"How do you know?"

Because Roy was like that I wanted to say but didn't. My skin rippled at the memory, and I shivered despite the heat of the water.

Ramsey took hold of a nearby towel and held it out for me. I stepped into it, letting him tuck it around me as he would a child. Once I was wrapped in it, he led me to the bedroom and sat on the edge of the bed, carefully drying me off.

"Tell me about the guy that turned you," he said.

"I'd rather not."

"Sara." He tugged me into his arms and held me against his chest. His hands slid to my ass, skin slightly damp. "Tell me. Right now I want to kill the bastard. I want to kill the wolves for trying to claim you. So tell me about him, or I'm going to go find me some Andersons and start pounding heads in."

I looked up at his serious face, his lovely, hard mouth drawn into a frown. I traced my fingers lightly over his features. How much could I trust him? It wasn't just my secret, after all. It was Bath's, too. "I don't know if I can," I said softly. "You're not mine."

He buried his face against the small rise of my breasts, kissing my flesh fiercely. "You can trust me."

"That's not what I was saying," I said gently, running my fingers through his messy blond hair. "I said you weren't mine, Ramsey. You're Nikolina's. You belong to the bear clan. This is all still pretend. As much as I'm attracted to you, and you're attracted to me, this can't go on forever. Either the wolves will win, or we'll win and you can go back to the bear clan and your family . . . and your fiancée. But this is only temporary—I can't tell you about Roy because you're not mine."

The look he gave me was half fury, half frustration. Very carefully, he cupped my face, kissed my nose, and then said softly, "Get some sleep."

Chapter Sixteen

*T*he next morning, I awoke to the sounds of hammers and drills. A quick peek out the window showed that the Wilder Handyman van was parked out front. I heard hammering on the roof and the faint call of one voice to another—Jackson asking Ramsey to hand him something. I should have been irritated that they'd woken me up, but I felt an odd rush of happiness instead. I liked seeing the old house take shape and wondered what it would look like when it was all done.

And then I wondered if I'd be around to see it. I sighed and dressed in a T-shirt and paint-splattered jeans. Maybe they could use some help.

Downstairs, I found Dan wiring in a new stove. He retreated a few feet at the sight of me.

I shoved my hands in my pockets and gave him a sheepish look. "I'm okay. Jackson and Ramsey on the roof?"

"Yep. I'm supposed to tell you that you're not allowed to go in to work today. Ramsey says that you're supposed to get him when you wake up."

"I'll get him soon enough," I said, not in any kind of rush to see him at the moment.

Dan gave me a quick smile and then went back to fussing with the new stove. It was shiny and black and had a glass top. I liked it already. "You and Jackson did a great job, Dan," I said, running my fingertips over the new stove. "You Wilders should be proud."

"My last name's St. James," Dan said. "No relation to Jackson. He's just my alpha."

"But I thought packs were family based?" I sat on the counter and picked up an apple, biting into it.

"Most are," Dan agreed. "My family is . . . they aren't around anymore." He swallowed hard and averted his face, concentrating on the stove. "Could you hand me those pliers?"

I plucked them out of the nearby toolbox and handed them to him, feeling like an ass. I didn't want to ask about his family—he'd told me they'd passed on recently, and the wound was clearly still fresh—but I needed to know more about how packs worked. I was desperate for this knowledge.

Dan must have sensed my anxiety. After a moment, he looked up, re-handed me the pliers, and added, "We didn't have an alpha when Jackson came in. When the others passed on, I stayed with him."

Interesting. I thought for a moment, then delicately phrased my next question. "So you two don't have a pack right now?"

"We *are* a pack—of two. I could join another

pack, but Jackson can't. He'd be immediately challenged by the alpha—if one even let him get near. So we just mind our own business and try to stay out of everyone's territory."

That sounded lonely. But it might be perfect for my needs. "What if someone wanted to join your pack?"

He gave me a surprised look. "You want to mate with Jackson?"

"*What?* No! Is that the only way I can join?"

He shrugged. "That's how it's done."

"That's barbaric."

"It may not seem right to regular humans, but wolf instinct is real hard to override."

I couldn't argue with that.

"'Sides," Dan continued in a careful voice. "If you joined our pack, I imagine the other pack would challenge Jackson for you."

I blew out a sigh of frustration. Jackson was a nice man, but he was one man, and there were eight redneck Andersons. "I was just thinking aloud. I'm not joining anyone's pack."

A relieved look shot over his face, quickly masked. Outcast even among the wolves, that's me. I decided to change topics. "The new stove is nice."

He grinned over at me. "Got a new washer-dryer to install, too. And new toilets, but they want to do that after the roof has been patched."

I smiled at the thought. "This place will seem almost like home once it's all done. Wonder why Ramsey let it get so run-down?"

Dan gave me a funny look. "I guess the instinct finally kicked in."

I didn't know a thing about shifter instincts, so I had to ask. "What kind of instinct?"

"You know. Bears and their dens. Family stuff." He shrugged. "He took a mate and he's making a home for you."

Before I could reply, I heard the sound of truck tires on the gravel driveway. "Another delivery?" I asked Dan with a smile.

He didn't look happy. "No, ma'am."

An anxious quiver erupted in my stomach and I hopped down off the counter, moving to the big, open window in the kitchen. Behind the Wilder van I saw the bright green pickup of the Anderson family, and as I watched, Levi, Wyatt, Maynard, and Gracie piled out of the truck. They sniffed the air, then began to head toward the house. The hammering on the roof stopped short.

My heart pounded in my chest. Every bone in my body screamed for me to run, but I knew that wolves didn't respect a coward. Any weakness I showed would just make things worse. Clenching my hands, I walked onto the porch and paused at the front of the porch steps.

Levi saw me and took a few steps in my direction. Maynard and Wyatt were smirking, but Gracie seemed sullen. Levi waved a hand at me, beckoning me forward. "Come here, girl."

My muscles locked and I bit down the whimper in my throat, compelled to obey the alpha. His gaze was staring me down, and I took a step down the stairs, then a second, dragging my feet as much as I could. I didn't want to obey, but the alpha's will was overwhelming.

Before my feet could touch the ground, Ramsey dropped from the roof. He landed in front of me in a crouch, blocking me from the alpha, preventing me from answering his call. He stood, one hand going protectively behind him to shield me.

"Leave her alone," he snarled. His voice sounded more bestial than I had ever heard it.

"Howdy, Papa Bear," Gracie drawled, unafraid. "We've come to check on your girl. Daddy wants a pop quiz."

"You need to leave this property," Ramsey said. "Now." His back bristled, and I could have sworn he was about to sprout fur. His hands clenched, and I noticed that he'd grown claws. His entire form trembled with rage.

This was the closest I'd ever seen Ramsey come to losing his shit.

Levi seemed to notice just how on edge Ramsey was, because he paused and raised a hand, commanding his wolves to stop. "I came to check on the girl. See how her shifting is doing, since you decided to send her wolf companion home. If she ain't controlling her shift, she's ours. I won't let you destroy her."

The low rumble in Ramsey's voice continued, and I realized it was a full-on growl. His back began to ripple with the shift of muscles. "You're the ones that forced her to change. You knew that if you scared her—"

"Don't matter one way or another," Levi said smugly. "If she was learning the way she was supposed to be, it wouldn't have happened, would it?"

"You're not going to fucking touch her."

"Our pact said you were going to show her how to shift, and that she'd keep a wolf at her side. But I found out this morning that Gracie ain't welcome, and one of my boys has footage of your woman vomiting blood." He lifted his chin, staring directly at me around Ramsey's massive, tense form. "So I want to see her shift. See what progress she's making."

I froze. I still felt shredded from last night's ugly shift. If they forced me to shift now, it'd be just as hard, and just as painful. They knew that, too.

"She will shift for you," Ramsey said, his words slurred as if he was speaking them around a mouthful of fangs, "over my dead fucking body."

Levi's eyes flared green. "That can be arranged, Bjorn. Four against one. Mighty big words."

I stepped out from behind him. "Four against two."

Gracie's mouth curled into a sneer. Why had I ever thought we could be friends? She was friendly to me as long as she thought she would get something out of it.

"Four against three," said another voice, and Jackson hopped down off the roof, walking to our side.

"Four against four," a voice called behind me, and I saw Dan emerge from the house, hammer in his hand.

Levi's lips drew back in a snarl. "So you're saying our treaty's over, Bjorn?"

"You broke it. Touch my mate and you'll lose your hand."

Maynard made a fist, but Levi put a hand up. "So be it. Better watch your back, then. If we have to go through you to get her, we will."

I held my breath as the wolves turned and piled back into the pickup, then left. No one breathed until their truck had disappeared down the highway. When it was gone, I suddenly gasped for breath, feeling dizzy.

Ramsey turned and grasped my face in his hands, his still wild eyes searching mine. "Are you all right?"

I nodded, then pulled out of his embrace. "You shouldn't have done that," I said softly. "The gloves are off now."

"The gloves were off last night when they tried to attack you," he said, his voice nearly animalistic with fury. "The gloves were off when they deliberately scared you to force a change, and then showed up here to try and force another. Would you have been able to turn to show them?"

I shook my head.

"Exactly. They knew that, too." As I watched, his claws receded and his hand stroked over my hair, touched my jaw, my shoulders, constantly touching and smoothing me. "They're playing games with us, Sara. I'm tired of playing."

I looked up at him, so strong and furious on my behalf, and wondered just what he was thinking. Jackson and Dan headed to the side of the house, no doubt to give us privacy. "But we're playing games, too," I whispered, my own emotions in a turmoil. "This thing between us—it's just a game to trick them. They know it. We know it. Why are we bothering?"

I didn't think it was possible for Ramsey to look more furious. I was wrong. His eyes grew to narrow slits and his mouth clenched into a hard line. "No one's playing at anything anymore. You belong to me, and this is where you're staying."

I wanted to believe him. Somehow, I doubted the wolves would let that happen, though.

Shortly after the wolves had been run off, Ellis and Joshua showed up, and I caught a whiff of Beau as well. He stayed outside with Ramsey, and I saw them head out to patrol the grounds, likely to sniff out any hints of wolves prowling around the property. Ellis and Joshua shadowed me closely. I left them to play Xbox while I worked on my computer. My gaming accounts had gone unused in the past few weeks, but I didn't feel like losing myself in a game. There was too much going on.

Too much going on—and nothing for me to do. Every time I suggested heading in to work, someone gave me an ugly look. If I picked up a paintbrush or a hammer, someone took it out of my hand. I tried to make lunch for the crew, and Savannah dropped by the house with a couple of sub sandwiches.

The remaining dates that I had scheduled with Ramsey were canceled. It was too dangerous for us to go out for a casual night on the town when the wolves were determined to harass me. That left me homebound with nothing to do while everyone around me scrambled to save my ass.

It rankled. Here I was trying to be stronger, more confident, and I was still sheltered and protected from everyone and everything.

I logged on to the Liaisons website and scrolled through my in-box, skimming over everything without stopping on anything in particular. I felt out of sorts, not right in my skin. I couldn't focus. I poked at a few things, then thought for a minute and searched the database for were-bears. Only a handful popped up—they weren't the most common shifters—and most were out of state. I sucked in a breath at the sight of Nikolina's name and clicked on her profile. I stared at her picture, then looked at her stats. Six foot one. One hundred eighty pounds—I bet that was all muscle, too. She looked strong. Her profile was inactive, meaning that she hadn't logged on in quite some time. She'd be a good match for Ramsey; he wouldn't have to be careful with her. They'd make cute little bear cubs together. I could just see them, roaming the woods together, two bears on a leisurely stroll—

I slammed the laptop shut, scowling.

Jackson and Dan finished up for the day and I wandered back into the kitchen, made a sandwich, and then sat back down on the couch, waiting.

When dusk hit, Ellis and Joshua left and Jeremiah and Austin showed up. They chatted with Ramsey and Beau for a short while, then left without coming into the house. At my quirked eyebrow, Ramsey said, "They're going to patrol the grounds tonight."

"What about shifting?" I asked.

He shook his head. "It can wait for tomorrow." His hand brushed over my hair and he dropped a kiss on my forehead before heading deeper into the house to check the windows and doors.

I followed him as he went upstairs and into our room. "Are you coming to bed with me tonight?"

"Yes."

I ground my teeth, frustrated. He hadn't slept with me for the past two nights. "Is it because I need protection, or because you want to?"

"Both."

A surge of desire rushed through me, making my nipples hard. I pushed the feeling away, crossing my arms over my chest. "I don't understand you, Ramsey."

He remained standing where he was. "Do you want me to sleep somewhere else?"

"No! I just . . . I don't know what you're thinking." The frustration and the tension of the day got to me and I sat on the edge of the bed, trying not to throw something at the wall in frustration.

"What do you mean?"

"I mean this," I said, gesturing wildly at the bed. "Me and you. You and me. In bed together, making out but not having actual, all-the-way sex. And the Nikolina thing. I don't know where all of this is going, and it makes me crazy."

He'd grown very still. "And where do you think this should go?"

I wanted to choke him for saying that. "I want you to tell me how you *feel* about me," I snarled. "I want you to quit being so quiet and strong, and just freaking tell me how you feel about me, already! Is this you-and-me thing going somewhere, or is it just a momentary diversion on the road to Nikolina-land? That's what I need to know, because you're throwing me mixed signals here. One moment you can't wait to kiss me, but you won't have sex with me. You want to hold me and cuddle me close at night, but then you don't."

"Sara—"

"Is it so freaking hard to say if you love me or not?"

He sat next to me on the bed, then pulled me into his lap so we were face-to-face. I wore nothing but my panties and T-shirt and could feel the heat of his erection between my legs.

His dark eyes met mine. "Sara, you know how I feel about you."

"No, I don't. I'd really like you to say it out loud."

"I love you," he said simply, and I felt a surge

of triumph. "I've loved you since you climbed me like a tree and called me that stupid name. You were scared, but you refused to show it. I admired that. My feelings for you have only grown."

"Then Nikolina is out of the picture?" I blurted.

"Never *in* the picture," he said gently, his thumbs rubbing at the bare patch of skin above my panty line. "My life with her and the bear clan ended when I was fifteen. I thought I might go back someday if I missed the clan. If I missed my family. If I wanted to settle down. It was there waiting for me if I wanted it."

I hardly dared to breathe.

His fingertips traced along my body, moving up my breastbone and dancing lightly over my fragile collarbones. Ramsey seemed fascinated by his fingers on my skin, his gaze following them instead of looking me in the eye. "When I claimed you as my mate, I committed myself to you. That was my path forward. *Not* the bear clan. With you, and with the Alliance. I gave you my house and my protection because those are things I can give to you to show that I care."

I pressed my hand to his chest, feeling the warm skin through his shirt. "And your heart?"

"You have always had it," he said gruffly.

I reached for his unruly hair. "Then why hold me at arm's length—"

He gently grasped my hand in his own, stopping me before I could touch him. "Because this relationship is not about what *I* want, Sara."

I frowned at him, not liking the ominous tone of his voice.

"This is about you, Sara. It has always been about you." His dark eyes were so, so serious. Not a hint of a smile on his stern face. "I am no Roy, to force you into a life that you do not want. I am no Levi, to force a mate on you that you do not choose."

My breath caught in my throat. "Is that why you won't have sex with me?"

His gaze caressed my face. "I won't because that would tie you to me. So many other freedoms in your life have been taken from you—I won't force my wants and needs onto you. When you are done with the wolves and are free to choose—really *free*— then we can have sex if you want to. And if not, that is fine, too."

"But it's not forcing." I brushed my fingers over his cheek, feeling the hard line of his jaw. "I'm glad that you love me." So freaking glad.

"I know," he said in a soft rumble. "And I don't want you to feel like you have to say anything back. I will not push."

I froze at his knowing gaze. I *should* have said something back. Claimed him. Claimed the relationship. But I was suddenly paralyzed with fear.

A flash of pain shot over Ramsey's gaze, and he very gently kissed my forehead. "You need to decide what you want, Sara. I won't force a decision or a relationship on you. I'm not like Roy. And I'm not like Levi. I *am* very patient. And I will wait until you are sure."

With that, he slid me off his lap, brushed his fingers over my cheek, and left the room.

I stared after him, my heart pounding. *I know you're not like them.* But the words stuck in my throat, just like the *I love you, too*, that I'd been too terrified to utter.

Did I love Ramsey? Or did I simply want him because he was safe and good to me? I lay back on the bed and stared at the ceiling, wondering when life had gotten so very confusing.

I didn't sleep well that night. Every time I closed my eyes, I saw wolves. And when I dreamed, Roy was there in my dreams, bullying me. I jerked awake after another bad dream, drenched in sweat, and realized that Ramsey still hadn't come to bed. I tiptoed across the floor and cracked the bedroom door—now leveled and hinges greased—and peered down the hall. Ramsey sat in a folding chair at the end of the hall, staring into the darkness, his gaze out the window. I smelled a bit of a breeze and realized he had it cracked so he could scent changes in the air. Across his lap lay a shotgun.

A funny tingle went through me at the sight. I crept back into the bedroom and shut the door, then leaned against it. Seeing that gun in his lap made me feel all kinds of things. Horror that we might have come to this. Fear that the wolves might attack and hurt Ramsey.

And a deep, warm sensation that he cared enough about me to go that far.

—————

When dawn finally came, I woke to what sounded like a shot being fired, and I sprang out of bed. I raced down the stairs, nostrils flaring, frightened out of my wits. The sound went off again, and I followed it into the kitchen . . .

Only to be greeted by Dan and Savannah sitting on the floor, a stack of ceramic tile in front of them. Savannah looked up from the tile cutter, her long, dark hair spilling over her shoulders. "Did we wake you up? Sorry."

I clasped my hands at my waist, willing them to stop shaking. "I just . . . I thought . . . never mind."

She gave me a mild look, then pumped the handle on the tile cutter again. It made a cracking sound like a shotgun once more, and she laid the resized tile to the side. A pretty black and white for a checkerboard floor, unless I missed my guess.

"The tile's nice."

"Ramsey thought you might like it," Savannah said coolly. "You can help us lay the tile if you want."

"Okay."

"Probably'll go easier if you put some pants on," she commented. "So Dan can stop staring at the floor."

Oh. In my haste, I hadn't paid a lick of attention to what I was wearing. I dashed back upstairs, grabbed my old jeans and threw them on, then dashed back down to the kitchen again. There was no sign of Ramsey, and it was weird how my heart plummeted at that. "Have you seen Ramsey?"

"He went out. He and Beau had some big plan today. My brothers are crawling all over the land, though; don't you worry."

I sat cross-legged on the floor. I wasn't worried. If Ramsey thought I was safe with all the Russells breathing down my neck, then I was safe. Just . . . disappointed that I didn't see him. I felt the oddest need to touch his hand, let him know that I was all right.

Dan straightened as I sat down. "If you guys are good, I'm going to go help Jackson with the roof," he said and disappeared.

I gave Savannah a questioning look.

"It's the cat in me," she said. "He's young enough that it probably still unsettles him."

"Oh," I said, pulling my knees up. I hadn't noticed anything jarring about Savannah—or the rest of the Russells. Perhaps it was a "born" shifter thing? "Do most species get along as badly as wolves and were-cats?"

"Mostly those two," she said cheerfully. "Though most find were-snakes untrustworthy. And vampires smell amazing, but other than that, they're unsettling."

I made a mental note to add this to my sister's database. Perhaps we *were* missing some vital elements by not having a natural-born shifter working there.

Savannah went back to cutting tile, handing me each piece as it was trimmed. "You want to do this?"

"No," I said. "You're doing just fine. I appreciate the help."

"Gives me a chance to get out of the house," she said. "I'm afraid the same doesn't go for you, though. House arrest until Ramsey gives the order."

"I'm not going anywhere." I shuddered at the thought. "Though I should probably call my sister and make sure she has coverage at the agency."

I didn't get up, though. I had too many questions running through my mind. I picked up a piece of the marble tile and ran my fingers along the rough, gritty edge. Expensive tile. I wondered if what Dan had said about Ramsey making a den—a home—for his mate was true.

Why did I doubt it? Why was I running scared now? I couldn't imagine being with anyone other than Ramsey. Yet whenever I thought of the reins of the relationship being in my hands, I got scared. The last time I'd picked who I'd wanted to be with, he'd been a monster. What if I was being stupid again? Worse, what if I ruined Ramsey's life instead of just my own?

After six years of being at the mercy of others, I was in charge of my own destiny, and I was terrified at the thought.

I swallowed. "Hey, Savannah? Can I ask you something?"

Her expression grew instantly wary. "Of course."

I continued to run my fingers along the edge of the tile. So pretty and smooth, but so rough around the edges. "What were the wolves like when you were captured?"

She thought for a minute, and then offered, "Indifferent."

That wasn't the answer I'd been expecting. "Indifferent? How so?"

She shrugged. "They're massive assholes, but when they stole me they were careful not to hurt me. I think it was more to call a bluff than anything else. They kept me in a cabin in the middle of the woods. I was chained to the wall, but other than that, they left me my privacy. Fed me three times a day. They didn't harass me. They just didn't seem to care at all. Totally uninterested. It's the cat thing."

I could think of one particular wolf who was very interested, but I said nothing. "And Gracie?"

"She's an odd one. She was friendly to me, but every time her father came around, she'd clam up. I think her family brings out the worst in her."

I nodded. "And . . . Connor?"

Savannah's eyes narrowed, and for a minute she looked just like Beau when he got angry. "Why are you asking me about him?"

"Because he's sick with love for you and I'm trying to understand it, since they were all so indifferent to you."

Her mouth softened a little. "Not Connor."

"Not Connor what?"

"He's not like the others. When I count the Anderson pack, I don't count him. He's different."

"Then why won't you talk to him?"

She gave me a sad smile and picked up another tile. "Because he's not different enough."

That struck me as rather unfair. "You don't know that."

"Don't I? I begged him to send me home because I was in heat, to send me back to my boyfriend. Connor didn't listen, though. At the end of the day, he still obeyed his alpha. I can't love a man like that. I need my needs—and my child's needs—to be first in his mind." Her voice had grown hard. "He slept with me knowing he was destroying my relationship with my boyfriend, and he didn't care."

I shook my head. "Are you sure he wasn't just doing what was best for you? What if he'd let you go and the alpha killed you? Levi and the others are ruthless, but that doesn't mean that Connor is. Or that he doesn't have the capacity to love."

She said nothing.

It really bothered me, so I continued. "Just because he's different doesn't mean he's your enemy. Judge him by his actions, Savannah, not the actions of others."

She still said nothing.

My stomach gave a funny little twist, and I pulled the tile from her hands, forcing her to look at me. "He's sick with love for you. He wants you at his side but doesn't know how to accomplish it. He wants to share his life with you, and you won't let him in."

"You think so?"

"I think if you asked him, he'd give up everything for you. Pack, family—they don't matter to him. *You* do. It's obvious that he adores you . . . and that you won't give him a chance."

She gave me an odd look, and then a wry smile curved her mouth. "Are we talking about my relationship . . . or yours?"

I had no answer for her. *Was* I shutting Ramsey out? I handed the tile back to her and got to my feet, mumbling something about needing fresh air. I stepped out onto the porch and noticed that the warped wooden steps had been repaired. I walked to the front of the house and turned, studying the house. The fresh coat of paint had given it new life, and the holes in the roof were patched and reshingled. The porch still sagged at the edges, but that could be easily fixed. I knew it would be in the coming weeks.

Ramsey had started making this a home ever since I'd moved in. It was me who asked about the bears. Me who asked about Nikolina. He'd never volunteered it because it hadn't mattered to him, and he'd never lied, either. Why was I so certain that I was forcing him to stay here? That I was going to get hurt?

What if he stayed because . . . he wanted to? Because he wanted to be with me?

I rubbed my arms and knew the answer. He wanted me to be free to love him. And he'd stand, waiting for me with his hand outstretched, until I was ready to take it. He wanted me to be sure. Really sure. He wanted to know that I wanted him because I *wanted* to be in a relationship with him, not because I was simply lining up another protector.

I knew what was in my heart.

But the trick was admitting it.

Chapter Seventeen

*B*eing stuck at the house with a handful of Russells and no Ramsey drove me insane. I fidgeted and paced until I heard his big truck pull up into the driveway. I stayed in the kitchen, waiting, as he exchanged a few words with Savannah and Joshua. They talked for a moment, then I heard the smaller truck drive away, and Ramsey entered the front door. I smiled at him from behind the kitchen island, feeling oddly hesitant and uncertain after my revelation this afternoon. If I came on to him, would he trust it, or would he simply think I was using him?

Ramsey looked tired, though, his eyes hollow. "Long day?" I asked.

He nodded. "I need a shower. Still smell like sweat."

I had a million things I wanted to ask him. Why was he so tired? Where had he gone? Was everything okay? But they could wait. "I'll start dinner," I said.

While he showered upstairs, I double-checked all the locks on the windows and doors just to be on the safe side, then started the pasta. By the time he came back, I had French bread cut into thick slices and the microwave pasta served on paper plates. His mouth curved into a faint smile at the sight of it. "Appreciate the dinner."

"I'm just warning you now that I'm not much of a homemaker," I teased. "If it can't be zapped in the microwave, it's out of my league."

"But I made you this enormous kitchen," he said gruffly, taking a beer out of the fridge and sitting down.

My jaw dropped a little.

He winked at me and twisted the cap off his beer.

"Did you just make a joke?" I asked, baffled at his playfulness.

"Wanted to see the expression on your face," he admitted.

I laughed despite myself.

We had a pleasant meal, talking about inconsequential things—home repair, what he planned to do next in the house, the weather—avoiding topics that would bother either of us.

Until I couldn't stand it any longer. "Where were you?" I blurted.

A hint of a smile tugged at his mouth.

I blushed. "I worried about you. You were gone all day. Is something wrong?"

The look in his eyes grew possessive and heated, and my nipples hardened. "Thinking about me all day?" he asked huskily.

"Don't change the subject."

The hint of a smile that lingered on his mouth said that he was humoring me. "Beau and I went looking for Tony."

"Who?"

He gave a short nod, toying with the empty longneck in front of him, the bottle nearly dwarfed by his hand. "Tony Anderson. Beau thinks he's the weak link. We thought if anyone was going to give us details on what the wolves plan, it'd be Tony."

I swallowed hard. "You weren't going to torture him, were you?"

"Nope." He stood, his massive form nearly blotting out the lights in the kitchen. "But I can be real convincing if need be."

No kidding. I shivered.

The hard expression on his face faded. "I'm scaring you," he said quietly. "I'm sorry."

"Oh, no," I said hastily, but he ignored my protests.

"Go upstairs. I'll be up shortly."

I brightened. "So we can keep talking?"

"So you can get some sleep. It's late, and you're fragile."

Fragile? "I feel like shoving my fragile fist through your fragile brain," I muttered.

His mouth twitched, and I realized he was holding back another smile. "You need to rest."

"Shouldn't I at least shift tonight?" I wanted to keep in the habit. Now that I had an ounce of control again, there was no way I'd give it up.

"That can wait for the morning. I'll ask Savannah to come over again. She can supervise."

My heart plummeted. "You won't help me?"

He shook his head. "You need someone with more patience."

No one had more patience than Ramsey. I stared at his back, hurt. I knew what this was. He was giving me space. He wasn't going to crowd me.

Well goddamn it, I wanted to be crowded. I didn't want space—I wanted him *in* my space. I went upstairs, chewing on my lip, and slammed the bedroom door behind me. So I'd show him just how hard it'd be to let me go, then. I crossed the room and pulled the small lingerie bag out of the closet. I'd been saving the unveiling for a special occasion, and now was the time. I changed into the skimpy lace bra and panties and then put my jeans and T-shirt over them. Before playtime, I needed to have a serious conversation with Ramsey. About the man who'd changed me and what had happened to him.

He knocked on the door as I sat on the edge of the bed, running my palms over my jeans. "Come in."

He entered and scanned the room, then shut the door behind him. "Everything all right?"

I nodded and patted the mattress next to me. "I want to talk to you."

He hesitated for a moment, then walked in and sat next to me. I always felt tiniest sitting next to him. Odd that he could be so very enormous and not scare me in the slightest. Roy had been small and compact, and he'd scared the living daylights out of me.

I sighed. I couldn't put this off any longer. I

reached over and grasped Ramsey's big hand, and his fingers curled over mine. "So what did Beau tell you about Roy? Because it's time we talked about him."

"Nothing."

I raised an eyebrow at that.

"He told me that it was in your past, and Bathsheba's, and that it was not to be worried over. He wouldn't say more."

Beau was a good guy. I liked that he'd protect my sister even from his best friend. I took a slow breath, composing myself, then stared at his hand as I talked.

"When I was sixteen, I met an older guy," I began, feeling a little sick and relieved all at once. "I was kind of a wild kid. My mother was a drunk and my dad was never home. My sister took care of me. Bathsheba was always the adult in our little family, taking care of Mom and me, running the house, making sure the bills were paid, you name it. When she got a full scholarship to college, I encouraged her to take it. I was going to miss her like hell, but it was the best thing for her." I smiled a little at the memory, thinking of her joyful face on that day. "Bath deserved to be someone amazing, and smart, and educated. I wasn't going to hold her back."

Ramsey said nothing, squeezing my hand a little. I ran my free hand over his knuckles.

"I met a guy named Roy a few weeks after she'd left. I was out drinking with some friends and went to a college party. Roy was there, but he wasn't in college. He was a mechanic, and he was twenty-five, and he was handsome and just a little bit dangerous."

How dumb and completely naïve I'd been then. I'd been so dazzled by his rakish smile and his thick black hair. "I was totally in love with him the moment I saw him. We dated once or twice, and then he started declaring his love for me. And I was a stupid sixteen-year-old, so I was totally on board with it. I didn't really mind that he was possessive or tried to run my life. Bath had always told me what to do, and my mother was stoned or drunk more than she wasn't."

I looked over at Ramsey. "At the time, I liked that a man was going to step in and take charge of my life. Someone else had always been in the lead, and I'd never known what to do without someone there to guide me. Kind of sad, looking back."

"Not sad," he said gruffly. "You were young. Scared."

Yes, but I'm not young anymore, and I'm still scared. I shook my head, picking up the reins of my story again. "After we'd been dating for a month or two, Roy insisted that I move in with him. He wanted me there in his house to take care of all his needs at any time. My mother didn't like the idea, but I didn't care. I threatened to call the cops on her drugging if she didn't let me go, so she let me. I moved in with Roy, and we played house for a time. I dropped out of high school so I could spend all my time with him. If I wasn't with him, I was doing things to please him, like cleaning the house. Roy liked the house to be spotless. If I left a dish in the sink, he'd slap me. It was his way of teaching me how to be a proper girlfriend, he said, and that I was lazy and didn't respond well—but I responded to the slaps."

Ramsey's hand tightened over mine. I squeezed his hand to calm him, because the story was going to get worse.

"As time passed, I couldn't seem to make Roy happy. We'd been together for six months or so when he really started to hit me. One time he lost his temper and began to change, and that's when I realized he was a werewolf. It all fell into place after that—his weird buddies that came over every night for just a short period of time, the way he'd disappear for hours and then come back smelling like the woods. I didn't ask—I was too desperate to make him happy with me. We got into a fight one night. We fought almost every night, but this time it was worse than ever. And that night, he bit me."

Ramsey's hand clenched mine, hard. "Sara—"

I wasn't going to stop; I needed to tell him all of this. "Roy was always very fastidious before that. He'd never drink out of the same glass as me. Never let me use his toothbrush. Always careful to use condoms. I just thought he was a bit OCD. Turns out, not so much." I laughed, but it sounded hollow. "That night, he nearly tore out my throat. I don't think he meant to. It was just the heat of the moment, and I was pretty delicate, and boom. There

I am, bleeding all over the place. At first he was shocked, but then he started to bite me over and over again, and I didn't know what he was doing. It wasn't until my bites started to heal that I realized what he was doing—and what he'd done. At that point it was either turn me or let me die, so he must have cared for me a little to try and save me, right?"

My hand tightened on his and I continued to trace his knuckles, my voice growing tight. "I was so freaked out back then. I didn't know what was happening. The first change was just . . . awful. I bled like crazy, and I think I stayed in wolf form for three days." I remembered the horror of those days. The sheer terror that I hadn't known what had happened to me. The loneliness and bewilderment. I sighed. "I also ate the neighbor's cat."

He didn't smile.

I continued, "Roy disappeared on me, and I had to suffer through it alone. It was so painful to change back, and the entire time, I wasn't convinced that I hadn't gone crazy somehow. Until it happened again, and again. Roy didn't like that I had become a wolf, but he didn't know what else to do with me. And I cried a lot, because I was a kid and I was scared, and he liked that even less. Roy wanted me to be strong, so he hit me even more, trying to toughen me up. It didn't work. It just made him angrier, and me more frightened."

I heard a faint grinding noise and looked up to see Ramsey's jaw clenched so hard that I thought he might break his teeth. "Go on," he gritted.

"Bath heard from my mother that I'd gone off to live with a man, and she didn't approve. She drove her little beat-up car ten hours to come and talk some sense into me."

"Your sister is a good person," he said softly.

I nodded. "I couldn't control the changes at all back then. When Bath showed up on my doorstep, I panicked at the sight of her and began to change. It was awful. My sister didn't know what to do. She thought I was having a seizure. I didn't know what to do, either. Roy was off on another of his nightly jaunts. That was just . . . ugly. And having to explain it to my sister was even worse. When I changed back, my clothes were gone, of course, and she saw all my bruises, and the cigarette burns, and the bites."

The low growl started in Ramsey's throat.

I touched his arm to calm him. It all felt like so long ago. Distant, sad memories. "Bath insisted that I go home with her. And I was so rattled and unsure of myself that I told her no. I believed that I was no good, and stupid, and that Roy was right to beat me to make me stronger. He'd brainwashed me."

Again that grinding of teeth. "I hope this story has a happy ending, or I'm going to have to put my fist through a wall."

I rubbed his arm. "I'm getting there. Anyhow. Roy got home and saw my sister packing a bag for me. He attacked her—he was getting really bad at controlling himself. I managed to get him off of her, and then he started attacking me. The next thing

I knew, Bath had a gun out and . . . she shot him. Through the head. She thought he was going to kill me—and maybe he would have."

I peeked through my lashes over at him, hating the tremor in my voice. He said nothing.

"We buried him on the side of the road in the middle of nowhere," I said. "And then we left New Mexico for good. We tried to get my mom to go with us, but she thought I was the devil after I'd been changed, and she didn't understand . . ." I shrugged. "She attacked me when I tried to talk to her, but Momma was always a bad drunk and a worse druggie. We gave up on her and left the state. Started over. And here we are today. Your mate is an accomplice to murder, and not at all sorry about it."

He gave me a solemn look. "You wouldn't tell me about Roy before because that would endanger your sister?"

I nodded. "She gave up everything for me. I wouldn't sell her out."

"Then why tell me now?"

I stood up, placed my hands on his shoulders, and looked him squarely in the eye. "Because I've been thinking about what you said. That this relationship was mine to steer, and that you'd let me lead."

"And?" His voice was a warm rumble.

"And I've decided that I want to be your mate, Ramsey Bjorn. I love you. I love you for being warm and protective, and still giving me the freedom to be me. I was scared to think that I'd have to make the decision, but then I realized that I was even more scared of a life without you by my side." My fingers tangled in his hair, and I gazed with satisfaction at the mate marks I'd left on his neck. I leaned in and licked them, long and slow.

I felt a tremor run through his large body, and delighted in it.

"So I'm taking control of this relationship," I said softly, leaning back to look him in the eye again. "I want you as my mate, and I'm not taking no for an answer."

And with that, I tugged off my shirt.

Ramsey stared at my small breasts, cupped by the naughty bra. It was a red lace demi-cup with just enough padding to push my small chest into something magnificent. As he stared, I slid out of my jeans and tossed them to the side, displaying my matching thong, which did wonderful things to my ass. Bright red lace, because Ramsey said he liked red.

Ramsey licked his lips as if his mouth had gone suddenly dry, and looked up at me. "Sara, I—"

I pressed a finger to his lips. "You said you wanted this to be my choice. I'm choosing."

"Shouldn't you take a few more days to decide?" His gaze was glued to my décolletage.

I crawled forward, pushing him backward on the bed. "I'm sure about this. I had a long talk with Savannah earlier, and it made me realize that I was holding things against you and I didn't even realize it. Moreover, I realized that I was being a coward."

With the barest touch of my fingers, he fell backward into the bed, and I straddled him. His hands brushed my thighs, now straddling his chest. "You don't seem very cowardly at the moment," he murmured.

"Nope," I said cheerfully, looking down at him. "I want this. And I want you—forever. Mates in every sense of the word. I know you're not like Roy, or Levi, or the others. I've always known that. I just had a hard time admitting it to myself." I leaned in and brushed a light kiss on his mouth. "And now I want to show you."

He flipped over and suddenly I was under him, legs spread wide, his weight pressing between them. I felt the hard length of his erection against the scrap of my panties and resisted the urge to rub up against it.

"Ramsey," I said softly, brushing my lips against his as I spoke. "I'm the one leading this relationship, aren't I?"

His hips flexed against mine involuntarily, and his eyes flared with need. He leaned in and kissed me, hard, and then pulled back, burying his face against my neck. "You are, but—"

"We'll go fast the first time, and then slower afterward. All right?"

He nodded. I wiggled out from under him and went over to the dresser. "I have something we can use," I said, sparks of excitement racing through my body. My nipples were hard with need, and he'd barely touched me.

I showed him the tube of lubricant and he actually blushed a little. I dropped it on the bed and my hands went to his waist, undoing the buckle of his belt and then sliding his jeans down his legs. His cock was so hard and thick already that it brushed against me as I moved, and I leaned in to give the head a light kiss. He groaned. "Sara," he warned, his breathing ragged. "About to come."

I reached up to his cock, took the crown of it in my grasp, and squeezed, waiting.

His body stiffened and his eyes flashed, and then he reached for me again, as if desperate to put his hands on my body.

I leaned in and kissed him, nipping at his mouth. "Normally we don't need this, but you're a big guy. Let's be careful this first time. Plus I really just want to get my hands all over you," I said and flipped the cap of the lube, squirting a small amount into my hand. I rubbed my palms together and then, my gaze locked to his, I brushed them over the hard, silky length of his cock.

He groaned like a man dying. "*Sara.*"

Pleased, I wrapped my slick fingers around the massive length of it, stroking up and down. His breath bit sharply, telling me he was about to lose control, and I dropped my hands and leaned in to kiss him. "Now do me?"

He closed his eyes, breathing hard for a long moment, then sat up. His hands gripped me and he pulled me down onto the bed, pressing kisses to my stomach, as if unable to contain himself. I wriggled in pleasure at the sensation, my still-slick fingers going to tangle in his hair. "Please, Ramsey," I said. "I need you inside me."

For a long moment he hovered over me, then stood. He stared down at me, then gently tugged my dainty, lacy little thong down my legs and tossed it on the floor. His hand cupped my mound and his thumb grazed the slit of my sex. "You're already so wet."

God, that felt so good. I needed him so badly. I lifted my hips, pressing against his thumb. "This first time, let's go for really, really wet, all right?"

He nodded and grasped the lubricant, applied some to his hands, and slicked them, mimicking my actions from just a minute ago. His fingers returned to my sex, brushing along my folds, making them slippery with lubricant. I cried out when his fingers brushed over my clit, my hands teasing the tips of my breasts through my lacy bra. "Put your finger inside me."

He did as I commanded, and I nearly came at the feeling of that thick finger pushing deep into me. My breathing became quick and panting, and I bit my lip, trying not to buck against his hand and ruin the moment. He pushed in with his finger, his gaze fascinated as he watched my body, then withdrew and stroked the finger deep inside me again.

I moaned. "Another finger."

When he added the second one, I sucked in a breath, the feeling incredibly tight and full. He pushed deep inside me with both fingers, then withdrew. "Sara. You're so tight. I don't want to hurt you."

"Shh," I said, wrapping a leg around his waist and pulling him in. I felt the head of his cock butt against my leg, hard and slick. "You won't. We're just being extra careful this first time." When he still hesitated, I sat up and kissed him fiercely, until his hips jerked against my own, and I knew he was close. I gave him one last kiss and then lay back down on the bed. "Just go slow," I whispered. "You'll be just fine."

He grasped my hips and pulled me closer, then leaned over me. Ramsey had an intense look of concentration on his face, and I wanted to kiss him all over again. He was so worried he was going to hurt me.

With good reason, I found out a moment later. The head of his cock brushed against my sex and he inched in, a hiss of breath escaping him. I bit my lip to prevent my own hiss. It had been six years since I'd had sex, and Ramsey was a very, very big man. To say the fit was tight was an understatement. I felt the burn as he pushed just a little, sinking the head of his cock in. It felt good, but it also smarted.

"Going slow," he gritted.

"Slow," I agreed, brushing my fingers over his shoulders, encouraging him.

His hips gave a little surge, pushing deeper. I gasped, the burn giving way to an intense fullness that made me quiver. Oh, God. He was so big and so deep inside me, and it suddenly felt so incredibly good. My hands slid back to my breasts, and I began to pluck at my nipples again.

"Good?" he asked.

"Very good," I breathed. "*Really* good."

He groaned and I felt his hips surge again. There was a sharp stretching pain that made me suck in my breath, and then nothing but pleasure again. He leaned in to kiss me and groaned against my mouth. "Sara . . . I don't know . . . feels so tight . . ."

"Deeper, Ramsey." I showered his face with small kisses, then tugged at his lower lip with my teeth. "*Please.* I need you."

He surged forward, seating himself to the hilt, and I gasped. He froze, terrified that he'd hurt me.

"No, it's good," I said softly, lifting my hips a little. "Are you . . . ?"

"Amazing." His voice was tight with strain and wonder. "God. I love you, Sara."

My heart gave a funny little thump in my chest. "I love you, too, Ramsey."

His breath hissed out of him again at that, and his hips surged, pushing hard against my own. "Won't last long."

"Me, either," I brushed my fingers over his nipple and then reached up to bite at his shoulder. "Please, please, don't stop."

The growl came low in his throat again, and he withdrew a little, leaving me aching and hollow, until he surged deep again. I gave a little gasp at the overwhelming sensation. Oh, wow. That was . . . amazing. When he surged again, I raised my hips to meet his. His strokes started out slow and smooth, then his hand slid to my hips and he anchored me. He began to move hard and fast, deep inside me with wild force. The panting, frenzied look on his face a thing of wildness as he drove into me, once, twice, three times and then shouted, his entire body going rigid.

I felt his climax deep inside me and pushed my hips up frantically, almost there myself. "Ramsey, please," I said as he rocked into me.

He drew in a long, ragged breath and then leaned in to kiss me.

I writhed and kissed him back, biting his lip hard. He was still buried deep inside of me and I didn't care that he'd come, only that I was so close and I wasn't going to get to come, too. He ran a hand over my hips and stroked my flesh, and I moaned. My hands fisted in the blankets pushed up behind my head. "Please, Ramsey, I need to come."

He rocked his hips against mine, his eyes heavily lidded as he watched me, as if fascinated by my needy writhing. His hand slid between us and found my clit, and I nearly rose off the bed at the small touch. He rocked against me again and rubbed that small, lovely spot, just brushing his fingers over it, watching me arch on the bed. His hand slid up to cup my breast, pinching at my nipple as his other brushed against my clit, and my panting turned into pleading. "Please. Oh, God, yes. Please. Do that again."

When he pushed down the cup of the bra and

leaned down to take my nipple in his mouth, I nearly wept at how good it felt. His teeth grazed along the hard, aching nub, then licked the soft skin, teasing.

"Please, Ramsey," I breathed. "I need—"

"Not yet," he murmured against the peak of my breast, then bit at it lightly, which sent another moan rocketing through me.

"Why not?" I moaned.

He sat up and ran a hand down my belly, fascinated by my body. Fascinated by everything about me. I loved that intense look on his face so much.

"Not done with you," he growled low in his throat, and I felt him thrust deep inside me again. I moaned as the orgasm began to build again.

His eyes were gleaming, the look in them intensely possessive. He was ready again? But it had only been a few moments.

"Are you—"

He kissed me, lightly, on the mouth, taking my words.

I sucked in a breath as he pulled me into a sitting position. My return kiss was fierce. I needed him.

He licked at my mouth, his hand moving to my hair and grasping it, holding me against him. I reveled in it—loved that he was so wildly needing me. "This is a fantasy of mine," he rasped harshly. "You. Against me. Writhing with need. Calling my name."

Just the thought of that made me incredibly hot. "Even better—reality. Every night for the rest of our lives."

He growled low and nipped at my jaw and I gasped, raking my nails on his chest. He was so hard, still so deep inside me. I raised my hips, rocking against him, and he groaned. "I want . . ." he breathed.

"What?" I asked breathlessly, excited.

"On your knees," he said with a fierce nip at my jaw again, and I felt him withdraw from me, pulling his wonderful, amazing cock from my body. I whimpered a protest, which died when he tugged me to my knees. Then he turned me until I was on my stomach, my ass in the air. His hands went to my ass and palmed the soft, rounded curves. "So beautiful."

The breath sucked out of me when I felt the head of his cock against my wet, aching sex. That was all the warning I got before he sank deep inside me again, filling me with that intense pleasure. The breath died in my throat, and his hands grasped my hips, and he began to pump into me from behind. Ramsey hadn't learned "slow" or "leisurely" in bed yet; he needed me and he took. He thrust into me so hard and rough that the bed shook and his skin slapped against my own.

I was delirious with desire, feeling the orgasm spiraling up through me, so close, my body aching with intense need. I needed to come with him deep inside me. So bad. One hand slipped to my sex and I touched my clit as he thrust roughly inside me. As soon as I did, an orgasmic sob escaped my lips and I came, my entire body clenching hard, my legs stiff and locking.

Ramsey gave a fierce growl, his movements jerky. "I . . . can feel you . . . coming. Keep touching yourself."

I'd stopped, panting, waiting for the orgasm to ebb.

He growled low again and then I felt his fingers searching for my clit as he thrust hard, and then I was spiraling into the next orgasm all over again, moaning his name over and over.

The climax rocked through me and I shuddered, but he wouldn't stop rubbing, just kept touching and touching as he made love to me, and my words became a low, endless moan of pleasure. I was boneless when he thrust hard once more, and then shouted my name, his body stiffening over me. This time, I felt him withdraw, and he flopped to the bed, pulling my boneless form with him.

"Fuck," he panted.

"Yeah," I agreed breathlessly, dreamy. That was the longest, most intense orgasm I'd ever had.

"That was . . . ," he trailed off, speechless.

"Yeah," I sighed happily.

He pulled me close and buried his face in my hair. "God, I love you."

I smiled and curled my hands in his hair. "Love you, too, Huggy Bear."

I was pretty sure I heard him laugh.

Chapter Eighteen

The next morning, I woke up to Ramsey pressing kisses on my neck. His arms were wrapped around me, and I sighed in pure bliss.

I could wake up like this for the rest of my life.

"No hammers this morning?" I said sleepily as he continued to kiss my throat. His tongue licked across my collarbone, and I gave a shiver of pleasure.

"Not today," he agreed. His thumb grazed the tip of my breast and I made a noise of pleasure in my throat, which made him growl low in response.

"Are we staying in bed then?" I asked sleepily. I was sore, but it was a delicious kind of sore. He'd woken me up twice in the night for more sex, and I'd been happy to oblige.

He sighed, then pressed a kiss to my breast. "No. I need to meet Beau today. He wants to check out a few more places. See if we can find Tony."

"Mmm. I should see my sister. Go in to work."

He gently bit my nipple, and the ripple of pleasure almost distracted me enough to miss his quick "No."

"What do you mean, no?"

He passed my breasts and began to kiss a line down my flat stomach. "Not safe."

"I'm just as safe there as I am here, Ramsey. I'll be surrounded by Russells. Joshua and Ellis are big"—I gasped when he kissed my belly button and then moved lower—"and strong. They can take care of me."

He licked the inside of my thigh, and my bones went to Jell-O. "If I say yes, will you stop talking about other men when I'm trying to kiss you?"

"Absolutely," I breathed, and completely forgot all about Russells and the agency when his mouth hit my sex.

Two hours later, we pulled into the Midnight Liaisons parking lot but were reluctant to part. When I leaned over to give Ramsey a good-bye peck, he pulled me into his lap and we began to kiss all over again, our mouths locked in a sultry thrusting of tongues as I straddled his hips, rocking against his erection.

Ramsey finally broke off our kiss, his glazed eyes caressing my face. I leaned in to bite at his neck anew, right over the mark that I'd created there. Seeing that mark always inflamed me, made me want to bite him all over his skin and in secret places so I would see those teeth marks everywhere as he undressed.

"You should go to work," he rumbled, his hand sliding to cup my ass.

I groaned against his neck and brushed my nipples against his chest. "Why must you be so responsible?"

He ignored my grumbling, continuing on. "If there's even a sniff of trouble, you call me." He looked less and less pleased with the thought of me going to work. "I don't like leaving you here by yourself. You should go back to the house."

"I'll be fine," I told him. "Bath needs my help. The agency is shorthanded as it is. And I refuse to hide in your house for the rest of my life, waiting for the wolves to strike. If I cower, they'll know I'm afraid."

His big hand cupped my face. "Don't leave the agency. Stay in sight of the Russells at all times. I'll be back in a few hours."

I leaned in and bit his earlobe. "I'm fine," I said again. "And I love you."

"I'm going to the gas station to fill up," he said, leaning in to kiss me again. "Want me to get you anything while I'm there? Stop by Starbucks?"

"Starbucks is good," I agreed. "Pick up a coffee for Bath, too, while you're at it. Actually, better make it four. Two for whichever Russells are babysitting today."

"Four coffees," he agreed, looking frustrated as I slid to the far side of the seat, like he wanted to grab me and stuff me in his pocket so we could never be apart.

I blew him a kiss. "When you get back with the coffee, maybe we'll have time for an office quickie, Huggy Bear."

"Don't tempt me."

"If I was going to tempt you, I'd tell you that you need to come inside so I'm not forced to take care of matters myself." I winked and hopped out of the truck. "Love you."

Hands clenched on the steering wheel, he watched me go inside. I waved when I got inside and then blew him another kiss.

"Look what the cat dragged in," my sister drawled.

"I should be saying that to you," I teased, breathless. My mood was so light it could have been air. "Miss me?"

"God, yes," Bath said, crossing the room to give me a quick hug. "We're still swamped from the dance. Every time I try to clean out my in-box, thirty more emails show up. How about you? Everything okay?"

I nodded. "Just trying to get back to a normal schedule. Well, as normal as you can be with bodyguards everywhere."

She nodded sympathetically. "Joshua and Ellis are in back. I put them to work filing. So I guess Savannah and Jeremiah are at the house?"

"Yup. And Ramsey and Beau are off chasing down Tony."

She shivered. "I met Tony once. He's a nasty sort."

"I'm starting to think they all are," I returned, and then thought for a minute. "Well, not Connor."

"No," she said thoughtfully. "How are you holding up?"

I gave her a genuine smile. The world seemed a little brighter today—guess a night of loving would do that to a girl. "I'm great. Ramsey's protecting me."

She gave me a knowing look. "Everything okay on the other front, too?"

To my mortification, I blushed. "Just fine."

She grinned.

"I told him our secret," I blurted, then glanced around to see if the others had returned. But they were nowhere nearby. "About . . . Roy."

She nodded. "I'd wondered if Beau had mentioned it."

"No, he was protecting you. But I trust Ramsey. I trust him with my life."

"I know," she said softly. "I'm glad."

I sat at my desk to tackle the workload that was building. My sister was making plans for future events, but we had to clear the backlog from this one first. Joshua and Ellis hung out in the back room, playing the Xbox that had been set up. While I liked gaming, I was occupied with other things— Ramsey's house. *My* house. I spent the morning browsing the internet and looking for appliances that would match my new floor. In between work, of course. Other than the constant presence of Russells, things settled back to a normal pace.

I should have guessed that it wouldn't last. The door to the agency opened early that afternoon, and I glanced up.

And sucked in a breath. The woman who came in had a hunted look on her face that I recognized all too well. She glanced around the small office as if frightened, hugging her arms to her chest, her shoulders hunched.

I looked over at my sister, but Bath was on the phone, soothing a high-maintenance client. Her shoulder cradled the phone against her ear as she typed, attention focused on her computer monitor.

I stood and invited the woman to sit down in front of me. The scent that touched my nostrils told me she was were-otter. "Good afternoon," I said brightly. "Can I help you?"

"I . . . I think I want to cancel my account."

"All right. I can help you with that. Your Alliance ID number?"

She gave it to me, and I pulled up her profile. Amanda Michigo. Twenty-seven. Unattached. She'd been a client of the agency for six years. Odd. "Is there a problem?"

She leaned forward and rested her arms on my desk. "I think . . . I'd really just like to close it. I'm not going to be dating for a while."

I stared at her arms. They were covered in faint bruises, most of them finger-shaped. Alarm raced through me. I recognized those sorts of bruises.

I glanced over at my sister, but she was still on the phone. I kept my voice low as I asked, "Did someone hurt you?"

Her nervousness seemed to double. She fidgeted in her chair and pulled her arms back, tucking them close to her body. "Not as much as they could have," she said in a small voice.

I felt sick to my stomach with rage. On a hunch, I pulled up her dating history.

Maynard Anderson—date—last night.

I wanted to bury my head in my hands and weep. His profile was active because I'd been so distracted with my own problems that I'd forgotten to go back in and deactivate it. This was my fault. I looked over at Amanda, and how twitchy she seemed. "I'll cancel your account," I said softly. "You could have done it online, though."

"I know," she said, and her voice trembled a little. "But someone . . . someone told me to come at this time. And give you a message."

"Oh?" I could barely hear from the blood roaring in my ears. "Who? What did they say?"

She swallowed hard. "They said that . . . that they were tired of waiting for you. And that you'll be coming to them, begging for them to take you."

I stared at her.

Behind us, Bath put down her phone. Immediately it rang again and she picked it up with an exasperated sigh. "Midnight Liaisons."

"Is Ramsey there with you, baby?" I heard Beau's voice clearly from across the room.

My sister looked over at me with wide eyes. I sat frozen in my chair. My stomach threatened to lurch out of my mouth.

"No," Bath said, her gaze on me. "Sara said he was meeting you."

No, no.

Beau sighed. "He's not answering his phone. I'll try him again."

I stood, my entire body trembling.

They said that they were tired of waiting for you. That you're going to come to them, begging.

"Maybe he got stuck in traffic. Or had a flat."

"I'm going to the gas station to fill up," he'd said. *"Want me to get you anything while I'm there? Stop by Starbucks?"*

He'd never come back to deliver the coffee. I'd been so immersed in work that I'd completely forgotten. I turned toward the front door.

You're going to come to them, begging.

They were tired of waiting for me. I had a mate in the way, and since I wasn't coming around, they'd just get rid of the mate.

"Sara?" my sister said, her voice questioning. "You okay?"

My fists clenched, and I ran for the front door and slammed through it, hearing the clang of the decorative cowbell against the glass. My sneakers crunched on the gravel and I sprinted, dashing down the highway.

"Sara," my sister yelled from the front door. "Where are you going?"

Anguish gutted me. I ran though my legs burned, the muscles twitching to shift. I raced out of the parking lot and down the street, past the Dollar Mart and ripping down the road, as fast as I could run, my mind picturing the gas station on the corner of the intersection. I raced there and stopped, panting, breathing hard. A car rolled past and honked; I was blocking the pumps. I moved out of the way and lifted my nose, sniffing the air for the slightest hint of bear. The gasoline smell was overwhelming, and I wanted to scream in frustration.

I couldn't smell him. Too much traffic had come through. I paced around each of the pumps furiously. If I had to put my nose to the damn concrete, I would.

There! A scent! I ran to the last pump, even though there was no car parked there. I ran my hands over the pump, looking for a scent of anything—a leftover, a hint.

A twisted piece of metal hanging out of the garbage caught my eye. I pulled it out and sucked in a breath—Ramsey's license plate. The edges were clawed, as if someone very strong—and half-transformed—had yanked it off.

The garbage began to ring, and my eyes widened. Ignoring the bees buzzing around the trash, I reached my hand in and pulled out Ramsey's phone.

I clicked to answer.

"Ramsey? Hey, man, you had me worried—," Beau began.

"I just found his phone," I said in a trembling voice, interrupting. "He's not here."

"Sara? Where is he?"

"He's gone," I said harshly. "They took him. They took him because they want me to find him."

"Sara—"

The growl started low in my throat. "And I'm going to do it," I said, my lips tightening. *Nobody* stood in the way of me and my mate.

"Let's be calm about this," Beau began, but I hung up and tossed the phone aside. I barely made it behind the gas station before I began to shift. Grim with determination, I encouraged the change to ripple over me, mentally leaned into it. I needed the aid of my wolf side.

And . . . the change came. Slowly but steadily, my muscles adjusting and tensing, bones flexing as if they'd been made of rubber. In a few minutes, I was down on all fours, and my body sank into the last of the changes with relative ease. It twinged and stung, but it wasn't the earth-shattering pain it had been in the past.

The trick was simply to embrace it. Much like in my relationship with Ramsey, my own fear had gotten in the way of things.

I lifted my canine nose to the breeze. The scents were ten times stronger as a wolf, and I easily caught the scent of bear—and wolf. Werewolves in human form have a slightly differently tinged scent—much like a howl sounds different to wolf ears—and I could tell they'd been human when they'd grabbed him. All but one, that is.

I circled the parking lot, nose to the asphalt. A child cried for his mother at the sight of me, but I ignored them. Ramsey's scent disappeared on the asphalt—they'd driven away with him. I wanted to cry out in grief at the thought. Ramsey would have never let them drive away with him while conscious—he would have fought to the death. And he could have taken them, too—so something must have happened. The scent of the wolf continued back behind the gas station, and I circled the scent trail for a minute, puzzled.

Then I realized—they were trying to lead me somewhere. Of course. This was all part of the elaborate, sneaky trap they were laying for me. The scent went across the next parking lot as well, and then down the street. I crossed the street and slunk through a suburban neighborhood before crossing into a field. The wolf's trail—Wyatt, I could tell by the smell—continued on forward, so I followed it. They were leading me northwest, out of the city and into the sticks.

On my wolf feet I was able to travel fast. The trail cut through yards and over structures, and at some points it circled around buildings. I knew it was designed to lead a canine nose. As a human, I'd have been able to follow the trail, but not as clearly and as quickly.

By the time the sun was high in the sky, I was deep into private property and out of the city. My skin twitched with the need to change back, but I ignored it. The trail grew heavy with the scent of wolves, the scent older and foul. I was close.

Deep in the woods, thick in the brambles and weeds that overgrew the land, I found an old ranch-style house. It was surrounded by a tumbledown barbed-wire fence, and I approached, the scent of wolves in my nose. The house had been abandoned long ago. The wooden shingled walls needed a coat of paint, and every window seemed to be broken. There was a large porch up front, and several wolves lay there, lolling in the shade. Their ears pricked at the sight of me and one raised his head. I'd found the Anderson hangout.

This was where they had taken Savannah. This was where Ramsey would be.

Wary, I paced in the front. One of the wolves slunk into the house as the others regarded me, waiting. One wolf lay his head back down on the porch, and his mouth curved into the canine version of a smile.

That made me furious. I lowered my head and began to make the difficult shift back to my human form. They wanted to play games? I wouldn't play by their rules. I crouched low, my back arching as I shifted. Now all the wolves on the porch watched me. I didn't care. I *had* this. Fury or determination made the shift surprisingly easy to manage. Within a minute or two, my human form crouched on the ground instead of my wolf form, and I brushed my sweaty hair out of my eyes.

The others hadn't changed—maybe they spent more time in their wolf form than human? I knew the Russells didn't. Then again, the Russells were sane. I couldn't say the same about the Andersons.

A high-pitched whine cut through the air, then someone appeared in the doorway. Gracie, still wearing one of her too-short-too-tight sundresses, her feet bare. Her curly hair was pulled over one shoulder and she smiled broadly at the sight of me. "Hey, girl. Was wondering when you'd show up."

I stared at her, resisting the urge to bare my teeth and snarl at her. I didn't understand her friendly words. We weren't friends.

She approached me with a knowing smile, her hands on her hips. She had a towel thrown over her shoulder and she offered it so I could cover up.

I ignored her and stood, easing my stiff muscles. I was adapting. I didn't need the wolves.

She pushed forward, trying to wrap the towel around me. "Here, girl—"

I pushed her aside with a snarl, baring my teeth. Surprised, Gracie took a step backward and then averted her eyes.

A surge of elation rushed through me. Her bossiness was a challenge, and I'd won it. She couldn't deal with the confidence that anger had brought to me, and she was yielding. In the pack, I now outranked her until she challenged me again. She kept her eyes averted and took another step backward.

I resolved then and there that I wouldn't yield to another wolf. They wanted to see me strong? They got it.

"I want to see Ramsey."

"Why would your boyfriend be here?" someone asked, and I looked up to see Tony.

"Because you wanted me to come here," I said calmly. "I'm here, and I want to talk to Levi."

Tony looked me up and down with a leer, then

nodded his head. "Come in, then, if you're so brave."

I went. There was nothing else the wolves could do to me, after all. My jaw set, I stalked inside behind Tony.

There were a few other wolves lounging in the living room of the house. The place smelled like stale cigarettes, weed, and so many wolves that it was impossible to pick out any other scent.

Connor jumped up at the sight of me, immediately removing his shirt and offering it to me.

This was different than Gracie's smug offer of a towel. As a male wolf, Connor couldn't really compete with me, so I took the shirt and shrugged it on.

"Sara? What are you doing here?" His face went pale. "Is Savannah all right?"

I gave him a cold look. "I'm here for my mate."

Sprawled on the couch nearby was Maynard. He gestured at his body and winked at me. "Here I am, baby doll."

I ignored him, sniffing the air for Ramsey's scent. The smell of wolves and weed was too thick to pinpoint anything else.

Tony moved past and slapped my ass, and I jumped in surprise, then glared at him. He was trying to unnerve me, make me doubt myself.

Connor shook his head. "I don't understand. Why would Ramsey be here?"

"Ask your cousins," I said. Either Connor was playing stupid or he wasn't being included in the games of the others. I didn't know which one it was—Gracie turned on a dime, after all.

But Connor gave me an uneasy look and raced for the stairs.

"Now, boy," I heard Maynard call after him, teasing. "We didn't tell you 'cause you know how you get. Can't have you fucking *all* the captives . . ."

My heart raced and I followed him as he stomped up the narrow stairs. "Uncle Levi? Levi! Where are you!"

He tried the first door, which led to an empty room. He tried the next door, and I tried the one opposite. The room I stared into was empty, filth and leaves scattered on the floor. This had obviously been a nesting ground for the wolves for years.

Across the hall, Connor groaned and disappeared into one of the rooms. Heart pounding, I followed him in . . . and gasped.

Ramsey lay on a filthy mattress on the floor. Dried blood crusted his nose, and a massive bruise shone at one of his temples. His feet were manacled together, the chain hooked to a support beam in the wall.

He didn't stir as Connor stood over him, fists clenching. My heart slammed in my throat at the sight. Oh, Ramsey.

"Levi!" Connor called again.

I crouched next to Ramsey, an enormous knot in my throat. Oh, God. Oh, God. My fingers fluttered over his face, smoothing his hair back so I could see the damage. He was pale, his skin with an odd cast to it. I brushed my fingers over his face . . . he was warm. Too warm. I lay my cheek against his chest, and his heart seemed to be pounding unnaturally fast. His breathing was rapid, and underneath his eyelids, his pupils darted as if stuck in a nightmare.

"Ramsey," I said softly, brushing my fingers over his cheek. "Ramsey, wake up."

He didn't answer—his body didn't respond to my touch. Fear washed over me, and I looked up at Connor. "What's wrong with him?"

"Drugged," he said thickly.

"Actually, he's poisoned," Levi said from the doorway, slouched casually against the frame.

I turned with a snarl, my teeth baring automatically as I placed myself between Levi and my mate. "You *poisoned* him?"

The leader of the wolves was sporting a black eye himself. His mouth drew up in a smirk at the sight of me, crouching in nothing but Connor's T-shirt. "I don't know if you noticed, but bears have incredible stamina." He leered at me. "Though you probably already guessed that. Your boy here wouldn't stay under with tranqs, so we gave him a little something extra."

My fingers curled and I could practically feel my claws coming out again. "What did you give him?"

Levi continued to study me. "Family secret. As in, only members of the pack get to know."

"I'm in your pack," I said bitterly. "Remember?"

"Are you, girl?" His gaze seared into mine. "Because saying you're in the pack and actually *being* in the pack are two different things."

I bared my teeth at him. "I said I was pack."

"You're not," he snarled. "Do you run with the pack? Do you hunt with us? Do you mate with us? Those are the things a wolf female does with her pack. And since you haven't done any of those things, you're still an outsider, aren't you?"

I wanted to *kill* him. Rip his throat out with my bare teeth and watch him bleed out on the floor. Rage consumed me, and I clenched my fists, ignoring the bite of my claws into my palms. "Give me the antidote to the poison."

He continued to stare at me with those hateful yellow eyes. "Pack secret. You can have it . . . for a price."

"What do you want from me?"

His eyes gleamed. "Same thing we've always wanted from you, baby doll. You need to join the pack."

Hunt with us. Run with us. Mate with us. That's what a pack female does.

I bit the inside of my cheek. I wanted to scream my outrage, but I couldn't. I needed to know what was wrong with Ramsey.

"Fine," I bit out. "I'll join your pack."

"In all ways?" Levi led on, raising an eyebrow. "Be a shame to get the boys' hopes up for nothing."

"In all ways," I gritted, ignoring the tremor of fear that passed through my body.

"This is wrong," Connor said, stepping in front of me. "Uncle Levi, you know this is wrong."

Levi shoved Connor aside. "Why's it wrong, boy? Because you don't want to fuck this one? This is about your *pack*. We need a female. A mate for Maynard so he can take over the pack when I step down. Mating ain't about a girl you want to stick your dick in, boy. It's about the blood. It's about making sure there are more wolves to keep the bloodlines strong. You need to stand down." He glared into Connor's eyes, his voice hard. "Or are you challenging me?"

I sucked in a breath. There was a long moment of silence, and then Connor shook his head. "No. No challenge."

"Good." Levi gripped Connor by the arm and threw him aside. Connor crashed into the wall and waited, crouching low, his face averted, flushed with anger. Levi approached me, that smug smile on his face. "Let's take our newest family member out for a run, shall we? Break her in nice and easy."

I stood still, though the will of the alpha was so overwhelming that it took the effort of every muscle in my body to do so. "I want the poison antidote first."

He reached out and snarled his hand in my hair, pulling me close. His yellow eyes ate up my vision until all I could see was them. "You don't get to make demands," he told me softly. "I'm the alpha."

And I found I could not disagree.

Levi stood, and I watched the others look over at him with a look of hungry anticipation. "Who's hungry?"

A low chorus of affirmative, happy growls met his question.

"Time for a dinner hunt, then," Levi said, his eyes more yellow than ever. "I'm in the mood for some fresh, bloody rabbit."

I hated that my stomach growled.

Wyatt and Tony looked over at me and grinned.

They all stood and began to strip off their clothing. I watched as Maynard was the first to drop to all fours, transforming. The others followed suit just as quickly. I longed to go upstairs and check on Ramsey, but as long as he was chained to the wall, I needed to play along. So I stripped off Connor's shirt and bent to change as well.

My change took longer than the others. When they raced out of the house, howling with excitement, I was only half-transformed. Out of the corner of my eye, I saw Levi had waited for me, as well as Connor. I continued my shift to wolf and was relieved when everything slid into place smoothly.

Once I was wolfen, Levi nipped at my flank, herding me in line, and I fell into place behind him. It felt natural to fall in behind the alpha, to race through the woods. The human part of me was screaming to run for help—to get Beau and the others. But if I left Ramsey, what would happen to him? He was helpless. And if I ran, they'd just hunt me again. They'd made it quite clear that I wasn't allowed to leave.

Why keep fighting it, if it put my life and the lives of those I loved in danger? Better to just give in. I would never win, and I was tired of fighting.

Ramsey's life was in danger, and I wouldn't let him die because of me.

I joined the wolves, and we took off into the underbrush. The air was crisp with oncoming night, and the smells of the earth were all around me, in my nostrils and influencing my wolf side, making my mind wild with the scents and sounds of dusk.

As we raced, the other wolves ran into me, nipped at my flanks and danced circles around me. They were feeling playful, a sensation I couldn't share.

The scent of a rabbit crossed our path, and Levi turned and bolted after it. The pack followed, all eagerly chasing the same goddamn rabbit. I followed as well, lest I earn another nip to my flanks if I fell back. The chase went on, but the rabbit was doomed. Within a short time, it was tracked, attacked, and then the wolves fell back as Levi dismembered his kill. We'd get a taste if he deigned to leave us anything. That suited me just fine. I didn't want any of it. That rabbit reminded me of myself a little too much right now.

Maynard circled around my flanks and I turned slightly, baring my teeth in the anticipation of another nip. His leg moved over mine. Confused, I sidestepped only to have him nip my flank again, and then push at my hips again, trying to get over me.

He was trying to mount me!

I tried to scream, but nothing came out of my

throat but a whine. He pushed against me again, and when I tried to scuttle away, Wyatt's wolf form was suddenly there, trapping me in.

Run with us. Mate with us.

I was suddenly furious. I snarled and bit at Maynard when he tried to mount me again. He growled low and pushed at me, and this time his nip wasn't quite so gentle. It was a warning instead.

I attacked him, flinging myself at him in fury, jaws snapping. I bit at his face, and he yelped in surprise.

A large, heavy form slammed into me, and it was my turn to yelp. Suddenly the forest was alive with fighting wolves, and we swarmed over one another, biting, kicking, and snarling. I tore at throats and felt teeth claw at mine. Something bit my hind leg and I yelped in pain, then another attacked me and I flew backward.

A hand grasped me by the scruff, and I snarled, snapping at the hand. "Change back, girl." Levi stared down at me.

I snapped at his hand.

His fist plowed into my muzzle. I yelped, and when he flung me to the ground, I stayed there. My muscles shivered and then I began to change back, the transformation grating but swift.

A few moments later, I crouched on my hind legs. I had a massive bite on my thigh and wiped blood from my mouth, now swollen and throbbing from Levi's hit. Around me the others were changing, and I noticed that Maynard and Tony were both changing back with erections.

"What the fuck is wrong with you?" Levi said, striding over to me and grabbing me by my hair.

I lashed my arms out at him, striking. "I will run with you, but I'm not going to let your wolves mount me."

He bared his teeth, the human version of a wolf snarl. "If my boys want to mate with you, you're gonna sit there and smile while they do it, you dumb little bitch."

My fist slammed into his mouth.

The clearing grew quiet, the only sound my own harsh breathing. Levi dropped me and I clutched at my throbbing scalp, waiting for him to do something.

He touched the corner of his mouth. "Did you . . . did you just challenge me, baby doll?"

I trembled with fear and outrage, but I held my ground. "I'm not your fucking baby doll. I'm not your plaything, and I'm not the mate of your sons. I may be wolf, but that doesn't mean I belong to you."

He stared at me, amazed. "That *is* a challenge, isn't it?"

I said nothing.

He sprang at me, knocking me to the ground. The earth slammed against my back and the wind flew from my lungs. I gasped, trying to suck in breath, but his fist plowed into my face again. Stars exploded behind my eyes.

"No girl challenges the alpha, you stupid little bitch," he snarled, grabbing me by my hair again. "I'm gonna teach you a lesson about wolf packs. First rule is that when the alpha tells you to do something, you do it, and you show your throat while you do it."

I shoved my hands at his face, clawing.

"Daddy," Gracie said off to the side, uncertainly. "She's just new. Cut her a little slack—"

"You telling me what to do, girl?" He turned feral yellow eyes on her.

Gracie shrank back, giving me a worried look. I felt a surge of gratitude at the help, even if she hadn't been strong enough to stand up to her father.

He flung me down to the ground and I felt my ribs creak in protest, the air slamming out of me a second time. I crawled backward as he began to stalk toward me, the wolves milling nervously behind him.

"Let me teach you another lesson about wolf packs, baby doll," he sneered. "You *always* submit to the alpha."

With that, he grabbed my legs. I kicked at him, but his strong hands grasped one of my ankles and yanked it apart from the other. He knelt between my legs.

My scrambling hands clasped a rock, and I slammed it into his jaw.

The crack of it echoed through the clearing. It would have been enough to fell a regular man. The supe over me blinked, and swayed.

Crack! I slammed it into his jaw again.

He toppled, falling backward onto the forest floor. I scrambled to my feet, panting hard, and shoved my foot against his throat. He wasn't quite out cold—but he was dazed, his jaw bloody.

With my foot, I pushed all of my weight down on his throat. "Show your throat to your new alpha," I hissed. "Bitch."

Chapter Nineteen

There was a long, long moment of silence.

Then Maynard began to snarl. Tony began to snarl. Wyatt began to snarl. My skin prickled as they stared at me standing over their fallen alpha.

They were snarls of anger . . . and snarls of challenge. The others hovered nearby, uncertain. Connor's eyes were shining, but his expression was blank. Gracie looked dismayed.

My heart thudded in my throat. I'd taken Levi by the skin of my teeth, but there was no way I'd be able to beat the others if they all lined up to challenge me.

"I don't want to lead," I panted, throwing down the rock. "I just want Ramsey."

"You challenged. You won," Maynard snarled, stepping forward. "Now you gotta keep it . . . until one of us takes it from you."

"No," I breathed, taking a step backward.

Before Maynard could pounce at me, Connor shoved him aside and crouched low, his yellow eyes focused on me. "I challenge her first."

I blinked at him in surprise. I had thought Connor was on my side.

He gave me a meaningful look, then bared his teeth in a snarl and sprang on me.

I barely had time to suck in a breath before he'd pounced on me, and we rolled to the dirt, clawing at each other. He was all hard muscle and sinewy strength, and I shoved my hands at his face as he twisted a hand around my waist, trying to grasp me and flip me to the ground. His arm snaked around my throat and he locked me against him. I struggled hard.

"Make it look good," he whispered against my ear. "Don't give in too easy."

Then he bit me, sinking his teeth into my ear. I screeched in outrage, digging my fingers into his gut, and I was pleased at his grunt of pain. We tumbled to the ground again, clawing and fighting, and when my gaze met his again, he widened his eyes a little to let me know that he was pulling his punches. I openhanded slapped him across the face. I was going to make this look good, all right.

We rolled again, his nails gouging a long scratch across my face. "Sorry," he hissed even as we rolled again and I desperately tried to get the upper hand.

My weight was no match for him, though. His foot connected with my belly, and he kicked me off of him with such force that I flew through the air, slammed into a nearby tree with a crack, and then fell to the ground, unconscious.

I awoke in a blur of pain a short time later. I sat up, shaking my head, focusing my gaze on the clearing. Maynard nursed a black eye and a swollen jaw against a nearby tree, his body covered in dirt and scratches. Tony squatted next to him in the same condition. Ditto Wyatt. In the center of the clearing, Connor pounded his fist into Levi's face—Levi had apparently awoken and decided to challenge for leadership once more.

It was clear that young, strong Connor was holding the alpha position quite firmly. I glanced over at the other watchers, who didn't seem like they were going to challenge.

As I stood up on wobbly, aching legs, Levi raised a hand and bared his throat, yielding to Connor. The older man's jaw was set with anger, but his hand trembled. The beating he'd taken was enough. Breathing hard, Connor hauled himself to his feet and looked around the clearing, baring his teeth. "Anyone else?"

Silence.

"Anyone?" he demanded, the sound almost feral. I felt the overwhelming urge to drop to my knees and whine for mercy, so the alpha thing must have been kicking in.

He gave a firm nod and straightened, wiping away the blood on his lip. He glanced over at me, then at Levi. "Uncle, you're going to give Sara the key to Ramsey's manacles."

"And the poison," I said quickly, thinking of Ramsey. "I want the antidote."

"We'll get it for you." Connor turned his angry gaze back on the pack. "She gets to leave with him, and no one's going to fuck with them." He turned to Maynard and Tony. "Especially not you two. Find your own goddamn mates. You don't have to steal someone else's."

"Like you found that little cougar," Maynard sneered, then flinched when Connor turned the force of his gaze on him.

"If that cougar will have me, yes," Connor said. "I don't care if she's a cat or a rat or a goddamn snake. If I want her to be my mate and she wants to be my mate, there's not a damn thing you or anyone else will do about it. Understand me?"

No one said a thing.

"And we're going to join that goddamn Alliance and we're going to act like fucking humans, not like animals just because we don't agree with someone. Our days of terrorizing others are over. I'm tired of wolves being synonymous with bullies. We're better than that, and we all know it."

He looked over at me. "If you want to run with this pack, Sara, you are always welcome here. You and your mate."

It would take a lot of trust and time before I could believe that, but I nodded. "Thank you."

"Now let's get you back to him," he said. "We haven't got much time."

When we got back to the house, I dashed up to Ramsey's room. He was pale and sweating, and his heart thrummed even more rapidly than before.

Tears brimmed in my eyes. "Where's that anti-dote?"

Gracie showed up with the keys a minute later and gave me an awkward smile. "I'm sorry, Sara. You know how it is with the pack. We have to obey our elders."

I said nothing. Until Gracie showed a real heart and not just whatever the pack told her, we'd never be friends.

She unlocked his manacles and said, "I'll get Connor."

When Ramsey awoke I was by his bedside, holding his hand. I stroked the sweaty locks of hair from his forehead tenderly, my heart unknotting a little at the sight of his eyes opening.

"Hey," I said softly.

He looked over at me, and his mouth firmed into a hard frown. "You're hurt."

My jaw was sore and bruised, but it was nothing that wouldn't heal. "I'm all right. How are *you* feeling?"

He struggled to sit up.

"Take it easy," I said. "You're probably a little woozy." From what Connor had told me, the cure was almost as bad as the poison.

A low growl started in his throat. Alarmed, I placed a hand on his chest. He surged past me, and with a snarl, he lunged for Connor. I hadn't realized he'd been standing in the doorway.

"You . . . threatened my mate . . ." His big hands closed around Connor's neck. To my surprise, Connor didn't fight back at all. He gave me a helpless look, as if pleading with me that he didn't want to answer Ramsey's challenge.

"Ramsey, love," I said, putting my hands over his and prying at them. "It's okay."

"Fucking . . . bastards. Going to kill them all for hurting you."

"Ramsey, it's *okay*. Levi and Maynard were behind everything. Connor defended me. He's taken over the pack."

It took a moment for my words to sink in. He slowly unwrapped his fingers from Connor's neck and then turned to me, listing heavily. He reached for my cheek, and I could have wept at the look on his face. "You're . . ."

"I'm all right," I said softly. "The pack isn't going to bother us anymore."

"I don't believe you," he rasped, his throat dry.

"I don't blame you," Connor said, his voice harsh. "That's twice now that my kind has attacked and injured your kind. We can't make it right in a day, but we can make a start." He looked over at me. "And we're going to start with meeting with the Alliance."

Well, technically, we started with getting Ramsey home. He was exhausted and weak, and every time he saw one of the other wolves, he'd start snarling, anger burning through him. It took a while for Connor and me to half drag, half carry his big body through the woods, but we made it to Connor's car, and he drove us back to where Ramsey's truck had been abandoned.

"I'll meet you tomorrow morning," Connor said. "Alliance and pack meeting. There, we'll decide what to do with Maynard and Levi. As long as they're here, they're going to keep breaking the rules we've established. I can't have that if we're to bring the pack to any sort of order." He said the words heavily, suddenly looking much older.

"What did you have in mind?" Ramsey said wearily.

"Ritual execution?" I said cheerfully.

"I don't know if that'd be such a good idea," Connor said.

"I do," I muttered. "And you know as well as I do that the Russells aren't going to be happy with a slap on the hand and a warning. Neither am I. They attacked my mate."

And that, I wouldn't forgive.

When we got into Ramsey's car, he stripped off his T-shirt. To my surprise, he tugged me close and pulled it over my head.

I'd forgotten I was naked.

"Where are your clothes?" he asked me.

"Probably back at the gas station." A hysterical laugh bubbled out of me, a mixture of relief and absurdity.

He hugged me against him, plastering my body

to his. The steering wheel bit into my back, but I didn't care—I breathed in his scent, sweaty and faintly medicinal from the antidote. He smelled so familiar and wonderful that I wanted to suddenly weep. The laughter died in my throat, and I snuggled in as he tucked me close against his arm and wrapped his arms around me.

"Did they hurt you?" he asked quietly. "Tell me the truth. If they hurt one hair on your head, I'll go in there and break every single one of their necks."

"They tried," I admitted softly. "I fought back, and I think that Maynard and Levi didn't know how to handle that."

The rumble in his chest was low and approving. "So I only need to snap two necks."

"No," I said softly. "You just need to hold me for a bit longer. We'll let someone else take care of the details."

His grip on me tightened and he pressed a fierce kiss to my shoulder. "You were all I could think about," he said roughly. "When they attacked me, when they drugged me, I fought. I kept fighting because all I could think about was how I was leaving you unprotected. It drove me insane. I thought I would die if anything happened to you. I would never leave you—ever. You know that, right?"

My hand moved down his chest, and I pressed against his heart. I could feel the slow, steady beat of it, his muscles tensing with emotion even as he cradled me close, and knew he was moments away from turning right back around, going into that house, and making the others sorry they were ever born. So I stroked my hands over his body to soothe him and pressed a kiss to his neck.

"I'm free of them, Ramsey. I fought back when they tried to cow me and make me step into place. I fought back and I *won*. They can't try and force me to obey anymore. Connor's in charge now, and things will be different."

"Until the next alpha comes along and tries to think you're his," he said darkly.

"I don't think so," I said thoughtfully. "It's hard to explain, but . . . I'm not scared anymore. Not of the wolves or what they can do to me. When I was frightened, I was frightened for *you* and what they'd do to you. And I realized that I didn't have to be afraid anymore. There's a strong core inside me that I've found and they can't take away." I knew now that if shit hit the fan, I could take care of myself, and I would. I was no longer the scared rabbit but the wolf.

I was my own alpha. It was a feeling I liked.

I smiled, then leaned in and kissed his neck again. I'd never get used to the wonderful taste of him. I wanted to lick him all over and eat him up. I wanted to crawl inside his skin and never come out again. He captured my mouth in a searing kiss.

"I love you," I breathed against his mouth when we pulled apart.

"I love you, Sara." His fingers brushed over the bruise on my cheek. "But if we don't drive away soon, I might have to go back in there and crush some skulls."

I slid out of his lap and onto the passenger seat. "Then take me home."

Ramsey went instead to Midnight Liaisons, where Beau and my sister were armed with shotguns, and Russells were preparing to send a posse out to the Andersons. We quickly explained what had happened and arranged the meet-up with the wolf pack in the morning.

My sister hugged me and demanded that I sit and let my wounds be taken care of, and an extra set of clothing (I always kept a spare at the office) was dragged out for me. I didn't mind my sister's fussing—I knew it was her way of coping with stress—but as soon as I was dressed and covered in Band-Aids, I returned to Ramsey's side.

When he saw me, he extended his hand, inviting me to return to him.

I always, always would.

After a long, tense morning meeting, the wolf pack and Alliance came to an agreement: Maynard and Levi would be exiled.

"This is a joke," Maynard sneered. "Exile?"

"Exile," Connor said firmly.

"What for? For following pack law?" Levi looked belligerent, crossing his arms over his chest.

"Pack law has nothing to do with this," Beau said, looming menacingly over both seated men. "You're also part human, and human law condemns kidnapping, attempted rape, and assault. You're lucky you're getting away with just exile."

"Exile," Levi said in a dull voice. "From pack territory?"

"From both pack and Alliance territory."

"How far does that spread?" Maynard asked with a frown.

"Lower forty-eight," Beau said, and I had to admit that I felt a little gleeful at the shocked looks on the Anderson faces. "And most of Canada."

"If you return to this territory, your life is forfeit. You'll be fair game for anyone. My suggestion is that you explore your Alaskan roots, Uncle Levi." Connor turned his hard-eyed gaze to the other wolves in attendance—the remnants of his new pack. "That goes for anyone else that thinks that they cannot follow both human and pack law."

No one spoke up. I was pretty impressed. I hadn't been sure if Connor was strong enough to hold the alpha position initially, but overnight he'd seemed to become a new man—strong, confident. Perhaps he'd found his inner core as well.

As the assembly scattered, I moved through the crowd to find the massive man who stood head and shoulders above the rest—in all ways. He'd been guarding the door, ever the protector.

Gracie stopped me on the way. "Hey, Sara . . . I just . . ." She fidgeted. "I just wanted to say I'm sorry. I never really thought about what we were doing."

I said nothing. This didn't sound quite like an apology.

Gracie squirmed under my stare. "I just . . . I wanted to let you know that we're turning over a new leaf, and that includes me. And I wanted to let you know that I really enjoyed helping with the agency, and I wanted to keep my record updated. I liked dating all those men," she said shyly. "I don't get to do a lot of dating in the wolf pack. And if you ever have a job at the agency, well, please think of me."

I blinked in surprise. "We'll keep you in mind," I said politely.

Gracie smiled. "I'm glad. I know you can't trust me, but maybe in a while, if I've been a good girl."

She looked like she was anxious to please me. Uncertainty over her new pack status? I patted her shoulder and slipped away before she could say anything else.

As I approached Ramsey, I overheard Beau and Connor talking.

"Will she ever forgive me?" Connor was saying.

Beau put his hand on Connor's shoulder. "Forgiveness takes time. This is a step in the right direction, though. Give her time to learn to trust, and maybe she'll come around. But if she doesn't . . ."

"Then it's no one's fault but my own," Connor said grimly. "We have a lot to make up for."

I couldn't disagree with that.

Beau gave him a friendly smile. "Well, you're still invited to my wedding. I think the more the pack spends time with the Alliance, the more they'll see that it's not such a bad thing to be a part of."

A large hand dropped over my shoulder and a familiar scent enveloped me. I leaned in to Ramsey's kiss as his mouth brushed my hair.

"Are you satisfied with the outcome?" he asked, his voice low to ensure that only I heard him.

"And if I'm not?"

"I'd snap every neck in this room to bring a smile to your face."

"That is the sweetest, most bloodthirsty thing anyone's said to me."

He grunted. "It's the truth."

"Which makes it even sweeter. I'm satisfied," I said. "It'll take some time before I can fully trust the wolf pack, but I trust Connor to do the right thing."

"And why is that?"

I looked at the determined expression of the new pack alpha. "Because he wants Savannah back, and he'll do whatever it takes."

Ramsey was still fatigued after his poisoning, and I wasn't in top shape either, thanks to my ordeal. We'd gone home early after promising Beau that we'd stop by for lunch the next day. My sister was back to planning her wedding, and I'd gladly volunteered to help.

When we got to the house, I regarded the re-painted porch, the repaired roof, the fresh lumber, and new windows. Ramsey had done all this to provide me with a safe home, and it felt odd to return and not have a wolf or a Russell tailing us. It was just the two of us.

A rush of uncertainty hit me. Did I know for sure this relationship of ours was *his* choosing?

He moved beside me and gave me an odd look. "What?"

"It's just . . ." I fiddled with the hem of my T-shirt. "For years you've dreamed about rejoining the bear clan. Are you sure you don't want to—"

He scowled at me. "You've got to be kidding."

I bristled at that. "I'm *not* kidding. You've had all your choices taken from you by me. I just want you to know that if you want to go back, I'm okay with that—"

"I'm here because I want to be."

"But you were forced—"

He shook his head. "I volunteered. I told Beau I wanted to watch over you. From the moment I saw you, I thought you were amazing."

I stared up at him in shock. The weeks I'd spent with the Russells, he'd had feelings for me? I'd had no idea. "You did?"

"Here you were, this tiny, beautiful little human, snarling with fear. You were surrounded by shifters and strangers, and trying to hide in plain sight." His mouth quirked. "While pretending you weren't hiding. I liked that. You were fascinating. I wanted you, even then."

My heart melted into a big puddle of goo. "But . . . your clan . . ."

"Exiled me years ago for my friendship with

Beau. Like the wolves, the bears don't consort with outside shifters. I think it makes them weaker. I won't miss them. My family is here."

"And am I your family?"

His dark eyes stared down at me hotly. "You are my mate. My reason for living. I would do anything for you."

Now I really was going to melt into a puddle. I trailed my fingers up his shirt. "Then would you do me a favor?"

"Anything."

My fingers grazed one of his nipples through the fabric of his shirt, and I heard the sharp intake of his breath. "I was wondering if you would demonstrate this amazing bear shifter stamina I keep hearing so much about . . ."

He grabbed me by the waist and pulled me against him, and I wrapped my limbs around him. My mouth met his, my tongue brushing against his.

He groaned with need and we stumbled toward the house. I loved the taste of him, loved the taste of his mouth, the way his tongue moved against mine. Each flick of it sent a surge of liquid heat straight to my apex, and by the time we managed to slam the door shut, I was whimpering with need. I needed him deep inside me, and I told him that, whispering naughty words against his mouth.

His breath hissed from his throat, and he pulled away from my hungrily seeking mouth, staring at me with passion-glazed eyes. "Couch?"

"Couch," I breathed, agreeing.

In two seconds flat, I was down on the couch and he was undoing the button on my jeans. My fingers fumbled with his, and as soon as the button was free, he tugged the jeans off of me and down my legs. As soon as I'd divested myself of my shirt, I wiggled to help, tugging at his clothes even as he undressed me. "Take this off. I want to feel your skin against mine."

He growled low in his throat, a sound of pleasure, and then he bent over me, his massive form covering mine. I felt his lightly furred chest brush against my nipples. They stiffened into hard points, and I deliberately pushed them against his chest. "Bite me, Ramsey."

He groaned low in his throat and leaned down to take one aching nipple in his mouth. I felt the scrape of his teeth against the peak and gasped at the intense flare of pleasure/pain. My fingers slid to his nipples, flicking them in response, then trailed down his stomach. I felt the head of his cock brush against my fingers, and I curled them around it. So big and hard, the tip already slick.

He nipped my nipple again and then nuzzled it, teasing the point with his tongue. Each sweep of it over the tip made my sex clench, and I wanted him so fast and hard that I dug my fingers into his skin. "How's your stamina?"

A harder bite on my aching nipple was his response, and I nearly came off the couch. "First time . . . not gonna be a long time."

"That's okay," I breathed. "We'll get it right on the second try."

"Or the third," he agreed.

I dug my fingers into his hair, reveling in the feel of his body against mine. "I won't count if you won't."

"Deal," he growled, and pulled me closer.

Epilogue

I dyed my hair a cheery hot pink for my sister's
wedding. It went well with the peacock-green,
taffeta minidress she'd picked out for her brides-
maids. Marie, Ryder, and I held small bouquets of
pale roses as we stood in a line up the steps of the
chapel. I'd promised myself I wouldn't cry at the
sight of my sister in her wedding dress, but I started
weeping as soon as the music keyed up.

Bathsheba arrived at the base of the steps in her
wedding dress, her face radiant and utterly gorgeous. Her long, pale-blond hair had been left loose,
and a small circlet headband anchored the veil cas-
cading down her back. Her dress was beautiful,
with a creamy white sweetheart bodice of thick satin
and a flowing organza princess skirt. She looked like
something out of a fairy tale, and her face glowed
with happiness. We preceded her into the church
and down the aisle, her gaze on Beau the entire time
as she placed her hand in his and they turned to the
preacher to begin the ceremony.

Across the aisle, Ramsey shifted uncomfortably

in his tuxedo. He hated it when I cried. I gave him a watery smile and turned my attention back to the ceremony.

It was lovely and brief, and before long, Bath and Beau endured the rounds of photos and well-wishes, and then were racing out of the chapel to a rain of birdseed.

I sidled up to Ramsey, still clutching my bouquet. He looked so tall and handsome in his tuxedo. "Hey there, hot stuff. I like the tux."

He yanked at the collar. "I don't."

I straightened his lapels, giving him a possessive look. I could see the bites I'd left on his neck, and it made me want to drag him somewhere private and do dirty things to him. "You look delicious. I want to climb you like a monkey."

His mouth twitched at the corner, a sure sign that he was fighting a smile.

I leaned in closer, encouraged. "And then make sweet monkey love to you."

Someone coughed behind us, and Ramsey's ears turned bright red as Joshua and Ellis Russell sauntered past with a laugh.

"Climb the monkey bars later," Joshua teased as he walked out of the chapel. "Time for the reception first."

My hand in Ramsey's, we went to the door just in time to watch Bathsheba and Beau get into the back of the rented limo. Beau's hand slid around my sister's waist, pulling her into his lap, and they were kissing madly by the time someone shut the door. "Looks like my sister is Bathsheba Russell now," I said with a watery sniff. "She looks so beautiful."

Ramsey pulled out his peacock-green handkerchief and handed it to me. "You're supposed to be happy."

"I *am* happy," I told him. "That's why I'm crying."

He gave me a skeptical look, and then leaned in close. "Do you need a few minutes alone with your Huggy Bear?"

I threw my bouquet aside, wrapping my arms around his neck. "God, it is so sexy when you say your pet name like that." I kissed him, hard, feeling the need to brand him as my own. When someone coughed politely behind us, I broke the kiss off. "Where's private around here?"

"My truck's pretty private," Ramsey said and hauled me up against him as we headed out to the parking lot.

We showed up at the reception about a half hour later, just a little disheveled. My sister was on the dance floor with Jeremiah Russell, laughing and blushing as the other Russell brothers tried to pin dollars onto her bodice. The band—a were-badger family—played cheerful, up-tempo songs, and the reception hall was packed with Alliance supernaturals. The heavy scents of tiger, badger, cougar, jaguar, mink, fox, and just about everything else I could think of were thick. I even caught the scent of the fey. Ryder and Marie stood in one corner, looking like they felt awkward being the only humans in a room full of supes.

I pushed a lock of my pink hair back behind my ear and looked up at Ramsey. "Want to dance?"

"No?" he said hopefully.

I laughed. "You always say that." I nudged him toward Ryder, who watched the dance floor with a bit of longing. "Go dance with her. No one's approaching them because they're human. If you dance with one of them, that'll make it okay."

With a heavy sigh, Ramsey crossed the room, and I watched Ryder break into a smile as he led her out on the dance floor. I went over to keep Marie company. "How's it going?"

Marie gave me a wan smile. "The wedding's lovely."

"You feeling okay?"

She nodded a bit too quickly. "Just a migraine. It'll go away soon."

Joshua Russell sauntered over, all cocky smiles and broad shoulders. His normally mussed brown hair had been combed down, and his signature baseball cap was nowhere in sight. He looked handsome, and he also looked as if he knew it. He swaggered over to Marie and leaned against the wall, looming over her.

"Hey, kitten. You ever had a wildcat in your bed?"

She rolled her eyes. "Does that line ever work on anyone?"

"Only needs to work once." Joshua grinned down at her. "How about it?"

"How about you go find some nice were-raccoon to harass," Marie said smoothly. "I have a headache."

He just winked and pushed himself off the wall. "Okay, but don't come crying to me later when you're jealous of all the ladies hanging on my every word."

"If that scenario ever comes to pass, I'll try not to weep too loudly," she said dryly.

Joshua headed off, a swagger in his step, as if he hadn't just been turned down by a human. My amusement faded when Marie sat down heavily, as if all the strength had drained from her body.

This wasn't the first time Marie hadn't been feeling well lately. I gave her a concerned look, but she wore a determined smile, watching Ryder dance a flirtatious cha-cha around my man, who looked as if he'd like to run away. "You sure you're okay?"

"I'm fine," she repeated, then nodded at the far side of the room. "Look over there."

At the back of the room, Connor and Savannah sat next to each other, heads bent together. Neither was touching the other, but the fact that they were talking was a good start. I crossed my fingers behind my back for him and sat next to Marie to keep her company.

The wedding reception was a lively event, and my sister was the belle of the ball. I danced a few times but was mostly content to watch her enjoying herself. She didn't leave the dance floor, and whenever a slow song came on, Beau muscled his way in with a possessive look on his face, and I watched my sister melt. It made me teary-eyed all over again.

As a slow song played, Ramsey showed up at my side and extended his hand. Waiting for me, always there to take my hand. My heart swelled with love, and I placed my hand in his, letting him lead me out onto the dance floor. I could stay in his arms forever.

When the reception began to wind down, a cheer went up from the crowd as a chair was brought forward. Bathsheba, blushing furiously, lowered her garter and Beau tossed it into the air, where it was caught by Joshua. He grinned and tucked it into his pocket while his brothers elbowed him with glee.

Ryder rushed forward with the bouquet, and Bath moved to the center of the dance floor and turned her back to the crowd. Women began to gather behind her.

Marie nudged me. "You going to go catch it?"

I interlocked my fingers with Ramsey's and leaned back against him, quite content where I was. "I'm good."

Marie wasn't rushing forward, either. She sat next to us, and I noticed her hands were shaking slightly. She looked a bit pale.

At the front of the room, Bathsheba laughed. "Everybody ready?" She did a fake throw, and then peeked over her shoulder. "On the count of three, then. One, two . . ."

The bouquet sailed through the air. All eyes

turned to it, and as I watched, women flung themselves forward to try and grab at it. . . .

Only to have it sail over their heads and land directly into Marie's lap.

Marie stared at it with horror. "You've got to be kidding me."

*Turn the page for a special look
at the next tantalizing novel
in the Midnight Liaisons series
from Jessica Sims*

Coming Summer 2013 from Pocket Books

*T*here was a time that I'd have been excited about going out to a late-night dinner with a gorgeous man. A time when, if he put his hand on the small of my back to guide me down the sidewalk, I'd have shivered with delight. Tonight? I had a handsome, gorgeous man with his hand on my back right now, walking at my side, and it just bothered me. I was filled with annoyance and a mild curiosity that I tried to stomp out of existence. What did Josh so arrogantly think he could teach me about dating a male vampire? I was the one that worked at a dating agency, after all.

I strode down the sidewalk, my steps quick and irritated. I tried not to think about Ryder, who was having a bad night, and focused on my situation, since it was a worse night for me. I didn't pause to see if Josh was keeping up with my angry strides, though I could feel his bigger form hovering close and protective. As we walked, I felt his hand press on the small of my back even as he came to my side. I stiffened in response, but he only gestured at a nearby sign. "How about that?"

I eyed the yellow sign with a frown. "A diner?"

He grinned down at me, and I was distracted by how close he was. "Why not? Open all night."

"It just seems so . . ."

"Casual? It's not a date." His hand nudged on my lower back again, directing me toward the restaurant's lit parking lot.

My mouth tightened. Of course it wasn't a date. The creep. Did he think I'd forgotten? "I know it's not a date. You don't have to keep reminding me," I said. "And since you picked, you're paying."

"Why? It's not a date."

I gritted my teeth. "Fine."

We crossed the street and my body was all too aware of the hand that lingered on the small of my back. I could insist that he remove it, but then that would mean acknowledging his body so close to mine and that it was bothering me. So I ignored it the best I could.

When we got inside, the elderly waitress lit up at the sight of Josh. "There's my boy," she crowed in a voice that sounded as if it had smoked too many cigarettes. "How are you, Josh darlin'?"

He strolled forward to give the small, stout woman a bear hug. "I'm pining away with love for you, Carol."

She gave a raspy chuckle and swatted his bottom, then reached up and tugged on the brim of his baseball cap. "You want your usual?"

"You know I do," he said with a grin, then

nodded at me. "I brought a friend. She'll probably want a menu."

The waitress glanced over at me, her nest of overly bleached curls tilting as she studied me. "Fine," she said flatly, then squeezed him in a half hug. "You go pick a table, anywhere. I'll get your food started."

"You're an angel," he said, then looked back at me and gestured. "Come on."

I rolled my eyes and followed him to a curved booth in the far corner of the nearly empty restaurant. When I slid in on one side, Josh began to slide in right next to me. I immediately scooted all the way around to the far side, putting some distance between us.

That just seemed to amuse him, which only made me more irritated.

"I see why you wanted to come here. You get free food every night just because you flirt with the old ladies?"

He smiled. "Not every night, and I don't flirt. They just love me."

As if to prove this point, Carol showed up with two glasses of water and a coffee for Josh. She set it down in front of him and then tugged his cap off his head in a proprietary move that surprised me. She smoothed his hair. "No hats inside, young man."

Josh gave her a rueful smile. "Sorry."

I stared at my companion. He looked even more boyish with his hair sticking up wildly. If it wasn't for the scruff on his face, he would have looked far too young.

"This one's too charming for his own good," Carol said affectionately, chucking Josh's unshaved chin as if she were a doting mother—or grandmother.

"He only thinks he's charming," I pointed out. "He just expects everyone else to think it too."

She chuckled again, that horrible smoker's rasp. "I like this one, Josh."

My face colored in response, which only made Josh grin.

"You want the same thing he's having, honey?" she asked me.

Why not. Anything to get her away from the table and the two of us. "Sure. Thank you."

She put a coffee mug down in front of me and poured it as well, and then left with another smile at Josh. He grinned back at her.

"So that's your schtick?" I said irritably. "Is that your goal in life, to be a charming freeloader?"

"First of all," he said, lifting the coffee cup to his lips. "I pay for everything. Carol doesn't make enough to buy me dinner on a regular basis." He sipped it and grimaced. "Her coffee is shit, though."

But I noticed he still drank it. Maybe telling her would hurt her feelings.

"And second?" I prompted, opening a few sugar packets and dumping them into my own cup.

"I'm not here every night. Carol works four nights a week. Her husband died three years ago and she lives in a small apartment on the bad side of town. It scares her to take the bus, so she tries to get a ride with friends. I stop in to check on her and give her a ride when she needs it."

That was . . . unexpectedly nice of him. "So she's a shifter, then?"

"No," he said. "Just an old woman with no one to look after her. So I do."

I said nothing. Carol swung out of the kitchen with two massive stacks of pancakes and plopped them down in front of us, then dropped a bottle of syrup on the table. I stared at the stack. That was a lot of pancakes.

Josh put a hand over his heart and gave Carol a pleased look. "You make my heart melt with your delicious food, Carol."

She chuckled again. "You flirt. I'll be back with the rest when it comes off the grill. Dig in."

As she left, I eyed the pancake mountain and then looked at Josh. "The rest?"

He leaned in as if sharing a secret. "You ordered the same thing I get, right? Perhaps you didn't realize that shifters eat a lot?"

I admit it hadn't been the first thing on my mind. "So what exactly did I order?"

"Two club sandwiches, a skillet scramble, these pancakes," he said, pointing, "and a steak."

"A freaking steak? With all this? That's revolting."

"Does that mean I get to eat yours?"

"Only if you want to buy it from me," I said,

mashing my fork into the pat of butter on top of the pancake mountain. "That's what I get for trusting a pretty face."

"So you think I'm pretty? Marie, you flirt you."

"*Voyons*. It's a figure of speech, *tabarnak*."

"And more French. You know that's sexy, right?"

"You know I just called you vile things, right?"

"I'm figuring you out. That's how you flirt."

"I hate you."

"More flirting."

I ground my teeth and forced myself not to reply, since he'd consider it practically a declaration of love. Instead, I focused on swamping my pancakes with syrup, and then taking a bite. Delicious. I'd be totally wound up from the sugar and coffee later, but it didn't matter. It wasn't like I could sleep anyhow. I ate a few more bites in companionable silence as Josh cut his pancakes into perfect triangles and ate them without a bit of syrup.

Carol stopped by with the rest of the food by the time I'd eaten three pancakes and was feeling nauseated and full. Josh, meanwhile, had polished off all of his pancakes and was more than ready for the next course. He dug into the sandwiches, scrambled eggs, and steak, and chatted with Carol while I sat quietly. He asked her how her job was going, listening attentively when she complained about a co-worker who was taking all the extra shifts. He asked about her hot water heater, which hadn't been working properly in the last month, and he volunteered to take a look at it, and she turned him down with a wave of her hand. He even asked about her cat. They talked easily for a few more minutes while Josh ate, until Carol left, smiling.

I digested it all in silence. It was clear that Josh knew the woman well and took an interest in her life. That seemed odd to me. Josh was such a playboy, a love-them-and-leave-them type that I hadn't suspected him to be the kind to chat with lonely old women about their cats and whether or not their hot water was working.

There was another side to the incorrigible flirt. Either that or this was all an elaborate ruse to get women to fall into his arms. Take them to a low-key diner, charm them with his relationship with a down-on-her-luck old woman, and then they'd tumble into his bed faster than the speed of light.

Even as I told myself that, it didn't fit.

"So," I said when we were alone again. "You were going to tell me what I'm doing wrong?"

He stopped eating, wiped his mouth with his napkin, and nodded. "But first, I need to know the whole thing. How many vampires have you gone out with?"

I hesitated, wondering if I should tell him everything. It wouldn't matter if I couldn't get a vampire to show up for a date. I had to take my chances with Josh. "I've gone out with three. At least, I *tried* to go out with three. First there was Valjean—"

Josh shook his head immediately. "He's hooked up and left for Europe. You know Ruby Sommers? Pretty little were-jaguar? Sister to Jayde?"

No, I didn't, but it was clear that he knew Jayde pretty intimately. He probably knew all the "pretty little were-jaguars" in town, which made my teeth grit. "I know he's hooked up. Anyhow. Then I went out with Bert."

He laughed. "No way. Seriously? Bert? World of Hurt Bert?"

I wasn't going to have any teeth left if I kept grinding them all night. "He's a vampire, isn't he?"

"Only in the barest sense of the word," Josh said with a grin. "The man's a loser. I can't believe you went out with him."

And he'd told me that I wasn't his type. That stung a bit more right now than it should have. "It was only one date."

He nodded. "Turned you down, didn't he?"

I gaped. "How did you know that?"

"I did a spin of guard duty for Bert last summer. He likes 'em"—he began to gesture, indicating a rather large butt, and then began to jiggle his hands.

"Yes, I know," I hissed, slapping his hands down. "Badonkadonk."

"I was going to say 'big booty ho's,' but that works," he said with a laugh. "Anyhow, that's why he's single. He's selective and the dating pool is kind of lean when it comes to that sort of thing. No pun intended."

I rolled my eyes. "Yes, well, number three turned me down, too. He didn't even show up to our date."

He nodded. "I'm not surprised."

"Why are you not surprised? I am."

"Vampires are sketchy. I don't know if you've noticed, but I make a full-time living out of being a bodyguard to the fanged persuasion."

I eyed the Russell Security T-shirt he wore. It was tightly stretched over his large shoulders, outlining his pectorals and firm stomach. "I noticed. So they're paranoid?"

"To the extreme," he agreed, sipping his coffee again with a grimace. "Vampires are a dog-eat-dog society. You look at someone's blood partner the wrong way and you could find yourself with a contract on your head. You go into someone's territory and set up shop—contract on your head. It's like the mafia, but with fangs. The smart ones lay low or leave town fast."

There was so much that I didn't know about vampires, and I was quickly realizing that Josh could bring into focus some of the fuzzy edges. "So what's a blood partner?"

"A vampire's mate is called a blood partner. Blood partners only drink from each other. And since vampire women are rare, you'll find a lot more single male vampires, since every female that isn't already partnered pretty much has her choice of men."

Interesting. That sounded like it could work in my favor. If vampire females were highly prized, my willingness to become a vampire female would probably be looked upon positively. "So why aren't there many vampire females?"

"Same thing as female shifters, I imagine," he

said in a low voice. "You're marrying into a family that's not exactly the most fun to get along with. And I hear it's quite painful for the victim if the turning doesn't take—or it kills them."

That wasn't a deterrent for me. I was dying anyhow. I had only months before I was going to totally deteriorate, so I'd take my chances on a vampire turning me. The alternative was worse. I rubbed my eyes, feeling suddenly tired. The more I found out about vampires, the less I wanted to become one, but I was low on choices. Very low. "So vampires are skittish and think everyone is out to get them. Is that why my date didn't show up?"

"That's my guess. Either that, or he didn't like the way you looked and had second thoughts."

I scowled. "I look perfectly acceptable."

"You're beautiful," he agreed.

I was momentarily flabbergasted. "I . . . thank you."

"To me," he amended. "Vampires like different things."

Oh, I remembered. Badonkadonk. Still, I felt warm under Josh's flattery. "So what is it about me you'd change?"

He studied me for a long moment, an intense scrutiny that made my cheeks flush. His gaze swept over my face, then my chest, then back over my face again. That knowing, arrogant smile curved his sexy mouth. "I wouldn't change anything."

My cheeks felt like they were on fire.

"But we're not talking about me. You're talking

about hooking a vampire . . . unless you changed your mind and decided you want me instead of a vampire?"

Figured that he'd bring the conversation back around to how sexy he was. I kicked him under the table. "I didn't change my mind. Tell me about what I need to do to get a vampire."

"You girls and your weird vampire fetishes," he said with a shake of his head. "You know dating a vampire's not like it is on TV, right?"

"I'm not stupid."

"No, you're not, but I'm questioning your taste in men." At my glare, he raised a placating hand. "Fine. Let's start with the basics. You went through the agency?"

I said nothing, suddenly nervous. Josh was the brother-in-law of my boss. If she knew that I was using the database for my own personal needs, I'd be fired in a red hot minute. That was a big no no in her eyes, especially since I was human and only a marginal member of the Alliance.

Of course, Bathsheba had dated through the agency herself, once upon a time. Anytime it came up, however, she was quick to explain that it hadn't been her choice—she'd been more or less blackmailed into it to hide the fact that Sara was a werewolf. She didn't want Ryder or me dating through the agency, because the fact that a human had used the service stirred up a real hornet's nest amongst the shifter clans. Some wanted to date humans, but more of them didn't want us contaminating the works. I could understand it, even if it countered my own plans.

Josh sighed at my reluctance. "I'm not going to rat on you, Marie. If I was, would we be here?"

That was the thing. I had no idea. But I supposed I had to trust someone—I was getting nowhere fast on my own, and there wasn't a ton of vampires in the database to experiment with. "I'm in the database. As Minnie Michigo. Were-otter."

The nod of approval came slowly. "Michigo was a good choice. Lots of them in the area."

Strange how flustered I felt when I had his approval. "That's why I picked them. Plus, they're not a bigger predator that could be intimidating."

He nodded again, his expression thoughtful. "Vampires are a bit paranoid. He could have ran a background check and found out that Minnie doesn't exist."

As I watched, he pulled out his phone and began to flip through screens. "What are you doing?" I asked warily.

"Looking up Minnie's profile," he said with a grin. Then he frowned, looking back up at me. "No picture?"

"I send it if they ask for it," I said defensively. "Why should looks matter?"

"Because you're dealing with men," he said bluntly. "Did you send a picture to this last guy? Send it to me."

I had. I hadn't wanted to send one that looked like me, and I'd wanted to make sure to hook him, so I'd simply looked up "sexy girls with glasses and dark hair," picked one that looked kind of like me, and sent him a hopefully enticing picture. I sent the photo to Josh's profile.

His eyes widened. "What the hell is this?"

I crossed my arms over my chest, feeling defensive. "Just a picture I pulled off the internet. I thought it might convey fun and lighthearted silliness." You know, all those things I wasn't. "It's kind of a silly pose but I thought it might look natural."

Josh continued to stare at the picture, and then back at me. "That's not you, right?"

I snorted. "Nope, that's not me. She's putting her fist in her mouth, and I can't do that."

"Marie," he said slowly. "That's not her fist. That's not even *her* body part."

I snatched the phone away from him and studied it for a minute. That definitely wasn't a fist . . . good God. "I . . . oh." A hot flush crept over my face and I quickly handed the phone back to him.

He threw back his head and laughed. "Well, I think I'm beginning to see why date number three was afraid to meet you."

"Shut *up.*"

Josh only grinned at me. He glanced back down at the picture, shook his head, and then clicked his phone off and tossed it on the table. He slouched in the booth, his gaze moving up and down over me.

I internally squirmed at the perusal and grew wary. "What?"

"I see three main problems."

"Well, what are they?"

"You sure you want to know?"

Now he was just torturing me. "Of course I want to know," I said, feeling exasperated. "Would I be sitting here in the middle of the night with you if I didn't?"

He winced and clutched a hand to his chest. Those long-lashed eyes closed dramatically. "Marie, that hurts me. Deeply." His tone was playful, but I got the impression that I had actually hurt his feelings.

"You knew why I was coming here," I said defensively. "Either help me or leave me alone."

"I'll help you, but I have conditions."

I crossed my arms over my chest, glaring at him. "What kind of conditions?"

"If you want to find a vampire, you have to let me help you."

"Isn't that what I'm doing?"

"No," he said. "I mean, *really* help you. You work at a dating agency, right? You help clients make a match." He tapped his chest with a finger, and my gaze went to that tight shirt, straining over his muscled shoulders. "I'm an expert on women."

I snorted. "I'll just bet you are."

Josh tilted his head, as if studying me. "Don't believe that I'm good with women? I think my track record speaks for itself."

"Oh, it says something all right," I said cattily. "It says that you might know how to bait the hook, but I haven't seen anything that tells me that you know how to have a relationship. You never stick around long enough to find out. I know all about you and your legendary dating excursions, Joshua Russell. You like the chase. You get a girl, date her, and then you dump her."

"If we're going to compare fishing to women," he said softly, leaning across the table toward me, how about you let me give it a shot?" His eyes gleamed dangerously.

"Very well. Go ahead."

"I might know how to bait the hook, but I also know how to reel in my catch. If I'm throwing back what I'm getting, it's because I'm after a different sort of fish."

"The one that got away?" I said dryly.

He laughed, and the tension of the moment was gone. "Something like that."

I chewed on my lower lip, feeling suddenly confused. How had this turned from Josh flirting with me to Josh talking about other women? And worse, how had he made his endless string of dates sound so . . . practical? He was fishing and he just threw them back because they weren't what he was looking for. Why did that sound so incredibly reasonable? Was I crazy? Or just falling under his spell? I sighed. "All right, you win this round." Before he could say something smug I quickly added, "But I don't need to know how to catch a woman. I need to know how to catch a *man*."

"No, you need to *be caught* by a vampire. There's

a difference. Both in the vampire and the fact that you're going to be the one that's caught. That's where I come in. I'll help you bag a vampire, but you have to take my advice seriously if this is going to work."

I continued to stare at him across the table, uneasy. He was offering to be my dating guide. It was a generous offer, and yet— "I don't understand you. What are you getting out of this?"

"How about the knowledge that you'll be safe?" His mouth tightened and I found my gaze going there, to a warm, curving mouth framed by a day's growth of stubble. "You're human and you're pretty much approaching every vampire asking them to date you. That's not the safest situation, Marie. Get mixed up with the wrong vampire, and you could be in trouble."

Danger hadn't been on my mind, it was true. I *wanted* someone to turn me; I didn't care about the consequences. I hated that he was making me slow down and think about them. "So this is your knight in shining armor schtick? Like you do with her?" I thumbed a gesture at Carol, currently on the far side of the restaurant, taking an order from a trucker. "You feel the need to chaperone women? Patron saint of lost causes?"

"No," he said bluntly. "This is about me giving you what you think you want. I don't know why on earth you want a vampire, but you're determined to get one. And since you are fixed on this course of action, I'm going to help you." He picked up his coffee cup, realized it was empty, sighed, and put it back down on the table, reaching for mine instead. "I want you to see that you really *don't* want a vampire. They're not like in the movies."

"I'm not that shallow," I said quickly. As he placed his mouth directly over where I'd been drinking, a funny flush went through my body.

"All right. But I think that maybe, if I show you how vampires really are, you'll change your mind." Those gorgeous eyes focused on my face, making my mouth go dry. A slow, lazy grin began to spread over his face as he drained my coffee and put the cup down. "Maybe you'll go cougar instead."

Somehow, I didn't think he was referring to dating younger men.

I frowned at him and adjusted my glasses. He had no clue why I wanted a vampire because I hadn't offered any information. To him, it probably *was* a weird fetish.

I should have told him the truth. But the words caught in my throat as he continued to look at me expectantly. The way he was smiling at me, laughing with me, flirting with me . . .

He wouldn't flirt with me if he knew I was dying. And call me crazy, but I liked being attractive to him.

"Why me?" I couldn't help but ask. I wasn't pretty, like Ryder, or flirty. I wasn't soft and feminine like Bathsheba. I was all hard angles, dark hair, and glasses. I didn't laugh and joke around like Sara. I was acerbic and cold. I wasn't easy around him. What did he see in me that made him stay here? Made him flirt relentlessly? Made him more or less offer a one-night stand if I changed my mind about dating a vampire?

"Because," he said slowly, spinning the small coffee cup with his big fingers, "I've never met anyone as alone as you, Marie. You hold everyone away from you with that icy frown. You need a thawing."

He leaned forward, all devastating grin again. "And I'm pretty sure I could make you melt."

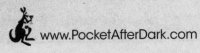